BUREAU ARCANA
THE TWISTS OF FATE

By R.G. Grayson

Bureau Arcana: The Twists of Fate
Written by R.G. Grayson
Published by MammothVision Inc.
Copyright © R.G. Grayson 2025
All rights reserved.
No part of this publication may be reproduced or distributed in any form without express permission of the copyright holder.
Edited by Zachary Liebreich-Johnsen
Bureau Arcana Logo: Misha "Cych0" Petrov
Cover by Misha "Cych0" Petrov
Special Thanks to George Johnsen
ISBN: 979-8-9939489-0-4

This is a work of fiction. The events described here are imaginary: The names, settings, places, and characters are fictitious and not intended to represent specific places or persons, living or dead. Any resemblance to actual events or persons is entirely coincidental.

No part of this work has used generative AI at any point in its creation.

www.bureauarcana.com

Bureau Arcana: The Twists of Fate

Table Of Contents

Chapter 00: The Canary of Capstone Creek

Chapter 01: The Wolf of Westridge

Chapter 02: The Prince of The Old Gods

Chapter 03: The Inferno of Beaumont Heights

Chapter 04: The Shadow of Sharp Manor

Chapter 05: The Wanderer of the Astral Frontier

Chapter 06: The Twins of Electric Avenue

Chapter 07: The Academy Arcana

Chapter 08: The Phases of The Moon

Chapter 09: The Full Moon

Chapter 10: The Twists of Fate

Chapter 11: The Aftermath

"It was too late for me to regret what had occurred during the day."
-The King in Yellow (1895)
-Robert W. Chambers

Chapter 00:
The Canary of Capstone Creek

00:

Everything was still as Elliott Harding stood in the corner of his bedroom. The room was ice cold, but he found himself unable to shiver. The room was dark, the only light being the dark blue of early morning penetrating through the broken window. The few cold streaks of light illuminated a body slumped over his desk.

Elliott flicked the light switch, but nothing happened. He reached into his pocket for his cellphone but couldn't find it.

"Okay!" Elliott thought to himself, "It's just a normal investigation. Examine the crime scene... even if the crime scene is your own room."

Elliott's eyes flicked to the window. There was a clear bullet hole, with shattered glass on the inside windowsill indicating that the shot came from outside. Outside the window was nothing but the thick, still darkness of the last moments before the sun breached the horizon.

Elliott turned to his desk. There was a broken computer monitor with a bullet hole in it that lined up perfectly with the hole in the window. Slumped over the desk was a body. It was difficult to make out details through the haze of blue darkness, but the body was a young man with a small frame. There was some hard to identify damage on their right shoulder and severe damage to his right hand, like it was bitten by a large dog. Long hair flowed from the victim's head, soaked in blood from the gunshot wound to the back of their skull.

Elliott felt panic grip him. He reflexively reached for his chest expecting a pounding heartbeat, but his chest was still. He shook his head and focused.

The victim wore a sharp, well-tailored trench coat that looked right out of a noir thriller. Its once grey color was now stained red with blood. Elliott recognized the clothes as his own.

"Why was the victim wearing my clothes? In my

apartment?" Elliott thought out loud. The victim was slumped over Elliott's desk. What was he doing there? Elliott carefully moved the victim revealing a scattering of Elliott's notes, illegible from being soaked in blood. He sighed and turned to face the victim. Elliott gasped. His own dead eyes stared back at him. Elliott fell backwards and screamed out. The lack of pounding in his chest became all the more alarming. His mind raced as it searched for an explanation. The obvious one was this was simply a nightmare.

Alas... It was not.

Elliott slapped his face to try and wake up, but it felt too real. Everything felt too... solid to be a dream.

He shot up and rushed through the door. He was expecting his living room, expecting his roommate Adam to be sitting on the couch... He expected something familiar.

Beyond the threshold of his bedroom, Elliott found himself in a warmly lit corridor. The walls were lined with luxurious art deco wallpaper adorned with elegant candelabra-esque light fixtures that radiated a welcoming, but ethereal light. An endless row of doors stretched on until the light faded into the distance.

Elliott turned back to see into his bedroom, but it was too dark now. There was a label beside the door, reminiscent of the number of a hotel room that read "Elliott Harding." He gulped and stepped fully into the hallway. The faint melody of a piano filled the air but didn't seem to come from any one place of origin.

"Hello?" Elliott called out, nothing but his echo greeted him in response. He began to walk down the hall. Each door had a label, and each label had a name, none of which Elliott recognized. Out of curiosity, he tried some of the doors, but none of them opened.

Elliott walked and walked. He expected his legs to tire out, but wherever he was, he seemed to have infinite stamina. His endless march came to a sudden halt when he came across a door labeled "Harris Flemming.". The name rang familiar in his head, but he couldn't quite place why. He tried the door. To his surprise, it opened.

01:

Stepping through the door was like stepping into a memory. Everything that happened beyond the door happened exactly as he remembered it.

This is the fourth murder this month. Elliott didn't think that a potential serial killer could start to become tedious, but here he was, standing over the fourth victim, Harris Flemming. Same M.O., same lack of new clues, same dumb cops.

Uniformed officers buzzed around the victim's apartment as they marked evidence and took pictures. Elliott heard snarky comments about the young private detective's presence, but he ignored them. If they had done their job properly, he wouldn't have to be here.

Elliott brushed his long ginger hair behind his ear, snapped on a pair of gloves that he pulled from his trench coat pocket, and crouched down to examine the body. The victim's skin was deathly pale. Cause of death: Blood Loss. The victim's limbs were twisted and contorted, as if the assailant was violently wringing them of their blood. The most vexing detail, though, was the lack of any blood at the scene. Yup. Same M.O.

Elliott delicately ran his finger along the victim's body. No matter how carefully he looked, there was no puncture wound. Elliott stood and looked around. The walls were slammed in, mirrors broken, and other clear signs of a struggle, so Elliott ruled out the murder taking place somewhere else. Why and how did the killer drain the blood? Same lack of new clues.

Elliott stood up. One of the uniformed officers immediately spoke up.

"What's the deduction, Mini Holmes?" the lead officer said, laughing. The nickname made Elliott visibly cringe. It was always his height. That was always the choice of insult thrown his way. Same dumb cops...

"Still think it's someone the victim knew?" another cop said.

"I do," Elliott said, still intensely studying the body. Elliott's voice was best described as cute, something he did his best to hide by speaking with a confident theatricality that even two words, two syllables could convey.

"Keh. You're not as smart as they say, then." the lead officer said.

"KEH!" Elliott repeated mockingly, "Oh yeah?"

"You only had that theory because the last three incidents had no signs of forced entry? Look," the lead officer gestured confidently to the apartment's shattered sliding glass door that led to the backyard. "Forced entry. Bashed in."

The officers snickered; their eyes fixated on Elliott.

Elliott shook his head and let out a theatrical, exasperated sigh which quieted the heckling. He then stepped over to the shattered glass door, crouched down, and gestured at the carpet inside the apartment.

"Look!" Elliott said. "No glass."

Then he took a hop backwards over the threshold and onto the back patio. There was a distinct sound of crackling broken glass. Elliott picked up one of the broken pieces and posed with an exasperated "tah-dah" pose.

"The glass door wasn't bashed in. It was bashed *out*," he said, "Signs of struggle. Same as the rest."

The other officers turned to the lead officer who was red in the face. Elliott snickered and strutted over to the front door. He propped his arm on one of the rookie officers who was keeping his head down.

"Report?" Elliott said.

"He doesn't take orders from you!" the lead officer shouted through grit teeth.

Elliott sighed and raised his hands up in resignation.

The lead officer cleared his throat and spoke, "Report?"

The rookie officer looked to Elliott, then to the lead officer nervously, then said, "W-well… No signs of forced entry… b-but… we did find boot prints that matched ones found at the other scenes…"

"Bam!" Elliott said and clapped his hands together, "Invited in!"

"Fine," the lead detective said, eyes narrowed at Elliott with disdain, "But so what? There is *no* connection between any of the victims. They are all perfect strangers. How can they all recognize the same person?"

"That's the mystery, isn't it?" Elliott said with an almost giddy smirk.

The lead officer flared his nose in annoyance. "Better figure it out, then. The feds are coming to take over, and I doubt they will be as… charmed by your Jr. Holmes act."

Elliott groaned at the nickname once more which made the lead officer chuckle.

"Well, I, for one, look forward to working with some actual professionals," Elliott said with a cocky smirk.

The lead officer's face somehow turned a darker red than before as Elliott turned around and gave a dismissive wave. He could hear the lead officer rant and rave, but he didn't much care to fully listen to what he was saying. He put his hand on the doorknob and opened the door.

On the other side of the door, Elliott found himself back in the hotel hallway.

02:

Elliott gasped and shook his head. He turned back to look inside the room with the door labeled "Harris Flemming." Beyond the threshold was the crime scene of the poor man's death. The lead officer was still red in the face as the other police pretended to look busy. But it was all perfectly suspended in time.

Elliott turned back around to see a dark figure leaning against the wall. He yelped in surprise.

The figure was a man dressed in a pure black suit with a bone gray tie. His pitch black dress shirt was lined with horizontal gray lines that, combined with the tie, looked like a rib cage. He was a sickly thin man with a ghostly white face that was obscured by the shadow of a straight, long brimmed hat. The man in black was looking down at the dull bronze pocket watch in his gloved hand. At the sound of Elliott's gasp, he closed the watch.

"It's too soon for you to be here," the man in black, said. His voice was soft, with an ethereal rasp to it.

"W-what do you mean? And who are you?"

A smirk could barely be seen under the shadow covering the man in black's face.

"Who am I? I'm busy. Too busy to be dealing with someone checking in this early," he said.

"Wh-wha? You don't look too busy to me."

The man in black simply chuckled and walked away, hands formally behind his back.

"Hey! Come back!" Elliot said, chasing after the man in black, but no matter how fast he ran, the man in black only got further and further away.

As Elliott ran, the elegant hallways slowly turned into an alleyway. Elliott stopped. This alley looked familiar... His head flooded with an intense sense of deja vu. The same feeling as when he opened Harris Flemming's door. Yes... He had walked down this alleyway right after investigating that man's apartment... Again, he was reliving a memory.

He stepped out of the alley and onto a familiar street.

03:

Elliott found himself downtown, or the closest thing the small town of Capstone Creek had to a downtown. There was a quaint little coffee shop that he was especially fond of that he made a habit of going to after an investigation to think things through. The rich, pungent smell of the fresh ground beans always stimulated his synapses. His roommate, Adam, was waiting there for him, sitting at one of the outdoor tables.

Adam Nolan was a fresh-faced young man with excited eyes that he constantly tried to make look more serious and stern than he could pull off. His hair was a light brown that, while he tried to keep it neat, had a habit of falling in front of his eyes in the heat of the moment. He wore an untucked button-down shirt and straight legged black jeans. He locked eyes with Elliott and raised his coffee cup as his friend approached.

"How'd it go?" Adam said, his voice bright and naturally charming.

Elliott groaned and slumped in his chair.

"Not well?" Adam asked.

"It's truly baffling. No human should be able to do what this killer is doing," Elliott said before he took his coffee cup and held it to his temple. The heat radiated from the coffee and soothed Elliott's head.

"Maybe it isn't a human after all," Adam said casually. He closed his eyes and took a long sip of his coffee.

"At this rate, I'm willing to consider anything," Elliott said dryly

Adam choked on his coffee and sat up straight, surprised. "Gosh! You're that stumped, eh?"

Elliott nodded and brought the coffee to his lips.

As the two enjoyed their coffee, a tall man approached their table.

"Do my eyes deceive me?" the tall man said in a deep voice that rang familiar to the two roommates.

Elliott and Adam turned to the voice, both of their faces lit up.

Before them stood James Graves, a man who radiated pure professionalism. His facial features were sharp. His black hair was neat and tidy, brushed back with no chance of falling in front of his field of view. His dark gray eyes were deep and focused. He was wearing a raven black suit with a pristine white dress shirt underneath. His silk black tie was tied with perfect symmetry. On the lapel of his suit jacket was a silver, stately lapel pin that depicted a raven perched on an eye surrounded by a rather oceanic looking wreath. Elliot swore it looked like tentacles.

James's face was cracked with a smile. The kind of smile that was only reserved for close friends one hasn't seen in years.

Adam gasped, jumped up from the table, and rushed to hug James.

James was surprised by the sudden affection and looked to Elliott.

Elliott cackled and leaned back in his chair as he spoke, "Don't look at me, big shot."

"Where the hell have you been all these years?" Adam asked as he let go of James.

"Training," James said, bluntly.

"Oh? Military?" Adam asked.

"Looks more like a fed to me," Elliott said and held out a finger pointed to James's breast pocket. "I don't recognize the pin, but I can see the outline of a badge in his inner suit pocket."

Adam took a step back, eyed James up and down, and said, "You do look very secret agent-y."

James appeared to be fighting the urge to roll his eyes and chuckled.

"If I looked like a secret agent, I wouldn't be doing a very good job, would I?" James said, "What about you, two?"

"W-well!" Adam began, "I just started college, and Elliott turned being a smartass into a career!"

James let out a dry chuckle and said, "Private detective, then?"

Elliott smirked wide and propped his hands behind his head, still leaning back in his chair.

"That's right! In fact… I bet I know why you're here."

James's eyebrow twitched up for just a fraction of a second. Adam didn't notice, but Elliott did. "Oh?" James said.

Elliott locked eyes with James and spoke in a low voice, almost a whisper, "Bloodless murders."

04:

Elliott closed his eyes and took a sip of his coffee. When he put his coffee back down and opened his eyes, the morning blue sky was now a late-night black. Adam was gone and James was at the table. In the back of Elliott's mind, he recalled spending the whole day here with Adam, catching up with James and discussing the case. James was vague about his involvement up until Adam had to leave for class.

Elliott blinked to reorient himself to the current memory playing out before him. James leaned in.

"These murders. They seem impossible, don't they?" James asked in a low, covert voice.

"Well clearly not," Elliott said, one eyebrow cocked curiously, "They happened."

James smirked. It was a competitive smirk that Elliott recognized making himself in the many chess games he won against James in the past. He had never seen such a face on James before. He didn't think the stone-faced man was capable of it. Elliott's other eyebrow cocked up, fully invested.

"With everything you know, with everything you understand of this world, it is impossible," James said.

Elliott eyed James's pin. "You haven't joined a cult, have you?"

James let out a dry chuckle and shook his head. "I can see how you would assume as much."

"Well then do enlighten me, Mr. Federal Agent," Elliott said with a slight teasing tone, "Just as long as no Kool-Aid is involved."

James smiled warmly and let out a polite laugh. "Of course. We will simply solve this impossible case together."

"You say that with such certainty," Elliott said as he kicked his feet back and propped them up on the coffee table.

"The agency I work for," James began, "has resources that make finding the... perpetrator of these events nearly trivial. The hard part is apprehending them. Our intelligence points to the next attack taking place at Capstone College. Your experience as a local investigator-"

Elliott fell back in his chair, but James grabbed Elliott by the ankle, keeping them from hitting the floor. "What? Adam goes there!" Elliott yelped.

James nodded, "Indeed. We have no time to waste."

The town of Capstone Creek was quiet this late at night, which was an almost mocking foil to the pounding anxiety in Elliott's chest. James drove the two of them in an unmarked black sedan to the Capstone College campus with a speedy but measured pace. The radio was playing classical piano, which came as no surprise to Elliott, but it still made Elliott roll his eyes. Admittedly, the piano music and the sleek government coded interior of the car helped ease a bit of Elliott's anxieties.

Once at the campus, James parked and turned to Elliott. "Are you sure Adam is still here this late?" James asked.

"Yeah. He stays until the last bus comes. He says he can't study unless he's the only one in the library."

James's already perpetually dour face somehow soured further and said, "Convenient... Or inconvenient. Depending on perspective."

"Doesn't the attacker only kill people in their own homes though? He should be safe... Right?" Elliott said.

"No. Our agents have found several bodies in the Capstone Creek outskirts that matched the contorted nature of the others. Local law enforcement simply never discovered them."

Elliott cursed under his breath, "Useless p-"

James snapped his fingers in front of Elliott's face. "Yeah yeah. There's a reason I took you along instead of one of them. Now let's go. But be quiet."

Elliott nodded and James got out of the car and moved to the trunk. He popped it open where inside, a small arsenal of guns was stored. A pump action shotgun, a hunting rifle, and a pair of revolvers laid alongside boxes of ammo labeled, ".45 pure silver," "12 gauge blessed salt," and such.

"James... is what we are hunting... human?" Elliott asked, eyes wide as they scanned across the munitions.

James equipped himself with the pump shotgun and bluntly said, "No."

Elliott stared at James in shock. All this talk of the inhuman and the supernatural... He had been skeptical... until now.

James began making his way towards the campus library. Elliott stayed at a distance and watched as James moved with a natural and stealthy caution. He looked well trained. Whatever agency James worked for, they were legit. James didn't look like he was sneaking, but as Elliott followed, he noticed that James's steps made absolutely no sound.

Once inside the library, the campus librarian looked up from her desk and saw James. She immediately shot up, as if she'd been caught slacking on the job. Before she could say anything, James reached in and pulled out his badge. Inside was an emblem that looked the same as his lapel pin, but with the words "Bureau Arcana" inscribed around it. Above the emblem was an I.D. card that had a picture of James, his name, and the words "Clearance:

Arcana 00. Fool."

"Hello. I am rookie agent James Graves with the Bureau Arcana. Is there anyone else here?" James asked the bewildered librarian as she reached for her phone.

"Yes. In the back near the study rooms. Like I told you before," she said.

James's face didn't move, but his eyes widened. "Like you told me before? Thank you," he said politely, the slightest edge of worry in his voice before bolting towards where the librarian pointed. Elliott rushed behind, shocked by the sudden urgency.

At the back of the library, Adam sat at a desk. James sat next to Adam, an arm around him in an uncharacteristically casual manner.

Elliott blinked in confusion. His eyes went from James, who was standing next to him, to James, who was sitting next to Adam. Adam gulped. Was whatever this was... stealing faces? Was that why all the victims let their attacker in?

"Adam!" Elliott screamed.

Adam looked up to see Elliott and James, then turned to the other James. His warm and excited face twisted with worry. The other James's head snapped towards Adam, its facial features twitched unnaturally into a wide, insidious smile. Its eyes were wide... pitch black... hungry...

"Detec-tive. Spec-ial agen-t," the other James said, his voice a near perfect echo of James, but ever so slightly wrong. As it spoke, its arms began to ratchet themselves jerkily around Adam's neck. "We were jus-t t-alking ab-out you."

"James?" Adam said, eyes fixated helplessly on the real James. His voice sounded choked.

James swiftly brought the shotgun up and racked a shell into the chamber with an unnerving ka-chunk.

The creature let out a mocking cackle, as if it were used to humans trying to use guns on it. Its arms continued to tighten around Adam, making an unsettling click with each twitchy movement.

"What are you waiting for?" Elliott said to James.

"I'll hit Adam..." James said, his voice cold.

"I'll hi-t A-dam..." The creature parroted.

Elliott grit his teeth and took a step forward. The creature that looked like James tilted its head at an unnatural angle. James made a sound of objection that Elliott didn't comprehend, then Elliott took off in a sprint. He jumped across the desk and tackled the creature to the ground.

Elliott decked the creature in the face. The impact made a wet crunch.

"What are you?!" Elliott screamed, readying his fist for another punch as his eyes refocused. Adam stared back up at him.

"Ellio-tt! I-ts me!" Adam said. No, not Adam.

Elliott hesitated. That moment was all the creature needed. The face that looked like Adam's split out from the corners of its mouth and revealed a grotesque set of sharp teeth. The creature's head jittered up and bit Elliott's fist.

Elliott screamed in shock and agony as the creature overpowered Elliott, its arms now locked around Elliott's head, tightening more and more, clicking like a machine, relentlessly. Elliott could feel his neck twisting. The necks and limbs of the previous victims flashed before his eyes. He was about to be drained of all of his blood…

There was a bright flash, a loud crack, and a heavy force blasted the creature off of Elliott. James pumped the shotgun and fired again. The creature screeched, its form morphed into a twisted copy of Elliott. Without hesitation, James continued to fire, taking a step forward with each shot, until the shotgun was empty.

James stood over the creature. It twitched and cracked and writhed until it finally went still. Without his gaze leaving the monstrous copy-cat, he pulled out a shell, chambered it in the shotgun, racked it, and fired into the creature's skull.

"Elliott… are you okay?" James asked, his eyes seemed to glow.

Elliott looked at his hand. It was torn up by the creature's bite. He felt an intense burning in his shoulder and reached up to touch where the pain came from. He winced as his fingers touched raw and bloodied skin. It seemed like some of the initial shotgun blast grazed Elliott.

"In pain, but just dandy… How's Adam?" Elliott said.

"I'm… fine…" Adam said, voice shaken.

James's eyes were focused on Elliott's torn up hand. "It got you, eh? That was damn reckless," James said. He tried to make his voice sound calm and cold, but it was shaky and rattled.

"Saved him, didn't I?" Elliott said, trying to sound humorous, but equally shaken, "So... is that it?"

James reloaded the shotgun. "Very likely. Backup will arrive soon. Go home. Recover."

Elliott opened his mouth to protest, but Adam put an arm on their good shoulder. Elliott immediately silenced himself and nodded.

Adam helped Elliott out of the library despite his objections that he could take care of himself. A handful of agents rushed in, all of them dressed like James was, all of them with the same silver lapel pin. Some of the agents had another pin below that one. This secondary pin depicted a sword and a roman numeral, as if denoting rank. One of the agents, who introduced herself as Agent Strength, tended to Adam and Elliott. She patched up Elliott's wounds and drove the two home.

05:

Despite being told to rest, Elliott was feverishly at work at his desk, typing his report on the night's events. Elliott typed with his left hand, as his right throbbed with pain from the monstrosity's bite. As he typed, Elliott got an email notification. He opened it.

From: JGraves@BureauArcana.gov

Subject: Doppelganger report for local law enforcement.

Elliott. Attached is a copy from our archives describing the creature we encountered. Make use of it as you will.
Best regards, James.

[[Director of Research, Agent Moon's report on the entity labeled "Doppelganger

██████████."]]

The entity's anatomy appears humanoid, but with a series of extra joints and muscles in its limbs. The purpose of these extra joints appears to be related to how it hunts its prey: A doppelganger, once getting close to its target, wraps its arms around its victim, the joints locking, only able to constrict further until the victim is squeezed to death.

Analysis of the subjects' digestive tracts show a structure consistent with other vampiric beings designed to primarily take nutrients from human blood. Unlike other vampiric creatures, instead of biting onto the victim to create an opening for the blood, the Doppelganger squeezes and contorts the victim, forcing internal bleeding that the creature then sucks from the mouth upon which the doppelganger wrings the victim dry. This explains why victims have no open wounds and no blood is found at the feeding site.

Analysis of the skin shows a heightened sensitivity to sunlight consistent with other vampiric beings. It is theorized that this is a tradeoff to accommodate the shapeshifting properties displayed in the subjects, hence the label of Doppelganger.

Analysis of the brain shows a significant degradation of higher brain function, heightening neurotransmission in the hunger and facial/voice recognition skills on a more instinctual level at the cost of conscious, theoretical understanding. Notably, however, is the preservation of the part of the brain most associated with social interaction. It

```
should be noted that a doppelganger, in
every reported case, will attack the host's
closest social link before going after those
completely unrelated to itself or each
other. We are still theorizing the exact
purpose of this behavior, but our initial
theory is ▇▇▇▇▇▇▇▇▇▇
     Transmission is rare due to the
Doppelganger's uniquely brutal M.O. but,
like other vampiric beings-
```

That was the last thing Elliott was conscious of in this life.

06:

Everything was dead still as Elliott Harding stood in the corner of his bedroom.

Elliott gasped. He clutched his chest to ease its pounding, but there was none. He stared over the room, frozen in time at the moment of his own death.

He turned from his corpse and out the broken window. He tried to see through the haze of darkness, in the hopes of making out who shot him, but nothing could be seen.

His last memories of Adam and James played through his mind. He wondered what they were doing now, how they had reacted to his death, or if they even noticed he was gone yet.

A deep loneliness gripped Elliott's heart. The realization that he will never again be able to share a coffee with Adam brought Elliott to his knees. He wanted to weep, but his body simply did not respond. He was dead after all, what body did he really have that could produce tears?

It was impossible for Elliott to comprehend how long he stayed there, grieving for the loss of everyone, everything he knew. Days could have passed, but nothing changed.

Eventually, Elliott forced himself to stand and opened the door of his bedroom. Outside, the hotel hallway awaited him. He hesitated but forced himself over the threshold. He lumbered down the halls in a daze. He had no idea what he was searching for, or if he even was searching for anything... Maybe this hotel had some sort of recreation.

A sharp ding snapped Elliott from his lamenting daze. He turned around to see the man in black. The ornate bell of a reception desk sat upon his open palm as his other hand hovered just above.

Elliott stared at the face obscured by a long-brimmed hat. He was relieved. It was a comfort to see that he wasn't alone, but it was outweighed by the uncertainty of what this man had in store for him.

The man in black spoke with a soft, slow meter. Every word felt carefully chosen and deliberately delivered. "I... apologize for your... hasty accommodations. It has been a... puzzle to figure out how best to handle your... abrupt arrival."

"W-what do you mean by that?" Elliott asked, "Was I... not supposed to die?"

Under the shadow of his long-brimmed hat, the man in black smiled. His long, bony fingers caressed the reception bell, as if inspecting it for any imperfection.

"Supposed to? Nothing is quite so... preordained," the man in black said.

"Then what the hell do you mean?" Elliott asked.

"Hell? No, not quite," said the man in black with a grave chuckle.

"I don't have time for games," Elliott said.

The man in black slowly alternated the position of his hands, the reception bell that was held in one hand fell into the other, transformed, and now appeared as a pocket watch.

"Don't you?" the man in black said, a smirk ever so slightly visible.

Elliott let out a defeated sigh. "This eternal rest is turning out to be quite exhausting. Why are you here anyway?"

The man in black waved his hand. The pocket watch now morphed into an archaic looking skeleton key. "The scales of fate must be rebalanced. You will be brought to a time and a place that will best carry out such a feat."

The man in black dropped the key then moved his hands behind his back. The key hung in the air, suspended from the ceiling by a thin chain.

Elliott cautiously approached the key. He wrapped his hand around it and pulled. As if pulling the switch on a lamp, there was a loud, mechanical ka-chunk. A bright spotlight shone down on Elliott. The hotel hallway was drenched in darkness. The man in black was gone. Elliott looked around to see nothing but a lone door, highlighted by the spotlight.

Elliott held the key in his hand and approached the door. It didn't look like the same kind of door the rest of the hotel had. It looked more... academic. It was reminiscent of a door to a classroom, or dorm room. He tried the key; it fit into the keyhole of the door perfectly. He turned the key until there was a satisfying click.

Elliott opened the door...

07:

The executive director of the Bureau Arcana was a man named Arthur Gecko, codenamed The Emperor. He was an older man whose face was perpetually shrouded in smoke, nothing but the glare of his round glasses indicating where his eyes were. He sat behind a sleek black slate desk, arms propped up on his elbows, sleeves rolled up to show off a strong set of forearms. His fingers were laced together in front of the cloud of smoke that was his face. On the desk lay an ashtray with a smoldering cigarette.

The Executive Director's office was vast and sparsely furnished. Nothing there was without purpose. The walls were brutalist and of bare concrete. The only decorations on the wall were a series of portraits of all of The Bureau's previous executive directors. Each portrait had a silver plaque with the executive director's name and date of appointment. The first in the series was the Bureau Arcana's founder. It read "1895: Harvey Ashford."

The floor of the office was cold, polished stone with a large Bureau Arcana emblem embedded into it.

James Graves sat on the other side of the desk and stared calmly into the hazy reflection from Executive Director Gecko's glasses.

"Congratulations on your promotion, Magician Graves,"

Gecko said, his voice smooth and professional, with a political confidence that came from decades working in government.

"Thank you, sir," James said, bluntly. He hid it well, but he hated the executive director's office. It reeked of a bureaucratic indifference to humanity... and tobacco...

"You were supposed to recruit that detective... Mr. Harding, was it? What happened?" Gecko asked, the vague swirl of smoke shifting to indicate a head tilt.

"Elliot- Mr. Harding became... un-viable as a candidate," James said, face stone still.

"How unfortunate. And this Adam Nolan fellow... He has no special talents, no metanatural markers... Why do you think he will be a suitable agent?"

"He may seem unremarkable but think of him as clay. We can- I can train him to be the best agent in the Bureau Arcana's history," James said, a hint of passion colored his voice.

There was an ominous silence as Executive Director Gecko considered James's words. He picked up his cigarette from his ashtray, the smoke from its tip flowed into the cloud surrounding Gecko's head.

"So be it," Gecko said. He waved James off, and the smoke enveloped the rest of his frame. After a few seconds, the smoke dissipated, leaving an empty leather chair where Gecko once sat.

James sat silently, listening, as if waiting to be sure Gecko was gone. Eventually, after a solid minute of silence, James allowed himself to stand.

James walked through the halls of the Bureau Arcana; his footsteps echoed down the concrete and linoleum. It all looked like any other office, but the arcane secrets that lurked among them invigorated James.

There was so much more to the universe that the mundane world simply couldn't comprehend. The Bureau Arcana was the first line of defense against the eldritch infinity, the first pioneers into the astral frontier. They were chroniclers of impossible knowledge, the bridge between the physical and metaphysical.

Back in his office, James Graves picked up a file on his desk and looked through his next mission briefing.

Chapter 01:
The Wolf of Westridge

01:

Local news stations tend to be run by skeleton crews. The only ones in the control room being the technical director, the producer, and the sound engineer. The studio only has the camera operators and the news anchors. If they are lucky, they have an intern.

Royce Grayson was working as an intern at this particular station, working in the control room for the nightly news. He was in his final semester at Westridge Community College working on his associates degree, and if this internship could become a job, he could skip going to university. Royce was enamored by the TV Studio. The darkness of the control room was only illuminated by the glow of the wall of tv monitors, some with live feeds of the various cameras in the studio, some dedicated to pre-edited news segments.

Behind Royce, the producer leaned into an intercom microphone. "We go live in five. Four. Three. Two..." and instead of saying one, she snapped her fingers.

Royce sat beside the technical director and watched how they operated the switchboard. At the sound of the producer's snap, the technical director pressed a button on the switcher and the opening theme played. A simple button press, and the entire county was getting their news.

Once the theme finished playing, the technical director pressed another button and the main camera in the studio went live. Moments prior, the two anchors were on their phones as if they were simply in their living room and not a button press away from being broadcast to thousands of people, but once the camera went live, Royce blinked and they seemed like completely different people. They were bright and full of life, professionally comfortable, the kind of public comfort that came from years of live broadcasting.

"Hello, and welcome to the evening news," the lead anchor

began, "Coming up: In the north, The Jack of Diamonds strikes again! Master thief pulls off another impossible heist. In the south, we celebrate the grand opening of the record-breaking skyscraper Beaumont Heights. Inland near the valley, we have reports of a potentially haunted mansion."

The co-anchor took over, "And now for our top story tonight: Mysterious maulings in the gem of the wooded coast, Greencrest Forest. Local authorities report an increase in violent attacks taking place off the main trails of the woods occurring during last week's full moon. Police have confirmed fatalities but have yet to release a total number. Eyewitness accounts from survivors claim they saw..."

The technical director lowered a lever on the switcher and a sketch of what could only be described as a wolf man faded in on screen.

Royce turned to the technical director and whispered, "Do you believe this crap?"

The technical director, with an unnerving casualness to his voice said, "Oh yeah. This wouldn't be the first werewolf outbreak we've covered," he said, cutting to a prerecorded interview with an eyewitness.

Royce's eyes shot open. "What?! You can't be serious." He turned to the sound engineer who side-eyed Royce and nodded.

Royce blinked in disbelief and turned around to the producer. She nodded as well. He let out an exasperated breath and sat back in his chair in disbelief. He watched the rest of the news segment only half focused. Once the technical director faded out into commercials, Royce stood up.

"So," he began, "You all can't honestly believe this is actually werewolves, right? You're just pranking the gullible new intern, right?"

The technical director shook his head and said, "I wish,"

"This is the third time we've covered werewolf attacks," the producer said, sounding almost annoyed, "You'd think people would stop going into the forest on full moons."

Royce stood there, mouth agape and full of the hot-headed incredulity that came with inexperience. "Maybe it's because all they get is bigfoot-ass sketches. We can get real actual video evidence! We have cameras, why don't we go out and get some *real* evidence?"

"Pff!" the technical director scoffed, "Too dangerous. Let the Bureau handle it."

"Wha, who?" Royce said.

"If the Bureau thought that would help, they would have given us footage to show," the producer said.

"Sounds like a cover up to me. Next full moon, I'm goin' out there," Royce said.

The technical director looked at Royce with a dismissive expression. "Go get your Pulitzer then, kid."

"KID?!" Royce shouted, immediately being shushed by the producer.

"We are live again," the producer said sharply.

Royce tisked and sat down, watching the rest of the broadcast as it aired.

02:

The next few weeks, Royce carried on as normal, but with a nagging thought in the back of his head. That nagging thought became an obsession. When Royce became obsessed with something, it consumed him. Whether it was a gift or a curse, he wasn't sure. On one hand, he was one year out of high school and already finishing up college. On the other hand, he got there by sacrificing his social life and hobbies.

He was just about done with school, so this new obsession was especially dangerous. He had nothing else to focus on, his classes were a means to get this internship, and now catching a werewolf on film would, in Royce's mind, further his chances of making a name for himself at the station. He fixated on his fantasies of glory and fame.

Royce argued with the station's producer, saying how half-baked conspiracy theories and fairy tales wouldn't convince people to stay out of the forest. He said their curiosity would overcome their fear. Royce used himself as a prime example. His arguments fell on deaf ears. The producer kept mentioning the Bureau.

"They are the experts in these matters. Leave it in their

hands," she said.

Come the next full moon, Royce did the nightly broadcast as usual. The main story was a reminder not to enter the woods. He felt like it was directed specifically at him, but he was undeterred.
Royce helped close up the studio. He used that time to hide a field reporter's camera in his backpack. As he left, he waved off the last of the staff, and walked out, right past his producer, the film equipment successfully smuggled out.
Royce's body shook with excitement, adrenaline coursing through his veins as he biked out into the forest, the full moon illuminating the way, almost guiding him to his destination.
Greencrest Forest was at the northern end of town, along the northernmost border of Westridge county. It was a thick, dense forest with only somewhat maintained hiking and bike paths. Once Royce was at the mouth of the forest, he parked his bike, then pulled out his map and flashlight. The map had the site of each confirmed mauling highlighted with a red circle. All incidents seemed to emanate from the Greencrest Wick, a grove near the heart of the forest that centers around a once giant tree that was struck by lightning, causing the biggest forest fire in the county's history. It is famous locally for now being one of the most lush and thriving parts of the forest, though the "wick" that started the fire, the centerpiece of this area, has remained a charred husk. Royce began his trek through the forest.
It was much darker there. The full moon, once bright and beaming down on the town, was now blocked out by the dense woods. The emotional part of his brain was screaming with fear, his fight or flight instincts trying to seize him to run. Royce ignored such impulses.
He hiked deeper and deeper into the forest. His surroundings got darker and darker, his flashlight dimmer and dimmer... Hard to afford a long-lasting flashlight with a student's budget. He heard rustling behind him and swiftly turned around. He saw nothing... Not even the path he thought he was following.
Royce frantically looked around. He quickly began to realize that the fear, the panic he felt wasn't just nonsensical

emotions: he was alone... far away from civilization... looking for something that has caused the death of several people... of course his brain was telling him this was a bad idea...

Royce hoped it was just the wind. Then he froze. He didn't want it to be the wind. Royce wanted it, he *craved* it to be a monster. He quickly pulled the camera out from his backpack and mounted it on his shoulder. He smiled with determination and continued deeper into the forest. He started whistling loudly, quickly turning the flashlight on and off, taunting whatever may or may not be out there.

He was almost frustrated when he reached Greencrest Wick without incident. He sighed and sat against the blackened tree, staring out into the near wall of trees surrounding the grove. He set the flashlight down and used both hands to point the hefty portable broadcast camera at himself, then hit record.

"Hello hello! Royce Grayson reporting from the heart of Greencrest Wick! The recent..." Royce thought for a moment. He realized no one had given these events a catchy name. Then he stared into the camera with a proud smirk. "...Full Moon Maulings have been occurring right around here. We are here to catch, on film, exactly what has been causing this!"

Royce stopped the recording and sighed. "I can do better than that..."

He did another take, saying the same thing, but more energetic and without a pause in the middle.

Unhappy with that take... He did another.

Then another.

Then another...

Royce ended up propping the camera up on one of the burnt branches of the Wick, then propped the ever-dimming flashlight up on another branch to use as a makeshift spotlight. Full of energy, Royce stood in front of the camera, the shot framed perfectly to show off the shirt and tie he wore the whole hike here. He had to look good on camera, after all. He spoke into the camera feeling like a proper news anchor.

"Hello hello! Royce Grayson reporting from the heart of Greencrest Wick! The recent Full Moon Maulings have reportedly been caused by..." Royce said with a now well-rehearsed cadence.

He was so focused on delivering the perfect opening that he was completely unaware of the creature that emerged from the woods...

The creature stood at least seven feet tall, covered in a thick black coat of fur, and had a feral, snarling wolf's maw.

Royce was almost done with the perfect take before being cut off by an ear-piercing howl. Royce jumped and turned to the creature, his eyes wide, his mouth agape. He was frozen in awe.

"...W-werewolves..." Royce said in disbelief.

Then the flashlight died.

03:

Earlier that night, along a heavily wooded ridge overlooking the Greencrest Wick, two men laid prone near the edge of their makeshift camp. There was no campfire and all the lights they brought were turned off. One man had a pair of night vision binoculars, and one man had a rustic bolt-action hunting rifle. The rifle was a well-used and equally well maintained modified Winchester Model 70 that was specifically designed to fire silver bullets.

The man with the binoculars was a fresh faced young man named Adam Nolan. He looked up from his binoculars into the dark night sky and sighed.

"James? Will they even show up since it's so cloudy out? I mean we can't even see the full moon," Adam said.

James Graves, the man with the rifle, looked a few years older than his partner. His eyes were normally dark gray but currently they were glowing a bright arcane white, allowing him to look though the darkness without night vision goggles. He wore a dark black peacoat over his standard issue Bureau Arcana suit.

Without looking away from the scope, James let out a short, "Yes."

Adam nodded silently and continued scouting the wilderness....

Until he got bored again.

"Are you certain?" Adam said.

"Yes, Adam," James said, hyper focused.

Adam sighed and stood up. He cracked a glowstick to see. "We have been here for hours. I need to stretch my legs."

James immediately turned his head away from the scope for the first time since they started their watch. Having lost focus, the white glow in his eyes dissipated with a blink.

"Adam…" he said, a noticeable twinge of worry in James's voice, "That is ill advised."

"Relax. Jacqueline is in her tent. Just holler if you need her," Adam said.

"Use our code names," James said.

"Pardon me. Agent Strength is asleep in her tent and Hanged Man is perched up somewhere- wait, why don't you use *my* codename?"

James sighed and glanced at the Bureau Arcana pin shining on the lapel of Adam's Bureau Arcana black suit. He smiled with pride. "I'm still not used to you being an official agent, Agent Fool."

Adam smiled back but cringed at his codename. "You guys really couldn't call rookies something else?"

James let out a dry chuckle. As he chuckled, a tired woman emerged from one of the tents set up behind James and Adam's sniper's nest. Jacqueline Wells, AKA Jaq, AKA Agent Strength, crawled out of the tent and looked between the two agents before letting out a loud yawn. Despite being woken up, her eyes were energetic and full of life. As she left the tent, she put her medical satchel on around her waist.

"Ah! Doctor," James said, making his way to his feet, "Talk some sense in the rookie: going out by yourself is dangerous."

Adam sighed and pulled out a custom revolver that most closely resembled a Colt Python. Like the rifle, it too had been designed specifically for shooting silver bullets.

"I'll be fine," Adam said, "Agent Tower gave us these bad boys, and you know I'm a crack shot."

"In this darkness?" James argued.

Adam opened his mouth before being cut off by Jaq.

"Agent Magician," she said, "He's not some Minor Arcana grunt. Have some faith in your protégé."

"I didn't get here because of faith," James said before closing his eyes and taking a deep breath. When he opened them, they glowed white, and he scanned the forest line.

Adam watched his mentor and friend James Graves scan the forest with his heightened vision. The glow of James's eyes illuminated him just enough for the Bureau Arcana's silver Raven and Eye pin to glisten on his lapel. He smiled with a bit of nostalgia and touched his own pin. He remembered when James first introduced him to the Bureau Arcana. His smile turned bittersweet when he remembered his closest friend, Elliott, who died protecting him from a monstrous beast. That's when James recruited him.

While Adam was still at the Academy, James would often sneak him into the Bureau headquarters to teach him spells, but he was never good at it. Adam was always too impatient to master any spell and always wanted to learn something new. Now here he was, after years of study and training, he was an official agent.

"How's it look, *Agent Magician?*" Adam said.

"Looks clear, but it is a dense forest out there," James replied, "Be careful."

"Thank ya," Adam said with a nod and a smile, his hair falling over one of his eyes. He hastily brushed it back into place with his hand.

Before Adam could take a step away, however, a voice crackled in over the radio.

"Unidentified human subject," said the voice through a faint hiss of static. It was a strong voice with clear enunciation, a voice that was experienced with trying to be understood over the radio. The voice came from Agent Hanged Man, the Bureau Arcana's director of Intelligence, and James's mentor. Adam had never met the man in person, only ever heard his voice over radio chatter or read his reports. Even now, Adam had no earthly idea where Agent Hanged Man was posted.

"Hold on, wha- ACK!!" Adam said before being choked out as Jaq grabbed the binoculars hanging from his neck.

Jaq put the binoculars to her eyes. "Who the hell… is that a *vlogger?*" she said.

"What?!" James said, taking the binoculars and looking

through them with his glowing eyes.

"ACCCKKK!!!" Adam yelped, further choked out by the binoculars strap.

Sure enough, from the cliff, James saw a kid overly dressed for someone just hiking through the forest. James watched them in awe as they seemed to record take after take of an amateur vlog intro as they fumbled with equipment that was comically over-engineered for a one man cast and crew.

With one hand still holding the binoculars, James used his free hand to put two fingers to his ear. "Are those news cameras? I thought we told the media not to come out here tonight."

"We did," Agent Hanged Man said, "I called my old contacts in this town. There are no news vans or crew coming. This kid is alone. Quite the dedication to finding the truth. Heh. The kid reminds me of... me."

Adam swiped the binoculars back from James and finally took a breath. "Let me see!" he said, looking through the binoculars. He gasped. Right as he focused on the over eager kid, a large black beast emerged from the woods and slowly approached the distracted vlogger. Adam was awestruck. It was the first time he had seen a werewolf in person, and the gravity of his role as an agent of the Bureau Arcana hit him.

"T-t-target spotted..." Adam stuttered, his voice shaky and nervous.

James immediately brought the rifle up and looked down the scope. James was a good shot, but he was standing instead of prone and was not prepared for the added time pressure of saving some overly ambitious brat wanting to make a name for himself. He had the werewolf in his sights but was struggling to steady himself.

"James... It's getting closer..." Adam said.

"I know," James said through grit teeth. He gulped and tried desperately to steady himself. The closer the werewolf approached its prey, the higher the risk of hitting the civilian, the more James hesitated. The more James hesitated, the closer the werewolf approached its prey...

"Ace," Hanged Man said to James, "If you don't take the shot... The kid will die.

Adam watched through the binoculars as the kid finally locked eyes with the beast. The beast appeared to snarl, as if ready to pounce...

The kid's flashlight, the only source allowing Adam and Jaq to see, went completely dead.

"JAMES!" Adam yelled.

James took his shot.

04:

James, Adam, and Jaq rushed down the cliff. James approached the limp werewolf, aimed his rifle right between the downed beast's eyes and pulled the trigger, double tapping the wolf. Adam picked up the video camera and checked the footage this kid managed to capture. Jaq rushed to the unconscious vlogger.

"Status?" James asked, pulling the bolt of the rifle back and ejecting a spent shell.

Adam caught the shell casing and rolled it between his fingers as he examined the footage. "Kid says on film his name is Royce Grayson. Werewolf was in frame and well lit. We were not captured on camera," he said, looking over to Jaq.

Jaq cleaned the blood off of Royce and immediately went to work patching them up with her first aid pouch. "Deep lacerations on the left arm consistent with beast claws. Bite marks on his shoulder consistent with werewolf jaws," she said, focused solely on keeping Royce alive.

After he heard the report, James raised the rifle. His usually stony face soured as he aimed the rifle at the unconscious Royce.

Adam gasped and jumped in front of James.

"He will turn. There is nothing we can do." James said, eyes locked on Adam's. His aim quivered.

"With all the resources of the Bureau, we can't help him?" Adam asked, refusing to move from in front of James's aim.

"We can't. He will only hurt more people," James said, teeth grit tight.

"I refuse to believe that. It's one night a month. We can do *something!*" Adam screamed.

Jaq finished patching Royce up and looked down at the boy. His face was pale from blood loss. His clothes were soaked red. His breath was slow and labored... Jaq looked back to James.

"We have a month before he turns. We can figure something out," she said.

"We must!" Adam said, "We aren't exterminators! That's not why I joined the Bureau!"

James's lip twitched with worry. His eyes flicked to Royce. He swore he saw the face of his old friend Elliott. He winced and looked away, lowering the gun.

"You're right," James said. After hearing that, Adam let out a relieved sigh.

Jaq, on the other hand, shook her head at James, "I cannot believe you were seriously considering-"

"Look alive, or else you won't be," Agent Hanged Man's voice said through the radio, "We have six more lycanthropic subjects inbound."

The agents' debate was cut cold. There was a chilling silence, an eerie stillness. A deep shiver ran down Adam's spine. From the surrounding trees came an ear splitting, feral howl, followed by five more, coming from all around. The three agents were surrounded.

A tremendous beast pounced from the forest, its massive maw snarling. In that exact moment, James, with one swift motion, brought the rifle up and fired. He shot the werewolf square in the heart, and it collapsed at James's feet. He swiftly racked the bolt and turned his eyes to Adam.

Adam un-holstered his revolver right as two more werewolves jumped from the forest line, one for Adam, and one for James. Adam rolled out of the way and fired two shots into the beast, staggering it.

James blocked the second beast with the rifle as it tried to overpower and bite him. Adam, blood rushing with adrenaline, rushed to James and fired four shots into the second beast, killing it. James gave his protégé a nod of approval right before the beast that attacked Adam recovered and growled at the two men. Adam raised his gun and pulled the trigger. The gun clicked. Adam went wide-eyed with panic before the sound of James's rifle cracked from behind and put the beast down with a shot right between the eyes.

"I'm out!" Adam shouted as three more beasts pounced from the forest line.

James, steady as stone, stared down the scope of his rifle as the beasts flew towards them. He only had two shots left in his rifle... He could not afford to miss... Even then, that leaves one ravenous beast...

No time to think.

Bang!

Rack bolt.

Bang!

Each silver bullet landed true, and stopped two of the beasts dead, but he had no time to celebrate. The last beast was about to pounce onto Jaq. In a blink, James warped across the grove and intercepted the beast just before it got Jaq. The final beast's claws were just about to pierce James's suit when a powerful magical white flash erupted from him, filling the grove and sending the beast flying back. With this new opening, James pulled a silver bullet from his coat pocket and with surgical precision, chambered it into the rifle.

He stared down the scope at the final beast, the glow in his eyes dimming... His vision swayed and he fell to his knees.

The final beast growled and stared at James with a hungry gaze. It slowly recovered from James's arcane flashbang and was nearly ready to pounce again.

Adam rushed to James and grabbed the rifle. James, with the last of his strength, smiled at Adam and gave them a pat on the back.

"Don't miss," he said, before falling unconscious besides Royce.

Adam, heart racing, locked eyes with the final beast, aimed, and pulled the trigger.

The forest fell silent.

No more howls. No more growls. No more gunshots.

Jaq moved to check on James. She felt along his suit and felt where the wolf made contact. It cut the suit, but upon closer examination didn't break the skin. She checked his pulse.

"How's he doing, doc?" Adam asked, brushing the hair from his eyes and catching his breath.

"He is fine. Exhausted, but uninjured," Jaq said and continued to thoroughly check James for injury.

"And the kid? Royce?"

"He will be fine... if you let him," Jaq said, watching Adam carefully.

"I mean... c-can you ensure he won't spread the... scourge?" Adam asked anxiously.

Jaq sighed and smiled, "I will make sure of it."

Adam sighed with intense relief and collapsed beside James. There was nothing left to do but clean up and extract.

Jaq rolled her eyes and chuckled.

"Nice shot, rookie," Agent Hanged Man said through the radio.

"Good job, rookie," Jaq said with a warm smile.

05:

Royce awoke to the rhythmic sound of a heart monitor beeping in his ear, and the sterile burn of antiseptic in his nose. His mind was fuzzy and his vision blurry. He blinked to clear the haze from his eyes and slowly looked around. The room was colored with various shades of beige. In the corner of the room stood a woman in a long crisp doctor's coat and white scrubs with a medical satchel on her hip. She had a warm, immediately disarming smile. Two things in particular stood out to Royce: one, she looked far less exhausted than any doctor he had ever seen before; and two, the silver emblem of a raven and eye pinned to her lapel...

"Hello, Royce. My name is Doctor Jacqueline Wells," she said, her tone warm and soothing, "How are you feeling this morning?"

Royce found himself smiling back, "I uh... well- ow!" His shoulder twinged hard, so he reached back to rub his muscle, but he felt a bandage on it. That was when he also noticed that his arm was wrapped in bandages, a wide claw mark bleeding through ever so slightly. Royce's eyes widened in shock, his brain registering the injuries and wracking him with pain.

"Nnnngh... Like I got mauled by a..."

"A werewolf?" Jaq said with a knowing smile.

Royce gulped and couldn't help but fixate on Jaq's lapel pin. "N-no, that would be crazy," he said, nervously. Was this The Bureau his producer told him about? Was he about to be disappeared for interfering? Royce tried to mask his anxiety but was immediately sold out by the increased beeping of the heart monitor.

Jaq laughed and shook her head. "Ah yes, I am also the Director of Medicine of the Bureau Arcana, and no, you are not in trouble," she said in a way that soothed Royce's anxiety, slowing the beeping of the heart monitor.

It was only a fleeting moment before a whole new anxiety spiked his blood pressure. Royce locked eyes with Jaq with a look of dread.

"I... am I gonna turn?" he asked, his heart sinking.

Jaq's expression darkened. She moved to sit right beside Royce.

"Yes," she said, bluntly, "But that is why I am here."

"You can cure me?" Royce asked.

"Unfortunately, no," Jaq said, "But... I'm hoping with some intervention we can help you manage this."

Royce was staring straight into Jaq's eyes, but his vision went gray. He could hear Jaq talking, explaining her plan for how to deal with this, but Royce struggled to hear over a growing ringing in his ears. Jaq's instructions were fragmented in Royce's head: "Lock yourself somewhere secure... Will be provided silver laced restraints... keep track of the moon..." Royce couldn't comprehend the rest. He sunk into his hospital bed and stared into the ceiling.

Jaq noticed that Royce was dissociating, and she snapped sharply in front of his eyes.

"And keep an eye out for that... Stay in touch with yourself," she said,

Royce blinked and groaned, his fists clenched reflexively. Jaq pointed at his clenched fists.

"That's why. Even when it isn't a full moon, you are more

susceptible to mood swings... Although I think with counseling... I can help you with at least that part," Jaq said, a hint of optimism in her voice.

Royce sighed and relaxed his fists. He continued staring into the ceiling, but he was focusing hard to not disassociate again. He turned to look at Jaq.

"Am I just supposed to live with this?" Royce asked, his voice weak and defeated.

"Until we find a cure."

Royce let out a dry chuckle. "How would that even happen? Is there a university that teaches werewolf biology?" He said, laughing at the idea.

Jaq chuckled with Royce before looking him in the eyes, "Actually... yes. Where do you think we learn about our field?"

Royce went silent, his eyes immediately blazed with the familiar burn of obsession. This was stronger, more intense than ever before. Normally his obsessions were rooted in curiosity or ambition, but this... his very wellbeing was at stake.

Jaq smiled wide, seeing the flame of passion in Royce's eyes. "Safe to assume that you are interested?"

Royce nodded eagerly.

Jaq bubbled with excitement and said, "Then let's begin."

06:

[[Director Of Medicine, Agent Strength's report: Royce Grayson's recovery:]]

Royce Grayson's physical recovery was slower than I liked. He frequently ignored my medical advice for rest and insisted on getting an early start on his studies. My fear is that if he doesn't fully heal before the next full moon, transformation will reopen his wounds and make them even harder to heal. Thankfully, we worked out a way where he could study without overexerting

> himself and should be sufficiently healed come the next full moon. I will also have to prove that it is possible to safely contain a werewolf.

    James Graves put down the report. The full moon was here, and he had spent the previous month working with Jaq and the director of engineering, Agent Chariot, to develop humane but effective werewolf restraints. The restraints were set up in the observation room in the Bureau Arcana's science and medical wing. The room was set up like an old-fashioned operating theater, with rows of audience seating raised and encircling a glass enclosure. The glass was reinforced to be both bulletproof and magic proof, able to contain, or at least slow, any subject mundane or otherwise.

    James had hoped that the test would be a discreet affair, but word spread around the Bureau and the operations theater was packed with curious observers. Over the idle murmur from the Bureau agents, one voice was heard above the rest.

    "Director Gecko, this is absurd!" Jaq argued, "Have you even considered the psychological harm such a crowd will cause?"

    Executive Director of the Bureau Arcana, Arthur Gecko, AKA Agent Emperor, stood in the back of the theater, one hand in his pocket while another casually gripped a cigarette. The smoke produced from his cigarette didn't disperse or fill the room but instead drifted up to mix with the swirl of smoke that perpetually engulfed Gecko's head.

    "My dear Doctor Strength," Gecko began, "We must test these restraints under the most intense of circumstances, don't you think? We wouldn't want to half-measure the testing only to see a... catastrophic failure in the field, hmm?"

    "Sir, this is endangering everyone here," Jaq responded.

    "We can handle one lone fledgling werewolf, my dear."

    Among the agents in the audience was a large man with a military haircut whose Bureau Arcana raven black suit struggled to contain his muscles. He had an automatic tranquilizer rifle slung over his shoulder. Jaq knew him as the director of munitions, Agent Tower. Along with Agent Tower and his tranq gun, James had his hunting rifle loaded with silver bullets besides him.

Jaq sighed in defeat. "So be it," she said, turning to leave.

"One last thing, doctor!" another voice said. The voice was full of a smug self-importance that made Jaq shudder.

It was the voice of the director of research, AKA Agent Moon. He was a tall, thin man with slicked back hair and a narrow face. He stood with a crooked posture that made him come off like a snake getting ready to strike.

Agent Moon handed a report to Director Gecko, who flipped through it. Agent Moon explained, "This is the first time in Bureau history that we have a live werewolf specimen."

"His name is Royce," Jaq said.

Agent Moon gave a dismissive wave and continued, "The research possibilities here are extraordinary. We must make use of this opportunity while we have it. This report details a list of samples I require from the subject. Blood, hair, DNA, standard stuff. All things that should be no problem for Agent Strength to extract during the full moon."

"What? You want me in there with him while he's turned?" Jaq exclaimed.

"What?" Gecko retorted, "Are you not confident in the restraints? The whole reason he's even alive is due to your faith in them."

"Sir-" Jaq began to argue.

"Approved," Director Gecko said, pulling out a pen and signing Agent Moon's report.

Agent Moon flashed a satisfied smile at Jaq, "See you when the sun sets, Doctor."

07:

As the sun began to set, Jaq led Royce into the observation cell. He froze as he saw all the Bureau agents in the theater audience. Royce forced a confident smirk and waved at his onlookers, then turned to Jaq and whispered.

"I feel like a circus attraction," Royce said with quiet anxiety.

"Most of them have never seen a live werewolf before.

You've caused quite a stir around here," Jaq said with a kind smile that immediately relaxed Royce.

Jaq attached a series of vital monitors onto Royce then helped him onto a hospital bed, and started strapping him in. As she tightened the straps, she narrated her procedure both to reassure Royce and to appease the audience.

"The straps were engineered by Agent Chariot and are made primarily of Kevlar with thin silver wire weaved throughout. Testing has shown the straps to be quite resilient, so I am confident it will sufficiently contain Royce," she said.

"When I turn... Is it gonna hurt?" Royce asked, his heart rate was elevated, blood pressure high. His body was shivering as he broke out in a cold sweat.

Jaq's smile wavered before responding, "Well, we're not certain. Some reports say it feels like intense growing pains, but that's it."

Royce put on a brave, proud smile, "I'll write a detailed report on how it feels, then!"

"That's the spirit!" Jaq said, matching Royce's smile. She looked up at the audience. James was there with his hunting rifle, his face as cold as ever. Next to him stood Adam, who was fidgeting anxiously. At the other end of the theater audience, Executive Director Gecko stood with his arms crossed, his perfectly circular glasses shimmering dimly behind his aura of smoke, reminiscent of two full moons. Beside Gecko was Agent Moon whose twisted smirk made Jaq's blood run cold. It was obvious to Jaq that Royce wasn't the only test subject here, she was one, too. Right behind Agent Moon, Agent Tower sat in shadow, the shimmer of his tranq rifle scope the only indication of where he sat. Jaq could feel agent Tower's crosshairs on her.

Royce's vitals suddenly spiked. His body tensed up, and he let out a groan. He gripped the sheet tight as his groan slowly morphed into a growl.

"I think... It's happening, doc..." Royce said through grit teeth. Jaq looked up at the smirking Agent Moon and took a step closer to Royce. She placed a comforting hand on their forehead. "Indeed, it is. But it will be okay, I swear," she said.

Royce flashed a smile before his body thrashed against the

restraints but remained constrained. His face twisted into a snarl, his muscles bulged and grew. A thick black fur covered his body. Royce's hands became sharp claws, his teeth huge and monstrous. The boy that was Royce was now a feral beast who growled and snapped at Jaq, but Jaq remained close, confident the restraints would protect her. As she stroked Royce's fur, she looked up and flashed a smile. James and Adam smiled back, Adam visibly cheering with excitement. Moon's smirk was suddenly absent, and that made Jaq smile even more.

Once it became clear that Royce was thoroughly restrained, much of the audience dispersed. Moon was notably the first to leave, and as the night went on, only Adam, James, and Agent Tower remained. Jaq drew the demanded samples with little trouble. The most painful part about it was the volume of Royce's howls.

Once she was done, she got herself comfortable in the observation room. She stayed close to Royce, observing him up close. She took notes, more for Royce's sake than Moon's.

"A live werewolf in the middle of the Bureau Arcana. Can you believe it, James?" Jaq said, turning to look into the theater.

James looked on with a curious glint in his eye, "Times sure are changing. I just hope they are changing for the better."

Chapter 02:
The Prince of The Old Gods

01:

The Arcadia Gala has been hosted by the Prince family for generations. The Gala is hosted once a year at the Prince Estate as one of, if not *the* highest class gathering of the year. All the glamorous socialites show up wearing their most elegant tuxedos and most opulent dresses, everyone trying to one-up each other. In recent years, the Gala was the Prince family's way to flex their private collection, always holding the event in their personal art gallery, using the event to showcase some priceless one of a kind something or other. It never mattered what it was, it only mattered that they had it and no one else could.

Miles Prince was an only child and heir to the Prince fortune. His champagne blonde hair was meticulously brushed to the side in a wonderfully suave fashion to perfectly frame his young face and bright blue eyes. He walked with a straight, dignified posture as he effortlessly floated through the party, moving his head as little as possible to avoid accidentally messing up his hair. He once suggested pomade to keep his hair in place, but his family stylist insisted that hair products looked "cheap."

He hated every moment of it. The tuxedos were uncomfortable, the drinks were disgusting, and the conversations were vapid and drowned out the music. The only time he didn't have to feign interest was when the topic of "The Jack Of Diamonds" came up. Miles always perked up when the master thief was mentioned. Everyone at the Gala had a story about their priceless such and such going missing without a trace, nothing but an everyday playing card left behind. Every conversation ended up talking about this "bothersome thief" and every time, the conversation turned to Miles. They all said the same thing.

"The Arcadia Gala is the perfect place for someone like that to strike. I do wonder what your family will reveal today, or if it will be naught but a playing card," they all said, almost verbatim every time. The gaudy posh laugh grated on Miles's ears.

Every time Miles would let out a cheeky laugh in response and say, "Oh you are trying to get me to reveal our treasure early, aren't you?"

They would always laugh in response, and he would take his leave to the next guest or group of guests to repeat the same social dance. It was exhausting, but he was good at it. It was his role in the family to keep up public appearances. He hated it, so it was quite a bother when he was told to be the one to reveal this year's artifact.

After doing the rounds of socialization, he retreated behind the stage where the string quartet was playing. Miles was let into a vault with a handful of armed guards. Inside was this year's "Treasure Of Arcadia," an ancient looking wooden chest which held an obsidian chalice decorated with a ring of deep green crystals. Each crystal had a unique, unidentifiable symbol carved into it. Even in the darkness, the crystals seemed to glow.

The obsidian chalice came from a group that claimed it once had occult properties, or whatever. Miles didn't really listen. All he knew was that this item now symbolized the Prince Family's status over not only the other guests and the Jack of Diamonds, but the gods, whatever gods there may or may not be.

Miles picked up the obsidian chalice and turned it side to side, examining each esoteric gem before rolling his eyes.

Back in the heart of the gallery, the socialites were all talking amongst themselves. They all looked around at the increase in security and wondered if the Jack of Diamonds would even dare make a move tonight. The string quartet finished their song, and a spotlight illuminated the stage. Miles emerged from behind the curtain and placed the chest upon a pedestal. The crowd went silent and all eyes fell upon Miles.

"Good evening esteemed guests!" Miles said, sounding crisp and clear even without a microphone, "It is a pleasure and an honor to have you all here tonight. As you all know, the Prince family..." blah blah blah blah. Miles's body was giving an engaging, charismatic, and well-rehearsed speech about the glory of the Prince family, but his mind was completely elsewhere. The words he was saying were self-aggrandizing nonsense to him, but it made the audience feel special and "in the inner circle." He made eye contact with members of the crowd, as his hands moved elegantly and theatrically to emphasize his words and enthrall the audience. Every member of the crowd hung on to every word as Miles caressed the chest and teased what was inside.

"Now. Without further ado, it is my honor to reveal..." Then he opened the chest. The crowd gasped in shock as they laid eyes on the contents of the box. Miles, with a proud and self-assured smirk, turned to admire what was inside...

Miles's eyebrows shot up as nothing but a Jack of Diamonds playing card stared back at him. He turned back to the crowd as they erupted into a cacophony of scandalous murmurs. Miles grit his teeth and retreated backstage as a duo of security guards emerged on stage to bark instructions at the crowd, organizing a lockdown.

Miles's heart pounded as more security rushed him away to his bedroom. Miles locked the door behind him and collapsed in a thick, cushy leather chair. The silence of the room was intense compared to the constant noise of the party outside. He took a deep breath and relaxed.

Then he pulled out the obsidian chalice and smiled.

"The Jack of Diamonds strikes again," he said with a chuckle, letting his hair fall in front of his eyes, the tension of having to put a face on all night finally fading. He let the adrenaline dissipate from his blood before putting the obsidian chalice away with the rest of the Jack Of Diamonds's loot. He had no material need for any of this hodge podge of valuables. It was just his way of sticking it to the blue bloods like him who cared about appearances over anything else. Plus, it was simply quite the thrill.

He undid his bow tie and moved across the room to put a vinyl on his record player. He closed his eyes and listened as the needle caught the groove with a satisfying crackle. Just as the music was about to start, there was a knock on the door. Miles sighed. He had practiced what he would say to security but was surprised how fast they decided to question him. He thought they would lock down the rest of the estate first.

He opened the door with a warm smile that froze when the security guard was pointing a taser at him. Before Miles could even attempt to charm the guard, a jolt of pain shot through him.

Reflexively, he turned to the drawer where he had stashed the obsidian chalice.

Everything went black.

02:

[[Director Of Intelligence, Agent Hanged Man's report: Obsidian Chalice.]]

History:
A private archeology firm, while excavating a possible native burial site north of Mount Saint Helens, excavated a tomb that predated even the earliest documented native civilizations. When opened, the crypt was full of cremated human remains and volcanic ash. Buried in the ash was a miraculously polished obsidian chalice encrusted with gems or crystals of a dark green color with ancient symbols carved into them. When shown the symbols, Local scholars could not determine any language they belonged to. Based on photographs of the obsidian chalice and markings inside the tomb, and with help from the Director of Archives, Agent Hierophant, I was able to determine that the symbols are of eldritch origin. The chalice was possibly used to channel eldritch power to one who drank from it, but I was unable to pinpoint any specific god or gods or how powerful its effects were on its users.

Location:
The Obsidian chalice went on auction soon after its recent discovery. We were unable to obtain the obsidian chalice due to being outbid by a private collector. The chalice was transported to the Prince family

estate in ▮▮▮▮▮▮▮▮▮▮ It seems the Prince family has no interest in its potential eldritch properties, and simply want it as a piece of art.

Conclusion:

While the obsidian chalice itself seems dormant and inert, it has drawn the attention of local cults who may want to use it for dangerous occult rituals. The Prince estate's security is high, so it is recommended we don't exert significant resources into its protection, but my department will be keeping eyes on it just in case.

03:

Miles Prince slowly awakened. He tried to stand only to find that his legs and arms were bound to a tree. He looked around to see himself in the middle of an intricate drawn sigil, surrounded by hooded figures clothed in dark robes. They were watching someone wearing a more ornate green cloak give what sounded like a sermon.

The green-robed leader spoke in a powerful and manic voice, but Miles was still too dazed to understand all the words. He heard "Vessel" and "puppet."

Miles started to panic and thrash about in his bindings, which caused the congregation to turn their focus to him. The green-robed leader even turned and tilted his head at Miles.

Miles gulped. His mind was racing with possible things to say. Threatening? No, they clearly knew who he was and determined the risk of kidnapping him was worth it. Appeal to sympathy? To an apparent cult? Not a chance… Appeal to greed? No… if they wanted money they would ransom him…

"Hello!" Miles said with a forced warmth. He tried to make eye contact with the leader. "L-lovely evening for a sermon, eh?" Then he let out a chuckle, but his voice cracked, revealing his fear.

The congregation laughed.

"BEHOLD!" said the green robed leader. "Our vessel! The final piece of our plan!"

After every sentence from the leader, the congregation would mutter short chants of approval.

"And what a plan it is! It is truly an honor to be a part of it! There is no need for these restraints. I am happy to serve," Miles said in a vain attempt at talking his way out of this. The congregation laughed again.

"And serve he shall!" the leader continued, gesturing wide, the obsidian chalice in hand. "It was prophesied that the famed Jack of Diamonds would go after the obsidian chalice, and it was prophesied we could capture him AND the chalice together!"

"Well done! You caught me. As is a thief's honor, my treasure is yours," Miles tried, only to get laughed at. The constant laughing frazzled him.

"And not only will the famed thief be our puppet," the leader continued, "We will also control the heir to the Prince family! Truly the gods have smiled upon us."

Miles was not used to his charm falling on deaf ears. The reality that he indeed couldn't talk his way out of this sunk in. Panic gripped his heart.

"Grrr! What do you want with me?" Miles screamed, his facade fully breaking as he thrashed in his bindings, eyes wide with fear.

The green-robed leader stepped up and cupped Miles's chin. "Be still, my child," he whispered in an insidiously sweet tone that made Miles shiver, "You are about to become host to a great power."

As the leader spoke, he brought the obsidian chalice up to Miles's lips. Before Miles could even think about fighting, though, the leader placed his free hand over Miles's forehead, holding him against the tree so he couldn't struggle, then forced a thick, bitter black liquid down Miles's throat.

As he swallowed, he stared out at the congregation, eyes burning with rage. Once the obsidian chalice was empty, the deep green crystals lining its rim seemed to fade, turning colorless.

Miles coughed, shaking with fury. "You better hope you can control this power... because I swear to whatever god you are summoning..." he said.

The congregation seemed to, for a brief moment, lose confidence before the leader pulled a long, thin ritual dagger from the sleeve of his elegant green robe.

"Now... we sever the mortal link and allow our god to claim its vessel."

Miles watched the dagger glisten in the moonlight as he felt whatever he drank writhe inside him. He grit his teeth and silently prayed to whatever god they were trying to summon. It felt like his last possibility. The congregation began to chant in unison, growing louder and louder and louder... The chant filled Miles's mind. He was unable to think anymore, nothing but the ever-loudening chant echoing in his own thoughts.

Miles's bright blue eyes refused to break eye contact with the dagger, even when it began to descend for his heart.

Then, there was a bright white flash.

For the briefest of moments, Miles thought he was dead. But when the light faded, there were no pearly gates. Instead, there was a smirking man in a black suit gripping the wrist of the cult leader.

"See that, James? I *can* learn your tricks!" Adam Nolan said. In one swift motion, Adam managed to disarm the cult leader, elbow them in the jaw, and use the dagger to slash the ropes binding Miles.

"Sorry for cutting it close there," Adam said, holding a hand out for Miles, "our intel guy had us running around the forest for a while. Seriously, two forest missions in a row?" Then he turned to another black suited man.

James Graves stood over a pile of unconscious bodies, reloading a handful of tranquilizer darts into his rifle.

"Codenames," James said coldly as he slowly scanned around, his eyes glowing white to see into the dark woods.

"Uhg. Magician," Adam said, turning back to dust Miles off, "Is it clear?"

"It appears to be," James said. He blinked, the glow in his eyes dissipating. His stone face cracked a smile at Adam. "Well done."

Miles was shaking uncontrollably. He looked between the

two agents before letting out a shaken "b-bwah?"

James straightened his tie and approached Miles. "Hello," he said, "I am special agent James Graves with the Bureau Arcana."

"Codenames?" Adam said with a smug smirk.

James sighed and gave Adam a patient smile. "Codenames are for us. Not civilians."

Adam shrugged and scooped up the obsidian chalice, examining it thoroughly.

James turned back to Miles. "How are you feeling? Are you hurt?"

Miles caught his breath. "I... I think I'm fine... but whatever they made me drink... feels weird..."

Adam swabbed the inside of the chalice and put it in what looked like an evidence bag. Adorning the bag was the same eye and raven symbol that decorated the agents' lapel.

"What was that stuff anyway?" Adam asked.

"Agent Hierophant should know when we get back to the extraction site," James said, checking Miles for nicks, cuts or other wounds. "If not him, Agent Moon will run an analysis."

"Am I gonna be okay?" Miles said, feeling his legs about to give out.

James stared into Miles's eyes. "We will make sure of it. This is what we do." He sounded genuine.

After hearing that, Miles's body felt it was safe enough to check out, and he immediately passed out.

James chuckled and shook his head. He put his finger to his ear. "Hanged Man. Status?"

There was a brief hiss of static before a voice spoke through James's earpiece.

"Local law enforcement are en route. ETA seven minutes. Ensure suspects are restrained, then it is safe to extract," the voice, agent Hanged Man said.

"Copy," James said, before turning to Adam. "You heard him. Let's handcuff the cultists and take this poor kid back."

"Kid? He looks my age!" Adam huffed as made the rounds to restrain the cultists.

"Exactly," Agent Hanged Man said over the radio.

Adam tisked and rolled his eyes. There was an eerie silence

that made Adam anxious, so as he worked he held his hand to his ear and spoke, "Hey, Hanged Man, what was it like mentoring Jam-Agent Magician when *he* was a rookie?"

"Heh. He was a beast," Agent Hanged Man said, a clear hint of admiration in his voice.

"Oh yeah? Tell me more," Adam said, looking over to James.

James gave Adam a tired look. "We're busy right now. You can read the files later if you must," he said before kneeling beside Miles. He reached out and placed two fingers to Miles's neck, right on their carotid artery. James struggled to find a pulse when Miles began to convulse and writhe.

Adam raised his eyebrows with concern and leaned against the tree that Miles was previously bound to. "I-is he okay?"

Miles's pulse suddenly shot up, his body contorting and twisting unnaturally. The back of Miles's coat ripped, and an inky black tentacle spewed out. James jolted back in shock, blinking back several feet with a soft flash of white light as Miles's body erupted in a flurry of tentacles. The tentacles thrashed about horrifically like the creature from The Thing.

"What in the hell is that!?" Adam shouted in horror, reflexively pointing the ceremonial dagger towards Miles's corrupted figure.

Miles's face snapped towards Adam. Miles, or what was left of Miles, stared at the dagger with deep green eyes, and let out a horrible screech. The tentacles attached to Miles's back whipped out in a panic, grasping for whatever it could grab. In this case, the tentacles gripped the branches above him and pulled. Miles was flung into the air and the tentacles, apparently moving solely on impulse, flew into the forest, using the trees and branches to propel them at speed.

Adam dropped the knife and stared wide eyed. Throughout all his training, this was the first time he had encountered any sort of eldritch anything. He turned to James, and although he hid it well, Adam could tell that even he was shaken just a bit.

A voice broke in through the earpieces.

"What the hell was that, Ace? Something on the scan just

took off like a bat out of hell." Agent Hanged Man said.

James put his hand to his ear to respond. "Unidentified eldritch entity. It appears to be using Miles Prince as a host and-"

"WHERE THE HELL IS THE ROOKIE GOING?" Agent hanged man interrupted. James blinked and turned to where Adam was, only to see him right as he dashed into the darkness of the forest.

04:

Deep in the forest was a small, abandoned chapel. It was originally used as the meeting ground for the cult that kidnapped Miles, but as the congregation grew, it no longer had room for them. Inside, Miles thrashed about, the tentacles from his back whipping and wrecking the pews as he gripped his head. Except... was it Miles anymore? The being that was once Miles collapsed to the floor, arms and legs spasming as it tried to acclimate to its new body.

Eventually, the being managed to stand, though its limbs moved rigid and jerkily. It brought its new hands up to its face.

"No... Not again!" it said, the sounds coming out of Miles's throat sounded harsh and rough, like someone trying to use an instrument they hadn't used in years. The being stared at its hands; it recognized them as that of a human. It knew this wasn't its body. It was stolen. It was forced to steal this body.

"I'm sorry... I'm so sorry..." it sobbed, wrapping its stolen arms around itself as it stumbled to the altar of the chapel. It fell to its knees and looked up at the altar.

"Please... help me... I'm no good at being human..." it begged.

Maybe I can help... A voice said in the back of the being's mind. The being recognized it as its own voice. No... The voice of the body it inhabited... No... the voice of the human whose body this was supposed to be.

The being gasped, "Y-you're still here?"

So it seems... Miles's voice said. Miles was still there, in the back of his own mind... He was completely conscious, fully aware of what was happening to him, to his body. At first, he felt like he should panic... but throughout his entire life, he felt like his person was just a means for his family's end. Being literally possessed felt almost cathartic compared to being figuratively possessed.

"H-how?" the being asked.

How would I know that? Miles replied.

The being gripped its hair and started laughing nervously. "Sorry sorry sorry sorry!"

Take a deep breath... We will figure this out. Let's start with the basics. My name is Miles Prince. Do you have a name?

The being took a deep breath, "Uhm... The closest human pronunciation I think is... Z'ak'Aroth."

Z'ak'Aroth... Mind if I call you Zak?

"Zak... I like that... It sounds... human," Zak said, flashing a twitchy smile.

Nice to meet you, Zak! Circumstances notwithstanding... Now...can you tell me what you are?

"W-well... I uhm..." Zak let out an anxious whimper as he searched through Miles's brain, trying to translate the incomprehensible reality of his existence using words and concepts Miles understood. "I am Z'ak'Aroth! Heir to the Cosmic Court of Aroth!" Zak said, trying his best to stand proud, like he was trying to impress Miles, but he still struggled to articulate the meat bag the way he wanted, and he fell to his knees. "Nngh... My family... we don't really understand you humans... so we made that Chalice as a way to... learn more about you all."

Zak could feel Miles's judgment burning inside his mind.

"We didn't know it would kill the host! We didn't understand what death was! I'm sorry! I-I tried to hide the chalice where nobody could ever find it so I couldn't hurt anyone ever again! I didn't want this to happen again!" Zak screamed, body seizing up as he tried to cope with these human emotions.

Take a breath...

Zak tried to take a breath again, but his body spasmed. He gasped for air but just couldn't figure out how to breathe.

"Help... me..." Zak choked out.

Okay! Focus... I'm still here so maybe... let me lead?

Zak slammed his eyes shut and focused. He focused on an abstract image of Miles and tried to pull them forward. Miles felt himself being pulled from a thick, inky black pool and brought under a spotlight. In the spotlight, he became hyper aware of his/Zak's body. He became aware of every sensation running along their shared skin, aware of every thought running through their shared brain. It felt less like Miles was taking back control, and more like Zak had tuned a radio to Miles's signal. Miles broadcast his moves, and Zak chose to listen. Miles took a deep breath.

Zak took a deep breath.

Miles smiled, and Zak smiled.

Feeling better? Miles thought.

"Yeah," Zak said.

A knock on the chapel door snapped Zak around, yanking the mental receiver away and sending Miles back into darkness.

Hey!

Zak wanted to apologize, but he moved on impulse and turned to where the knocking came from, his tentacles splayed out in a threat display.

Adam Nolan stood there, hands raised, eyes wide with fear.

"I come in peace?" Adam said, putting on a brave face despite his frightened shivering.

"WHO ARE YOU?!?" Zak screamed.

I recognize him! He saved me!

Zak's tentacles fell to the floor and he backed away. "W-what do you want?"

Adam straightened his tie and took a careful step forward. "H-hi! I'm special agent Adam Nolan with the Bureau Arcana! Well... Not *special* agent yet. Technically I'm still a rookie but... Anyway!" he said, rubbing the back of his head, "I overheard you say your name was Z'ak'Aroth?"

"I prefer Zak... I think..." Zak said.

"Yes, Zak!" Adam laughed nervously.

Zak nodded shyly and gave another twitchy smile. He looked into Adam's eyes and Zak, like a radio picking up interference, could vaguely sense Adam's thoughts. Adam was scared. Scared for his own wellbeing, yes, but more so Miles's wellbeing.

I can hear his thoughts... Miles thought to Zak.

Zak nodded. "M-Miles is fine..." he said.

Adam nodded. "He's still in there? I was wondering who you were talking to all alone in here," he said, attempting to let out a lighthearted laugh.

Zak rubbed his shoulder anxiously. "So, you heard what I am. A-are you scared of me?"

Zak could hear that Adam was indeed scared of him.

"Oh yeah. My colleagues even more so, I'm sure," Adam said, bluntly.

"Wh-what are they gonna do to me?" Zak shivered.

Adam's mind raced with possibilities: some innocent, and some gruesome. Zak panicked and backed away, tentacles rising defensively.

Adam took a step back and raised his hands higher, trying to seem unthreatening. "That depends on you, I think. My team is incoming, and... if you aren't an immediate threat, I'm sure we can work something peaceful out."

Zak whimpered and hugged himself. His life, or rather... Miles's life depended on seeming unthreatening. He didn't know how to do that. His body shook, his tentacles writhed involuntarily. He tried to smile, but he could immediately sense Adam tense up with anxiety. It must have looked unnatural, twisted.

More mental frequences jammed Zak's mind. It was the rest of Adam's team. Their anxiety only amplified Zak's and he curled up. Miles was going to die here because he was too incompetent to pilot a human body...

Let me handle this. Miles said inside their shared mind.

Zak closed his eyes and let Miles come forward, center stage in the limelight of his own mind.

Miles opened his eyes and stood up straight and tall, as dignified as the heir to the Prince family fortune should be, as calm and collected as a master thief should be.

Adam looked into Miles's eyes to see one bright blue eye and one deep green eye. Adam chuckled.

James kicked open the door and stormed in, rifle raised and pointed directly at Miles/Zak.

Miles! Help! Zak thought.

Miles smiled brightly and calmly walked towards James.

"James Graves, correct?" Miles said, holding out a hand in formal greeting.

James kept the rifle raised until Adam gently took it from him. James looked to Adam, who only smiled.

"I must thank you for saving my life," Miles continued, and he and Zak were able to sense the anxiety and fear in James shift to cautious bafflement. "I am sure you have many questions, as do I. Let's figure this out together."

05:

"Aroth… Aroth…" Executive Director Gecko said, deep in thought. The ashtray on his desk was nearly overflowing in cigarette butts. Agent Moon noticed that Gecko was smoking a notably higher quantity than usual since Miles/Zak was brought in.

"Is there a problem, sir?" Agent Moon asked.

"It's eldritch… The eldritch have been nothing but a problem for us. The last thing we need is another monarch in color prancing around, carelessly making a muck of things," Gecko said, snuffing out the butt of his most recent cigarette before immediately lighting another.

"If I may, sir," Agent Moon began, "So were werewolves, yet I've found a way to make use of our recent… domestication efforts. Plus, I think we could leverage its connection with Prince Pharmaceuticals as a private sector investment into Project Moonlight."

Director Gecko stared at Agent Moon, the cigarette rapidly burning between his fingers. Eventually, the reflective circles that were Director Gecko's glasses shimmered, indicating a nod.

"Approved," Gecko said.

06:

Zak stared at himself in the mirror and ran his hands up and down his own face. He was slowly getting used to recognizing this face as his face.

"You're so… how do you say… pretty!" Zak said, ruffling his own hair, thoroughly fixated on the sensation of fingers through hair.

If a disembodied consciousness could blush, Miles would be bright red.

Focus, Miles said. He had no idea what to expect from his and Zak's debrief with the Bureau Arcana, but an offer to join the Academy Arcana and train to be a potential agent was not on his short list of possibilities. He hated the idea of going back to university, but Zak begged Miles to accept. Miles agreed. It would be hard to go back to the life of a socialite/thief with a socially anxious eldritch being in the driver's seat.

"Right!" Zak said, fiddling with an untied necktie.

I'm not gonna take control this time. You can do it.

"I got this." Zak said and shakily began tying the necktie. Once he was finished, he stared at himself in the mirror and tried to smile. It looked awkward and unnatural, just like his tie. Zak felt Miles's disapproval, and he hastily undid the tie.

"I'm sorry! These finger things are weird!" Zak cried.

I know. Let's take a break for the night.

Zak sighed and turned to view his dorm room. It was a stark contrast to the opulent splendor Miles was used to, but he only insisted on keeping his record player and vinyl collection. Miles wanted to put a record on, but Zak was too nervous about scratching the disk. He would call Miles forth to do it, but the two learned that doing so was incredibly exhausting, so Zak simply collapsed in bed.

"I'm not ready for this…" Zak lamented.

Don't worry. We are in this together.

07:

Upon returning to the Bureau Arcana headquarters, as Adam Nolan wrote his report on the Obsidian Chalice incident, his mind began to wander. Why was he writing this report? Who was reading them? Are they stored anywhere? That made him think back to his first encounter with the Bureau, back in his hometown. He wondered if there was a report about that… he wondered what was in it.

Adam finished up his report and explored the Bureau's

grounds. Besides the directors that were associated with the Major Arcana, The Bureau was also staffed with agents associated with the Minor Arcana. Each Minor Arcana was associated with a suit that designated their department, and number that designated their rank. Aces were rookies and glorified interns, 10s were senior agents, etc. The face cards were management. Kings were the department managers, Queens were Vice Managers, Knights were assistant Managers, and Pages are jr. managers. A Six of Swords, for example, was a medium ranked agent working as security.

The Pentacles were associated with administration and ran the day to day operations of The Bureau Arcana. Desk jockeys, pencil pushers, accountants, etc. They tended to blend into the bureaucratic haze of cubicles, water coolers, and business casual.

The Cups were associated with Research, IT, Engineering, or anything similarly related. They tended to scurry around The Bureau in lab coats and scrubs with the anxious energy of someone with too many tasks and not enough daylight.

The Wands were associated with Education and Training. They are in charge of running the Academy Arcana. Originally named the Acclimation Department, they are responsible for ensuring a potential agent's smooth transition to the understanding of the otherworldly. Adam hadn't seen them since his time at the Academy, but he recalled them as floating around with a preppy air of intellectualism.

Swords were security and field agents, both internal and external. They acted as guards inside The Bureau and acted as general field agents outside The Bureau. They patrolled the halls and perimeter with a self-seriousness that unsettled Adam. There were notably more Swords than there were in any other department. The proverbial deck that was the Bureau Arcana was stacked with extra Swords.

Adam continued to wander the cold, bureaucratic corridors of the administrative department. The walls were sparsely dotted with motivational posters that seemed at a glance to be just like anything else one would find in an office, but upon closer inspection, had an otherworldly or eldritch tone to them that unsettled Adam. One was a picture of a cat hanging from its tentacle arms with the caption "Hang In There." Another was a picture of what appeared to be a swarm of octopus eyes with the caption "SUCCESS: The Path to Success Is Seen by Those Who Dare to Gaze; Look Beyond What Your Eyes Can See." The worst one was a picture of a human figure in a mirror with a thousand copies in the reflection, the caption read, "COMPANY: Don't Worry! You Are Never Really Alone!"

Eventually, Adam found a door labeled Archives. He stepped inside.

Inside, the Bureau Arcana archives were deliberately labyrinthine. Every aisle was labeled with a runic character that Adam simply could not comprehend. To make matters worse, every time he tried to read the spine of any given folder in the farfetched hopes of getting his bearings that way, his eyes glazed over before he could parse a single word. It was like trying to read something in a dream. The words individually made sense, but together, they simply had no discernible meaning.

He turned one of the countless corners in the hope of finding some semblance of direction. A man was waiting for him. Adam jumped in surprise.

"Even senior agents avoid just wandering into the archives," the man said. He was dressed in a black Bureau Arcana suit but modified to look like a priest. Draped over the blazer was a white stole with the Bureau Arcana's eye and raven logo embroidered on it, and instead of the white shirt and black tie, he had a black shirt and roman collar. He had a wizened face with soft but intense pale eyes. He had salt and pepper hair and stood with a strong posture. His voice was soothing yet commanding, one that felt right at home speaking to a crowd.

"You must be the new agent Fool," he said. He reached a hand into one of the bookshelves and pulled out a file that was clearly labeled, "Adam Nolan. Arcana 00. Fool. Recruit." He started flipping through it.

"Handpicked by Mr. Graves. Very interesting," he said.

Adam blinked and asked, "Hi… Who are you?"

"My name is Nathanial Cross. I am the director of Archival here at the Bureau Arcana. Agent Hierophant if you are fond of the codenames."

As Nathanial, AKA agent Hierophant spoke, he put the

file back on the shelf. Adam looked to see where he put it, but it was lost in the sea of nonsense.

"What, pray tell, are you hoping to find here?" Nathaniel asked.

Adam anxiously fiddled with a random file on the shelf as he answered, "A couple years ago, there was an incident in my hometown. I-it was the first time I learned of The Bureau, actually."

"Ahh yes," Nathaniel said, "The Capstone Creek Doppelganger. Here." Nathaniel ran his fingers along the archive as if searching for the right file and stopped. He pulled out a folder labeled "Capstone creek, 12/12/2010," and handed it to Adam.

Adam flipped through it. There was a report from Hanged Man detailing reports consistent with doppelganger vampires, a biological report of what a doppelganger was, and a series of field agent reports, including from James. As he read, his face twisted in confusion. Every detail was exactly as he remembered it... except one.

"Is this a redacted report?" Adam asked, flipping through the file, his eyes scanning fast and thorough, searching through as if there was something just under the surface.

"No. I detest redactions. Knowledge, history, etc., should not be censored, no matter how inconvenient it may be. Sometimes agents request copies with redactions, but the originals will never be removed, never redacted, never erased from *my* archives," Nathaniel said as if the comment was aimed at someone specific. Adam imagined it aimed at Director Gecko, whose constant smoke made him seem like a walking redaction.

"Isn't that a security risk?" Adam asked.

Nathaniel chuckled and gestured to the vast rows of documents around him. "Find me the words that would bring The Bureau Arcana to its knees."

Adam's mind was immediately overwhelmed by the sheer scale of parsing through the archive word for word. He shook his head and raised the Capstone Creek file. "How come Elliott isn't mentioned in this at all, then?"

Nathaniel's eyebrows raised with concern. "That name... it rings familiar. Why?"

"He was... killed," Adam said, voice sounding distant, sheepish.

Nathanial turned to the wall of archives and searched with an intense focus that he hadn't shown before. It almost appeared like he was struggling. Eventually, he pulled a thick file form the bookshelf labeled "ELLIOTT HARDING"

"That's him!" Adam said as he excitedly moved beside Nathanial as they opened the file.

Every page was blank.

Chapter 03:
The Inferno of Beaumont Heights

01:

Killian Wilkes got quite a thrill from wearing his most expletive laden t-shirt under his collared "business-casual" shirt mandated by his temp agency. He sat in his cubicle, doing his work. It was mind-numbing clerical work, but there was one thing that kept him sane. He was damn good at his job. He made it a point to do all the "unprofessional" things that drove his rotation of middle managers absolutely insane, such as "forgetting" to take his piercings out, keeping his shirt unbuttoned in his cubicle, keeping his cubicle messy, responding late to emails, and usually responding with a nothing more than "k." etc. The best part was seeing their face redden more and more when they inevitably chewed him out, and he would just smile and smile, because whenever it got higher up… Killian's exceptional productivity meant on paper, Killian was too valuable to fire.

Killian was typing away at his computer, headphones on only one ear, when he heard the unmistakable sound of self-important footsteps coming his way. He turned his music off and covered his exposed ear. He continued to work and pretend to listen to music until…

"Mister Wilkes!" said some stuffy man in a cheap suit with a dark blue shirt that he hoped would hide his sweat stains. His hair was thinning, but the way he styled it showed he was in denial. A name tag around his neck read "Bob"

Killian didn't respond. He just kept typing away, swaying to his imaginary music.

Stuffy Bob's eye twitched and he cleared his throat, as if it was some spell that could pierce headphones. When that too got no response, Stuffy Bob spun Killian around by their chair.

Stuffy Bob immediately grit his teeth when he saw Killian's feet dug into the office chair, his tongue out, idly clicking his tongue piercing against his teeth. The brown roots of Killian's hair were just coming in under his dyed black hair.

Killian spent the least amount of effort possible to look up at the man who just interrupted his work. Killian had a young yet severe face that constantly looked like it was on the verge of snarling. His eyebrows raised dismissively, and he could hardly contain the slight smile already forming from seeing the blood vessel on his yuppy boss's forehead bulge with rage.

"Eh?" Killian said flatly.

Stuffy Bob's eyes twitched before he smirked. He crossed his arms and leaned against the edge of the cubicle entrance.

"Someone is here to see you," Bob said, sounding more smug than Killian expected.

Killian's eyebrow twitched ever so slightly before he rolled his eyes. "Tell 'em I'm busy," he said before starting to turn his chair back to his desk.

Stuffy Bob stopped the chair and snickered. "They're feds. They insist on seeing you this instant."

A sharp chill shot up Killian's spine, making him sit in his chair with good posture for the first time since he started working there.

"Thrilling" Killian said with a curious smile. He stood up and let out a deep yawn as he stretched his arms. Stuffy bob tapped his foot impatiently. Killian responded by sticking his pierced tongue out as he buttoned his shirt.

"Smoke break first." Killian said as he stepped out of his cubicle and waved Stuffy Bob off, barely concealing the fact he was flipping the bird.

Killian appeared calm, but his heart was pounding. He walked down the hall and stared into the frosted glass of the conference room. He saw the sharp silhouette of at least half a dozen figures, shivered, and kept walking until he reached the balcony.

Once outside, he reached in his pocket and pulled out a brand new carton of cigarettes. He pulled one out and placed it between his lips. He looked around to make sure no one was around, and using his other hand, snapped his fingers. A flame appeared on his thumb, and he used that to light the cigarette. Killian didn't smoke, it was just the most socially acceptable way to light things on fire, and when you can spawn fire from your fingertips, it was hard not to pick up the habit.

Killian watched the flame dance between his fingertips as the cigarette burned in his mouth without him sucking in the smoke. Maybe that's why the feds were interested in him. While there were no laws on the books relating to those with arcane abilities, his foster parents always told him horror stories of a clandestine federal bureau disappearing anyone they discover with potentially dangerous powers. As a kid, it was an effective way to make him conceal his powers, but it had the side effect of further brewing his hatred and distrust for authority. As an adult, he tried to reason it away as just a way for his foster parents to keep him from burning his clothes, but the fear that it was true always lingered.

He let the fires on his fingertips dissipate as he looked 30 stories down to the streets below Beaumont Heights. He watched as a bit of ash fell from his cigarette.

Killian was startled when the door to the balcony flung open. He steadied himself and nonchalantly turned to see a man whose getup almost made Killian laugh out loud. He was wearing a black suit, black tie, dark sunglasses and a black fedora. The man couldn't look more like a federal agent if he tried, he even had a bronze pin with a raven perched on an eye.

Although it was impossible to see behind the shades, it was clear the agent looked directly at Killian. The man smiled and approached, leaning his forearms against the balcony railing right next to Killian.

"It's weird to see such a young guy smoking an honest to god cigarette these days. Most guys your age prefer vapes," the man said. It sounded like an attempt at small talk, but Killian had talked to enough cops to assume every sentence was a deliberate attempt at getting information.

Killian shrugged. "Call me old fashioned," he said.

The man in black held out a hand in greeting and said, "Well mister old fashioned. I'm a special agent Magician with the Bureau Arcana."

Killian chuckled and shook the Magician's hand, "Code names? Really? Got a name I can call you instead?"

The Magician chuckled with Killian before smirking and

saying, "That information is classified." The smug way he said it made Killian cringe.

The Magician seemed to sense the shift in Killian's demeanor, and after a pause, said, "I haven't had a proper smoke in ages, and with a view like this? I think I could relapse for a day." His words sounded so charming that Killian couldn't help but smile.

Killian suspected it was another attempt at social engineering, but he didn't want to play his hand too quickly, so he pulled out the cig carton, whereupon the Magician eagerly swiped a cigarette from within.

He put the cig in his mouth before letting out a frustrated tisk. "Ah hell. I don't carry a lighter on me. Mind if I borrow yours?"

Killian's face remained still. His smile didn't falter, and his eyes remained politely fixed on the Magician's sunglasses. Killian was only able to see the reflection of his own smoldering eyes. His pupils twitched.

"Sorry. I don't have a lighter," Killian said, trying to sound as natural as possible. "All I use are matches and... wouldn't you know it; I just used my last one."

The Magician let out an almost obnoxious laugh and shook his head. "Oh, just my luck. I found the one smoker in Beaumont Heights who buys a brand new carton of cigarettes but neglects to buy a new case of matches to go with it."

Killian's blood ran cold. The corners of his smile twitched. He stared out over the railing. Deep in the back of his mind was a call telling him to jump. He grit his teeth and turned to see the Magician. His brown eyes were just barely peeking up from behind the top of his sunglasses. And he was smirking. That smug little smirk.

Killian did his best to smirk back. He opened his mouth to speak but was immediately cut off.

"Plus, I don't see a discarded match anywhere. And it would be dangerous to just toss a lit match off a building... That could cause a fire. You don't want to do that, do you Mister Wilkes?" the Magician said, placing a firm hand on Killian's shoulder, not-so-subtly guiding them to the conference room.

02:

As soon as Killian and The Magician were inside the conference room, The Magician's demeanor changed. His professional stiffness loosened and he cocked his hip. His head tilted from side to side like a snake sizing up its prey. He gestured to his fellow agents whom populated the conference room. One agent went to lock and guard the door, and two others swiftly grabbed Killian.

Killian, cooperative up to this point, started struggling.

"Hey! Hands off! I'm cooperating! OW!" Killian screamed before The Magician decked Killian in the nose, stunning him enough for the two agents to force Killian into an office chair and handcuffed each wrist to one of its arms.

Killian shook his head and snarled at the group of agents. The Magician sat down in his own chair and scooted right up in front of Killian.

"Show us the magic," The Magician said. His voice sounded different than before. Instead of the familiar cadence of a cop, it was... the familiar drawl of a thug.

Killian narrowed his eyes. "I don't know what you're talking about."

The Magician snickered and slapped Killian hard across the face. Killian's eyes shot open in shock as the slap forced his head to turn and look through the frosted conference room glass. He saw the silhouettes of his coworkers puttering about, blissfully unaware of what was happening to him.

The Magician grabbed Killian's chin and forced Killian to look him in the eyes. In the reflection of the magician's sunglasses, Killian saw his lips quiver and his eyes begin to water.

"Show. Us," The Magician demanded.

Killian's arms shook with rage. He looked around, surrounded by authority figures who were all smiling with an almost perverted glee as they abused their power. Killian locked eyes with the Magician as best he could and spit a flame square into their face.

The Magician recoiled as the other agents laughed and

clapped. Killian smiled wide, proud as he stared at the Magician's freshly singed eyebrows.

"What else can I do for ya?" Killian asked, sounding calm, but face twitching with fury.

"That's confirmation enough for me," one of the agents said.

"Yeah. Terminate him before he causes any more problems in our world," said another.

"Don't you mean extinguish?" said a third before they all started laughing.

"WHAT?" Killian screamed before the Magician gagged him by stuffing a thick cloth in his mouth.

The Magician cracked his neck and casually pulled out a silenced pistol. He pointed it right against Killian's forehead.

This is how Killian always imagined it would go. A shadowy government organization killing him for being... inconvenient. Murdered in cold blood and disposed of like nothing more than a piece of trash to maintain the status quo, no one to mourn him, no one to remember or care. No fanfare. No explanation. No remorse.

Screw that.

03:

[[Director Of Intelligence, Agent Hanged Man's memo: Imposters.]]
I have been receiving an increasing number of reports from around the southern California region detailing encounters with a group who claim to be agents of the Bureau Arcana. I have cross referenced the reports with our archives and can see no connection to any of our operations. I asked Executive Director Emperor if they were perhaps black ops that would have no report, and he responded with a no. I am inclined to believe this because usually when he is

working on something clandestine, he simply doesn't respond. See my report on ███████████ procurement for Moon's Project

All of the incidents involving these seemingly imposter Bureau Agents all have a similar M.O. A group of individuals in black suits show up claiming to be special agents of the Bureau Arcana investigating a "person of interest." This "person of interest" then ends up going missing.

Upon further investigation of these persons of interest, they all seem to have, at some point in their life, exhibited some sort of metahuman, arcane, or cosmic affinity. It is too early to speculate on their exact motives, but they seem to have a strong distaste for anything outside the mundane plane.

Director of Communications, Agent Empress, has asked for any information that could help identify an imposter agent, especially if our agents clash with them in the field. Based on my investigation into these incidents, there is one telltale detail that pegs these faux agents as imposters: their pins are bronze instead of silver.

04:

Adam Nolan stood, hands in the pockets of his deliberately tailored black suit, leaned against the side of the Bureau Arcana intel van, and stared up at Beaumont Heights as it towered above them. He pulled a spent rifle shell out of his pocket and began idly rolling it between his fingers. He focused intensely on the shell, rolling it between his knuckles with less and less effort until he flicked his wrist, launching the shell into the air and caught it in his hand. Or rather... right above his hand. Adam lit up with excitement as he held the shell casing suspended in the air right above his palm.

"Yes!" Adam exclaimed, immediately losing focus and dropping the shell. He stumbled to catch it and hit the ground. The shell rolled away and into a well-worn dress shoe. Adam looked up to see James Graves standing over him.

James raised an eyebrow, the faintest hint of a smirk cracking his stone serious face.

"S-status?" Adam said, grabbing the shell and hurrying back to his feet.

The radio in Adam and James's ear crackled to life, it was a crackle that Adam had grown to associate strongly with a certain Director Of Intelligence, Agent Hanged Man.

"Men in black suits spotted on the 30th floor. Reception confirmed seeing bronze lapel pins."

"Hanged Man, am I ever gonna actually see you?" Adam asked.

There was silence on the other end of the radio before an amused chuckle emerged from the crackle of static. "If you are seeing me on the scene, things have gone very wrong. But don't worry, I'm here. Always watching," Agent Hanged Man said. Coming from anyone else, the words would have sounded sinister, but with Agent Hanged Man's voice, it was reassuring.

"Besides, with Ace with you, I'd just get in the way," Agent Hanged Man added. James sighed, suppressing a blush.

"Well then, *Ace*, What's the plan?" Adam asked, gazing at James with admiration.

James opened his mouth to respond but was cut off by a loud boom and the sound of shattering glass. Thirty or so stories up, a torrent of flame burst from the side of Beaumont Heights.

James whipped around to see what happened, then immediately pinned Adam to the side of the intel van to shield them from the showering glass.

Adam pushed James away and said, "Too late for plans! We gotta go!"

The two agents rushed into the building. The flame had already begun to burn the floors above.

05:

Killian was dazed. At first, he thought that the inferno surrounding him was the gates of Hell, but as his vision cleared, he could make out the revolting corporate art that adorned the walls of his office conference room. Not even hellfire could burn its hideousness away. He tried to stand but found himself still handcuffed to an office chair. That brought him fully to his senses and he looked around for the men in black suits. He saw that the windows of the conference room were completely blown out. He hoped he had blown the men in black out, but he wasn't gonna wait around just to be proven wrong.

Killian gripped the chains of his handcuffs and channeled an intense heat though his palms, melting the metal linking his wrists to the chair. Once freed, he got up and looked out over the blown-out edge of the building, his office shirt burning away to free his vulgar undershirt. When he looked down, he saw no bodies, and instead saw two more men in black suits rushing in.

He turned and the chaos around him became apparent. His co-workers were running around in a panic. Killian's heart pounded with adrenaline, but through his own panic, a stab of guilt overcame him.

He rushed out to better assess the damage. The fire was just starting to reach the open cubicle area, so Killian scanned about to find anyone in immediate danger. His focus was interrupted by a bullet hitting the wall next to his head. Sharp fragments from the wall sprayed from the impact onto the side of Killian's face. He briefly saw 'The Magician' pointing a gun at him from across the office as Killian's co-workers rushed out the door.

Killian swore out and dove to the floor. He rushed into the labyrinth of cubicles, head down and eyes peeled. He wanted to just escape, but with every cubicle he passed, he had to check to make sure it wasn't occupied. Thankfully, most cubicles he checked were empty, its inhabitants having already rushed off. The few colleagues that did stay were curled up under their desk, in each case, Killian slapped the shock out of them and screamed at them to leave. They complied.

The problem with rescuing his coworkers, Killian soon realized, was that it gave away his position. 'The Magician' turned a corner and locked eyes with Killian. The good news was that Killian was pretty certain the office was now clear of his coworkers, so when 'The Magician' raised his gun to Killian, Killian raised his hand and a woosh of flame rushed out. 'The Magician' shielded himself with his arms, the flames dissipating against the black fabric of his suit. The flames licked the nearby cubicles and lit them aflame. Killian used the moment to dive behind the cover of another cubicle.

"What are you doing?!" Killian screamed, "You'll burn to death here!"

"Look around!" 'The Magician' screamed back, gun outstretched, scanning for Killian, "If I let you leave, all this will happen again!"

"You tried to kill me!" Killian seethed, throwing a wisp of fire back to try and keep The Magician off balance.

'The Magician' hid behind cover and laughed. "Oh yeah?" he said with a hint of smugness to his voice, "Is that why you barbecued your pops?"

Killian's vision went white with fury. His mind flashed with memories of the incessant beatings at the hands of his father. Killian could feel his dad's hands around his neck.

Killian coughed and snapped out of it. The smoke that filled the office made it harder to breathe. He heard 'The Magician' laughing from behind his cover of cubicle walls. Killian placed his hand on the office carpet and narrowed his eyes. He focused on where he heard the laughing coming from, and slowly, a trail of burning carpet crept down the hallway to "The Magician's" position.

"Keep laughin', asshole…" Killian whispered to himself as the embers reached its target. Killian then slammed his fist into the carpet and a rush of fire erupted from the burnt trail, engulfing 'The Magician' in flame. Unless he had flame resistant underwear, this would surely set him alight.

'The Magician' screamed out in a mix of pain and fury, shooting blindly through the cubicle walls. Bullet holes appeared uncomfortably close to Killian's location.

After the shooting ceased, Killian poked his head out to assess, and he saw "The Magician." He looked like a furnace, his black suit remaining unharmed as everything inside was ablaze. He locked eyes with Killian and started sprinting towards them.

"ABOMINATION!" 'The Magician' screamed as he dove towards Killian.

Killian sidestepped, and "The Magician," unable to stop his momentum, tumbled into the glass wall overlooking the outside. The impact mixed with the extreme heat caused the glass to immediately shatter. 'The Magician' tumbled out and fell 30 plus stories to his demise.

Killian, shaking, looked around the office which was now engulfed in flames. He made his way to the stairway and stopped. He recalled the two agents rushing in from the entrance to the building. There would be agents waiting for him... This wasn't over yet.

06:

James and Adam rushed into the burning Beaumont Heights tower and began their ascent. The two agents only got a few floors up before a flood of the building's inhabitants spilled out. Since these floors were still low and far from the fire, the evacuation was still organized and orderly, only slowing the agents slightly. The further they climbed, the more... hampering the evacuation became. People got more and more anxious and tried to push past James and Adam.

James grabbed Adam and pulled them both into the now empty lobby of one of the floors.

"I think we have gotten as far as we can with the stairs." James said.

"So... Do you want to take an elevator?" Adam asked, catching his breath from the cardio and stress of fighting up a cramped stairwell.

James cracked a slight smile. "Of sorts." He said, walking deeper into the offices.

Adam followed and watched James curiously as they seemed to meander deep into the offices until they were in an especially open and empty space. Once James found a spot he seemed fond of, he looked up.

"My hope is... the floors above us will have this space in a similar layout. All we need to do is..." then James snapped his fingers and made a whooshing sound with his mouth. His eyes began to emit a dull glow.

Adam smiled with excitement and said, "Ahh, I see."

"You have been practicing, yes?"

"Of course," Adam said, hopping over to James's side.

"So, we are ten stories up," James said," We will need to blink twenty stories further. It will feel like sprinting those twenty floors. Don't push yourself if you feel exhausted. We still have to apprehend the targets."

"Aye," Adam said, before giving James a salute.

James nodded and took a deep breath. Adam mirrored James.

"Three..." James said, taking another steading breath.

"Two..." Adam said, matching his breaths with James.

"One." James said.

The sensation of blinking teleportation felt like an accelerated roller coaster launch followed immediately by a sudden stop. The most disorienting thing about it was the lack of g-force being exerted on the physical body when the mind was expecting it. James and Adam doing this back-to-back in such quick succession was bad enough, but when each blink led them to what appeared to be the exact same location, but with different paint, slightly different decor, and such, it was especially jarring.

Adam made it ten stories up before collapsing. His head was spinning, and stomach was churning with nausea. He crawled his way to the nearest potted plant only to curse when he discovered it was just plastic. He looked around the empty office, James kept going.

"Bleh," Adam said, laying on the floor and staring into the flickering fluorescent lights. He put his hand to his ear. "Status, Magician?"

Ten floors further up, James stood, dizzy but fighting it off as best he could. He wanted to relax and recover from his jaunt, but couldn't due to the six men in faux Bureau Arcana suits staring at him in shock. James carefully put his hand to his ear. "Six suspects spotted."

"What?!" Adam yelped as he jumped to his feet. He rushed to the stairwell, slamming into a man in a cheap business suit. "Ack! Sorry, uh… Bob!" Adam said after glancing down at their name badge. The stuffy looking man was too panicked and focused on escaping to really respond beyond hurrying quicker down the stairs. The flow of people was lessened this far up, but since it was so much closer to the fire, it was much more frantic. Still, Adam forced his way up the stairs.

Adam made his way up ten more flights of stairs and rushed into the lobby of the thirtieth floor. He stepped into the lobby and looked around. He looked down a hallway that led into the offices and saw James at the far end, hands raised as six men raised guns at him.

Adam gasped and took a breath and got ready to blink in when…

A hot blast of flame blazed past the side of Adam's head, singeing an unfortunate lock of hair that fell in front of Adam's eyes. He whipped around to see a young man with a furious gaze, his hand reeled back as a swirl of flame grew in his palm, ready to throw it at Adam. This new threat was now Adam's priority.

Adam's eyes went wide. "Did… you do this?"

Killian chuckled, "Another reason to off me, right?"

"What?!" Adam exclaimed before dodging out of the way as Killian's fireball scorched the wall where Adam once stood.

Killian snarled and wound up another fireball. Adam stared at Killian's hand, watching how they curled their fingers, watching how the fire swirled and grew.

Killian spoke, "Do you envy people like me?" he said before flinging the fireball at Adam.

As the fireball came towards him, Adam threw his hand out and focused hard on how he held his lucky shell casing suspended in air. Then, when the fireball made contact with Adam's hand…

Killian gasped. Adam blinked to see Killian's fireball held

firmly in his hand without feeling any heat or burning sensation.

Adam laughed and pumped his fist with his free hand. "Phew!" he said, flicking his wrist and making the fireball dissipate safely. "Thank goodness that worked."

Killian blinked with confusion. His eyes darted to Adam's lapel pin. Something clicked, but he didn't quite know what it meant.

Adam smiled and kept his hands raised. "People are pretending to be us. I'm guessing they tried to kill you?"

Killian kept his guard up but nodded.

"And... all this..." he carefully gestured above him where smoke was starting to seep in from the above floors, "Was self-defense, right?"

Killian grit his teeth. "I plead the fifth."

Adam chuckled and smiled. "Smart," he said. his glance shifted to the hall where James was held up. He didn't see James anymore and got nervous.

"What's wrong?" Killian said, his hands slipping casually into his pockets. He looked shockingly calm despite the slowly growing chaos around them.

"Dude. This building is on fire. You should leave," Adam said.

Killian chuckled. "Oh? You don't wanna question me?"

"Not in a burning building!" Adam wanted to command Killian to get to safety, but he was dressed like a punk. Adam assumed any demand would make him reflexively disregard it.

Killian let out a dry laugh, but he saw the genuine concern for his safety in Adam's eyes. It was something he wasn't used to seeing in law enforcement. "Yer pretty cool for a fed," he said as he strolled through the stairwell door.

Adam sighed and rushed down the hallway to the office. Once inside, He looked around and saw James standing over six handcuffed faux agents.

Adam blinked in disbelief.

James stared back. "Mundane humans are a cake walk. What was all that commotion in the lobby"

Adam rubbed the back of his hair, "Met the metahuman. He should be safely evacuating... like we should be doing too."

James nodded and brought the faux agents to their feet. "Lead the way down. I'll cover your back."

07:

The way down to the ground floor was hampered by the thickening smoke but was ultimately uneventful. Agent Hanged Man helped people evacuate, but he was gone before Adam could see him. The faux bureau agents were brought to headquarters and questioned by Agent Hanged Man. The smoldering body of their leader was found outside Beaumont Heights and was taken in for autopsy.

Adam wrote all of this in his report and had it filed to the archive. As he sent off the report, a pigeon landed on his desk, alerting Adam to its presence with a coo. Around the pigeon's neck hung a small scroll. Adam blinked. The pigeon stared.

Adam blinked again. The pigeon remained.

Slowly, Adam turned around in his office chair. Behind him, Agent Strength, Jaqueline, stood, sipping on a cup of coffee. "One of Empress's pigeons," she said, "That means someone needs you for something urgent."

"Is she too good for email?" Adam asked.

"Carrier pigeons are harder to ignore than an email and less intrusive than the intercom," she said.

Adam glanced at his computer monitor. He hesitantly opened his email tab to find three emails labeled "URGENT." Adam gulped and Jacqueline chuckled.

"Better get a move on, rookie," Jaq said as she walked off.

Adam reached for the scroll around the pigeon's neck. Upon making contact with the note, the pigeon vanished in a poof of ephemeral feathers. Adam sighed, he was still not used to all this magic stuff.

He unrolled the scroll to unveil an elegantly handwritten note that read, "You are formally and urgently requested to the legal department offices."

Gulp.

The legal department was a part of the Administrative wing and thus the route was dotted with cubicles housing lower ranked

Pentacles. The news coverage of the Beaumont Heights fire was on everyone's monitor. Adam tried to ignore it, but he couldn't help but gasp when even international news agencies were reporting on the incident.

Double Gulp.

Adam made his way to the office of Agent Devil, the director of legal, and gave a polite knock before stepping inside. Inside, Agent Devil sat behind a desk stacked with papers. He was a smooth, pale skinned man with sunken cheeks and dark circles surrounding his eyes. His hair was pitch black and slicked back, with not a hair out of place. Under his Bureau suit he wore a charcoal black shirt with a fiery red tie. He didn't even have to introduce himself; he *looked* like someone codenamed "Devil."

Also in the room stood James and Emperor Gecko who were hunched over a speaker phone. When Adam stepped in, Gecko turned towards Adam and pointed accusatorily at them.

"...And HE just let a pyromancer go? The one who blew up the building?" Gecko yelled, the smoke surrounding his head swirling angrily.

James spoke with a measured and calm tone, "We were focused on the primary, and more presently dangerous, objective. The imposter bureau."

"Dangerous?! They didn't start that fire! Did you even happen to get the name of the pyromancer?"

Everyone in the office turned to Adam, who stood frozen, eyes wide, the quintessential deer in the headlights.

"Ahem," came agent Hanged Man's voice from over the speaker phone, "His name is Killian Wilkes. He is the only employee listed as working on that floor who we haven't been able to account for. We found his apartment, but it looks like he packed up and fled town. Investigation of his apartment shows no involvement with the imposters."

"Find him," Gecko demanded, voice sharp and smoldering, "Find him and-"

Agent Devil put a hand on the desk in front of him. It only made the faintest of sounds, but everyone went silent. He rubbed his temples and spoke in a smooth, tired voice that sounded like an off the clock salesman. It was a voice that was used to getting people to listen. "Here's what we tell the media. The dead man dressed as a bureau agent was a terrorist who used our image in an attempt to stir fear. He self-immolated as an act of terror. Emphasize that no one else was even injured. The alleged pyromancer, Mr. Wilkes's involvement is negligible and can be redacted from any reports sent to the media. I will write the report, then you can sign off on it, then Empress will send it to the media. Now stop yelling in my office."

Despite the smoke surrounding Director Emperor's face, it was clear one of his eyes was twitching with aggravation.

"And Wilkes?" Gecko demanded, trying his damndest not to shout, "Do we just let him roam free?"

"Ace and I will handle it," Agent Hanged Man said from the speaker phone.

Gecko sighed and said, "Handling this stuff was so much easier before the internet." He hung up on Hanged Man and left. James followed and gave Adam a pat on the back as he exited.

Agent Devil eyes fixated on Adam, unblinking.

"Uhmm," Adam began, "A pigeon said you wanted to see me?"

Agent Devil nodded for Adam to have a seat. Hesitantly, Adam made himself comfortable, or at least as comfortable as he could be given the circumstances.

Once Adam sat, Agent Devil pulled out a file and placed it on the desk. It was the file from the archives labeled "Elliott Harding." Adam's eyes looked from the file to Agent Devil with excited eyes. Agent Devil's face smiled, but the kind of smile someone who always knows what to say makes when, for once, they don't have the right words.

Adam spoke first, "Emperor got your tongue?"

Agent Devil's smile turned genuine, and he let out a smoldering chuckle before he finally said, "This, for once, is a matter outside Director Emperor's control."

Adam leaned in with growing interest. "O-oh?"

Agent Devil leaned in, too. "Oh yes, but… Do you know why they chose the arcana Devil for the director of legal?"

Adam blinked, "Uhm.. Cuz lawyers are worse than the

devil?"

Agent Devil let out another smoldering, low snicker, showing off a bright white grin before he spoke. "Think about it, when you need to make a deal with the devil, who better to look at the contract than your own devil? The Devil's advocate? No, the devil IS the advocate. If you find a magic lamp, I write the contract to ensure the wish comes out *exactly* as you intend. A Witch puts a hex on you and rambles a cryptic riddle? I tell you what it really means. In other words, Faust would have ended a lot differently if he called me." As he spoke, his words came out measured and smooth, a constant slight smirk and focused gaze on his face, his hands gesturing to punctuate each statement.

"Okay, so what does this have to do with Elliott?" Adam asked.

"My point is, in our line of work, there are certain entities that follow certain rules. It is my job to know these rules and advise The Bureau on how to navigate them," Agent Devil said. He put the tips of his fingers on Elliott's file.

"This," he continued, "Whatever was in this file, it shouldn't have happened."

Adam tilted his head. "Like, it was against orders?"

Agent Devil shook his head, "Imagine the ones holding the cards of fate are sitting at a table. Someone plays a card that was never supposed to be in the deck. Let's say someone played a trading card in a game of poker. How do they proceed? Do they have a do over? Do they rewrite the rules? That's what's happening."

"So… Elliott wasn't supposed to exist?" Adam asked.

"No. He just wasn't supposed to be played in this game." Agent Devil explained.

"I don't think I like you referring to all of this as a game," Adam said with growing unease.

"I'm sure the King of Spades doesn't view itself as a part of a game, but we play the cards we are dealt regardless."

Adam frowned and looked at Elliott's file. It started to look like a playing card dealt to his opponent.

"Well," Adam began, "What 'game' was Elliott supposed to be played in?"

Agent Devil gave a half smile as he caressed the letters of Elliott's name on the file. "We can't know the cards dealt until they are played. If Elliott's game hasn't been played yet, we simply cannot know."

08:

James and Hanged Man's first course of action to find Killian was to check each seedy, derelict motel in a two county radius, but that investigation came up empty. It was Hanged Man's idea to check a more established motel in a small but populated town; somewhere that isn't an obvious place criminals go, somewhere people come and go so often a proprietor couldn't remember every face that checked in. Somewhere that had smoking rooms.

One week after the inferno at Beaumont heights, James Graves sat behind the wheel of an unmarked sedan, parked in absolute darkness overlooking a cheap, chain motel. From his car speakers, the faint tone of classical music played as quietly as the radio possibly could. The sounds of rain falling on the roof of the car almost drowned out the music. If someone were to look in James's direction they would see nothing but the dull white glow of his eyes refracted through the heavy rain. Adam would have been beside him, but he was assigned to a different mission.

A voice crackled into James's earpiece. "This is just like old times, isn't it, Ace?" Agent Hanged Man said, a hint of nostalgia in his voice.

"Stay focused, Hanged Man," James said in response, eyes perpetually scanning back and forth through his windshield.

Agent Hanged Man sighed, "Look at you bossing me around now, oh they grow up so fast."

"Please focus," James asked. He tried to sound stern and authoritative, but admittedly, it was still difficult to boss around his former mentor, even if he did technically outrank him now. James had to focus hard not to get swept up in the same nostalgia Agent Hanged Man did, though it was difficult not to reminisce just a bit about the times before he gained his… more cold-blooded reputation. James shook his head and focused ahead of him.

"Subject identified. Room 216," The Hanged Man said.

"Copy," James said. He excited his car and closed the door behind him, careful not to make a sound.

"Copy," came another, more gruff voice over the radio, the faintest hint of smug glee in their tone, as if they were stifling laughter. It was Agent Tower's voice. "Neutralizing subject."

James's eyes went wide. This was supposed to be a two-man job! Why was Gecko's muscle here? This was supposed to be an extraction, not an assassination! His gaze, originally focused only on the motel, quickly scanned all of his surroundings. Agent Hanged Man must have done the same because moments later, the radio crackled to life once more.

"Rooftop. 20 meters south, 15 east, 3 stories up." Agent Hanged Man said, quick but clear.

James blinked his eyes and blinked his body straight to the coordinates he was given. In an instant, James was on a roof overlooking the hotel. Agent Tower laid prone in front of him, scoped in with a sniper rifle on Killian's motel room window.

James swiftly kicked the rifle away, but Agent Tower kept his strong grip tight onto the rifle, the momentum of the kick instead rolling the agent onto his back. He angled the rifle to point at James's chest.

"Agent Tower, stand down!" Agent Hanged Man screamed through the radio.

Agent Tower slowly lowered the rifle as he stood. "Great investigation Hanged Man, now let the muscle do its job."

"We're not killing him," James said, voice so cold it seemed to freeze the rain around him.

"Not your call." Tower said bluntly.

"Gecko said that if we found him before he caused another fire, we wouldn't have to kill him," James said.

"Yeah, 'we' meaning you and Hanged man. *I* was ordered to follow you and kill him. Now stand back," he said, turning away and raising the rifle to his eye.

"Wait!" James cried. He grabbed the barrel of the rifle and tried to move it away, but with Agent Tower's strength, it hardly budged.

"Moon was right, ever since the new Fool showed up,

you've gone soft," Agent Tower growled.

James kept his grip on the rifle barrel, just enough to keep Tower's aim unsteady. He looked down into the motel and saw Killian lying on the motel bed, listening to music. James looked back to Agent Tower.

When James spoke again, his voice was calm and calculating, "He can make a great asset," the words were bitter on his tongue, but he didn't show the disgust he felt for Tower, for Moon, For Gecko... For himself.

Agent Tower kept his rifle up as he spoke, "Fine. If you can convince him to work for us, and convince Emperor that he's useful to us, he can live."

"Do you guys realize how evil that makes you sound?" Agent Hanged Man said.

"You say evil, we say pragmatic. Isn't that right, Magician?" Tower said, flashing a smirk towards James. James frowned imperceptibly. Hanged Man was silent, the radio static mixed and faded into the sound of the pouring rain.

09:

Killian Wilkes had his eyes closed, headphones in as they played music. Despite this motel being nicer than he was used to, he still couldn't bring himself to relax. The room was thick with the scent of cigarette smoke coming from the bathroom after idly burning through a whole pack.

A knock on the door jolted Killian out of his anxious daze. He gulped and, instead of answering the door, slowly made his way to the back window.

"I wouldn't go out that way, if I were you," James said through the door.

Killian froze. He stared out the window. He saw the unmistakable shimmer of a rifle scope in the distance.

"Don't give them any reason to shoot us." James said. His voice sounded as if it were right behind Killian. Killian jolted but took James's advice and fought the urge to ignite his fists.

"What do you mean, 'us?' Aren't you with 'em, fed?" Killian asked, doing his best not to sound intimidated. James's choice of words did manage to lower his guard.

James's face cracked into a half smile, "Upper management isn't fond of me."

Killian let out a cackle and turned to face James, "So, you aren't the followin' orders type, eh? Why are you here then?"

James looked out the window to Agent Tower, then back to Killian.

"My name is James Graves with the Bureau Arcana. I have a job offer for you."

Chapter 04:
The Shadow of Sharp Manor

01:

[[Director of Intelligence, Agent Hanged Man's report:
Sharp Estate Disappearances:]]
Background: The Sharp estate is home to Mason and Mary Sharp, two old money aristocrats who were well known eccentrics where they live. About 18 or 20 years ago, (reports vary,) The Sharps stopped appearing around town, yet their lights remained on. Sometime recently, approximately ▮▮▮▮▮▮▮▮ ago, the lights went out.

A series of disappearances have been reported in the inland town of ▮▮▮▮▮▮▮▮. Investigations by local authorities point to an abandoned mansion in the outskirts of town. The Estate is owned by the Sharp family who, according to the locals, became shut-ins, never going out, only having food and other essentials delivered to them. Around two years ago, calls for deliveries ceased. Local delinquents would allegedly break in to try and loot the place, but no one who intruded ever returned. There are no known reasons why. Local law enforcement sent inside the estate have not returned. Suspected occult cause. Recommendation: send field agents for further investigation.

02:

It was noon, and the sun was directly overhead. There were no clouds, and despite its position at the apex of a steep hill, the Sharp Estate seemed perpetually draped in shade. Adam Nolan stared up the hill at the imposing mansion and shivered. He looked around for his partner but found nothing but an empty field. He bit his lip anxiously and turned back around and jumped.

"Just my luck to be stuck with the Fool." Agent Hermit said, now standing in front of Adam as if he had appeared out of thin air. His arms were crossed, and he glared at Adam with a look of disdain in his eyes. The Hermit of the Bureau Arcana is the Director of Stealth Ops and dressed the part. He still wore a black suit, but instead of the shirt and tie, he wore a pitch black tactical turtleneck, and he did not wear a Bureau Arcana pin. His skin was pale, and his hair could only be described as emo. If it weren't for the sun overhead, Adam would have thought for sure he was a vampire.

"Ack!" Adam yelped, "Y-you know, I prefer being called rookie-"

"When you're with me, you are going to be called by your code name," The Hermit said coldly. "The Magician isn't here to coddle you this time."

"He doesn't coddle m-" Adam started to argue before being violently shushed by The Hermit.

"This mission doesn't involve speaking," he said before turning and hiking his way towards the mansion.

Adam huffed and replied under his breath, "You spoke first."

The Hermit twitched with annoyance but didn't respond. Adam stifled a snicker.

The two agents made their way up the hill. The closer they got, the darker the very air around them seemed to get. The garden that once bordered the path up the hill was dead, nothing but black, withered plant corpses sticking out of the dirt, like the hands of the dead trying to claw their way from their graves. Adam's every instinct was screaming at him to turn and run, but this was the very thing the Bureau was supposed to handle. He trekked on.

Once they reached the front door of the manor, The Hermit gripped the handles of the ornate and sturdy double doors and opened them. The two agents could see nothing beyond the threshold. It was pitch black... almost like there was nothing but empty void in front of them.

The Hermit looked at Adam and snickered. "Afraid of the dark?"

Adam scoffed and stepped through the threshold into the mansion. He held up his hand and slowly, a glowing white orb appeared and began to illuminate the foyer. The Hermit immediately grabbed Adam's wrist and forced it down. Instead, he turned on a flashlight.

"Save your energy. Use the equipment," he said.

"Oi!" Adam yelped.

"Shush," The Hermit said sharply, "I would like to maintain the advantage of silence."

Adam sighed and turned on his flashlight. God, he missed James right about now. He'd rather be on that mission, looking for Killian after the Beaumont Heights incident. He wondered why management was so adamant that they were separated for these missions.

Adam and The Hermit shined their flashlights and looked around. They were in a large open foyer with a grand double staircase leading to the second floor balcony. The architecture and decor was elegant yet rustic. Old school luxury. It reeked of old money.

Despite the flashlight, the darkness was thick and seemed to creep into the edge of their illumination. These were brand new powerful flashlights paid for out of the federal budget, but this darkness made them seem like dollar store trinkets. It was so disorienting that Adam lost track of where he was and bumped into a suit of armor. Adam jumped as the suit of armor fell, hit the floor with a loud series of crashes before crumbling into pieces.

Adam caught his footing, and the beam of the flashlight caught The Hermit in its sights. He was staring daggers at Adam.

"We are splitting up," The Hermit said.

"W-wha? Wouldn't it be safer to stick together?" Adam argued.

"No. You draw too much attention."

"Exactly! That's why I need backup!"

The Hermit shook his head and chuckled. "Sink or swim," he said. Then he turned off his flashlight and vanished into the darkness. Adam frantically waved his flashlight around to find him, but he was gone.

Sink or swim... It certainly felt like Adam was drowning in this darkness. He wished he could learn James's glowing eye magic, but no matter how hard he practiced, he just couldn't make it work.

He climbed the stairs to the second floor and began exploring. He cleared the second floor room by room, perhaps a bit hastily. He had no idea what they were looking for, if there even was anything to find, but Adam could swear something was watching him. He prayed it was just The Hermit.

The deeper into the mansion he traveled, the more the hallways seemed to look like each other. The more lost he felt, the more suffocating the darkness became. Adam started to focus less on investigating and focused more on possible escape routes. He was even willing to defenestrate himself just for a glimpse of the outside sun. It was then that a sickening realization hit him.

Adam hadn't seen a single window.

The darkness grew thicker, more suffocating. Adam's hands shook as he held the flashlight pointed down the hall. The dark wood of the halls absorbed the light that hit it. It made the flashlight feel almost useless at illuminating anything... which made the shimmer at the end of the hall all the more noticeable. Adam froze as his flashlight shined down a long, empty hallway with nothing but a solitary door at the end. The door was covered in chains hastily bolted to the walls around it. Where the rest of the manor's walls were dotted with photos of the Sharp family over the years, this hallway was completely barren.

Adam approached. His footsteps were silent; all he could hear was the pounding of his own heart. Once he got to the door, he examined the web of chains. All the chains were held together with a single padlock. Adam took hold of the lock. Everything about this door told him he shouldn't open it, but it was his damn job to do so...

Adam pinched the thinnest part of the metal and, thanks

to what he learned at Beaumont heights, slowly heated up his fingertips until the metal became red hot. Then he focused and gripped the lock with his mind and yanked. There was a sharp crack followed by the clatter of chains as the lock broke and the chains fell away. He gulped and opened the door.

The door creaked open on rusted, atrophied hinges, as if this was the first time the door had been open in years. On the other side of the door was a staircase that led up to the third floor. When Adam shined the flashlight to the top of the stairs, he was expecting more darkness.

What he saw instead was a face.

Adam yelped and locked eyes with the face... It was eerie and unnatural, porcelain white. Its eyes were empty and there was no mouth. The more Adam stared at it, the more he convinced himself it was just a mask, just a piece of wall decor... Then the mask moved, as if tilting its head curiously.

Adam's eyes widened. His voice was shaky. "H-Hello?" He said to the white mask, cold sweat dripping from his temples.

The moment it heard Adam's voice, the white face vanished behind a corner. Adam grit his teeth. Whatever it was, he was confident he could take it, he was a bureau agent after all. He wanted to call for Agent Hermit, but the words "sink or swim" rang in his ears. He still had to prove himself... So, he climbed the stairs.

The third floor was derelict and in disrepair, even more abandoned than the bottom two floors. On the top step, where the white face was, lay a piece of paper, the only other thing of white Adam had seen in this whole house. Adam approached it, eyes and flashlight darting anxiously around, but found no face.

He hastily picked up the paper. Hastily scrawled on it read:

THE DARKNESS IS ALIVE

Adam swore his flashlight flickered. The edges of the darkness seemed to wriggle with anticipation. Adam shook and started walking faster. He couldn't tell if it was just in his head or not, but he swore he felt the darkness clawing at him.

Adam clenched his fists and an aura of bright white light

appeared around him. The darkness hissed and scurried away. Adam felt like he could finally take a breath. He continued to explore the manor, but with every corner he turned, a blur of white disappeared behind the next. With no other leads, Adam followed. The walls were barren, the wood rotted. Whatever was up here was meant to be forgotten.

Adam followed the white face until he was led to a room. Adam prepared himself for a confrontation with whatever it was, and opened the door, leading with a glowing hand. He yelped as a dozen identical white faces stared back at him. He ignited a fireball in his hand, ready to fight, but slowly realized that none of the masks were moving. Carefully, he approached... These ones *were* merely wall decorations. Porcelain masks hung up for the atmosphere. What atmosphere? Adam couldn't say. He looked around the rest of the room.

Compared to the rest of the floor, this room felt eerily lived in. There were stacks of books and VHS tapes lining every foot of the room's diameter, some stacked neatly while others were a mess. The books ranged from textbooks of every subject and every grade, classic literature, science, psychology, foreign languages, but notably, no history. The VHS tapes were all silent movies, and some were played so often the magnetic tape inside was falling out. One wall was lined with cans and boxes of food, some unopened, some empty. Above the food supply was a small cubby that looked to be a conveyance to the floors below. Perhaps a lift to deliver food up and trash down. It seems at some point the deliveries stopped. Near the center of the room was an open book, a lamp, an old tv, and a VHS player. There was no other furniture. No bed, no chairs, nothing.

Adam shivered. He swore he had seen the white face go into this room, but as he looked around, there was no one else there.

"Hello? I am friendly if you are! Er... I didn't mean for that to sound threatening!" Adam said with a nervous tremble. He looked around the room more frantically, the anxiety and the exertion from using his powers making him feel tired. Adam sat before he could fully exhaust himself, right in the center of the room with the lamp and TV. He turned the lamp on, and a dim light glowed. Adam clung to it like a freezing man to a campfire. He stared out into the darkness, the faint haze of the masks staring at him, silent. Still.

Except one. One of the masks moved closer. Adam's fight or flight instinct kicked in, and a bright glow filled the room. With Adam's bright light, he could see the man attached to the white mask. Behind the mask his eyes were a bright blue, the mask itself framed by a head of thick pitch black hair. The masked man's build was tall and imposing. He was dressed in dark aristocratic looking clothes, clothes that would look out of place in most settings but looked ever so natural in this old estate.

The masked man froze. His bright blue eyes shone with fear. Slowly, he raised his hands, another piece of paper held in one of his hands. He seemed to offer it to Adam, as if offering a gift. Hesitantly, Adam took the paper.

THAT LIGHT. ILLUMINATE THE HEART OF THE ABYSS. DISPEL THIS SHADOW. PLEASE.

Adam looked up from the paper. The masked man continued to stare at Adam with an unnerving stillness. Adam shivered and tried to smile.

"Are you... friendly?" Adam asked.

The masked man nodded.

"Do you... talk?"

The masked man shook his head.

"Oh gosh... Do you know what happened here?"

The masked man fidgeted anxiously before pulling out a pen and a notebook. He scribbled in it before silently tearing the page out for Adam.

I WAS LOCKED HERE... FORGOTTEN...

Adam frowned. "I'm... so sorry..."

The masked man looked away, the large man seemed to deflate.

"I-I should probably introduce myself. I'm Adam Nolan. I am an agent with the Bureau Arcana. Do you have a name?"

The masked man turned to Adam. His fidgeting became more frantic. Eventually, the man wrote

MAXWELL.

Adam smiled warmly. "Pleasure to meetcha, Maxwell."
Maxwell stood upright, his towering height being all the more apparent. Adam prayed Maxwell was friendly. This man could easily break him. Maxwell then gave a deep, almost theatrical bow. It immediately made Adam think of the exaggerated way people moved in old silent films.
Adam couldn't help but giggle. "How well mannered. L-lead the way?"
Maxwell led Adam through the labyrinthine halls of the mansion with the confidence of someone who grew up in them. Adam followed. He trusted this masked man but was prepared to react if he was luring him into a trap. He wondered where The Hermit was.
Adam's arcane light kept the darkness at bay until Maxwell led them deep down into the cellar. The cellar was cold and musty. The wood of the manor was replaced with frigid stone. Maxwell brought Adam to a door and hesitated.
Adam looked at Maxwell who reached for the door's handle with a shaky gloved hand. He recoiled before he could open the door and hugged himself.
Adam's eyes opened with concern. "W-what's wrong?"
Maxwell gestured shakily, trying to wordlessly communicate something that Adam simply couldn't comprehend. When Maxwell saw that his efforts to communicate were in vain, he hugged himself and did his best to steady his panic.
Adam gulped. "I-I'll lead from here. Does that work?"
Maxwell gave a shaky thumbs up.
Adam nodded and reached for the door. When he made contact with the door handle, all the light around his hand vanished. Adam grit his teeth and opened the door. It groaned open and led to a staircase, a staircase that seemed to go down forever. An intense vertigo gripped Adam, and he felt as if he would fall and tumble down the endless stairs. He took a step

down, but before his foot could make contact with the next stair, Maxwell grabbed Adam by the collar and yanked him back. Adam fell back and hit the floor of the cellar, right at the threshold of the staircase.

There was a scream of pain. Adam turned in the direction of the noise to see Maxwell on the far side of the cellar, his gloved hands pinning The Hermit to the wall, one hand on his throat, and one hand on his wrist.

Adam scrambled to his feet and cried out, "Wait! He's an ally!"

Maxwell's eyes turned to Adam before skeptically locking back on The Hermit. He let him go.

The Hermit exhaled from his mouth and shook his head. "Made a friend, didja?"

"Yeah," Adam said, a bit excitedly, "I think down these stairs is the heart of what's happening here. A-an abyss!"

"You figured that out, eh?" The Hermit said, eyes twitching with annoyance, "That makes this more complicated."

Adam tilted his head and raised an eyebrow. "How do you mean? That's why we're here, isn't it?"

The Hermit sighed. In one swift motion, he pulled out a small, suppressed pistol and shot Maxwell square in the head.

Maxwell's mask shattered and he fell into the darkness.

"HERMIT, WHAT THE HELL!?" Adam screamed, ready to rush to Maxwell's side before the Hermit turned the gun on Adam.

"That's not why I'm here," The Hermit said, eyes trained on Adam. That abyss can be useful to the Bureau. It's perfect for... disposing of the things the Bureau needs rid of. Cleansing it doesn't align with our interests."

Adam stared into Agent Hermit's eyes. They were cold and heartless. Adam's eyes widened with realization. He was one of the things the Bureau "needs rid of." The Hermit smirked when he saw Adam's fear.

"This isn't what the Bureau is about..." Adam pleaded.

The Hermit tisked. "Things changed when you showed up. You turned the Magician from a ruthless agent to an idealistic nuisance."

"Wh-what? Ruthless?" Adam said.

The Hermit chuckled. "You'll see in the next life. Assuming the Abyss lets your soul pass."

The Hermit trained his aim between Adam's eyes. Adam stared down the barrel of the silencer, eyebrows furrowed. From the darkness behind the Hermit, a pair of bright blue eyes shimmered.

Maxwell locked the Hermit in a headlock which forced his gun arm up as he pulled the trigger. Adam dove to the ground as Maxwell effortlessly picked The Hermit up by their neck. The Hermit dropped the gun and grabbed Maxwell's wrists to try in vain to pry himself free as Maxwell dragged them to the open stairwell door. The Hermit's cocky look quickly turned to horror. Maxwell threw The Hermit down the stairs with such force that the Hermit never got his footing. The Hermit simply tumbled down the stairs, screaming in horror. Down… and down… and down…

Adam never heard a thud. The Hermit's screams simply faded out of existence.

Maxwell looked to Adam and immediately covered his face with his hands, rushing off to the darkness before Adam could catch a glimpse of his face.

Adam made it to his feet and looked around. Maxwell's mask was in pieces. The stairwell was still open. Adam put his hand to his chest and felt his heart pounding like crazy.

As Adam caught his breath, a piece of paper slid out of the darkness. Instead of words, Maxwell had drawn a picture of Adam. In the picture Adam was reeling back about to throw a fireball. Then beside the fireball, Maxwell drew a plus sign and a lightbulb and a question mark.

Adam looked into the darkness of the cellar and nodded. He stepped to the threshold of the stairwell and stared down, fighting the sense of vertigo as he grew a ball of fire in his hand. He took a breath and channeled his light magic, trying to mix the two. The flame in his hand swirled with a white light, and Adam giggled excitedly. He stared into the darkness and threw the light infused fireball down into the abyss.

There was a long moment of ominous silence. Adam

feared he would have to travel down deep into the darkness to try again when there was a sudden woosh. The darkness around seemed to burn away. It was still dark, of course, but it was no longer suffocating. Adam turned on his flashlight, and it illuminated the staircase perfectly. Without the abyss, it was a shallow staircase that simply seemed to lead to more cellars.

Adam swept the flashlight around until it illuminated Maxwell. Maxwell turned away, covering his face.

"Ack! Sorry sorry." Adam said, moving the flashlight off Maxwell.

As the now highest ranking agent on the mission, Adam decided to extract. He asked Maxwell to come with him, who, after replacing his face mask, was all too happy to escape the Sharp Estate.

03:

[[Director Of Medicine, Agent Strength's report: Physical and Mental examination: Maxwell Sharp.]]
Name: Maxwell Sharp
Age: 18 (approximately) It is estimated that his conception correlates with the time the Sharps began isolating themselves.
Birthdate: Unknown.
Sex: Male.
Height: 6'10"
Weight: 250 lbs (mostly muscle mass.)
Upon initial contact, Mr. Sharp was unresponsive to questions and reacted violently to any attempt to make physical contact. Mr. Sharp calmed down and became slightly more cooperative with Agent Fool's presence.
Physical examination of Mr. Sharp proved difficult. He was skittish and unwilling to accept physical contact, and

unwilling to remove his mask to check for injury. Mr. Sharp reported injury to his face resulting from ███████████. Visible dried blood indicates slight lacerations caused by the shattering of his mask, but there was apparently no bullet wound or any deep cuts. Mr. Sharp assures me he can take care of these injuries himself. Despite the scarcity of food and the malnutrition that caused, Maxwell has a far greater than average muscle mass. The muscles themselves are atrophied, but with a rehabilitating diet and minimal physical therapy, he should make a speedy recovery, at least physically.

Mental examination proved easier, if only slightly. Mr. Sharp is a selective mute but still communicates via handwritten notes and sign language. His inability/unwillingness to speak appears to stem from his upbringing. His birth was kept a secret, and he was kept locked in the Sharp estate for as long as he could remember. His mother, Mary Sharp, took exclusive care of him, while his father, Mason Sharp, would fly into a rage whenever Maxwell's presence was observed. This would result in Maxwell being locked in the Sharp Manor attic. Maxwell would scream and pound at the door until his vocal cords gave out, and only then, when he physically could not make any more noise, would he be let out. As he grew older, even his silence wasn't enough, and Mason Sharp chained the attic door shut, never to be unlocked again. Using a small service lift, food was transported up to the attic for Maxwell to live off, as well as books and VHS tapes to keep Maxwell occupied. Eventually, the deliveries stopped coming. Given the inability to easily tell the passage of time in such an environment, it is difficult to say for sure, but this end in contact seems to correlate to when the darkness engulfed the manor. He has somehow survived up there completely alone for almost two years.

Arcane examination of the subject showed no innate signs of arcane or other metanatural traits. His silent movement and ability to avoid being seen seem to be a direct result of his upbringing and habits. Even direct exposure to the Shadows of the manor seemed to have no effect. Director Moon will insist on more testing on Maxwell, but unlike Royce, Maxwell is unwilling. As his medical provider, I will deny any requests that attempt to prove his hypothesis at the expense of Maxwell's wellbeing. Some people are simply talented without arcane enhancements.

Diagnosis: Social Anxiety. Agoraphobia. Malnutrition. Facial lacerations.

Recommended action: I will slowly acclimate Maxwell to light and social activity until he is able to survive without direct guidance. Given Maxwell Sharp's ability to survive an arcane/eldritch event, enrollment at Academy Arcana would be an excellent place to further socialize him.

04:

Jacqueline Wells had installed blinds around the Bureau Arcana's Observation cell to provide Maxwell with the privacy he so desperately needed. If he was forced into any situation where he was observed, he would break down into a panic. She spent the next few weeks working with Maxwell to get him back to a healthy state while preparing them for enrollment at the Academy Arcana.

After the most recent session, James Graves stood waiting for her.

"Good afternoon, Agent Magician," Jacqueline said.

"Good afternoon indeed, Agent Strength," James replied, his face stoic as he looked at the door of the observation room.

"Something is on your mind. What is it?" Jaq asked.

"I was in the archive, and I read the unredacted reports, but Adam's hasn't been filed yet..." he said. His eyes were sharp and focused, full of anger despite his emotionless face.

"What are you getting at, James?"

"Why did Agent Hermit shoot at Maxwell? He is normally not sloppy enough to endanger civilians," James asked, turning to Jaq.

Jaq looked around, checking to make sure they weren't being watched. She leaned in and whispered to James, "Maxwell said he was protecting Adam."

James's face twitched. "Thank you."

"What are you planin-" Jaq began, but before she could finish her sentence, James had blinked away.

* * *

Director Gecko flicked the ashes into the crystal ashtray on his desk. Across the desk sat Agent Moon, leaning back, comfortable. Agent Tower was standing by the door as if on guard.

"Your private investor for Project Moonlight is growing impatient. I hope you can have something tangible to deliver soon," Director Gecko said, his voice grave and smokey.

"How very exciting. Don't worry your smokey little head, Arthur. Our asset is so focused on his pipe dream that it's easy to get hours of research out of him," Agent Moon replied. "Agent Chariot was even able to use our research to engineer a more... modern alternative to silver ammunition that can be used in our semi-automatic sidearms. No more carrying around those big heavy revolvers.

"Excellent. Very good," Gecko said, voice warm and pleased.

Suddenly, a hand rested itself upon Arthur Gecko's shoulder. Behind his desk chair stood James Graves, eyes a bright, glowing white.

Agent Moon froze. He did his best but failed to suppress an intense shiver. Director Gecko simply tilted his head.

"My dear Magician? We are busy, but for you? I can make time," Gecko said, measured, unbothered.

James spoke in a chilling voice, loud enough for Moon and Tower to hear even if the statement was intended just for Gecko. He said, "Leave Adam out of this."

If a swirl of smoke could smile, Directo Gecko was. "Are you threatening me, Mr. Graves?"

Agent Tower broke out in a hearty laugh, clapping with pride, "Now *that's* the Magician I've heard horror stories about!"

James did not respond. He stayed focused, a vice-like grip on Gecko's shoulder. Gecko's gaze moved from James's hand, to Agent Moon, to Agent Tower. After a long, poignant pause, he spoke.

"Agent Moon, Agent Tower, thank you for your time. We can continue this at a later date." Gecko said with executive professionalism. Agent Moon slowly stood, and backed away from James, as if he didn't trust to turn his back on him. Agent Tower was smiling like a child seeing his hero as he waited for Agent Moon to leave, whereupon he gave a gracious, if exaggerated bow before following Agent Moon out. Gecko and James were left alone.

Once alone with James, Director Gecko spoke again, his voice and demeanor completely unphased by James's imposing aura. "My dear Magician, first you begged me to accept that Adam boy into The Bureau, and now you disapprove of the methods in which I run said Bureau?"

"I wanted him in The Bureau so I could protect him," James said.

"And I wanted you in The Bureau so I could protect everyone else. I don't know if you are old enough to remember what happened in '95, but we don't have the luxury of being sentimental. When that happens, more people die. Your attachment to that boy has made you sloppy, made you weak." Gecko spoke as if he were a teacher explaining a mathematical equation to a student who just refuses to understand.

"Do not underestimate me, Director," James said, "If you continue to be a threat to him... Well... You promoted me to Magician for a reason, and it wasn't because of my winning personality."

"And I didn't become Emperor by kissing ass and playing politics," Gecko said. Then, in mere seconds, the smoke around Director Gecko grew to surround James. James tightened his grip around Gecko's shoulder, but it was like grabbing ephemeral whisps. The smoke reconverged behind James to again form Director Gecko. Gecko gave James a gentle pat on the back, and James felt something in his grip. Instead of Gecko, James was now holding onto the blade of a knife; had he gripped any tighter, he surely would have cut himself.

"Now. You are dismissed, my dear Magician," Gecko said.

When James turned around, there was nothing but fading smoke.

Chapter 05:
The Wanderer of the Astral Frontier

01:

Every night it was the same nightmare: Misha Woods was staring up at the stars in awe and wonderment until slowly, one by one, each star disappeared. The whole night sky turned black, and the world went silent. Misha stared up, paralyzed in fear, unable to turn away from the void. He desperately searched the sky for any hint of light, until he saw two dull stars hung in the night sky. The stars got bigger and bigger, as if getting closer and closer. They began to look like eyes… There was a deep groan from the sky as the darkness split open to reveal an abyssal maw. Slowly it engulfed the earth.

That's when Misha woke up. Every night it was like that, and every night he couldn't get back to sleep. Misha looked around his campsite as the sounds of nature calmed his nerves. As his heart rate lowered, he laid back down in his sleeping bag and stared up at the stars. They were still there, as bright and wondrous as ever before.

Misha spent a lot of time out in the wilderness and could tell by the stars that dawn was about an hour from breaking. He got up and, illuminated by nothing but the stars and moon, set up a campfire. Misha was camped out on a hill that overlooked a forest he had never explored, and he wanted to watch the sun rise while he enjoyed his morning campfire coffee.

Misha lit the fire, and it illuminated the hill he set up camp on. Despite his expertise and comfort in the outdoors, Misha was a young, rather frail boy with perpetual dark bags under his eyes and messy white hair that fell in front of one eye. He wore an oversized Victorian style long coat that, despite its wear and tear from heavy and rough use, still looked rather dashing draped over his small frame.

Misha had just finished brewing his coffee when the first rays of dawn broke from behind the forest. The strong scent of the hot coffee with the crisp aroma of the cold wilderness mixed to invigorate Misha. His soft face smiled as the sun slowly rose, illuminating the land, and highlighting what made this forest so intriguing to Misha: The treetops were a brilliant white, unlike anything he had ever seen or read about before.

Misha finished his coffee, put out his fire, packed up his campsite, and stuffed it all in his massive backpack. He set off with a sense of adventure and curiosity.

After a solid hour of hiking, Misha found himself inside the forest. He hiked deep into it, being sure to mark his path and make note of any landmarks he could, a mossy rock here, a uniquely shaped tree there, all to ensure he didn't get lost. The trees were thick and tall, with pale gray bark that stretched straight up to the vibrant white leaves atop them.

Misha closed his eyes and took a deep breath. The air felt stagnant, the forest was silent. He was used to hearing the rustling of wind or the commotion of wildlife, but here… there was nothing. Something didn't feel right. He turned around and carefully made his way back.

As he retreated, Misha noticed that the landmarks he had noted were not quite where he remembered them. He quickened his pace. His path became less and less familiar. He turned and backtracked… yet again, things were different.

When Misha looked up in the hopes of seeing the sun, he instead saw only trees, stretching on and on and on into the sky until they faded from view. He looked around, and a pale fog encroached. Misha wanted to break into a sprint, but that would only exhaust him. Instead, he grit his teeth and trekked on.

Misha didn't know what he was looking for, but he couldn't shake the feeling that he had to keep moving. The fog crept closer and closer to Misha, but never actually engulfed him. No matter how deep into the forest he went, the fog was just out of reach, yet also right behind him. For a brief moment, Misha broke into a jog to try and catch up to the mist. That was when he tripped.

Misha fell on top of a long log-like object that was shrouded in fog. Misha winced in pain and tried to push himself up using the object. As soon as his hand touched the fog, it scattered. Misha's hand was on what appeared to be the chest of a man in a black suit. There was a pained hiss coming from the man's face.

Misha gasped. He had found someone else here! He looked up to see the man's face. The hiss did not come from him; it came from the tiny worm like creatures that burrowed into it.

The worms, now exposed from the fog, writhed and wriggled from the skull and jaw of the black-suited corpse and jumped towards Misha, leaving a series of holes in the exposed bone.

Misha shrieked in horror and scrambled to his feet. The hiss from the worms grew louder as they landed on the corpse's shirt. They struggled to burrow into the corpse's chest. Misha cried out and swatted at himself in a panic as he ran off into the forest.

02:

[[Director Of Communications, Agent Empress's report: Agent Sun's absence.]]
Director Sun has not shown up for work in two weeks. I have tried to reach out to him with email, phone, text, even carrier pigeon. This is so very unlike him, really. We were just chatting the other day about him finding out something exciting about Moon's werewolf research. I was really looking forward to chatting about it over a cup of tea.

I have sent a request to Hanged Man to see if he could find anything out. Should he write a report, I will have it attached to this report. I do hope the dear boy is okay…

[[Director Of Intelligence, Agent Hanged Man's report: RE: Agent Sun's absence]]

[[REDACTED BY ORDER OF EXECUTIVE DIRECTOR EMPEROR]]

03:

"Another forest, eh?" Adam asked as he brushed the hair out of his eyes. He looked into the thick pale forest.

"This isn't just any forest," a tall, thin woman said. She was the Bureau's Star Arcana, the Director of Astrology. She had a spider-like elegance to her, reminiscent of a femme fatale but in a Bureau pantsuit instead of a cocktail dress. "It is an arcane hot spring of sorts, where the walls of the mundane and astral plane are weakened."

"That seems dangerous to just allow unchecked," Adam said.

Agent Star let out a chuckle that, to Adam, was dripping with smug superiority, "For those... astrally challenged like yourself, it will just amplify your magical powers. It poses no danger to our world."

Adam gave Agent Star a weary look but sighed. He turned around to the Bureau van that they traveled in to get here. James was poking his head into the back.

"Hey Magician! Cmon!" Adam shouted, hands cupped around his mouth to amplify his voice.

James leaned back to reveal his head from behind the van's back door and held out a hand with a "one more minute" gesture. Adam sighed and tapped his foot impatiently, but with a fond smile on his face. After exactly 59 seconds, James closed the van door and jogged up to Adam and Agent Star.

"Forgive me. I was helping Hanged Man set up some equipment," James said.

"I don't know why. Agent Moon has tested and analyzed every part of this region. This is just a waste of time and Bureau resources," Star said,

"Different departments need different data," James said curtly. He walked into the forest.

Agent Star suppressed an eye roll and followed after James. Adam followed as well.

Adam was never one to enjoy being out in nature much, but even he was awestruck by how majestic these almost otherworldly trees were. He stared up at the white leaves that populated the treetops and took a deep breath. The air wasn't nearly as crisp as he expected, but he could feel a surge of energy inside him.

He reached a hand in his pocket and pulled out his lucky shell casing. He held it in one hand before effortlessly, it started floating just above his palm. Adam snickered with pride and began to toss the shell casing back between his hands without ever actually touching it. Once he got into the rhythm, he focused a bit harder and started teleporting the shell casing between his hands in short blinks.

Adam's glee was overflowing. As he tossed and blinked the shell casing back and forth, he started imbuing it with other kinds of magic he'd learned. He engulfed the shell in bright light that he learned from James, then snuffed it out with darkness that he learned in Sharp Manor. Finally, he engulfed the casing in flames that he learned from Killian.

James looked behind to watch Adam so casually wield such diverse magical prowess. He turned to Agent Star.

"Perhaps he has some astral affinity, too," James said with a proud smile. Agent Star narrowed her eyes and didn't respond.

Eventually, after a long hike, the three agents saw a cabin in the distance. Adam's eyes widened.

"Oh hell no," Adam said with an indignant tone, "I've learned to deal with all the woods we end up in, but a CABIN in the woods? That's where I draw the line."

"Okay," Agent Star said coldly, "Feel free to make your way back. Hope you paid attention to the route we took."

Adam turned around. He had no idea how they got here since he was too focused on his magic. He sighed and followed James and Agent Star into the cabin.

The cabin was made from a dark oak, in contrast to the pale trees surrounding it. The bottom floor was sparsely furnished with an open layout. One side of the room had a large ornate mirror that took up half the wall. Around the mirror was a series of paintings that depicted the surrounding forest, but there was something uncanny about them. The other side of the cabin had a fireplace with a couple of armchairs and a set of cookware stationed around it. The only lighting was a series of oil lamps dotted along each wall. Upstairs was a basic bathroom and a sleeping area with four bunks. Downstairs was a cellar full of food and other supplies. The cabin was warm and quiet compared to outside. The smell was pleasant and oaky.

"This cabin is used as a literal spiritual retreat for agents who wish to hone certain magic talents," James said, taking off his coat and hanging it on the rack by the door, "There are enough supplies here to last a month in the dead of winter. You better like cold showers, though."

"We are not staying here that long, though. Only the strongest agents can handle that," Agent Star added with a cocky smirk, her eyes stabbing into Adam.

"If I recall, you only lasted fifteen days," James said as he rolled up his sleeves.

Adam stifled a laugh which made Agent Star's face sour.

"How long did you stay?" Adam asked.

James could hardly hide his smirk as he shook his head, "It doesn't matter. We are here to train, not brag."

Agent Star scoffed and cracked her knuckles, "He lasted the whole month."

Adam looked at James with starry eyes before James clapped his hand together, causing a supernaturally loud boom.

"Focus," James said as his hands glowed with brilliant luminescence.

04:

The three agents spent the next few hours training their abilities. James and Adam started out with basic formal exercises, but by the 2-hour mark, they were playing racquetball with an orb of light. Agent Star secluded herself in front of the fireplace and focused on meditating.

Out of breath, Adam called for a break. Adam went to the restroom to wash his face. The ice-cold water sent a jolt down his spine. When he came out of the restroom, James was doing stretches in front of the mirror, and Agent Star was still meditating.

Adam tilted his head. Something peculiar caught his eye.

One of the oil lamps was flickering. Adam went to investigate, but the lantern wasn't flickering. Adam blinked and turned around. In the reflection of the room, the lantern was clearly flickering. James picked up on Adam's confusion and looked between the lamp and its flickering reflection.

"S.O.S." James said.

"What?" Adam said.

"What?" Agent Star said as her eyes shot open.

"The lamp in the mirror. It is morse code," James explained as he stepped over to another wall lamp. He flicked it on and off.

"R E C E I V E D" he sent, James's lamp in the reflection didn't flicker.

The other lamp in the reflection stopped flickering for a moment. Then, it seemed to respond. "H E L P. L O S T. F O G. D E A D L Y."

Adam glanced out of the window. The forest was obscured by a thick fog.

"James... Outside," Adam said, his voice low and shaky as he pointed at the window.

"Fog... Deadly..." James said in a thoughtful tone.

"Quit screwing around," Agent Star barked, "Wasn't it you who said we are here to train?" The calm trance she had worked towards in her meditation was quickly replaced by a serious agitation.

"I think we have more pressing matters now," James said.

"What. Fog? Fog isn't dangerous here," Agent Star said, her tone growing more exasperated.

"What do you mean, 'here?'" Adam asked nervously.

"In the astral plane, the fog can hide some... unsavory things," Agent Star said, "But we are not in the astral plane."

"Wait, does that mean there's someone trapped in the astral plane?" Adam asked as he pointed at the flickering lamps.

"Impossible," Agent Star said, "Like I said, you can't accidentally stumble into the astral realm unless you are incredibly gifted."

"Well, it seems we found someone with such a gift," James said.

Agent Star's eye twitched, "Well, we should go get help, then," she said.

"On it!" Adam said as he rushed to the door.

James grabbed Adam's arm before they could leave. "Wait. The fog," James said.

"Like I said," Agent Star began.

"Silence," James barked with a sharpness that cut through the air like a razor. He rushed downstairs then came back up with a rope tied around a piece of dried meat. He opened the front door and, with his hand still on the rope, tossed the meat into the fog. A disgusting hiss escaped from the fog. Adam reflexively took a step back.

James carefully reeled the meat back to reveal that it was completely covered in what appeared to be a mass of worms. Exposed to the air, they all stiffened and jumped off the meat, scurrying back into the fog. James caught just a glimpse of the tiny holes left in the meat before slamming the door shut.

"What the hell was that?!" Adam shrieked, backpedaling with such vigor that he slammed himself into the wall.

James put his hand to his ear and said, "Hanged Man. Come in."

Hanged man's voice crackled in over the agents' earpieces, "I hear ya loud and clear, Ace."

"Is there any astral activity on your sensors?" James asked.

"Oh hell! The whole cabin area is surrounded by activity. What happened?"

"That's what we are trying to find out. There also appears to be a civilian in the Astral Plane. Attempting extraction," James reported.

"Copy, Ace," Hanged man said.

"You say that as if it's a simple matter to just… pull someone from the astral plane," Agent Star said.

"It is. Well… As simple as lifting a two-ton weight. Conceptually simple, but mechanically difficult," James said.

"Then how am I going to get them out? I'm skilled, but not that skilled." Agent Star retorted.

"I am going to help you," James replied with a matter-of-fact tone as he rolled up his sleeves, "There is a reason I was able to last the whole month alone here."

Agent Star tisked but couldn't help but crack a smile, "You are full of surprises, Mr. Graves."

James and Agent Star positioned themselves side by side near the center of the mirror. They both closed their eyes and entered a meditative state. The air around them started to glow.

James turned to Adam, "Ada- Rookie! Go to the oil lamp and transmit 'H A N D. O N. C E N T E R. O F. M I R R O R.'"

Adam scrambled to the oil lamp and quickly turned the light on and off to transmit the message in morse code.

The air pressure in the cabin slowly rose. Outside the window, Adam could see the fog growing thicker and encroaching closer and closer to the cabin.

"Jam- Er.. Magician... The fog is getting closer." Adam said.

"Good. That means things are coming through," James said, glancing over at Agent Star.

Agent Star looked at James with disdainful eyes but kept channeling her astral energy. Her fingernails began to glow with a blue magic.

The oil lamps began to flicker rapidly, the ones in the reflection out of sync with the ones outside the reflection. James let out a groan as if he were lifting a 500-pound weight, and the lamps' flickering slowly started to synchronize. As the lights synced up, a white-haired boy flickered into view behind the reflection.

The white-haired boy gasped. It seemed like he could see the three agents just as they could see him. He put his hand on the center of the mirror, right where James's hand was.

Suddenly, the light went out, and the air pressure dropped. James reached through the mirror and gripped onto the white-haired boy and yanked him through.

"Ack!" The white-haired boy yelped as he tumbled through the mirror and landed on James's chest.

"It worked!" Adam shouted. He rushed over to help the white-haired boy up. James got up without expelling much effort.

"H-hi there!" Adam said, "I'm Adam Nolan with the Bureau Arcana. What's your name?"

"Misha..." Misha said. He shakily brushed off his long, threadbare coat and looked up at Adam. He immediately locked eyes with Adam's coat and pin and yelped out. "Th-that pin! That suit! I-in the forest!"

James turned to Misha. "There's another agent out there?" he asked, his voice just a few semitones of excitement above his resting monotone.

Misha yelped, "N-no! Yes! But no! H-he's... He's dead... Th-the fog..."

"He's clearly in shock," Agent Star declared. She wrapped an arm around the boy to comfort them, "Save your interrogation for when we get back to the Bureau."

James gave Agent Star a brief but piercing look, his eyes narrowing ever so slightly with suspicion. Adam, too, wrapped a comforting arm around Misha, who clung to Adam and took deep, slow breaths to calm down.

"Wh-where was I?" Misha asked, voice shaky.

"The astral plane," James said, "It's very impressive that you managed to not only travel there but survive."

Misha looked up at James with confused eyes but nodded. "W-we're not there anymore, right?" he asked.

"Correct," James said. Then, before anyone could react, Misha rushed out the door in a panic. Adam screamed and tried to grab Misha, but they were already outside in the fog... but the fog dissipated; in a small diameter around Misha, the fog was gone.

The three agents gasped which made Misha freeze. He turned around and looked at the others. "D-did I do something wrong?" he stammered, then, hearing the hiss and cries of the fog, realized how reckless he was. He scurried back inside and curled up in the corner.

James' eyes traveled from the fog to Misha and said, "We may have our way home."

"You're gonna use the kid? You can't be serious," Agent Star demanded.

"I am open to alternatives," James said, then stared patiently at Agent Star, awaiting a response that never came.

Adam approached Misha, slowly and carefully. He crouched down next to them and gave them a comforting pat on the back. "Hey there. I know this is sudden, but... we could really use your help. We can't go through the fog but..." He paused and searched for the right words, "You know Rudolph The Red Nosed Reindeer?"

Misha looked up at Adam and nodded. Adam smiled reassuringly.

"Y-you want me to... guide you through the fog? Me? B-but I'm just..." his words trailed off.

Adam shook his head, "See that big scary man?" Adam asked, pointing to James, "He says you're special, and he's hard to impress."

Misha lit up with pride... and a dusting of embarrassment on his cheek. "Really?" he asked.

Adam nodded and held out a hand. Misha took it. Adam led Misha to the cabin door. James and Agent Star watched them closely. The two stepped outside, huddled close together. The sound of the worms beyond the fog made Adam shiver but... They remained at bay.

Adam turned to James and Agent Star. "Let's go. I can't stand it here anymore."

Hanged Man guided them over the radio as James made sure that all four of them were close and slowly, they entered the fog. The cabin vanished from view after only a few steps. They could see nothing around them but the obtrusive fog that, with each step, revealed a swarm of worms that hissed and squealed before escaping back into the fog. One misstep and their bones would be picked clean. Progress was slow... but careful.

05:

It took hours.

Hours of seeing nothing but the fog. After staring at it for so long, Adam swore he could see a pulsating mass waiting just beyond... waiting for someone to slip up.

Hours of hearing nothing but the ravenous hiss of the worms skittering and crawling around inches from their feet.

Hours of feeling the ground wriggle under them, waiting for them to trip.

Hours.

06:

The three agents and Misha breached from the fog and rushed into the open field. The sun was just starting to set and backlit the Bureau van. Adam and Misha sprinted as far as they could before they each collapsed, gasping for that crisp sweet air. James and Agent Star walked far past the van together. There was a long silence.

James broke the silence, "A Bureau agent found dead in the astral plane. I wonder how that could have happened. Since it's so hard to just wander in there. Quite curious, isn't it, Judeth?"

"Quite curious indeed," Agent Star, Judeth, said, "Director Emperor won't let you pursue that matter any further, you know."

"His orders, then?" James inquired, eyeing his fellow agent with a piercing gaze.

Agent Star stayed silent.

"You released the fog on his orders, too, didn't you?" James prodded.

Agent Star chuckled and shook her head. "You should know what happens to agents who outlive their usefulness."

Agent Star turned to walk back to the van, but James grabbed her wrist.

"I stopped playing Gecko's game. But if you so much as touch Adam..." he warned, eyes a powerful, bright white.

"You don't have to threaten me. I've seen your record. Graves really is a fitting name for you."

James Graves let go of Agent Star and looked away. Agent Star let out a sultry laugh and casually walked back to the van.

James stood there until the sun disappeared behind the hills. He lamented his early years in the Bureau. He did a lot of things in the name of the greater good, things he has been trying to atone for ever since.

"Cmon, Ace," Hanged Man said through the radio, "We're waiting for you. Let's go home."

07:

Back at the Bureau Arcana, in the observation theater, Adam led the interview with Misha Woods while James supervised. James did his best to remain professional and put together, and externally, he succeeded. Internally, however, the recent events caused a deep anxiety to well within him. The Bureau Arcana, the organization that gave him purpose, the place that gave him meaning, now felt like a beast. He wondered how much longer this pot could simmer before it boiled over.

"Mr. Nolan?" Misha asked, which snapped James out of his thoughts.

"Yeah?" Adam replied.

"If Mr. Graves is such a good guy… why does he have such a dark aura?"

James tilted his head but didn't react beyond that. He held up a clipboard and wrote something down, asking "You can read auras? You certainly are touched by the astral plane."

"What's my aura?" Adam asked excitedly, leaning in close to Misha.

Misha leaned back with wide eyes as he stared at Adam. After a long silence, Misha's face dropped, disappointed in himself. "U-uhm… I-I can't see your aura… I'm sorry."

Adam smiled to hide his disappointment and gave Misha a pat on the shoulder, "It's okay, I wasn't any good at using my powers when I first discovered them either."

"It seems you have this covered," James said suddenly, "I will file our reports." He gave Misha and Adam a distracted nod before leaving the room.

* * *

As James walked through the hallways of The Bureau Arcana, he walked past a closed door. Beyond that door, three agents sat around a poker table with a fourth chair left empty. At the table sat Agent Hierophant, Agent Devil, and the dealer. The dealer was dressed in a black vest made of the same material as the Bureau Arcana suits. His shirt was a crisp, white dress button-up with French cuffs adorned with silver cufflinks shaped like the Bureau Arcana logo. Instead of the standard issue black necktie, the dealer wore a black bow tie. A pair of designer sunglasses hid his bright green eyes, and a gambler's hat sat atop his dirty blonde hair. This man was Agent Wheel Of Fortune, Director of Statistics.

The dealer, Agent Wheel, dealt two cards to Director of Legal, Agent Devil.

"The Magician and The Fool. The Ace and The Wildcard. What a twist of fate they have brought upon us," Agent Devil said, before taking a look at his cards.

Agent Wheel dealt two cards to Director of Archival, Agent Hierophant.

"Indeed," Agent Hierophant didn't look at his cards and said, "Of all the things we deal with at the Bureau, Fate is still such an elusive, enigmatic entity."

Agent Wheel dealt two cards to the empty chair. The cards slid right up to a handheld radio. Agent Hierophant took the cards and held them up so neither he nor anyone else at the table could see.

The radio crackled to life, "And to think, if fate twisted differently, Elliott would have been the new Fool."

Agent Devil raised an eyebrow, "Oh? Do you know something we don't? Check," he said, knocking twice on the table.

"It's my business to know what others don't," Agent Hanged Man replied.

"He was at Capstone Creek with James that night. Raise," Agent Hierophant said, moving a blood red poker chip into the pot.

"Oh, Come now. You haven't even looked at your cards," Agent Devil said, arm gesturing with frustration towards Agent Hierophant.

"I do not toy with fate; it has a way of untwisting itself in unpredictable ways. I act on faith. Stable, unshakable faith," Agent Hierophant said.

Agent Devil tisked and turned to the empty chair, "Well then? What do you know about that night, Hanged Man?"

From the radio came nothing but static as the table waited for a response.

"Call." Agent Hanged Man eventually said. Agent Wheel took a chip from Agent Hanged Man's side of the table and moved it into the pot.

Agent Devil stared into the empty chair with a smoldering intensity as he tossed a chip into the pot as well.

Agent wheel burnt a card into the discard pile, then dealt the flop. Ace of Clubs, Ace of Spades, Eight of Clubs.

"Check," Agent Devil said, "What aren't you telling us, radio man? If Hierophant is right, and Fate decides to untwist itself, what happens then?"

"Raise," Agent Hierophant said, still refusing to look at his cards. Agent Devil groaned.

"Call," Agent Hanged Man said, "James chose to twist fate for Adam's sake. Let's leave it at that.

"Call," Agent Devil said, "And if fate does untwist itself? What then? What happens to the poor boy?"

Once all the chips were placed into the pot, Agent Wheel burnt another card and dealt the turn. Eight of Spades. Dead Man's hand. It felt as if that was the answer to Agent Devil's question.

Agent Devil hesitated for a moment before, with a measured voice, said, "Check."

"Raise," Agent Hierophant said.

Agent Devil slammed his fist on the table, "Why must you incessantly raise the stakes? You don't even know your hand!"

Agent Hierophant let out a dry chuckle before he spoke, "The game of fate we are intertwined in has much higher stakes than a silly poker game, yet I am in it no matter what. I have faith in our own... 'Ace and Wildcard' as you put it earlier. I will stand by them no matter the stakes, no matter what fate decides to deal us." Instead of raising one chip, Agent hierophant pushed the entirety of his chips into the pot. "Are you?"

There was a tense pause as everyone awaited the play from the radio. It was as if his response wasn't just about the poker game anymore.

"Call," was all Agent Hanged Man said. All eyes turned to Agent Devil.

Agent Devil smirked and shook his head in disbelief as he pushed his chips into the pot, "In for a penny, and all that."

Agent Wheel burnt a final card. He dealt the river card face down.

"It's fascinating watching how you each play your game," Agent Wheel said, a sharp, cocky smile on his face. His voice was bright and playful, relaxed. The voice of a man who held all the cards, literally and figuratively.

"One learns the rules and plays them better than anyone else…" Agent Wheel said, looking towards Agent Devil.

"One trusts in fate…" Agent Wheel said, moving his gaze towards Agent Hierophant.

"And one keeps their cards close to their chest..." he said, looking towards the empty chair.

"There is one other way to play the game," Agent Wheel said. As he spoke, he flipped the final card to reveal a joker.

"You can stack the deck and cheat fate."

Chapter 06:
The Twins of Electric Avenue

01:

Through the shake of a handheld camera and the digital compression of internet streaming, a video of a well-lit abandoned building buffered to life. Through the glitches and poor-quality footage, a young man walked into frame. He had bright lightning blonde hair that stuck up as if it was perpetually charged with static electricity. His eyes were electric blue and glimmered with a drive to create. He wore a mechanic's jumpsuit that was stained with oil and singed with electric burns. On his head rested a pair of goggles, and on his back was a backpack made seemingly completely of scrap metal. The straps of the backpack were made of a tangle of various colored wires with several exposed pieces of copper visible.

The young man turned towards the camera with a bright, performative smile, and struck a pose with his hand forming a peace sign.

"Hey hey! Quinton R. Cade here with RCadeBuilds! We're here at electric avenue to see if we can make Doc Oc's robotic arms in real life." His voice was bright with an electric passion as he described the technical aspects of his project. He turned to show off his mechanical backpack and explained what he hoped it would do. Once he finished his explanation, he flashed a peace sign to the camera again, but this time a band of electricity appeared between his fingers, climbing up them like a Jacob's ladder. He pressed the electrified fingers to two exposed wires on the straps of his backpack. There was a loud sparking sound that peaked the video's audio. The person behind the camera jumped and yelped with a voice identical to Quinton's.

Two mechanical arms about four feet in length sprang from the backpack, which caused both boys to laugh with excitement. Quinton moved his fingers up and down the exposed bits of copper wire and made the arms move in various ways. He made the arms flex, do the YMCA, and stick straight up.

From behind the camera, the operator said, "Oh my god it

works!"

"Of course it works! Your code is flawless, Andrew."

"Oh, shut uuuuup. The code would be useless if you didn't build the dang thing." The man behind the camera, Andrew, said sheepishly.

Suddenly, Quinton's eyes met the camera lens with a mischievous smirk, and he used one of the arms to snatch the camera. Using the robot arm, he held the camera in front of him as he grabbed Andrew and pulled them into frame. Andrew R. Cade was Quinton's brother and identical twin and thus shared the same features as his brother. Instead of his brother's jumpsuit, Andrew was dressed in an extra-large hoodie that hung almost to the knees of his skinny jeans. Instead of goggles, he had a pair of glasses that Quinton had often described as "nerdy."

Once Andrew was in frame, he gave a shy wave to the camera, the tips of his fingers crackling with small sparks of electricity. He glanced over to his brother and tapped one of the exposed copper wires which caused the robot arm to drop the camera. Andrew grabbed it and returned to his position, safe from the mischievous robot arms.

Quinton snickered and stuck out his tongue at the camera. Just then, a deep, deathly groan echoed from the abandoned hallways behind him. It was vaguely human sounding, but something was off about it. With the mediocre camera microphone, it sounded all the more haunting. The twins went silent with Quinton turning towards where the sound came from. With no hesitation, Quinton approached the open doorway where the noise came from.

"Hey, stupid! What are you doing?" Andrew whisper-shouted towards his brother.

Quinton turned back to face his brother, "What? It was just a noise."

"Noises come from things!" Andrew argued.

"And I wanna see what it came from!"

"Uhhggg," Andrew groaned before a deeper, more guttural groan drowned him out. The pained and hollow groans grew louder and louder until a humanoid figure shambled into the doorway. It froze, nothing but its silhouette visible to the twins and the camera. Despite standing upright, the creature looked as if it was hanging limp from a hastily constructed gallows.

"Uhm... Hey there? Can we help you?" Quinton asked.

It groaned again, the noise echoing throughout the empty room until decaying into silence. The creature stumbled forward and into the light.

It was hard to tell what happened next. The twins gasped, and the camera began to shake. There was the sound of an electric discharge, a nauseating motion blur, then it all stopped. The final frame lingered on the figure. It was hard to make out, but through the grain and pixels, rotted flesh sloughed from the figure's bone, a walking corpse.

02:

Adam stared at the last frame frozen on his computer monitor and shivered. He turned to James who was sitting right beside him.

"U-undead? Like... zombies?" Adam asked.

"Yes." James said, anxiously tapping on Adam's desk. His usually sharp and focused mind was concentrated elsewhere.

"Is this gonna cause like... an apocalypse?" Adam asked.

"No. That's why we're here. This is really quite a standard mission."

"So standard the Bureau's Ace agent is gonna be helping me out, eh?" Adam said, giving James a playful elbow.

"Huh? Oh, no, I won't be with you on this mission." James said, his eyes gazing out over the office, as if waiting for someone.

"Wh- huh?" Adam gulped. Memories of Sharp Manor and agent Hermit flashed in his mind. He wanted to object, to tell James he wasn't sure he could do the mission without James, but his pride made him keep quiet. "10-4, Agent Magician. But... What will you be doing?"

"Agent Hanged Man and I are working on something. He recommended that Agent Wheel Of Fortune be your partner so I wouldn't... worry," James said.

"Who?" Adam asked. No sooner than when the words came from Adam's mouth, the door to the office swung open.

Agent Wheel waltzed in wearing a long coat lined with white fur along the inside.

"So, this is our little twist of fate, eh?" Agent Wheel said with a winning smile, his eyes peeking ever so slightly over the top of his sunglasses. He leaned over Adam and extended a hand for him to shake.

"Twist of fate?" Adam asked, shyly taking Wheel's hand and giving it a shake. Those words snapped James out of his thoughts, and he glared sharply at Agent Wheel. Wheel's smile took on a more smirk-like quality as his eyes flicked over to James.

"Relax. I'll take good care of your wild card, or else Hanged Man will have my ass," Wheel said, giving James a wink.

James stared Wheel down. He didn't like the Wheel Of Fortune. He saw them as careless and flippant, succeeding through sheer luck. Where James took care and planning into his strategy, Wheel reminded him that one bad roll of the dice could undo it all. The thing he disliked most about Wheel was that he could never tell if he was cheating or was simply just that lucky. Despite that, Hanged Man trusted them, so James did too. He let his face crack into a smile and gave Agent Wheel a nod.

"Now c'mon. We gotta get to 'Electric Avenue' before that video goes viral. Heh, Viral. In more ways than one," Agent Wheel said, still gripping Adam's hand from their handshake. He started leaving, forcing Adam to follow.

James watched as they left, jaw clenched with anxiety.

03:

"Electric Avenue" was the name given to the industrial district of a town somewhere on the outskirts of Silicon Valley. It got its name from the abandoned power plant that stood as the heart of the district. Over time, like a rot, the surrounding buildings had shared the power plant's fate and became abandoned.

Agent Wheel led the way as Adam followed him through the labyrinth of derelict buildings. The overwhelming decay around them made Adam's mind wander. At least it wasn't another forest.

"So, we're hunting the undead right?" Adam asked, "Does

that mean there is like... an afterlife"

"There is," Wheel replied casually, hands in his coat pockets as his head swiveled around with curiosity, exploring and admiring the dead brutalist architecture.

"H-huh? How can you say that so confidently?" Adam said, voice cracking a bit with excitement.

"I've been there. Won a bet against the grim reaper," Wheel said, whistling. Again, he said it like it was obvious, mundane. Adam froze, jaw agape. When Agent Wheel turned to look at Adam, his whistling stopped.

"What?" Agent Wheel asked, almost defensively, "Agent World is literally a ghost. Agent Devil made a literal deal with the devil! Death and undeath is just a thing we deal with."

Adam was speechless for a long moment before breaking into a weak laugh. He looked up and imagined Elliott watching him from above.

"Maybe I will see him again," Adam said.

Agent Wheel couldn't help but smile at Adam. He had no idea what Fate had in store for the rookie agent. Agent Wheel thought that if he were a gambling man, he'd bet that whatever it was will have extraordinary repercussions for the Bureau Arcana.

Agent Wheel's ruminations were cut off by the sounds of a familiar voice coming from the next room over. Adam recognized it as the same voice as the one in the video.

"I heard something! Maybe it's the monster? What's the scanner say?"

An identical voice spoke up, sounding like it was coming in over a walkie talkie, the voice half obscured by a heavy static. "It's hard to read. The signal is weaker in these concrete buildings, and I can't see very well. Please be careful."

"What? Are you ragging on my drone design?"

"No! I just... Ugh. Even your genius is still bound by the physics of radio waves."

"Hehehe, copy that."

Agent Wheel walked into the next room without a care in the world and let out a warm, friendly, "Hi!"

The young man that Adam recognized as Quinton Cade yelped and threw his hands out, a haphazard web of lighting shot from his fingertips towards Agent Wheel. The electricity was immediately drawn to an exposed copper pipe only inches from Agent Wheel's face, leaving him completely unscathed.

"Well! That sure was lucky." Agent Wheel said, glancing over to Adam to give him a wink.

Quinton let out an exhilarated laugh, completely recovered from the scare. From behind Quinton, a drone flew up to Agent Wheel. A mini camera lens on the drone looked up and down. Agent Wheel almost seemed to pose.

From a speaker on the drone, Andrew spoke. "Are you... from the Bureau Arcana?"

Agent Wheel adjusted his shirt cuffs in such a way as to flash his Bureau-styled cufflinks, "Good eye. We saw your video and-"

Quinton gasped, a light blush dusting his cheeks, like he was star struck. He fidgeted with his goggles, trying to look slick. "No kidding? You know, My brother and I have a bit of metahuman in us if you're looking for recruits."

Agent Wheel ran a finger along the exposed copper pipe that saved his life. "You don't say?"

"See what happens when you're careless, Q?" Andrew said from the drone.

Quinton rubbed the back of his head, "Ahaha... sorry about that. But, but! Q! You know Q from James Bond? The guy who makes all the gadgets? Literally us! So, we're not *just* metahumans! Again... If you're looking for recruits."

Agent Wheel chuckled, a bright, charismatic smile on his face. "Let's take care of the undead before and see how it goes from there, eh?"

Adam finally poked his head into the room with the others and spoke up, "Are you sure that's a good idea? They are civilians after all."

Wheel tilted his head in thought. "Hmmm. It wouldn't be the first time the Bureau has recruited civilians, though."

Adam shuddered. The only time he knew of the Bureau working alongside civilians was... Elliott...

Before Adam could argue, Andrew's drone started beeping. "I think we found our monster. Follow me!" Andrew said before whipping the drone around and zipping off.

"Let's go monster hunting!" Quinton said, following the drone. Adam looked to Agent Wheel, who looked amused. He stuffed his hands into his coat pockets and nodded for Adam to follow the twins. Adam frowned and ran in front of the twins.

"H-hey guys!" Adam said, taking charge, "I appreciate your enthusiasm but… This is really dangerous. I don't wanna see you guys get hurt."

"Well duh. That's why I built a drone for Andrew to fly." Quinton said.

"He's talking about you!" Andrew retorted through the radio static.

Quinton rolled his eyes, "Pfff. I know, that's what makes it exciting!"

"I get it. Gambling is most fun when the stakes are highest," Agent Wheel said.

Adam snapped and he screamed. "This isn't a game! Lives are at stake!"

"Would you believe me if I said that wasn't even the highest the stakes could get?" Agent Wheel said, an ominous intensity hiding just behind his eyes. It was in direct competition with his playful, casual smile.

Adam went speechless. There was silence… just in time for a deep groan to echo through the halls. Everyone went still, waiting for another groan, waiting to hear if it was getting closer… and it was. The dead, mindless groan echoed and reverberated off the concrete. As the groan decayed, the silence was filled with a slow, relentless shuffle as the undead got closer and closer.

The spin of a revolver's cylinder cut through the silence, followed by the satisfying click of the hammer being pulled back. Adam turned to see Agent Wheel with a custom-made platinum plated Colt Peacemaker in his grip. Agent Wheel held the gun ever so naturally, like it was an extension of his fingers as he pointed the gun barrel lazily towards the ceiling.

"That machine of yours equipped with weapons or are you just gonna hover at it?" Agent Wheel asked, his coat pushed out of the way so one hand could fit into his pants pocket.

Quinton tisked and said, "c'mon. Don't you remember?" Then he held up his hands as they screeched to life with electricity.

Wheel chuckled and nodded, "I can't wait to see that in action... When not directed at me, I mean."

"Be careful..." Andrew said, hovering the drone right behind Quinton, as if hiding behind him.

Adam had already seen a lot in his brief tenure at the Bureau Arcana: werewolves, eldritch monstrosities, horrors beyond human comprehension. This struck the most palpable dread yet into Adam's heart. A walking corpse, flesh almost dripping from bone; A fellow human, forced from its rest to shamble on for eternity; it made Adam freeze as it creeped into the room. The hollow eye sockets of the undead seemed to bore into Adam's eyes. He wondered if Elliott could have ended up like this... He wasn't sure if he could have shot them. The stench of rotten flesh burned Adam's nostrils. It made him want to throw up.

Quinton cracked his neck then, with a screech of lighting, he sent a bolt straight into the heart of the undead. The corpse dropped to the ground with an empty thud.

Agent wheel let out an impressed whistle, slowly clapping as his revolver hung from his index finger.

"Bravo! One question, though," Agent Wheel said, "You know the movie Frankenstein, right?"

"Of course!" both twins chorused.

"And what happened right before the mad doctor screamed, 'it's alive'?"

"Oh oh!" Andrew said excitedly from the drone, "Lightning struck... the... o-oh..."

As he spoke, the corpse, like a marionette being pulled up by its strings, rose again. Slowly, relentlessly, it lumbered towards Quinton.

Adam grabbed Quinton by the collar and pulled him back. He drew his own side arm, a compact semi-automatic that seemed exceptionally modern compared to Wheel's revolver and aimed at the walking corpse. Quinton and the drone kept their distance.

"So," Adam said, heart pounding, "This is supposedly standard, right? What's the standard operating procedure, or whatever?"

"The usual. Destroy the brain. But that means *destroying* it. One shot to the head may not be enough," Agent Wheel said, a series of clicks punctuated his words as he fiddled with the hammer of his revolver.

"What are we waiting for then?" Adam asked, pulling back the hammer of his pistol.

It almost looked like Agent Wheel shrugged before aiming at the undead.

The sound of the gunshots bounced off the cold hard concrete, amplifying the sound again and again until it was deafening. All Adam could hear was the ringing in his ears.

The ringing slowly faded to heavy panting as Adam regained his orientation. The corpse was no longer standing… but would it stay down? Agent Wheel stepped up to the corps and nudged it with his shoe.

"It still has its head. Got any shots left?" Agent Wheel said.

Adam checked his gun and confirmed that it was empty. He shook his head at Agent Wheel.

"Reload?" Agent Wheel asked.

"I-I left the extra shots in the van," Adam admitted.

"Tisk. What bad luck," Agent Wheel said with a chuckle.

"What about you?" Adam asked.

Agent Wheel tilted his head. "Hmmm."

The corpse, that god forsaken corpse rose once more. Agent Wheel didn't seem to notice.

Agent Wheel started mumbling to himself, "Now did I fire six shots, or only five?"

"Wheel…" Adam started nervously, backing away to shield Quinton and the drone. Wheel continued to mumble to himself, like he was trying to exorcise an earworm from his brain.

The corpse got closer.

"Wheel!" Adam yelled.

Agent Wheel smiled wide and spun his revolver's cylinder. Slowly, he leveled the gun between the undead's empty eyes. The cylinder continued to spin like a roulette wheel.

"'Do I feel lucky?'" Agent Wheel asked.

The undead lunged, mouth agape and snarling. Agent

Wheel pulled the trigger.

With a loud bang, the corpse's head exploded. Adam swore the following ringing in his ears sounded like a slot machine that hit the jackpot.

04:

[[Director Of Statistics, Wheel Of Fortune's Report: Mission Debrief and recruitment recommendation.]]

Agent Fool and I eliminated the undead threat with the help of two civilians.

Standard operating procedure when dealing with the undead requires a thorough sweep of the surroundings to identify the cause of reanimation and to ensure no further threats or possibility for outbreak, so to please the bureaucrats reading this, here's what we found.

Thanks to the technical savvy of two civilians, ▮▮▮▮▮▮▮ and ▮▮▮▮▮▮▮ we were able to thoroughly scan the entirety of the area known as "electric avenue" and concluded that there were no further zombies or possibility for zombies. (I know that's not the official term, but they are zombies, damn it.)

Upon further investigation, we found the grave of the one zombie we eliminated. He was hastily buried underneath the main generator of the defunct power plant. The latent pollution and the electricity from the ▮▮▮▮▮▮▮ twins' constant tomfoolery triggered the reanimation. Yes, we did search the power plant thoroughly for any further graves or corpses, there were none. Why was the corpse there? That's Intel's department. Mine is stats, and I say the probability of there being further corpses there is about 0.003%. How I came to that calculation is detailed in the attached document.

As for the ▆▆▆▆▆▆▆ twins, given the growing number of vacancies (RIP Agent Sun and Hermit), I think they could make extraordinary candidates for potential Major Arcanas. I've sent their info over to Agent High Priestess for enrollment into the Academy.

05:

When Adam returned to the Bureau Arcana, his mind was occupied with the concept of the afterlife. He found himself wandering the maintenance halls of The Bureau. Compared to the polished, well-kept corridors of the Bureau offices, the maintenance tunnels were colder, darker, and cramped. The concrete walls were lined with various pipes and cables that ran along the entirety of the halls to supply the Bureau with its necessary utilities. The edges of the floor were lined with various janitorial equipment and miscellaneous storage, but it was never so cluttered to hamper one's ability to move through the halls. The air hung heavy with minerals and pine-scented cleaning products. There was something grounding about it all for Adam, that even an esoteric entity like the Bureau Arcana still had something as mundane as clutter.

Adam leaned against one of the walls and reached into his pocket to fiddle with the spent rifle shell casing he always kept there. He pulled it out and stared at it, rolling it around between his fingers. He closed his eyes and focused. He held the image of Quinton Cade crackling with electricity. Soon, he heard the shell casing spark to life.

He opened his eyes to see a man in front of him. Adam yelped and threw his electricity imbued casing at the man. The casing went through the man like he wasn't even there.

"It is a pleasure to meet you, too," said the man. He was

tall and thin, dressed in what looked to be a Bureau Arcana suit, but from a different era of fashion, perhaps a century ago. His face was a ghostly pale, with tragically young features. His hair and eyes were as pale as the rest of him. As he stood, he leaned on an elegant formal black cane with a silver handle. A Bureau Arcana lapel pin was fastened proudly to his suit jacket, but it wasn't quite right. Adam vaguely recalled seeing this version of the logo while reading through historical documents in the Bureau's Archive. He recognized it as the original design used for the Bureau Arcana's crest. This seemed to match with the era of suit he wore.

"Wha? S-sorry?" Adam stammered, reaching out to try and touch the man. His hand went right through them. The man's ghostly eyes rolled with silent exasperation, as if this were a regular occurrence for him.

"Cease," the man said with a firm but polite tone.

"Sorry sorry!" Adam said, rushing to retrieve the fallen shell casing. He secured it back in his pocket and turned to the tall, spectral figure.

Adam reached out a hand in greeting and said, "I uh... don't believe we've met. I'm Adam Nolan!"

The man glanced at the extended hand like it was a bad joke. "Osric Ashford. Also known as Agent World. Charmed," he said before giving an archaic bow.

Adam glanced at Osric, then down at his own hand. Agent World...

"You're the ghost Agent Wheel mentioned!" Adam blurted out.

Osric sighed and nodded.

Adam lit up with nervous excitement, a hopeful glimmer in his eye. He leaned in closer to Osric, "Forgive me if this is too personal but... How did you become a ghost? Not how you died but... Why aren't you just dead? How does the afterlife work? Why can some people come back and others can't?"

Osric crossed his arms, the hand not holding his cane tapping his arm in thought, "Alas, that is a difficult question to answer. I have on many an occasion requested study into the subject, but Research does not consider it a priority. The best I can provide is an account of my own ordeal, but who would want to listen to an old soul exposit about a time long since past?"

Adam leaned in closer. There was an intense cold emanating off of Osric. "I would love to hear it," Adam said.

Osric smiled nostalgically. "My brother and I were two of the first official operatives of the Bureau Arcana. When I swore my oath, I swore to protect the Bureau with my very soul. Looking back, knowing what we know now, perhaps I was a bit overzealous with my phraseology," Osric said with a laugh.

Osric continued, "I remember the sensation of dying very well. It was like being jolted from a dream. I was in my office, standing over my own dead body. I recall my office door opening, but beyond the door was unfamiliar to me. Death himself was waiting for me. He led me through what he called purgatory."

"What was it like?" Adam asked, enraptured by Osric's story.

"It was... eerily mundane," Osric explained, "Like a modest hotel in the middle of nowhere. The only indication of anything otherworldly was the halls that stretched on, eternally liminal."

"A-and Death? Was it like... the grim reaper?" Adam asked.

"Yes. Although his garb was far from the long robes of folklore. It was far more modern, for my time at least. He took me to a door. But it was unlike the other doors. It looked like the front door to the Bureau Arcana's offices. He repeated the oath I swore to The Bureau, to protect it with 'my very soul', then said that if that were the case, I could step through the door and carry out my oath. But he warned me that I would not be able to come back to the afterlife until the Bureau Arcana no longer needed me."

Osric chuckled and gazed down the long narrow corridors of the Bureau's maintenance halls. "So here I am. Bound to the grounds of the Bureau Arcana, doomed to haunt these halls until its purpose is no longer necessary. A fitting role for the so-called 'director of facilities.' As far as curses go, I am rather chuffed with the circumstances."

Adam let Osric's story hang in the air for a moment as he tried to comprehend what it could mean for his dead friend. The afterlife... It all felt unsettlingly tangible now. He didn't want to get his hopes up... but he did hope this all meant he could see his dear friend Elliott again.

Adam's eyes met Osric's spectral gaze. "It seems so easy to go to and from the afterlife... could you... take me there?" Adam's voice was nervous, but steadfast.

Osric let out a dry, hollow chuckle, "I would have to kill you. As for getting back... I do understand we here at the Bureau Arcana make it seem easy, but I assure you, we are simply beholden to the whims of Fate. Those who return from the afterlife must have purpose. We all have our role to play, even if we don't know the script."

Adam sighed.

Osric continued, "The Bureau Arcana's duty is to break down the barrier between the natural and the supernatural. It is inevitable that we would find ways to alter Fate to our whim. It is thus just as inevitable that Fate would push back against such efforts. I believe Death, the grim reaper, or whatever we choose to call him, is responsible for keeping that balance."

Adam nodded. "I see... I-I think."

Osric smiled. "Indeed? Well then, I must bid you adieu, rookie. I must tend to other parts of this facility." Then, with a polite bow, Osric floated straight through the solid concrete wall, and he was gone.

Adam leaned against the wall and stared up at the concrete ceiling. It was a lot to try and understand, but Adam felt like things were starting to click. He prayed he wasn't back in the denial stage of grief and simply finding every excuse he could to convince himself that Elliott could still be out there. The anxiety of waiting, of unknowing was driving Adam mad. What does fate have in store?

Chapter 07:
The Academy Arcana

01:

It was early in the morning, and dawn had yet to break. The moon had just set, and the sun was still an hour or so from breaching the horizon. When night comes, the full moon will rise. Director Gecko stood on the roof of the Bureau Arcana headquarters and looked over the surrounding redwood forest. A lit cigarette balanced on the guard railing that Gecko leaned against, letting its smoke naturally waft up and join the rest of the smoggy cloud around his head. Behind Gecko stood Agent Moon, Agent Tower, and Agent Star.

"Go on," Gecko said as he took a long, slow inhale. The cigarette on the railing burned faster and emitted thicker smoke.

Moon cleared his throat and spoke, "Project Moonlight is making great progress. I think we can expect to see promising results in just one month from now."

Gecko nodded. "And our student assets? Are they prepared for tonight?"

Agent Tower spoke next, "Yeup. The wolf boy knows the drill, be in bed by sundown. The other kid knows to shoot him if he isn't."

Gecko let out a pleased hum, "And our dear Magician and Hanged Man?"

Agent Star finally spoke, admiring the claws of astral energy that grew from her nails, "They are still snooping around, but we keep redacting their reports before they get to the other… more impressionable agents. In a month, they should no longer be a problem."

Gecko's cigarette smoldered out. He shook his head and chuckled.

"Well," Director Gecko began, "It seems Fate has blessed us with a red letter month."

02:

...Elliott opened the door. He found himself in what looked to be a barren dorm room. There was only one bed, one desk and one chair. On the desk was a black messenger bag, and an alarm clock. Notably, there were no windows.

He immediately felt his heart beating with life. He shivered hard and let out a sigh of relief. He opened the messenger bag. Inside was a notebook, binder, and various writing utensils. He flipped through the binder, and a plastic card fell out.

Elliott picked the card up to inspect. It was a student ID card for a school named "Academy Arcana." It was Elliott's. It had his picture, his name, and his date of birth. Looking back at the binder, there was a class schedule with a bunch of names that sounded absolutely insane to him: Spectral forensics, Analysis of astral activity, etc. It seemed like he had been provided with exactly what he needed to easily slip into being a student. He cringed at the idea. He skipped university, but fate somehow found a way to force him to study again anyway.

The bombardment of bafflement was starting to overwhelm Elliott, and he took a deep breath. He focused on the sound of his heartbeat. Slowly, he made some sense of things. The Man In Black had brought him back to life and he was now enrolled in a school. The name of the academy, and subject matter of the studies implied that it was related to the Bureau Arcana.

His train of thought was broken when the dorm room door opened, and he heard someone's voice.

"This floor is supposed to be empty..." The boy said. They were tall, but with a young, nervous face that suggested he was a student. He had thick black hair and sharp red eyes that were framed by a rectangular pair of glasses. They wore dark clothes with red accents that clung tight to his nerdy yet fit frame.

Elliott smiled nervously. "I uh... Just moved in," he said.

The fellow student anxiously bit his lip. He didn't know what to say in response.

Elliott gave the fellow student a concerned look, before putting on a warm smile. He held out his hand in greeting and said,

"My name is Elliott Harding."

The fellow student looked at the outstretched hand before he hesitantly reached out to shake. "R-Royce. Grayson.," he said, hesitating before giving his last name.

"Nice to meet y-" Elliot began before being cut off.

"Sorry! I would love to stay and chat but... I have class." Royce said before turning to scurry off. Suddenly, he stopped and whipped around, a grave look in his eyes.

"Tonight is a full moon..." he said, his voice low and shaky, "If this is indeed your dorm... Lock your door before nightfall."

Before Elliott could ask for clarification, Royce was gone.

Elliott shook his head and explored the dorm. There were two hallways, east and west, that connected to a central lounge. Attached to the lounge was a staircase that Royce ran up to get to class. The lounge was furnished to accommodate students socializing and studying, with comfy armchairs, tables, and snack machines. The snack machines were empty. The chairs looked unused.

It was eerily quiet. The carpet was nearly unsoiled. There were faint impressions of footprints of various shapes and sizes that Elliott was able to trace to only one room on the opposite wing to where Elliott's apparent dorm was. Was Royce really the only other student down here?

He made his way up the stairs. The stairs led to a door that opened to the ground floor of the dorms. The door closed behind him with a beep and the sound of an electronic deadbolt slamming home. Next to the door was a card scanner. Elliott pulled out his ID card and scanned it. The card scanner beeped and the door unlocked. Elliott took a mental note of the lock and explored the rest of the dorms. The other floors looked like they had seen use consistent with a busy college dorm. Each floor was separated by a door, but notably, none of these floors had an ID scanner, nor were they locked. The juxtaposition from the basement floor made Elliott shiver. Something felt oddly sinister about that detail.

Elliott flipped through his binder. He didn't have any class today, so he decided to use the day to explore, learn about exactly where, and when, he was. As he put his binder away, Elliott was overcome by the unshakable sensation that he was being watched. He whipped around to see an empty dorm hallway. As he stared down the hallway, he could have sworn there was a shadowy blur just outside his field of vision.

Again, Elliott shivered.

"One mystery at a time, Elliott," Elliott said to himself before continuing his exploration of the dorms. Along the walls were various posters advertising extracurricular events and other such student body activities. This was perfect for Elliott; they all had dates on them. As his eyes scanned the posters, he was suddenly gripped with dread... He checked the other posters in the hops that the first one was simply old, but each one listed the same year. It had been nearly four whole years since Elliott's death.

Elliott felt a pang in his heart... Like the world had moved on without him. He thought about where Adam may be now. He wondered if his own murder was ever solved... Elliott wanted to break down and weep, but someone interrupted his silent lamentation.

"Who the hell are you, pipsqueak?" demanded a soft voice that tried to sound gruffer than it could go. The voice came from a boy wearing ripped black jeans, a t-shirt with some underground punk band, and a scuffed-up leather jacket. Elliott noticed that the edges of the boy's sleeves were burnt. If the supernatural was real... Was magic real? Was pyromancy real?

"Huh?" Elliott said before the punk's words had fully registered.

"What, are you, short *and* deaf? Who. Are. You?" the boy repeated, more annoyed.

Elliott grit his teeth. It was always about his damn height... "The name's Elliott. You?"

"Killian, but call me Kia." The punk, Killian, said. He said it like he wanted to expend as little breath as he could uttering his name.

"Nice to meet you, Kia." Elliott said, forcing a smile and holding out a hand for Killian. Killian stared at the hand and deliberately stuffed his hands into his leather jacket's pockets.

"Uh huh," Killian said, glaring skeptically up and down

Elliott's frame. "New guys don't just show up here, ya know. What's your story?"

"What's yours?" Elliott asked.

Killian tisked, "None of ya business."

"Then why'd you ask me?" Elliott retorted.

"Don't matter. Just watch yourself around here, new kid," Killian said before unceremoniously walking outside.

Elliott watched them leave in disbelief. "Jeez. What a warm welcome…" he said to himself. Again, the feeling like he was being watched creeped up Elliott's spine. Again, he whipped around to see… nothing. He stared down the dorm halls for a long moment, waiting to perhaps catch the glimpse of whatever may be watching him… After several seconds of absolutely nothing catching his eye, Elliott left the dorms.

03:

As Elliott investigated, he did his best to avoid being seen. He was new, and he worried about what undue attention could cause him. To help him blend in, he held onto the notebook he found in his messenger bag. Along with making him look like a student, it was also useful for jotting down his notes about the academy's layout.

According to Elliott's investigation, The Academy Arcana was a series of surprisingly few buildings near the outskirts of a northern Californian forest. On paper, it was just a remote campus of the nearby state university. The Academy campus centerpiece was a circular plaza that sat as the pathway from each of the surrounding buildings. A keen-eyed observer could notice that the plaza and its buildings were constructed to function as a massive sundial.

Elliott Harding was one of those who noticed the campus's trick. With this knowledge, Elliott found a spot in the plaza that had a perfect view of the whole campus and watched as the sun began to set. He got to know a lot about his fellow classmates just from sitting here and watching. The student body of the Academy was fairly small, about 30 or 40 people.

As Elliott watched, a few specific students caught his eye.

He watched as a pair of twins whose hair looked like they had just stuck a fork in an electrical outlet both tinkered with a drone that looked to be cobbled together from half a dozen crashed quadcopters. The twins cheered as it took off, flying towards the roof of the library.

On the roof of the library sat that punk student who called himself Kia. His ripped jeans and combat boots hung off the ledge. The punk in the leather jacket let fire dance between his fingers as the twins' drone flew up to them. The punk flipped the drone a literally flaming bird, before shooing it away. The flames from his hand licked the drone and caused it to spark and plummet. Aha! Elliott was right! Pyromancy!

The drone fell and landed in a patch of flowers being tended to by a boy in a heavily worn, oversized Victorian long coat with white hair long enough to cover one eye. The emo-coded amateur gardener fell to his knees to mourn the death of his flowers as the twins rushed to apologize and recover the corpse of their drone.

As the twins crossed the quad, A tall, self-serious student Elliott recognized as Royce left the labs. Under his arms he carried a textbook on metahuman biology. Royce collided with one of the twins, knocking the twin to the ground. Despite his nerdy build, Royce was sturdy and kept going, in too much of a rush to offer more than a panicked "Sorry! 'Scuse me!" as he rushed into the dorms.

As Royce walked into the dorm building, Elliott shivered with the feeling of being watched. He gazed up at the dorms, eyes flicking between all the windows. Through one of the windows, he saw a tall man in a white mask staring at him. Elliott blinked and narrowed his eyes to get a clearer look, but the mask was gone.

Elliott shook his head. He scanned the plaza.

"What a motley crew," he thought to himself as he turned his head from right to left. Immediately to his left, only inches from his face was a champagne blonde student with deep green eyes. He was impeccably dressed, with the exception of his poorly tied tie.

"What's a motley crew?" The deep green-eyed student asked.

"Ack! What?" Elliott yelped.

He was only thinking that, Miles thought to the Eldritch being named Zak that he shared the well-dressed body with.

"Ack! Sorry!" Zak exclaimed, scrambling to his feet. He stood and reached his arm out, leaning over Elliott. "Hi! I didn't mean to startle you! It's just... I haven't seen you around before and I wanted to say hi! So... Hi!"

Elliott looked up at Zak, eyes wide with confusion.

A for effort but let me handle this. Miles said in Zak's head.

Zak blushed and pulled his hand away. "Sorry! Give me a moment!" Then he closed his eyes and took a deep breath. When he opened his eyes again, one was now a bright blue instead of deep green.

"Hello. My name is..." Miles began out loud before pausing.

Should I introduce ourselves as Miles or Zak? Miles asked in his head.

W-well... It's your body. I think Miles? Zak replied.

Elliott blinked rapidly, trying to comprehend what was happening.

"Miles. Miles Prince," Miles eventually said.

Elliott raised an eyebrow in recognition. "Prince like... *The* Prince Pharmaceuticals Prince?"

Miles chuckled with a hint of sheepishness. He sighed and said, "Yeah. That Prince."

Elliott raised both of his eyebrows and whistled. "My my! Well, it is an honor to make your acquaintance," he said, bowing. Although Elliott was sincere, his tone and mannerisms during the bow came off as a bit sarcastic.

Miles grit his teeth, his blush deepening. Normally, Miles was great at reading people, but he couldn't quite tell exactly how sincere Elliott was. Zak could sense Elliott's sincerity and psychically shared that information with Miles to soothe his anxiety.

Miles cleared his throat, "I'm just a student here. Same as you."

"Just a student," Elliott said, raising from his bow and eyeing Miles up and down, "What brought you here, I wonder."

Miles reflexively clenched his fist at Elliott's prodding. He flashed a warm, charismatic smile and said, "I was kidnapped by some cultists. The Bureau boys saved me." He did his best not to accidentally let slip that he was also a master thief.

Elliott tisked and shook his head, "How about I ask your co-pilot why *they* are here?"

Miles's eyebrows raised but kept his cool, "Whatever do you mean?"

Elliott snickered and theatrically put two fingers to his temple, "Like you, I'm psychic."

A hint of worry flashed in Miles's one blue eye. He looked to the side to silently consult with Zak.

Sorry! He isn't psychic. He's just very observant… Was I really that bad at acting normal? Zak thought to Miles.

Yeah, but it's okay. That's why we're here, isn't it? To help you practice. Miles thought back.

Thanks… Can I talk to him?

"Talkin' to your co-pilot?" Elliott said with a mischievous grin.

Miles sighed and closed his eyes. When he opened them, both of his eyes were deep green once again. His posture immediately went from straight and dignified to hunched and fidgety with nervous excitement.

"Hi!" Zak said, "I'm Z'ak'Aroth! But you can call me Zak!"

"Pleasure to meetcha!" Elliott said, grabbing Zak's hand and giving them a firm shake. Zak eagerly shook Elliott's hand, but didn't fully understand the mechanics of it, and just wiggled his arm in Elliott's grip.

Elliott stifled a chuckle at the awkward handshake. "It's getting late. How about we grab something to eat?" he said.

Zak lit up with excitement. "Borgor! Miles gave me a borgor and it was… Good!" he shouted, mouth watering.

Burger, Miles corrected.

"Brrr… grrr..?" Zak repeated, hesitantly.

Elliott laughed and wrapped an arm around Zak, "Yeah, we can get some burgers."

Zak wiggled excitedly as Elliott led the way to the campus cafeteria.

04:

The sun had set, and the sky was darkening. The outdoor lights of the academy campus buzzed to life with the glow of mercury vapor. As Elliott and Zak stepped into the cafeteria, Quinton and Andrew Cade stepped out carrying a tray of cookies. The lightning-yellow-haired twins made a beeline to Misha Woods, who was lying in a patch of grass near his still recently wrecked garden. Quinton, the older of the two twins, stood over Misha.

"We come bearing gifts," Quinton Cade declared, holding the tray of cookies out for Misha.

"As an apology for killing your flowers," Andrew Cade said in a deeply guilty tone, fidgeting with his fingers.

Misha gasped and leaped up, covering his face in embarrassment. "Wha? N-no you apologized enough! I should apologize for planting flowers that got so easily tangled in the rotors of your drone! Rotor? I-I mean propellers! R-right?"

The Cade twins looked at each other, each raising an eyebrow before turning back to Misha. As Misha continued to babble, Quinton pushed the snack tray closer towards them.

Misha blinked and looked at the tray, then back to the twins... Then back to the tray.

"Take the damn cookie," Quinton said, perhaps a bit too sharply.

Misha immediately took a cookie off the tray and shoved the whole thing in his mouth. He stared at the twins wide eyed.

"Sowwy..." Misha said, muffled with a mouth full of unchewed cookie.

Quinton sighed. Andrew's fidgeting intensified.

Misha quickly chewed and swallowed. "I-I mean thank you!"

Both twins relaxed, at least for a moment. That relaxation slowly turned to tension as all three remained silent, a silence that was only broken by the sound of Andrew biting into a cookie. Misha also took another cookie. Quinton stood there, feeling like an unwilling butler.

"Neither of you are werewolves, right?" Misha blurted out after he swallowed his most recent cookie.

The question came so far out of left field that Quinton recoiled so hard he dropped the tray of cookies. Andrew couldn't help but laugh, both from the suddenness of the question, and his brother's reaction to it.

Misha continued, "I mean... It's a full moon tonight. And you are a student here, so who knows what you could be! Not that I would care if you were a werewolf its just-"

"Relax," Andrew said with a bright, disarming smile, "We aren't werewolves."

Misha smiled and twiddled his fingers nervously. He looked down at his feet. "Well since you can- and you can say no if you're busy but... I was planning on going to the roof to admire the full moon tonight, yeah I know it's kinda dorky but-"

The twins once again looked at each other while Misha rambled nervously. They each moved to each side of Misha and wrapped an arm around his shoulders. "Relaaaaax!" the twins said in unison, "We'd be happy to!"

Misha let out a mouse like yelp at the physical contact and shrunk himself between the two. The twins snickered.

"Lead the way," Quinton said.

"Onward!" Andrew shouted, raising a pointed finger up to the roof.

The two twins ended up idly dragging Misha to the roof while Misha giggled anxiously.

05:

Come night, The sky was black except for the stars and bright full moon overhead. On the roof of the library of the Academy Arcana, Killian Wilkes lay on his back. He held his hand out, index and middle finger outstretched like a gun.

"Pew," he said as a lick of flame shot out into the night sky before dissipating. He let his arm fall back and hit the ground. He chewed on his lip. He had the insatiable urge to pull out a smoke and watch it burn, but the tobacco smell would make him flash back to Beaumont Heights and get nauseous. The cold night air made him shiver and he pulled his leather jacket tighter.

The doors to the roof opened and Killian tilted his head

back to see two lanky nerds and a small emo with white hair walk out onto the roof. The white-haired boy, Misha, ran up to the railing at the edge of the roof.

"Woooaaah! The moon looks so huge up here! Oh oh! Look look look!" Misha exclaimed as he gestured excitedly at the sky. "Look how bright Orion is!"

While Misha excitedly and breathlessly talked about the constellations in the night sky, Quinton and Andrew stood over Killian. Quinton with a sour expression, and Andrew with a sheepish, guilty one.

Killian chuckled and put his hands behind his head. He looked up at the twins looking cocky and comfy as he said, "Can I help you?"

"Our drone." Quinton said sternly, narrowing his eyes.

"Shouldn't have flown it in my face, then," Killian said, punctuating his sentence with a yawn.

"Th-that's probably my fault," Andrew cut in hesitantly, "My wind compensation programming may have been a bit… buggy…"

"See?" Killian said, flashing a sickeningly saccharin smile up at Quinton, "It was defective. I just made it easier to take apart."

Quinton's temples twitched with annoyance. Andrew looked at his brother nervously.

"Still mad?" Killian said as he got to his feet and cracked his neck, "Well, whatcha gonna do about it? Try me, two on one! I won't even use my powers against ya."

Quinton stepped in front of his slightly younger brother. "You can use your powers," he said. His eyes sparked, a flash of electricity jumped across his eyebrows, and his hair stood up like it was being filled with static electricity.

Killian's cheeky smile only grew before he suddenly threw up his hands. "A'ight. You called my bluff," he said before putting his hands into the pockets of his jacket and walking over to Misha.

"…And that's Polaris, aka the North Star! It's right ahead of us so this building must be the northernmost point of the campus!" Misha continued, oblivious of the preceding confrontation.

The doors to the roof opened yet again. Elliott and Zak

walked out.

"Awoooo!" Elliott howled, no longer worried about staying out of sight. Everyone else on the roof jolted and turned to the two new faces.

Zak froze, eyes wide and flicking between each of the faces, overwhelmed with the sudden assault of anxious emotions from each of them. Elliott raised his eyebrows in surprise.

"Oops." Elliott said, nonchalantly, "I wasn't expecting a party up here."

Killian let out a dry scoff and chuckled, "There wasn't supposed to be."

"D-did no one hear me talk about stars?" Misha said, face falling.

The twins looked at each other with intensely guilty faces.

"Perfect!" Zak blurted out. He spread his arms wide in a dramatic fashion. His wide eyes looked to the side. Elliott recognized it as Zak consulting with Miles. All eyes turned back to Zak, a feeling Miles was very familiar with, but Zak wasn't. Miles did his best to walk Zak through how to act and what to say without taking control.

"S-s... serendipi-tus!" Zak continued, "I mean serendipitous! That means we all get to hear about it! We're all up here to admire the full moon, right? Why not learn a bit from the Mystic Astronomy student?"

Misha blinked, his face turning a bit red as everyone turned to look at him.

"W-wha? How'd you know that's my major?"

That was in his head, Zak... Miles thought. *Just repeat after me...*

Zak grit his teeth then forced an attempt at a charming smile, "Why... anyone with such a passion for the stars must be studying them!"

Misha smiled sheepishly, "O-okay, well I-I'm Misha! Misha Woods! Wait... I don't know your names."

"I'm Z- er... Miles! I'm studying Paranatural Sociology. Pleasure to make all of your aqua-aint-dancees," Zak said before performing a formal bow. Miles mentally praised Zak for how well they pulled it off, "Er.. I mean... acquaintances..."

Elliott performed the same bow as Zak before introducing himself, "Elliott Harding. Paranatural Forensics."

"Hia hia!" Quinton said, "Quinton Robert Cade!"

"Andrew Robert Cade!" Andrew said.

"Metaquantum Mathematics!" the twins said in unison.

There was a beat of silence. Everyone's heads turned expectantly to Killian, who had his arms crossed. He sighed.

"Call me Kia," Killian said.

"Just Kia?" Misha asked.

"Yup," Killian said.

"Gonna tell us your major?" Quinton prodded.

"Nope," Killian said.

There was a brief silence before a faint howl broke through the night air. It came from the dorms. Everyone but Killian turned towards the noise.

"So, we do have a werewolf," Elliott said, walking to the edge of the roof and looking through each window of the dorms, trying to pinpoint which exact room the howl came from.

Killian's phone went off. He cursed under his breath as he pulled it out. He read the most recent message and frowned. While everyone else was now staring at the dorms, gossiping about the werewolf, Zak was staring at Killian. Killian looked up from his phone to see Zak.

"Mind your own business, rich boy," Killian said, his already rough tone sounding somehow more bitter than usual.

Before Miles could help Zak form a response, Killian walked through the exit.

Zak shivered at the intense resentment he felt coming from Killian. Eventually, he took a deep breath and turned to join the others to talk about werewolves and stars.

While everyone else stared at the night sky, Elliott looked down over the academy plaza. His mind buzzed... Why was he brought back here and now? He smiled to himself at the hum of social energy from the group around him. He sighed as he thought about Royce, and how skittish and nervous they were. Was he deliberately isolating himself from the others? Who was Killian communicating with this late at night on a full moon?

His thoughts were broken by a tingle down his spine. He

was being watched again. Reflexively, his eyes darted to a vague white shape that was peeking out from behind a tree in the plaza. Elliott smirked and moved away from the railing and went to leave. Zak intercepted them.

"H-hey! Where are you going? Th-the party is just getting started!" Zak said.

"We're missing something," Elliott said, giving Zak a friendly pat on the back, "I'll be back."

Before Zak could further object, Elliott pushed Zak back into the group and ran down the stairs.

Elliott made his way to the center of the plaza and looked up at the dorm windows, focusing on the reflection of the plaza. Soon enough, Elliott's spine tingled. Instinctively, he wanted to turn around, but he stayed calm. He kept his gaze focused on the dorm room windows. Barely visible in the plaza's reflection, amongst the shadows draped over the campus plaza, Elliott could see a monstrously tall figure in a blank white mask peering out from behind a tree. The same person, he suspected, who was following him around all day.

"Hey there, masked man. Care to introduce yourself?" Elliott said without turning to face his pursuer.

The man in the mask stiffened, his bright blue eyes pierced the darkness as they widened in surprise. Despite the plaza being empty and open, the masked man looked cornered.

Elliott took this moment to turn towards the masked man who stood frozen in horror at being seen, as if Elliott were staring at them completely naked. Elliott let out a gentle laugh.

"Hi. I'm Elliott," He said, "And you?"

The masked man slowly waved in response before making hand gestures that Elliott recognized as sign language. He gasped in excitement. In high school, Elliott volunteered at an old folks' home that specialized in deaf residents, so he had a lot of practice, and could understand sign language.

"Maxwell," The masked man signed hesitantly.

"Pleasure to meet you. Are you deaf? My sign language is rusty, but I can try," Elliott said, trying and failing to sign as he spoke.

Maxwell frantically waved his hands in a "nonono" gesture. *"I just don't like to talk,"* Maxwell signed.

Elliott nodded and asked, "I see... Why are you following me?"

"You weren't here yesterday. It's like you appeared out of nowhere," Maxwell signed.

Elliott rubbed the back of his head. He wondered just how accurate Maxwell knew that was, "Touche."

"How did you see me?" Maxwell signed as he fidgeted nervously.

"With my eyes?" Elliott said, his eyebrows raised curiously, "Look at how you're dressed. You're not exactly hard to spot."

"You are the first other student to notice me," Maxwell signed and looked away. He seemed embarrassed.

"Well Maxwell, I'm glad to have observed you." Elliott said with a snicker.

Maxwell looked down and bashfully kicked the ground. He fidgeted a series of hand gestures that weren't quite comprehensible sign language.

Elliott Smiled. The way Maxwell was acting, it was like his mask was blushing. He reached out a welcoming hand.

"Come with me to the roof," Elliott said, "We're having an impromptu full moon party."

Maxwell let out a barely audible gasp and took a step back, shaking his head nervously.

Elliott stood where he was, hand still outstretched, "Cmon, big man. We won't bite. Not as much as the werewolf anyway."

After a beat of silence, a muffled howl came from the dorms, punctuating Elliott's joke. Maxwell hardly reacted. He was far more scared of people than monsters. Still, after some thought, Maxwell took a step forward. His gloved hand gripped Elliott's and they shook hands.

Maxwell's height accentuated Elliott's lack thereof, a detail he didn't quite comprehend until Maxwell was casually towering over him. Elliott wondered how such a massive dude with such a conspicuous look could be so well hidden. He wanted to pry into why Maxwell felt the need to be so habitually hidden, but now was not the time to get so intimate.

Elliott returned to the roof with excited vigor. He kicked the door open with a theatrical flourish as he proclaimed, "I am back with a new friend!"

Everyone turned to the door. Nothing but an empty stairwell was on the other side. Everyone's eyes flicked between the empty door and Elliott, who was standing with his arms out in a vague gesture of "tah-dah!"

Elliott stared at the confused looks then turned to the empty doorway.

"Maxwell?" Elliott said.

Slowly, cautiously, Maxwell poked his bright blue eyes out from the edge of the doorway. He saw the small group of people all suddenly lock eyes with him, and he immediately retreated.

Elliott laughed nervously and took hold of Maxwell's arm to try and pull them out of hiding. Maxwell simply wouldn't budge.

Zak gulped and approached Elliott and Maxwell. He walked with the stiffness of someone trying to move comfortably in a body that had been raised with an obsessive strictness regarding proper posture.

Zak spoke with a soft and smooth voice, with only a slight nervous quiver that he did his best to suppress, "It's understandable to be frightened. I'm sure we've all been through a unique... hell... to end up at this academy. Let's not go through it alone."

Zak's words, or more likely Miles's words being spoken through Zak, immediately made Elliott feel at ease. It seemed to have a similar effect on Maxwell, because he fully emerged onto the roof. Once Maxwell was fully visible under the bright moonlight, Quinton, Andrew, and Misha approached to welcome Maxwell to the group.

The night went on, the hours passed, and the six students slowly warmed up to each other. They told stories, cracked jokes, and talked about their majors. Elliott was swept up in the growing camaraderie, but it felt bittersweet. He couldn't help but think about Adam.

Across the campus, in his dorm, Killian Wilkes sat in the

darkness of his room. The light of the full moon was just enough to illuminate the blood dried on his hands. He grimaced at how steady they were, at how desensitized to violence he had become.

He squeezed his hands tight until they caught fire, burning away the dried blood.

Chapter 08:
The Phases of The Moon

01: ☉
Moon phase: Waning Gibbous

The next morning, Royce Grayson was in the academy labs, hunched over a microscope. He was always full of manic energy the day after a full moon. A full moon always meant new data, and new data always meant progress. Progress meant being one step closer to the end of his rage-fueled nightmares. He always woke up the morning after the full moon terrified that he might find his chains broken and the campus a bloody mess.

The cold, sterile tiles of the lab, the highly controlled nature of the environment and his experiments, it always calmed Royce's mania. The quiet and rhythmic buzzing and whirring of the testing equipment were especially pleasing to Royce's hypersensitive ears.

When the door to the lab was rammed open, Royce yelped and jumped. Quinton and Andrew Cade barged in carrying a small CRT TV and an assortment of retro game consoles. The twins hastily put their haul down on one of the counters with a sound that made Royce's ears ring and teeth clench.

"Can you believe they threw this away?" Andrew said, immediately going to work trying to plug everything in. Andrew quickly got tangled in a gordian knot of cords and cables he didn't recognize. Quinton sighed and took over, knowing exactly what to plug in and where. The TV buzzed to life before an 8-bit chime rang from its aged speakers.

His flow sufficiently shattered, Royce slowly turned his head towards the twins. A fake smile twitched up as he looked at the two. Royce tried to make a polite noise, but it came out more like a growl.

The two twins turned to Royce, Andew smiled nervously while Quinton simply raised an eyebrow.

"Is that the werewolf?" Andrew asked.

"I don't know." Quinton said, adjusting his glasses before staring into Royce's eyes, "*Are* you the werewolf?"

Royce looked away nervously, which made Quinton crack a small smile.

"It doesn't matter to us. You're less dangerous than that fire guy if you ask me," Quinton said.

Royce mumbled something that neither twin could understand.

"What are you working on?" Andrew asked as he sat next to Royce.

Royce gulped before he spoke. "Just looking over some animal cells. Nothing too interesting…" Royce's voice trailed off.

"What kind of cells?" Quinton asked, sitting on the other side of Royce, leaning in with great interest.

Royce sighed sheepishly and said, "Werewolf cells."

Andrew gasped in awe and Quinton took the microscope to look at the werewolf cells.

"Are they yours?" Quinton asked with a tone of genuine curiosity. Royce relaxed a bit. He was expecting judgment and fear, so this display was very welcoming and broke through his closed-off nature.

"Y-yeah. Well… some of them are mine. The Bureau gives me some other werewolf samples too when I ask for them. I set up the freezer to freeze them at midnight so I could see them transformed. I've been trying to set up a camera that can record the transformation overnight, but I just can't figure out how to make that work with this equipment."

"I could build something for you." Quinton said with calm confidence. His hands worked the microscope with impeccable precision. As he spoke, his eyes never left the instrument's controls.

Royce blushed and rubbed the back of his head anxiously as he responded, "I mean… I don't want to be a bother or anything."

"Think of it as a trade for putting up with us tinkering with our retro gaming stuff," Quinton said as he looked up from the microscope.

"Wait. Do I not have a say in this?" Royce asked.

"Nope!" Andrew said, smiling wide and innocent.

Royce sighed, "Fine, but I get to use your gaming setup," he said, cracking a smile. It was nice to not feel so isolated and alone in his work for once. The old CRT looked surprisingly fitting in the lab. It reminded Royce of his time interning at the tv studio.

Just as Royce was coming down from his anxiety and stress of his night as a chained-up werewolf, Killian Wilkes kicked the door in. He strode in with his hands in his pocket. He saw the twins huddled around Royce, and his face twisted in disgust.

Royce immediately looked away, trying to hide in his notes. The Cade twins stared Killian down, though Andrew positioned himself slightly behind his brother. Quinton narrowed his eyes at Killian.

Killian chuckled dismissively and said, "Since when did monstrous beasts get groupies?"

"Since when do you care about others?" Quinton snapped back.

Killian laughed, "I dunno. Maybe I just don't wanna see even my worst enemies get mauled."

The words stung Royce's soul, and he buried himself deeper into his notes. He tried to act like he was writing something down, but his pen refused to move beyond the same one-inch line he kept redrawing up and down, up and down.

"We can take care of ourselves," Quinton said.

"I'm sure," Killian said, walking across the lab. He stopped near a freezer with a glass door that allowed one to see a collection of test tubes. Staring at them made Killian look sick.

"Who are these?" Killian asked, jerking his chin towards the direction of the frozen vials.

"They are werewolf samples," Royce said quietly.

Killian growled, "I didn't ask what, I asked *who!?*" he roared, voice shaking with a barely suppressed anger.

"Wh-what?" Royce stuttered.

"These samples came from *people!*" Killian screamed, "Real human beings who are now nothing more than a numbered label on a jar. Where are these people now, hmm? I don't see any other werewolves around campus. What makes you so special? Why aren't you just a vial like them?"

Royce's limbs shook. Without thinking, the pen in his

hands snapped and sprayed ink all over his lab coat. With nothing else to grab onto, he dug his fingers into his own thigh.

Quinton stood and stepped up to Killian, "Hey, why don't you back off, kay?"

Andrew shyly spoke up, "Yeah. It's not like he's going out at night to bite people! They keep him locked in his dorm on full moons, don't they?"

"Yeah!" Quinton continued, "And his entire damn floor is locked, so we couldn't accidentally wander down there. It's the damn Bureau Arcana. I'm sure they've gathered tons of werewolf samples over the years anyway."

Killian listened to the twins defend Royce. Killian shook his head and laughed like he was just told a brilliant joke. He continued to laugh as he walked back towards the exit. He took a hand out of his coat pocket and put his hand on the door. Before he opened it, he turned to the three students.

"Try not to end up as an unnamed numbered vial, eh?" Killian said.

02: ☾
Moon Phase: Third Quarter

The Academy Arcana's lecture hall was the largest classroom on the campus. It was designed to comfortably seat every student enrolled at once, which, given the esoteric and niche nature of its curriculum, was still quite intimate.

Elliott showed up to class as early as he could. He wasn't the most interested in the class itself but was incredibly interested in watching the other students file in and set up. His new role as a student at the Academy Arcana was a lot to take in, so he did his best to just observe from a distance. He was hoping to be the first one to class but was shocked to see Killian sitting in the back corner, headphones on, legs kicked up and resting on the back of the chair in front of him.

Elliott was fascinated by Killian; he may come off as a dick, but Elliott couldn't help but be curious about him. Elliott had to prod, had to learn more about him, so he sat right next to Killian. Killian sensed the presence of another, and his eyes shot open.

"Any seat to choose from, and you choose the only one that is directly next to me. Do you strike up conversations at the urinal, too?" Killian said, refusing to turn to look at Elliott.

"We missed you the other night," Elliott said, watching Killian's face closely.

Killian turned to Elliott with a reflexive look of shocked incredulity. The idea that anyone would want him around enough to miss him was inconceivable to him.

"My ass you did," Killian said. He turned away from Elliott and closed his eyes in the hopes Elliott would get the hint and leave him alone.

"Why do you do that? Why close yourself off like that?" Elliott asked. Elliott's eyes traveled up and down Killian, hoping to learn more about them through small details. His eyes fixated on Killian's headphone cable.

"I'm just trying to listen to my music, dude, damn," Killian said with a growing whine of annoyance, side-eying Elliott.

Elliott raised an eyebrow and lifted Killian's headphone cable to show that it wasn't connected. It must have become accidentally unplugged when Elliott sat down, either that, or Killian deliberately hadn't connected it in the first place.

Killian's eye twitched in annoyance. "Okay, smart ass. What do you want?"

Elliott shrugged, "Maybe I just wanna be friends."

"I don't," Killian said coldly as he swiped his headphone cable from Elliott's hand. In truth, Killian was indeed acting more closed off than he wanted to be, and Elliott could see it. In Killian's head, it would be better if he didn't make friends here, as painful as it was. The way Killian acted, of course, made Elliott all the more curious about the inner workings of Killian's brain.

"Why put on this act? We j-" as Elliott spoke, Killian grabbed Elliott's arm and stared them in the eyes, Killian's burning, almost orange, brown eyes quivered.

"Please... Please just don't," Killian almost pleaded, his eyes softened for just a moment.

Students started flowing in, and Killian threw Elliott's hand down. Elliott rubbed his wrist and watched the students flow in. Some of the students he didn't recognize, but those he did, he watched closely. Royce walked in first and sat at the direct front and center of the class. He got his binder and notebook out and was efficiently ready for when class began. The Cade twins followed and sat behind Royce, so they had a clear line of sight of Royce's notes. After a strong bout of analysis paralysis, Misha chose to sit somewhere in the middle and off to the side, one of the most inconspicuous seats he could have picked. Miles/Zak looked around until he saw Elliott, whereupon he waved and made his way to sit right in front of them with a polite greeting.

Killian audibly groaned. Miles/Zak ignored the groan, but they could sense Killian's intense resentment radiating off of them. He kept hearing the thoughts *"privileged prick"* emanate from Killian's mind. Miles hated to admit it, but Killian was right. Miles felt a constant pang of guilt growing up wealthy. He hated being handed his status just by being born to the right people. Part of why he became the Jack of Diamonds in the first place was a sort of atonement for his upbringing. Zak gently broke into his co-pilot's thoughts and coaxed them to focus on class instead.

Elliott looked over the lecture hall. This was supposed to be an Intro To The Esoteric class that everyone was required to take, so where was Maxwell?

Maxwell was sitting directly to Elliott's right. Elliott yelped in surprise when he finally noticed. Maxwell waved as a hiss-like snicker escaped from under his mask.

The murmur of students that filled the lecture hall was quickly silenced as a tall, professional woman in a pantsuit and glasses stepped in and walked up to the lectern. She had pitch black hair that went down to her shoulders, short enough for someone with a busy schedule to easily style. She wore sharp glasses in front of an equally sharp gaze. Her pantsuit was black, with a silver Bureau Arcana pin adorned on her lapel.

The professional woman spoke. Her voice was measured and clear. She was loud enough to be heard in the back, but not so loud it hurt the ears of those in the front. "Hello everyone. My name is Alexia Ward. I am the director of Academia at the Bureau Arcana, and I will be your instructor for this course." It was very clear she had given this lecture countless times.

"The purpose of this class," Alexia continued as a

slideshow listing a bunch of words and their definitions illuminated the wall behind her, "Is to provide a basic level of knowledge that will function as a solid foundation to the more specific areas of focus you are all studying."

Elliott looked around. Royce was taking furious notes. The Cade twins were taking less detailed notes while looking over at Royce's notes to check if they missed anything important. Misha took some notes but spent most of the lecture doodling. Miles/Zak spent the time between note taking twirling a pen between his fingers. The dexterity of the twirling seemed to increase and decrease as Miles or Zak took control over Miles's body. Killian was watching the lecture without taking notes. Maxwell transcribed the lecture word for word without once looking down at his notebook.

Elliott was never good at paying attention in class, but he forced himself to pay attention as best he could. Professor Ward spoke eloquently and explained these concepts in easy-to-understand ways. Her energy was surprisingly engaging and eccentric despite her deliberately sanitary appearance. Elliott was able to comprehend an analogy that compared the cosmic to the geological and the eldritch to the biological, but despite the professor's oration skills, Elliott's mind began to wander.

Elliott stared into the back of Miles/Zak's hair. It was brushed neatly, so Elliott deduced that Miles was probably in charge of getting ready today. He wondered if Miles/Zak could hear him if he thought really hard.

Elliott narrowed his eyes and focused his thoughts. *Hey Zak. Or Miles? Can you hear me?*

Miles/Zak stiffened in surprise. He turned in his seat, his deep green eye locking on to Elliott's eyes.

"I am thinking at you!" Elliott thought to Miles/Zak.

Miles/Zak smiled, and his eyes shined with excitement. He tried to telepathically respond.

If you are trying to say something back, I can't hear it. Elliott thought.

Miles/Zak nodded and turned back around. He scribbled on his notebook and moved it so Elliott could see what he wrote.

"I hear you loud and clear. This is so cool!" Miles/Zak

wrote. Elliott noticed that the first and second sentence seemed to have different handwriting. The first sentence was written in an elegant, practiced cursive, while the second sentence was a crude, rough scrawl.

Can you read other people's minds? Elliott thought.

"Yeah, but I try not to. It feels rude." Zak/Miles scrawled.

What about with Mr. wannabe badass next to me?

Zak/Miles thought for a moment then turned ever so slightly, as if listening to Killian. Eventually, Miles/Zak neatly printed, "It's hard to tell, but... He seems... upset that he had to leave the party that night."

Elliott cracked a proud, devious smile and turned to Killian.

Killian side-eyed Elliott with a confused, raised eyebrow. He whispered, "What now, shorty?"

"Nothing," Elliott whispered back before turning to Zak/Miles.

"He does indeed think you're short. Especially compared to the giant next to you," Zak/Miles wrote.

Why is it always about my damn height? Elliott thought.

"Well, looking around, you are the shortest one here. Even that kid Misha is taller."

Okay, thank you! Elliott thought harshly, face turning deep red.

Zak/Miles giggled. Elliott forced himself to focus on the rest of class.

03: ◐

Moon phase: Waning Crescent.

Every night it was the same nightmare... The stars disappeared... The eyes emerged from the void... The maw swallowed the earth.

Misha Woods shot awake in bed, just like he did every night. His dorm was dark, dark enough to see the stars outside his window. He took a series of deep breaths until his racing heart calmed. He got out of bed and checked his phone. It was 3:00 AM. That was later than usual, but that was still the last bit of sleep he'd get that night.

Misha put on a shirt and shorts then stepped outside his dorm. During the night, the Academy dorm hallways maintained a dim warm light. Misha was thankful for the illumination since he often wandered the halls this late, although by now he probably could traverse them in complete darkness. Every floor except the basement floor, Royce's floor. The locked floor.

Normally the dorm halls were silent, but tonight, Misha heard someone else's voice coming from this floor's lounge. It was an eloquent and dignified voice. It was Miles.

"... Yes, father," Miles said as Misha approached. Miles was facing the wall, staring at a corporate painting that decorated the lounge. He held one hand behind his back like a butler awaiting orders as his other hand held his phone to his ear. He stood there in silence as the person on the other end of the call talked at length.

"... Thank you, father," Miles said, before finally hanging up. He sighed and his body relaxed. His arms dropped to his side, and his shoulders loosened.

"Miles!" Misha said, perhaps a bit too loud for 3:00 in the morning, "What are you doing up?"

Miles jumped only slightly, "Oh? Mister Woods. Good evening," he said before turning to face Misha.

Misha locked eyes with Miles's and gasped in shock. One of Miles's eyes was a bright blue. Misha had only ever seen Miles with two deep green eyes. Miles blinked, and in that flash of darkness, Misha swore he could see the same eyes from his nightmares, only green. He froze in fear.

Miles tilted his head and cocked an eyebrow, "Mister Woods? Are you... okay?" he inquired.

He can see me. Zak thought to Miles. Zak's consciousness forced a heavy shiver down Miles's spine.

What? What do you mean? Miles thought back.

I... I don't know... Zak thought.

Miles looked at Misha for a moment before flashing a warm, slick smile. It was the same smile he always used to schmooze his parents' guests.

"You see him, don't you?" Miles asked in a soft, calming

tone.

Misha shook with fear but nodded.

Miles smiled and let out a soft chuckle, "Don't worry. He's friendly."

Misha looked at Miles skeptically, "H-he won't try to eat the earth?"

The question seemed absurd to Miles, so he couldn't help but laugh, "What? Of course not!"

Misha stared skeptically for a moment. Miles stared back, a bright, charming smile on his face. It seemed to disarm Misha enough for him to smile back.

"So!" Misha said after a long silence, "You were talking to your dad, right? Does your... uhm..."

"His name is Zak," Miles said.

"Zak! Does he have a dad, too? Does he talk to them? *Can* he talk to them?"

Miles tilted his head and said, "Hmm. Good question."

Do you? Miles thought.

I do. I don't speak to him. I don't want to speak to him...

Miles let out a dry chuckle and said, "Heh. It seems even elder gods have daddy issues."

Misha giggled, "How... human! My dad is a bit much, too. He's so overprotective... Gosh, you should have seen that agent deal with him. And my dad thought he knew better than the *federal agents!* He thinks I'm just crazy but... H-here... I finally feel understood. Sorry! I'm rambling! What's your dad like?"

Miles listened to Misha intently, amazed at how energetic and breathlessly this white-haired boy spoke at 3:00 AM. When asked about his own father, his eyebrows shot up.

"Mine?" Miles said sheepishly, "He treats me like an asset. He only calls when I can provide something to his company."

"Why'd he call tonight then? Is that too personal? Sorry! Wait, why did he even call this late? Is that normal for him?" Misha nattered.

A lot of words surely flow out of him. Zak though, which made Miles laugh, which made Misha shut up.

"It's okay," Miles said, "He's overseas and didn't care what time it was here. As for what he wanted... He told me to behave myself. Apparently he has some prospects with the Bureau Arcana, and I need to exude the elegance and grace of the Prince Family while I'm here."

"Gosh. He sounds... cold," Misha said.

Miles was about to respond when from the hallway came a dismissive groan. The two boys turned to see Killian with his arms crossed, his combat boot was kicked up behind him and pressed against the wall.

"Oh, boo hoo," Killian whined sarcastically, "My daddy pays for anything I want, but he's soooo demanding! Oh, woe is me!"

"Excuse me?" Miles said, suppressing a more emotional response. Misha looked around nervously before scurrying off.

"You heard me," Killian said with venom and vitriol, "The gall you have, sitting on your damn throne and complaining about the weight of the crown."

"I didn't choose this 'throne,'" Miles said calmly. He maintained a dignified demeanor, but kept his fist clenched tight behind his back. One of Zak's tentacles slid out from Miles's sleeve to wrap itself around Miles's fist in an attempt to calm his host.

"Oh, but you do choose to keep your privileged ass sat there, don't you?" Killian said, eyes blazing as he approached Miles. He poked an accusatory finger into Miles's chest.

Oh, this asshole! I am gonna- Zak thought, tentacle now squeezing Miles's fist empathetically.

No. It's fine. Miles thought back, even his internal voice was calm, almost cold like his father.

Miles said nothing, eyes locked to Killian's.

"Do you even care where all that money comes from?" Killian asked, inches from Miles's face.

Miles responded as if on autopilot, "Prince pharmaceuticals is at the forefront of innova-"

"Yeah yeah, I know what you *say* you do. But why are you interested in the boys in black? That's why dear papa gave ya a ring, right?" Killian leaned in closer, staring into Miles, as if trying to pierce into their brain and learn his secrets.

Miles grit his teeth and spoke, "We-... they are funding some of the Bureau's research. Royce's research. A cure for werewolfism. Should I be ashamed of that?"

Killian's eyes flashed. His wrathful demeanor seemed to calm down. He spoke in a low, gritty voice, "You don't even know..."

Miles's eyes twitched with curiosity. *Zak, what is he talking about?* he thought.

I... I don't know. All he's thinking is 'goddamn bureau, goddamn moon, goddamn fire...' And he is imagining blood... so much blood... Zak responded.

Miles gasped. He stared Killian in the eyes and leaned in with the same drilling gaze as Killian, but unlike him, Miles actually could drill into Killian's mind. The punk tried to suppress it, but the proximity to Miles made him blush. The jumble of emotions inside Killian's mind became even harder for Zak to translate. Killian was furious with Miles, that much was clear, but there was something else there. Zak could only translate the signal as an intense craving. For violence?

"Why are you even here?" Miles prodded.

Killian recoiled and turned away. "What kinda stupid question it that? Same reason most of us are. The boys in black saw I had powers and recruited me."

"How? How did they discover your... rather destructive power?" Miles said. Now it was his turn to look accusatory. He leaned in with a knowing smirk.

Through Killian's intense aggression, excitement, and guilt, Zak heard the words *Beaumont Heights* on Killian's mind. Zak immediately let Miles know.

Miles gasped, "It was you! The news said it was terrorists, but it was y-"

Killian pounced and grabbed Miles by the collar. He slammed Miles against the wall. Zak's tentacles instinctively extended from Miles's sleeves, but Miles gripped them tight to hold them at bay.

Killian leaned in close and whispered into Miles's ear. "The boys in black, the ones your dear papa are bankrolling, would rather that little factoid stay hidden. I would do what he says and behave," Killian said.

Miles stared into Killian's blazing eyes, "Self-righteous

Hypocrite," he said.

"Unlike you, I. Don't. Have. A. Choice," Killian growled.

A pair of doors opened in the hallway, and the twins, Quinton and Andrew wandered out, eyes sleepy and annoyed. Killian let go of Miles before the twins saw them.

"The hell's happening out here?" Quinton Cade said, looking from Miles to Killian.

Miles brushed himself off and spoke, "A heated philosophical debate. Nothing more."

"At three in the morning?" Andrew Cade asked, rubbing his eyes tiredly.

Killian chuckled and shook his head, "Insomnia is a bitch. This boring brat sure tired me out though."

The twins looked wearily at the punk and the rich kid, then turned to look at each other. They shrugged and both retreated back into their dorm.

Killian started to walk back to his dorm when Miles called out.

"What did you mean by not having a choice?" Miles asked.

"Don't worry your privileged little head, or your sword of Damocles may fall," he said as he walked to his dorm. He was stopped by Misha, who gently poked Killian on the arm.

"Mister Kia?" Misha asked, "Wh-what is your father like?"

"Wha?" Killian said, his face twisted in bafflement.

"I mean, that's what we were talking about when you showed up, and… you look all scary, but your aura is really kind, s-so I wanted to ask!"

Killian sighed and placed a hand on Misha's head to ruffle his hair.

"He was a prick," Killian said. He gently pushed Misha away and continued to his dorm.

"Was?" Misha asked.

"Goodnight," Killian said as he entered his dorm. He slammed the door behind him.

04: ●
Moon phase: New Moon

At night, the outskirts of the Academy were shrouded in shadow, the dull new moon providing very little light. Amongst the shadows, a man draped in all black dashed across the treetops, the cold night air rushing by. He silently made his way through the trees until he reached the spot he was looking for, a felled tree in an especially dense part of the academy's outskirts. The black-clad man sat on the fallen tree and carefully unraveled the cloth around his head, revealing his champagne blonde hair. He reached into his bag and pulled out an almost cartoonishly large ruby.

The Jack Of Diamonds returns! Zak said inside Miles's head.

Oh hush. This is necessary. If the Jack of Diamonds stopped... jacking diamonds after the obsidian grail, people might make the connection to me, Miles responded.

Hehe. I am inside your mind, Miles. I know you like it.

Miles chuckled and shook his head, *Little of column A, little of column B.*

So, what do we do with the ruby? Zak thought.

Eh. Ditch it, I think.

What?! Can I at least... hold it?

Uh... Sure?

Yippee! Zak thought, then instead of taking control of Miles's body, a tentacle slid out from Miles's sleeve and scooped the diamond from his hand. Zak held the ruby up to the stars which refracted beautifully though the gem.

What are these used for? Zak asked.

They have no use, Miles replied.

What? Then why is it so valuable?

To be valuable. Its only purpose is to show others that the owner is able to own it.

Oh... That's... Disappointing, Zak thought, *At least we stopped to get us something with actual value.*

That's right, Miles thought before reaching back into the bag. He pulled out a thick, juicy cheeseburger. Once the scent reached Miles's nose, Zak became the mental equivalent of a dog scratching at the door, begging to be let outside. Miles chuckled and let Zak take over.

Once Zak had full control over Miles's body, he tossed the ruby over his shoulder and used both hands to ravenously devour the burger. Miles was thankful no one could see his body behave so... animalistically. Then he heard a voice from the shadows.

"Ow!" yelped the voice

Zak/Miles whipped around to see where the voice came from. Barely visible in the darkness, Elliott Harding stood, rubbing his head where the ruby hit. He looked at Miles with a mischievous glint in his eye.

"Ya know, I used to be a private investigator. Gosh, imagine the battle of wits we could have had!" Elliott said.

Zak/Miles blushed as red as the stolen ruby, and rubbed the back of his head. Miles cringed as he felt the burger grease smear his perfectly groomed hair. "Ahaha! Should I say 'well done, detective?' Although, it is just your word against mine..."

As Zak spoke, Maxwell emerged from the shadows. His bright white mask seemed to appear from nothing as it caught the starlight. Without making a sound, Maxwell scooped up the ruby. Zak was so spooked by Maxwell's appearance that he retreated to let Miles take over.

"You were saying?" Elliott said with a wide, satisfied smirk.

Miles sighed in defeat and used his pant leg to wipe the burger grease off his hands. "What are you two doing out here anyway?"

Maxwell silently tossed the ruby to Elliott, who caught it and said, "We were playing chess in Maxwell's dorm and we saw you outside our window, so we set up camp and waited for you to come back."

As Miles spoke, Maxwell pantomimed everything Miles said with theatrical enthusiasm.

Miles and Zak were both enamored by Maxwell's antics and couldn't help but chuckle. "So, what now? Do you turn me in?" Miles asked.

Elliott and Maxwell both tilted their heads, Maxwell let out a hiss like snicker from under his mask. Elliott tossed the ruby back to Miles, who caught it, a puzzled look on his face.

"Of course not! We're buds!" Elliott said, "Though I do wonder what Zak would be willing to do to protect ya."

Zak snickered internally as a tentacle curled protectively around Miles's wrist.

Without seeing it, Maxwell ended up right beside Miles and swiped the ruby from them. Miles gasped and Zak shot a tentacle out to grab Maxwell's wrist. Maxwell didn't even flinch, he simply tilted his head as his blue eyes shimmered with curiosity behind his mask.

Down boy. Miles thought. Zak let go of Maxwell's wrist and the tentacle retreated back inside Miles's sleeve.

Elliott leaned casually against a tree. "The truth is, I could use the help of the Jack Of Diamonds."

Maxwell clapped with excitement and signed, *"Tell him, tell him!"* Miles didn't read sign language, but Zak read thoughts, so they both understood. Miles raised a curious eyebrow.

Elliott leaned in with a mischievous, cheshire cat grin, "I need to break into your family's estate."

Miles's curious eyebrows twisted further up in disbelief. He stared at Elliott with a look of incredulity. He opened his mouth to speak, but he was at a loss for words. The ever-eloquent Miles Prince, struck speechless. It made Elliott's eyes flash with pride.

"Maxwell told me about your spat with Kia the other night." Elliott said.

"Huh? But he wasn't there," Miles said, reflexively looking around. Maxwell was nowhere to be seen.

Maxwell is thinking, 'I am good at being where others think I am not,' Zak informed Miles.

To punctuate the point, when Miles turned to face Elliott, Maxwell was there in his place. Miles shivered.

"Anyway!" Elliott said, poking his head out from behind Maxwell's massive frame, "What Kia said got me curious. What is the Bureau brewing? What are they doing with private investors, like your father? I bet you're curious too, and I bet that's why your master thief has returned."

Damn, he's good, Zak thought. Miles wanted to deny it, but it was hard to lie to the person literally inside your head.

Elliott chuckled and let out a sigh, "I guess you get to have your game of wits after all."

05: ◐
Moon Phase: Waxing Crescent

Killian Wilkes entered his dorm room and tossed a compound crossbow onto his bed. He reached into his backpack and pulled out a paper target. It still had some dirt and detritus on it from being pinned to a tree in the campus outskirts. He brushed it off and wrote in sharpie at the top, "K.W. Compound Bow. 50 yards."

He admired his marksmanship with a proud half smile. It wasn't quite bullseyes, but his shots were grouped closer together than his previous attempts. He pinned it to the wall over his other targets with the same label. Next to that target was a collection of others, each one had a different weapon written on it. He looked at the target labeled "K.W. Hunting Rifle. 100 yards." and poked his finger through the hole over the bullseye. The edges of the bullet hole started to singe as Killian's finger ignited it.

Killian swore to himself and batted at the paper in a panic to try and extinguish the potential fire before it burned away the evidence of his accomplishments. His anxious state simply made the fire grow. He tore the target off the wall, which may have saved the rest of his targets, but doomed this one.

"Damn it," Killian said, staring at the ash from where his perfect target once was. The smoke from the deceased target wafted upward to the ceiling... Then the fire alarm went off.

"*Damn* it!" Killian yelled. He looked around to make sure nothing was left alight, and left his room. He exited casually, trying his best not to look guilty.

Amongst the evacuating students, the Cade twins stood, arms crossed and snickered at Killian.

"What are you two looking at?" Killian barked.

Quinton Cade held his hand to his ear and leaned towards Killian, "What? I can't hear you over the sound of the BLARING ALARM!"

Andrew Cade pushed his way through the students to peek into Killian's dorm, "What did you burn?"

Killian slammed his door shut. "None of your business."

"So, you did burn something!" Quinton said.

Killian rolled his eyes and evacuated with the rest of the students. Quinton and Andrew followed. Despite the "blaring" alarm, the Cades' snickering was heard loud and clear. It made Killian's cheeks burn hotter than his pyromancy.

Out in the plaza, the academy student body of around 30 students stood around impatiently. Killian tried to ignore the glares shot his way as his hands were stuffed deep into the pockets of his leather jacket to hide his balled up fists. The whispers were harder to ignore.

"Was it the pyro again?"

"That punk? Must have been."

"I heard he burned down that fancy skyscraper."

"What? Why did The Bureau let him in here then?"

"They're shady anyway."

"He's gonna burn us all down..."

Killian made his way to a dark corner to hide as best he could in such a public space. He closed his eyes and leaned against the wall. His head was racing with guilt and shame, and he was half tempted to just self-immolate. Killian grit his teeth. He had to endure; he had to play the villain for now.

Someone poked Killian's sides. Killian swore that if he opened his eyes and saw one of the Cade twins, he was just gonna deck them. He sighed and opened his eyes.

It was Misha. Killian sighed with relief.

"Kia... Is it true? Did you set off the alarm?"

Killian's relief immediately twisted back into guilt, "Uhg. Yeah... yeah it was. It happens sometimes."

"Gosh... That must be a pain to control... I'm sorry," Misha said, patting Killian's shoulder.

Killian tisked and shrugged Misha's hand off, "Don't pity me."

Misha looked up with a confused expression. Misha thought he was trying to be nice, so he didn't understand why Killian was still being so standoffish. Killian looked into Misha's big, innocent eyes and sighed.

"I'm just glad you're safe," Killian said, flashing a soft

smile.

"See? You're not as much of a dick as you want us to think," Elliott said, leaning against the wall to flank Killian.

Killian's smile twisted downward and his eyes twitched with annoyance. Killian questioned what it was that made these two so drawn to him. It made him anxious. He didn't want anyone tangled up with him and what he had to do.

"Yeah yeah, Don't get too close to me, you'll get burned," Elliott said, wrapping an arm around Killian, "You and Royce both need to lighten up."

"Do not compare me to that careless idiot!" Killian screamed, grabbing Elliott and picking them up by their shirt. Killian was shocked by just how easy it was. Some of the surrounding students turned to see the commotion; their whispering and gossiping intensified.

Misha yelped and grabbed at Killian's arm to release Elliott. Killian looked at the crowd, then to Misha, then to an obnoxiously giggling Elliott, then put Elliott down.

"Speaking of Royce," Elliott said, brushing himself off, "I haven't seen him out here. Did he not hear the alarm?"

Killian barely disguised the snarl of disgust overpowering his face as he spoke, "The world could burn around him and he wouldn't care. As long as he has his precious research, he doesn't care about anyone else."

Elliott sighed and rolled his eyes, "C'mon. Can you blame him?"

Misha mumbled under his breath, "Werewolfism must be tough…"

Killian stared Elliott dead in the eyes and said, "I can blame him, and I do."

Elliott met Killian's gaze, his mischievous smile never wavering, "What do you know that we don't?"

"Nothin'. Just a hunch is all," Killian said. He was staring into Elliott's eyes. They were scheming eyes, eyes Killian learned to recognize and distrust. There was something genuine in Elliott's eyes that was lacking in so many others. Most people try to hide their mischievous intent, but Elliott showed his off with pride.

"'Nothin" You say? Then I have a proposition that might

interest you."

Killin tried to seem disinterested, but his eyebrow perked up with curiosity. Elliott caught on and smiled wider.

"Meet me on the library roof," Elliott said before swiftly disappearing into the crowd.

Killian stood there for a moment and turned to Misha as if to silently ask, "What was that about?"

Misha smiled brightly and said, "You should follow! It'll be fun!"

Killian sighed dramatically, "If you insist..." he said with a playful sarcasm. He gave Misha a pat on the shoulder and made his way to the library roof.

On the roof of the academy library, Elliott leaned on the railing overlooking the plaza. Once he heard Killian arrive, he whipped around with excitement, arms wide.

"Kia, my buddy, my pal. My chum! You made it!" Elliott said with bright enthusiasm.

Killian cringed, "Nope." He turned around to leave. Elliott rushed to grab him by the arm.

"Woah woah wait!" Elliott pleaded, "Hear me out first. What's your opinion of the Jack of Diamonds?"

Killian stopped and smiled an almost dreamy smile, "I'm glad he's back. He's a damn hero in my book. He's showin' those snotty pretentious pricks like Miles that they ain't nothin'. I thought he got caught by some smartass detective like you."

"Aww, you think I'm smart?" Elliott teased.

"I think you're an ass," Killian replied dryly.

Elliott laughed out loud, and Killian rolled his eyes.

"Why did you call me up here?" Killion said, quickly losing patience.

"Right right! Check this out!" Elliott reached into his pocket and pulled out a folded piece of paper. He unfolded it to reveal what appeared to be the annotated schematics of a high-end estate. It was annotated with a permanent marker with notes and arrows and circles that looked like the blueprint for a heist.

Killian looked over the schematics and heist plan with intense interest. "What the hell is this?"

"It's the blueprint for the Jack of Diamond's next heist," Elliott said.

"What?! How did you get this? Wait… You're not…" Killian said, almost stammering.

"Nope. I'm the smart-ass detective that is gonna catch him. Unless…"

"Unless?" Killian said, staring at Elliott as if waiting for the punchline to a long-winded joke.

"We do a little heist of our own."

"What?!" Killian shouted before covering his mouth and looking around to make sure no one heard him. Since they were alone on a roof, it was all but certain no one except maybe Maxwell was listening.

"Oh yeah! I should probably mention who this mansion belongs to. It's the Prince estate," Elliott said, looking at Killian and savoring each of their shocked reactions. Killian was searching for the words to respond, but before he could, Elliott continued his monologue.

"I heard about you and Miles getting into it about Royce's research and, I have to admit, it got me interested. So! I thought, using The Jack's heist as a smoke screen, we *also* break in and dig around to find evidence. Everyone will be too busy focusing on the stolen priceless whatever to notice missing paperwork."

Killian had a feverish excitement blazing in his eyes. "Ohh this is rich. But why do you want me to go with you?"

"Because you know more than you let on, and something tells me you want a plausibly deniable reason to share with someone. So, what do you say? Game on?"

Killian looked at Elliott in awe for a long silent moment. Eventually, he leaned back until he was lying on his back, staring into the sky. He started laughing.

"Game on," Killian said.

06: ☽
Moon phase: First Quarter

Maxwell Sharp was the first one into the Prince estate. He was supposed to wait until Miles broke in, but he was getting far too anxious waiting silently with Elliott and Killian. He may have been partaking in a heist, but he was at ease in the dark, silent halls of the Prince estate. As he avoided the security patrolling the halls, Maxwell explored, admiring the art and architecture. It was a more modern and new-money palace than the rustic mansion he grew up in.

There was a radio crackle in his ear. Elliott had convinced the Cade twins to jury rig a set of small, receive-only radios that picked up whatever frequencies were being used nearby. Perfect for listening to security chatter on a heist.

"Breach in the private gallery. Requesting backup," said a serious voice over Maxwell's earpiece. Miles was in, distraction set. It was time to meet the others at the Prince Library.

Behind Maxwell, there was a sudden commotion. Maxwell dipped into the shadows as a pair of security guards rushed by. Despite Maxwell's size, he managed to squeeze into the tightest of spaces to hide. Once the coast was clear, Maxwell emerged and made his way to the rendezvous point.

Maxwell made sure the route his team took would be clear and still ended up at the library door before anyone else. He checked the massive mahogany double doors. Locked. No surprise. It was easy enough to pick.

Inside, the library was massive! There were rows and rows of books ranging from classic literature to historical nonfiction. Most of the spines were uncracked, unopened, unread. Deeper into the library was another locked door. The schematics said this was Mr. Prince's private office. Maxwell was jumping the gun by picking the lock, but the less time the team took unlocking doors meant the more time searching for documents. He cracked the lock and entered.

There was a massive, ornate desk made from polished dark oak in the center of a room lined with shelves and filing cabinets, lined and filled with binders and binders of Prince Corp paperwork. Behind the desk was a luscious, cushy executive chair. Maxwell promptly sat in it, leaned in, and got into a pose mimicking a stuffy executive with his hands folded in front of his face. Then he waited.

Killian was the first to walk into the office. His gaze fell onto Maxwell's white mask and jumped.

"Ack! Hey small fry, your giant is here already," Killian said.

Elliott snickered and walked in, holding a finger to his lips. "We're supposed to be stealthy. Try not to scream like a wuss."

Killian narrowed his eyes and said, "Wuss?! Tell your boyfriend not to s-"

"Shh! Stealth. Remember?" Elliott said. A soft hiss of quiet cackling came from Maxwell.

Killian grit his teeth and sighed, "Yeah yeah," he said as he made his way to one of the shelves of binders. He picked up a stack of binders he thought would be relevant. "I'll be in the main library to look through these and keep a lookout.

"10-4, hot shot," Elliott said, moving to another shelf to start searching.

"Uhg, is that a pun?" Killian asked, rolling his eyes, "Don't ever call me that again."

Killian snickered as Maxwell moved to Elliott's side. Maxwell searched the higher shelves while Elliott searched the lower ones.

As Elliott searched, his mind started to wander. He sighed.

Maxwell turned to Elliott and tilted his head. *"What weighs on your soul?"* Maxwell signed.

Elliott looked up at Maxwell and leaned against the shelves. "I just wonder what happened to my old friends sometimes. I wonder if any of them know I'm still alive. It's all so... overwhelming. Time passed me by."

Elliott looked at Maxwell, whose bright blue eyes stared back empathetically.

"I suppose it's the same for you, eh? Locked away for years, now suddenly you get to- no *have* to live a normal life. I guess we're both people time left behind."

Maxwell reached down and ruffled Elliott's long red hair. Elliott closed his eyes and leaned into Maxwell's touch. Elliott suddenly hugged Maxwell tight. Maxwell let out a gasp, eyes wide with shock. It was the first time he had ever felt human affection, the first time someone truly understood him. Slowly, he wrapped his arms around Elliott to return the hug.

In the main library, Killian was searching through his stack of binders. He came across a file labeled "Project Moonlight." Killian opened it with a keen eye. A lot of it was bureaucratic corpo-speak that made his eyes glaze over, but he forced himself to focus. The document appeared to be a technical schematic for a new kind of medicine, but it was hard to make out exactly what it was. It was filled with diagrams and technical knowledge that was far above anything Killian could comprehend. As he forced his eyes to read through the document, it slowly became clear. This was indeed a medication for werewolves, but not to cure them, it was to *create* them without a full moon!

Killian gasped and flipped through the folder. Technical jargon, technical jargon, then his heart stopped.

FWD: [[Director of Intelligence, Hanged Man's report:]]
Subject: Killian (Kia) Wilkes.
Background: Killian was born in the ghetto of a southern California town to a thug and a drifter. He led a stereotypically troubled upbringing being raised alone by his father. (Little was found about his mother. I couldn't even find any concrete evidence of her name.) He developed pyrokinetic powers at an early age, and his father made use of these abilities by taking him out to gas stations and convenience stores where he made Killian use his powers to rob the clerks, often physically abusing Killian to get him to cooperate.
At the age of twelve, Killian's childhood home was set ablaze with his father still inside. Neighbors at the time reported hearing a loud and violent clash between the two, even more violent than what they were used to hearing.

At the time, Bureau Arcana agents were not called to the scene. Local fire and law enforcement determined that the fire was due to natural causes (natural as in, not supernatural.) Upon future audit, no evidence was documented to support this claim. It is my professional opinion that these local agencies fabricated the report to prevent Bureau Arcana involvement.

Killian Wilkes spent the next few years bouncing from foster home to foster home, constantly getting into trouble and clashing with authority.

The incident at Beaumont Heights:

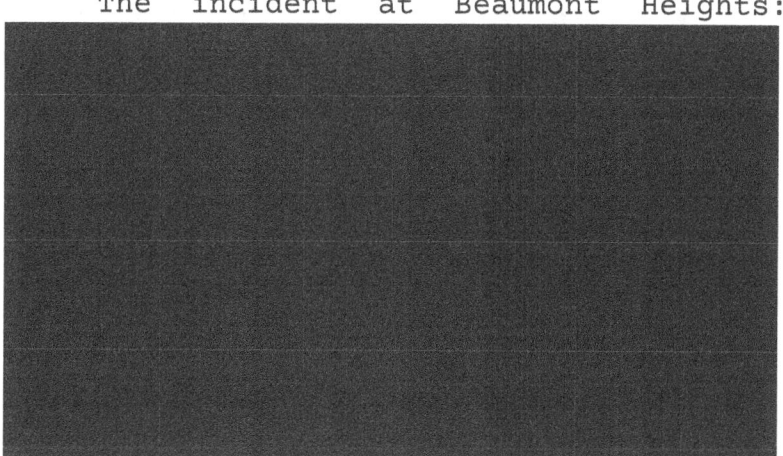

The rest of the document was fully blacked out, but under it there was a handwritten note:

"The redacted section details Killian's involvement as the cause of the inferno at Beaumont Heights. Killian Wilkes makes for an exceptional mercenary. Despite his authority issues, he knows that disobeying will result in... unignorable consequences. Under my command, I am willing to offer his services while we wait for Project Moonlight to be completed. I am sure some of your competition is proving exceptionally inconvenient."

The note was signed simply *"-G"*

Killian ripped the paper out with shaking hands. He was

ready to burn it... ready to burn the whole library down. The idea of being sold to bastards like the Prince family made Killian want to scream. He clutched the paper tight.

He was about to set it ablaze when Elliott poked his head out from the inner office.

"Sounds like you found something," Elliott said.

Killian quickly but subtly shoved his report into his pocket and showed Elliott the file on Project Moonlight.

"Yeah, I think we found it," Killian said, sounding shaken. Elliott's playful face went a bit somber at the sight of Killian's shocked white face.

"That bad, huh?" Elliott said, walking up to get a closer look at the document. His eyes scanned the document with a sharp gaze.

"Jeez... Royce is trying to cure werewolfism and they are using that research to do the opposite. That's... dark."

"Yeah... Can we leave now?" Killian said, his voice quivering.

"Yeah. Hey Big Man!" Elliott said, turning to the inner office.

Maxwell emerged and gave a salute before taking the file and leading the way out. Killian and Elliott followed.

On the way out, the radio crackled in their ears. A guard's voice was heard, "My god! We got him! All units regroup in the main hall. We're gonna unmask this punk."

Killian turned on his heels in an instant, "Like hell you are." Then he rushed back into the estate.

Elliott sighed and looked at Maxwell. "And it was going so smoothly... C'mon," he said, chasing after Killian. Maxwell shook his head and followed.

In the main hall, Miles, dressed in all black and still masked, was being dragged by the wrists to the center as all of the on-duty guards began to congregate. His eyes twitched and his fists clenched. It reminded him of being captured by the cult.

The guard captain approached and gripped the top of Miles's mask.

I can get us out of here, Zak thought.

No. That would make it obvious we were involved, Miles thought back.

It's gonna be obvious we're involved anyway! Zak thought-screamed.

Trust me. I'm just making it dramatic. I have a plan.

Miles! I'm inside your head! I know you don't! I'm taking over!

Miles writhed and spasmed under the grip of the guards as Zak took over. He looked up at the captain with his deep green eyes, glaring daggers at his captors. A tentacle began to wriggle out when suddenly-

A burst of flame hit the ground directly in front of the guard captain, making him let go of Zak/Miles's mask and jump back. Killian jumped down from a window and pointed finger guns at the guard captain, the tips of his fingers engulfed in fire. Zak quickly retracted his tentacles.

"Lay a hand on him and you're all going up in smoke," Killian shouted, his t-shirt pulled up to cover his face.

"Wha? A Meta?" one of the guards yelped, backing away from Killian. Killian took this opportunity to step in front of the still disguised Miles/Zak. He turned to them.

"Hey there, hero," Killian said with an almost messianic smile.

Miles narrowed their eyes and stood up. He looked at Killian with bewilderment on his face. Killian winked and turned to the guards. Behind the guards, Elliott locked eyes with Miles and slowly started pushing a vase off of a pedestal. He focused on the thought *Smokescreen* for Zak to hear.

Zak gasped, then with a deep gravelly tone to disguise his voice whispered to Killian what Elliott thought.

What happened next occurred in just a moment. Elliott pushed the vase onto the floor. Its shatter echoed in the vast main hall of the Prince estate. The guards whipped around. Killian sprayed fire onto the marble tile, causing a thick billow of smoke to fill the room. Now obscured by the smoke, Maxwell swooped in to scoop up Miles/Zak, Killian, and Elliott. By the time the smoke cleared, there was no one but the guards and a simple playing card depicting the Jack Of Diamonds.

Outside the estate, Maxwell put the three boys down. Miles, back in control of his body, faced away from Killian.

"Why did you do that?" He said, still disguising his voice.

Killian chuckled and rubbed the back of his head, "I couldn't let a fellow rebel like you get captured…"

Miles stifled a laugh. Killian calling him of all people a rebel. He was tempted to rip his mask off just to see the look on Killian's face. Instead, he just let out a gruff "Thanks."

Killian and Miles stood together for a long, uncomfortable moment.

"Man of few words, eh? I guess that makes sense," Killian said. He tried to control the trembling in his legs. He couldn't tell if it was the adrenalin of the heist, or the excitement of meeting someone he admired so intensely.

Miles nodded.

"Here…" Killian sighed and reached into his pocket. He nervously pulled out a playing card and thrust it into Miles's face. It was a common Jack of Spades with a slightly burnt corner. The Jack's face and outfit were drawn over to look like Killian's, and the Spade symbol was drawn to be engulfed in flames.

"You're a goddamn hero to me," Killian said, "You do what more people should: stand up against those rich pricks who think the world revolves around them. You show them that they ain't as invincible as they wanna pretend."

Miles took the playing card and stared at it.

Don't you dare laugh, Zak demanded.

Fine, Miles replied, putting the card safely into his pocket. He gave Killian a meaningful nod. Killian smiled like a starstruck kid, letting himself bask in the moment.

"Oi! Quit fanboying!" Elliott called out, "They'll be coming to search the perimeter. Let's go!"

Killian groaned and rolled his eyes, "Goddamn, we just pulled off a badass heist *and* rescue! Can't we enjoy our accomplishments for a bit! HEY! Let go of me!" Maxwell had picked Killian up by the collar and started dragging them away.

Hey! He gave you his card! Give him one of yours! Zak thought to Miles.

Miles sighed and called out, "Here. For saving me. It's just an ordinary playing card but..." Then he pulled out a jack of diamonds and threw it. It whizzed through the air, and Killian caught it.

"Hell yeah. Keep up the good fight!" Killian said as he admired the playing card.

Miles blushed under his mask, rolled his eyes, and dashed off into the night. Despite being dragged away, Killian watched the thief make his daring escape. Killian usually wasn't one to fantasize about stupid things like romance, but he could see himself dating someone like that. Killian quickly shook the thought from his head.

Along the way, Killian convinced Maxwell to let him walk on his own. Elliott and Maxwell seemed focused on making the journey back, so Killian took that opportunity to dip into the shadows. He pulled out the report about him and scowled. He turned to see if Elliott or Maxwell were around and, feeling confident in his solitude, set fire to the document.

Killian wished he could burn his past as easily as he burnt this report.

07: O
Moon Phase: Waxing Gibbous (One day before full moon.)

An amalgam of scrap electronics, miscellaneous cables, and frayed wires slowly amassed in its own corner of the Academy Arcana labs. It was the perfect facility for the Cade twins to tinker, fiddle, and engineer whatever idea came to their heads.

At first, Royce Grayson was wary of the twins. He was anxious of having to share the lab with anyone else and was especially anxious about having to shrink his workspace. Over the course of the past few weeks, Royce grew fond of the twins. Their excitement and energy rubbed off on Royce and made his long nights of experiments more enjoyable.

As the sun rose over the Academy, the Cade twins stepped into the lab. Quinton had a cup of coffee in each hand while Andrew followed with an energy drink in his. They were both shocked to see Royce already there. Well, judging by the dark circles under his eyes, was *still* there from the night before. He was staring at a screen that was hooked up to a microscope that Quinton modified.

Quinton walked up to Royce who didn't register his presence. He looked to Andrew who shrugged. Quinton sighed and cracked his neck, his hair raising as he built up a small charge. He set one of the coffees down and reached out to poke Royce in the ear, sending a small jolt through him.

"AYHEEEEEEOW!" Royce screeched, jumping up and clutching his ear. He turned to Quinton with a glare. Quinton couldn't tell if his ears were smoking because of anger, or because he accidentally caught his hair on fire.

"Mornin, wolf man," Quinton said, handing Royce one of the coffees. Andrew snickered as he sipped his energy drink.

"Already?! God dammit no! I still have so much work to do before tomorrow!" Royce said, frantically searching for his notes.

Quinton kept the coffee held out for Royce, moving his eyes just enough to give his brother a tired expression. He looked back at Royce. "Did you stay up all night?"

Royce rubbed the back of his disheveled head, "Heh. Oops." Then he reached for the coffee in Quinton's hands.

Quinton pulled the coffee away, "Then caffeine is the last thing you need."

Royce inhaled as if about to argue, but due to exhaustion, his breath simply escaped with a groan.

"I dunno," Andrew said, "I don't want him to be too tired for what we have planned!"

"Eh?" Royce said, his head lolling to one side.

"You're right! Here. Drink up!" Quinton said, thrusting the coffee towards Royce's face.

Royce eagerly accepted and, within seconds, chugged the entire scalding hot black coffee. He let out a satisfied and refreshed sigh and looked at the twins.

"Thanks! Anyway!" Royce said, turning back to his research.

"Oh no, you don't," Quinton said, grabbing Royce by the wrist. His eyes sparked threateningly with electricity. "We have plans for you."

"Okay okay! Jeez!" Royce said as he let himself be dragged away by Quinton and Andrew.

In the Academy plaza, Elliott was laying on the top of one of the picnic tables that he had just adorned with a full moon themed tablecloth. As he stared into the sky, Killian leaned over to block his view.

"Really?" Killian said with a disapproving voice. "You're throwing him a party?"

Elliott pushed Killian's face out of the way. "Yup. You should stick around and get to know your fellow classmates."

Killian paused, considering the possibility before frowning. "Pass."

"Oh, come on," Elliott pleaded. Just as he spoke, Misha and Miles walked up. Miles was hunched over in an awkward way that Elliott knew meant Zak was probably in control.

"Yay! Kia is here too!" Misha said, running up to Killian.

"No, I'm not," Killian said, turning his back to Misha. Zak could sense the hurt it caused him to turn Misha down.

"O-oh..." Misha said, looking down, dejected.

"Why do you do this to yourself?" Zak asked Killian.

"Why'd you let the Jack of Diamonds rob you again?" Killian responded.

"I am not my god damned family!" Zak shouted. He was sick of Miles just sitting there and taking all the bullying Killian dished out. He wanted to just scream that he was the Jack of Diamonds and throw all of his calling cards like shuriken. Miles tried to steer Zak away, but... honestly, he was sick of it too.

Killian turned his head and raised his eyebrow at Zak. "Aren't you?" he asked, though he didn't stick around for a response. Maxwell appeared to wrap an arm around Zak/Miles to try and calm them down. Reluctantly, they did. Now was not the time to be upset, now was the time for celebration and comradery. Soon after Killian left, the Cade twins walked out into the plaza, dragging Royce behind them.

"We have the wolf man!" Andrew called out as he reached the table. As Royce and the twins arrived, Maxwell snuck behind a tree and came back with a cake and placed it on the table. It was a round cake with a frosting depiction of the full moon on it. Royce stared at it with a growing blush, then looked around at all the people he was vaguely familiar with. They all seemed to have bright, welcoming smiles.

"Wh-what is all this?" Royce asked with a shy, quivering lip.

Quinton patted Royce on the back and said, "It was Andrew's idea."

"Yeah!" Andrew said, "Last month we all ended up hanging out during the full moon and... Well, I wanted to do that again this month and invite you, but... Ya know... So, I wanted to throw a party today so we can all hang out!"

Royce's blush deepened. He looked at Andrew and Quinton with a touched, albeit confused expression. "B-but why?"

Quinton gently nudged Royce towards the cake, "You're cooped up in the lab all day every day. We're worried about you."

Elliott stepped up and held out a card for Royce and said, "Yeah. Plus, your research is causing quite a stir. We thought it would be nice to get to know the man behind it."

"I-it is?" Royce asked as he took the card. It said, "Get well soon." The word choice made Royce laugh.

"The store didn't have any that said 'sorry about your werewolfism,' so I thought that was close enough."

"I mean it kind of works," Misha said, "It could be read as a, 'we believe you will get your cure made real soon!' B-but not that we are telling you to rush, we just think- ACK!" Misha's potential ramble was cut short by Maxwell who gave them a pat on the head.

"Yeah, that's exactly what I was going for," Elliott said unconvincingly.

"Suuure," Zak said.

Royce cracked a smile. The tension he had been building since he got to the academy felt like it had been relieved somewhat. He was so worried that no one would dare get close to him if he was a werewolf, yet here he was, being welcomed despite that.

Royce adjusted his glasses awkwardly, "It seems you all have me at a disadvantage. You seem to know about me but, besides Quinton and Andrew, I don't know any of you," he said as he sat at the table. Andrew cut the cake and passed everyone a slice.

Zak spoke up first, "Pleasure to meet you," he said in a formal, measured tone. His ability to mimic Miles's mannerisms was getting better, but to a keen-eyed observer, it was still not quite right. "I'm..." he looked around, most people at the table already knew about Zak, so he snickered mischievously, "Call me Zak. I'm what you humans call an eldritch being.

Quinton and Andrew audibly gasped.

"Eldritch?" Quinton asked,

"Coool!" Andrew said excitedly.

"Do you have tentacles?" Quinton demanded, rushing up to Miles,

"Show us the tentacles!" Andrew said, poking Zak/Miles's back.

"You can't just say that! What if it's like... intimate." Quinton snapped.

"Oh right, my bad. Is it?" Andrew asked Zak.

Zak's face was a dark red, he sighed sheepishly and a tentacle slithered out from the sleeve of his blazer. He used it to wave at the group.

"Woah." Quinton said.

"Awesome!" Andrew said.

"Wait," Quinton said, "Does that mean Miles...?"

Zak's posture straightened as he blinked and one of his eyes changed color. A more naturally dignified Miles stood, "I am also here. We share this body."

"Ooooo!" the twins said in unison.

Miles turned to Royce and gave a bow, "Pleasure to meet you. I am Miles Prince. I was... taken by a cult, and they used me to summon Zak."

Miles's blinked and his blue eye changed back to green, his posture became crooked, "I didn't have a choice, just so you know!" Zak said before giving control back to Miles.

"Yes. Neither of us had a choice in the matter, but the Bureau saved me from being fully killed in the summoning, and we have learned to work well together," Miles said.

"Prince?" Royce said, "I think they are the ones who gave me a research scholarship. Small world, eh?"

Miles kept a polite, warm smile, hiding his disgust without

even a hint of a crack in his facade. "The very same," he said.

Misha raised his hand. "Hi Royce! Doctor Royce? Erm, future Doctor Royce?" Misha said in a shy but excitable voice, "I'm Misha! Misha Woods! The folks at The Bureau say I have an astral affinity? I-I'm not sure what that means really, but they say that I can channel energy from the astral plane. I got lost in the astral plane once! There was this fog a-and... Anyway, The Bureau saved me, so here I am! Sorry if that was a long story."

Royce smiled warmly, "You're fine," he said. Then he turned to Maxwell.

Maxwell gave a deep, theatrical bow. Given his large stature, it was a wonder Maxwell kept his balance. He started signing his story.

Elliott cleared his throat, "He says, 'I'm Maxwell. My family home was consumed by shadows and The Bureau saved me, too.'"

"P-pardon me asking, but... What's with the mask?" Royce asked.

Maxwell signed, and Elliott translated, *"I got so used to being in the dark that I get anxious when people look at me without it. And my voice... Well, I haven't used it for so long that I simply lost it."*

"Aww. My sympathies." Royce said.

Maxwell shrugged and pulled Elliott close, *"It's okay. I'm making friends!"* he signed. Elliott laughed and translated with a growing blush. He playfully pushed Maxwell away to eat his cake. Elliott didn't introduce himself.

Slowly, everyone started to have the same realization and all eyes turned to Elliott. Why was he here?

Elliott munched away at his slice of cake before looking up to meet the swarm of curious eyes. "Eh? Royce and I have already met. Our dorms are on the same floor," he said dismissively.

"The locked basement floor?" Quinton asked. "I get why Royce is down there, but... why you?"

"Yeah!" Killian said, leaning against the threshold to the dorms, "What *is* your story? You come out of nowhere and start meddling with everyone's business. Why? Who are you?"

Elliott chuckled nervously, "I uhm... It's hard to explain. What about you, Killian? We don't know your story."

Everyone's eyes turned to Killian.

Killian narrowed his eyes, but, after a moment, his smirk widened, "I was in Beaumont Heights when it caught fire. The Bureau saved me like they did all of you. Well... Except your dear Elliott perhaps,"

All eyes turned back to Elliott, like a tennis match.

Elliott shook his head and let out a cornered laugh. He looked around at everyone he's gotten to know over the past month. He felt a kernel of resentment bubble up inside him.

Finally, he spoke, "The Bureau didn't save me. They let me die."

Elliott explained everything he knew: how he died, the hotel, the man in black, how he simply walked through a door to arrive in the academy.

"He said, 'The scales of fate must be rebalanced,'" Elliott said, "In my previous life, I didn't believe in fate, but after learning about magic, eldritch beings, the astral plane, werewolves... Fate doesn't seem so unbelievable. Why was I brought back here? Brought back now? How will this all rebalance the scales?"

Everyone was in somber silence as Elliott spoke, even the air was still. Elliott looked around at everyone's awestruck faces.

"So there. That's my story," Elliott said, flashing a weary smile. It was exhausting for him to be so serious.

Maxwell was the first to move. He placed a gentle, caring hand on Elliott's head, *"Whatever fate demands, we will balance the scales with you,"* he signed.

"Yeah!" Zak said, "We're a motley crew, right?"

"Heh. I guess you're right," Elliott said, grabbing Zak/Miles to ruffle their hair. The dire tone slowly melted into merriment as the newly christened "motley crew" bonded over how drastically their lives have changed since meeting the Bureau.

Killian rolled his eyes and turned around; He spoke quietly to himself. "Balancing the scales of fate, huh? Good luck."

Chapter 09: ○
The Full Moon

01:

The full moon hung high in the sky, shining down over the Academy Arcana. On the roof of the library building, Miles/Zak, Misha, Quinton, and Andrew were laying on their backs, staring up at the moon. Maxwell was pacing around anxiously. A howl pierced the cold night air.

"Hang in there, wolf man," Quinton said, raising a soda can into the air.

Miles sat up and looked at Maxwell, who's anxious pacing never slowed. Even behind his mask, it was clear their face was twisted with worry.

What's up with him? Miles asked Zak internally.

He's wondering where Elliott is. Zak replied.

Miles looked around, finally noticing a distinct lack of bite sized detective.

"Where *is* Elliott?" Miles wondered aloud.

Elliott was hiding in the shadows of the Academy outskirts. Something was bugging him about the last full moon. Ahead of him, lit clearly by the full moon, Killian Wilkes sat on a felled tree stump. In his lap he held a bolt action hunting rifle. In one hand he held a carton of cigarettes, and with his other, he pulled out a single cig, lit it on fire, then watched it burn down. Once the cigarette burned itself out, he pulled out another one. Elliott struggled not to cough from the secondhand smoke. If he did, his cover would be blown.

Suddenly, Killian's phone rang. Killian crushed the lit cigarette as his entire hand lit up in flames. The fire illuminated the deep pain, the intense fury in his face. Killian didn't even check his phone. He already knew what it said.

Killian slung the rifle onto his back and made his way back to the academy. Elliott followed, being sure to keep his distance. Once Killian was back in the dorms, he looked around. Elliott ducked behind cover and held his breath. Had he been caught? Elliott waited, listening for approaching footsteps, but none came. Instead, he heard the beep of the basement floor's lock being disengaged.

Killian went down the stairs.

02:

Agent Moon and Agent Tower waited at the far end of the east wing of the bottom floor of the Academy Arcana dorms, right outside Royce Grayson's room. Instead of his usual sidearm, Agent Tower carried a tranq gun in his holster. Agent Moon had a prototype device that looked vaguely like a megaphone. Next to Director Moon was an unconscious man strapped to a gurney.

"Where'd this one come from?" Director Tower asked in a tough, raspy voice, his chin flicking towards the unconscious man strapped to the gurney.

A thin-lipped smile crept across Agent Moon's face. "Just a cultist we apprehended during the Obsidian Chalice case. He has no eldritch influence inside him, so he will be perfect for our purposes."

A loud howl erupted from behind Royce's door.

"Does your protégé in there know how he's getting your test subjects?" Agent Tower asked, turning to Royce's door.

Agent Moon snickered, "No. And he's not going to."

Tower nodded gravely, "The price of progress, I suppose."

As the two Bureau Agents spoke, Killian Wilkes walked down the dorm hall, his rifle slung casually behind his back.

"Sup bitcheeeees!" Killian interjected in a deliberately loud and obnoxious voice as he propped himself up against the wall opposite Royce's door.

Agent Moon glared at Killian who simply snickered in response. Killian may be compelled to do Moon's bidding, but blackmail is a double-edged sword, and Killian was determined to see just how far he could push his luck. Sure, if he disobeyed, he'd be thrown in prison for causing the Beaumont Heights fire, but at the same time, that would mean Moon would have one less lackey. Agent Tower rolled his eyes and unlocked Royce's dorm. Inside, secured to his bed with silver-laced-kevlar chains, was a werewolf with pitch black hair and glowing red eyes. Royce, the werewolf, thrashed at the open door, but the chains kept him secured.

Agent Moon gestured to the unconscious cultist strapped to the gurney, "You know the drill, Mr. Wilkes."

Killian let out a tisk, as if to say "easy peasy," then took hold of the gurney. Outwardly he wanted to seem as unaffected by this as possible. To Killian, Agent Moon and his weaselly frame seemed like the kind of person who got off on making people do things they weren't comfortable with, so Killian did his best not to give the creep any satisfaction. Inwardly, of course... He was pushing a man in to be forcibly infected with werewolfism... for the sole purpose of being experimented on until he was inevitably killed... then on to the next unlucky soul. As he pushed the gurney in, he stared at his hands. He could already picture the blood that would soon soak them.

Elliott Harding watched all of this while crouching behind a pair of armchairs in the basement floor's lounge. His eyes were wide in shock, his mouth covered to keep his breath quiet. Was this what the Bureau Arcana did? Is this what James did? Was he brought back to be trained to do... this?

Elliott shook. He couldn't just sit here and let this happen... He took a deep breath and stood up. He looked down the east wing of the floor and stumbled out.

"Awooooo!" Elliott howled, then did his best impression of a drunk giggle and hiccup.

Killian, Agent Moon, and Agent Tower all immediately turned to Elliott.

"Halt! This is a restricted area!" Agent Tower commanded, immediately drawing his tranq gun and aiming it at Elliott.

Elliott looked at the gun in a pretend daze before swaying around and pointing to his dorm at the end of the western wing of the floor.

"B- hic- But I live here?" Elliott said, pointing at his dorm room.

Agent Tower turned to Agent Moon and said, "No one was supposed to be housed down here except Mr. Grayson."

Agent Moon looked back with a baffled expression. As the two agents tried to form a response, Elliott swaggered and swayed down the hallway towards Royce's room.

"K-Kia?" Elliott said with a convincing drunk slur, "You left right as the party got started! Whatcha doin' down here?"

Killian's eyes went wide, and a blush crept across his face. Did they actually want him at the party? Killian shook his head. There was no way Elliott could have gotten that drunk. Why was he doing this?

"Wh-what?" Killian said. He looked up at Agent Moon who was starting to snarl. Ahh, Moon was also the kind of man who couldn't handle things not going to plan.

Elliott ended up close enough to wrap his arms around Killian, who jumped.

"Wh-What are you DOING, Elliott?" Killian said, flustered and confused.

"Come back to the partyyyyy," Elliott begged.

While Killian was too stunned to respond, Agent Tower grabbed Elliott by the back of their shirt and yanked them into Royce's room. Royce began to snarl and thrash about with a ravenous hunger.

"You look familiar," Agent Tower said, "Where have I seen you before?"

Elliott stared into agent Tower's eyes. He had never seen this man before, but that doesn't mean they haven't met. Elliott's eyes flashed with sober awareness. Tower hadn't recognized him until he saw the back of Elliott's head. Elliott's eyes betrayed his lack of inebriation only to Agent Tower, but he kept up his ruse and said with a whisper only agent Tower could hear, "Maybe it was when you shot me?"

Agent Tower's eyes widened with recognition, "Heh. Fascinating."

Royce howled, reminding Elliott of his peril. He turned to his werewolf classmate.

"Eh? Royce?" Elliott slurred, heart racing. Still, Elliott

stayed in character. "You really are a floofy boy on full moons!"

"Hey! What are you doing?" Killian screamed.

Agent Moon cracked his neck and said, "Accidents happen at the academy." Elliott grit his teeth as Agent Tower forced Elliott closer and closer to the snarling werewolf. Killian watched Elliott. He could see the fear in their eyes, but by god, he refused to break character. Why? To save this stranger strapped to a gurney? Dumbass. Now he AND the cultist were going to die.

A pit of disgust welled in Killian's stomach. He raised the rifle. He didn't care what dirt The Bureau had on him. He wasn't going to be a party to it any longer. He focused his aim on the chains binding Royce.

"Accidents happen indeed," Killian said before he pulled the trigger.

03:

Killian had the hunting rifle to take down Royce should they somehow escape. The poetic irony of it being used to instead free the beast was absolutely delicious to Killian as his shot hit Royce's chains dead on. The chain shattered with a piercing metallic ring. Royce thrashed and began to break free of his weakened bonds.

In the brief moment of confusion, Elliott snapped out of his faked daze and delivered a strong elbow to Agent Tower before rushing from the room. He grabbed Killian by the wrist.

"Nice shot, tough guy," Elliott said with a cheeky grin.

"Shut up and run," Killian snapped and ran down the hall towards the lounge.

Agent Tower rushed from Royce's dorm and slammed the door shut just as Royce broke completely free. He drew his tranq gun and aimed at the two running students. Sharp zip sounds whizzed down the hall as Agent Tower shot two darts. One hit Elliott and one hit Killian.

The sting of the tranquilizer needle made Elliott jolt. His feet immediately became heavy and he tripped. Killian managed to struggle a couple more feet before he, too, fell.

Elliott watched as Agent Moon pulled out a device that looked like a jury-rigged megaphone. Royce burst through the door and lunged for Agent Moon. Before Royce could make contact, a loud, high-pitched sound erupted from the megaphone and the werewolf clutched his head and backed away from the two agents.

"Do you see, Tower? The efforts of our research," Agent Moon said. His face was smug and smarmy, and it made Elliott's skin crawl.

The two agents slowly made their way towards the lounge. They stopped and stood over Elliott and Killian.

"What do we do about these two?" Agent Tower asked.

"Leave them to the beast. It will be written off as a tragedy. Whoever housed another student down here will be to blame," Agent Moon said with a casual confidence that came from someone all too experienced and comfortable with burying mistakes in bureaucracy.

Agent Tower nodded as he led the way up the stairs. Once the two agents were at the floor's exit, Agent Tower turned off the device keeping Royce at bay. The two agents left, and the door at the top of the stairs locked with a beep. Elliott and Killian were trapped, alone as Royce recovered from Agent Moon's device.

Royce's growl echoed down the hall before he pounced on the gurney bound cultist. Elliott could do nothing but watch in horror as the man was torn apart. He had seen the aftermath of countless horrific murders in his brief time as a private detective… but never once had he seen one happen right in front of him. Elliott refused to look away. Royce's bloodlust unsatiated, the beast's red eyes locked onto the incapacitated Elliott.

"Welp…" Killian said, his voice sounding at peace, "At least I'm going out on my terms."

Royce Rushed down the hall.

04:

For Elliott, time slowed to a halt. Royce was mid pounce, midair just a couple of feet from Elliott. Elliott couldn't move his body, but his eyes darted around. The hall faded into a familiar art deco design. One of the doors in the hall opened and out stepped

The Full Moon

The Man In Black.

"Oh, my dear canary," The Man In Black began, his face shrouded in shadow, not turning to face Elliott, "Yet again, we meet far sooner than predicted. I suppose it is just in your nature to... meddle... and put yourself in harm's way for someone else."

The walls of the hall seemed to fade from the eerie warmth of the Hotel, and into a cold, bureaucratic concrete hall. The Man In Black morphed to nothing but a fading shadow on the wall. A sign on the wall read, "Bureau Arcana department of Intelligence: offices." The wood hotel doors morphed into secure metal ones. One of the doors read, "Hanged Man."

The door labeled "Hanged Man" opened, and The Man In Black stepped out again.

"Fortunately, I was prepared this time," The Man In Black said as he stepped over Elliott. He leaned down close, but Elliott was still unable to see his face beyond his dead, pale white smile. The Hallways faded yet again, this time back to that of the Academy Arcana dorm.

The Man In Black spoke softly, almost sensually into Elliott's ear, "It is time to rebalance the scales of fate."

05:

```
    [[Director of Intelligence, Hanged
Man's personal notes.]]
    Facts:
    1: The Bureau Arcana has not had any
incidents  or  even  reports  of  incidents
involving  werewolves  since  the  Westridge
incident.
    2: Personal  investigations  into  the
research  wing  of  the  Bureau  Arcana  have
revealed that Agent Moon has an abundance
of  lycanthropic  DNA  for  use  in  his
experiments.
    3: Audits of individuals involved with
crimes  of  an  occult  nature  who  are  in
custody in local prisons are inconsistent.
```

Numbers of individuals arrested often do not line up with those actually in custody. When this was brought to the attention of Executive Director Emperor, paperwork would always be retroactively changed to reflect the new numbers. In layman's terms, prisoners are going missing.
    Hypothesis:
    Since Royce Grayson is the only known living werewolf in The Bureau's records, it is my suspicion that Agent Moon is utilizing Mr. Grayson to infect convicts under Bureau Arcana jurisdiction and use them as subjects to further his research.
    Action: I have set up hidden cameras along the lower-level halls of the Academy dorms so Agent ███████ and I can observe what happens during the full moon. It is my hope that my theory is based on nothing but paranoia.

    Agent Hanged Man's eyes were sharp, focused, yet relaxed. They were the kind of eyes that effortlessly picked up the slightest of details, the kind of eyes one couldn't know just how closely watching you. The face that contained those eyes was a classically handsome man with short gray hair that never got long enough to obscure that piercing gaze.
    He sat in the back of a Bureau Arcana van as he stared at a series of monitors displaying the interior of the Academy Arcana's basement dorm rooms. His eyes watched one monitor, took in every detail, then casually flicked to the next monitor. Beside him sat James Graves, eyes intensely focused on each monitor. Eventually, both pairs of eyes stopped on the monitor that showed Killian Wilkes stepping down the stairs.
    "Poor Kid..." Agent Hanged Man said, his voice soft but grim.
    "Indeed..." James said, turning to Hanged Man, "You know, Agent Sun ended up killed and disposed of in the astral

forest for interfering with Director Emperor. This is painting a massive target on your back."

"I left the CIA because I wanted to get away from all the shady shit. I can't in good conscience just sit back and let it happen," Hanged Man said, his eyes fixated on the man strapped to the gurney, "Besides, you're here, too. I can't just let you do this alone."

James sighed, "You're not my mentor anymore. You shouldn't be doing this."

Agent Hanged Man laughed, "Too bad, you'll always be my protégé."

James tisked and shook his head. He tried to fight it, but he couldn't help but smile. He never would admit it, but he was thankful for Agent Hanged Man. He couldn't help but think that they were always looking out for him, even when they weren't on a mission together. He couldn't imagine what The Bureau would be like without him always lurking in the shadows, keeping an eye on everything.

The two watched the screens in front of them when suddenly, James gasped, eyes widening in horror as a face he never expected to see again appeared on screen. Elliott Harding.

"Wh... Impossible..." James whispered, his voice suddenly weak. His mind flashed back to that night in Capstone Creek... Elliott's death, and how James had to console Adam, eventually bringing him into the Bureau... Elliott was dead, James filed the report on it... Yet somehow, here he was.

Agent Hanged Man looked up at James. "What's wrong? That's the most emotion I've ever seen on your face."

James didn't answer. Instead, he bolted from the van.

"Oi! Ace! Where the hell are you-" Hanged Man rushed after James, being sure to grab a tranq gun before he left.

Soon after Agent Moon and Agent Tower left, Agent Hanged Man and James rushed in. James wanted to blink in, but due to his panic, he couldn't. Agent Hanged Man used his ID to unlock the door and rush down to where Elliott and Killion laid paralyzed.

Agent Hanged Man looked over to James and saw his eyes hyper focused on Elliott. James's eyes then darted to the werewolf.

Royce was getting ready to pounce.

James broke into a sprint to intercept the wolf man before it got to Elliott, but Agent Hanged Man shoved James with all his strength. Agent Hanged Man was now the only thing between Elliott and the werewolf. Royce pounced right as Agent Hanged Man fired his tranq gun wildly at the beast.

Agent Hanged Man took a claw slash across the chest but managed to keep Royce off Elliott as he emptied the rest of the tranq gun into Royce.

Royce was tough, but not invincible. The heavy dose of sedatives worked fast and staggered Royce enough for Agent Hanged Man to tackle Royce and push them back. A dazed Royce gnashed at Agent Hanged Man's neck and tore his claws into Hanged Man's back, but Hanged Man persisted, and managed to wrestle Royce back into his dorm. He used what was left of the chains to lock the sedated Royce up.

James grabbed the rifle lying beside Killian and rushed to Royce's dorm. Royce was chained to the bed, struggling but with heavy lethargy. Agent Hanged man stood beside Royce's bed and laughed.

"Hah. Hahah…" Agent Hanged Man said between labored breaths, "It's been a while since I've gotten that up close and personal on a mission."

"What was the damn point of that?" James demanded. His words were furious, but there was a hint of heartbreak in his voice. Agent Hanged Man's back was covered in deep lacerations and his neck was shredded. He was hemorrhaging blood rapidly, and no amount of first aid could stop it.

Agent Hanged Man staggered back until he hit the wall, where he slowly slumped to the floor, soaking the carpet with his blood. He chuckled, which made him cough up blood.

When Agent Hanged Man finally spoke again, it was with a labored, rapidly weakening voice, "I'm just… the director of intel… You're the Ace… Bad idea to burn the trump card so early when the deck is already stacked against us, eh?"

James stared at The Hanged Man, his face unmoving. Stone.

The Hanged Man smiled as a drop of blood ran down his

cheek. "You know I'm right."

"Shut up and rest," James said.

"Heh. I'll still never get used to you ordering me around," The Hanged Man rasped as he leaned his head back against the wall, "Mind if I give you one last order? For old time's sake?"

"Anything," James said. Tears welled up behind his eyes. It was a sensation he hadn't felt since Capstone Creek. He blinked. Not a single tear fell. James wondered if he was even capable of shedding tears anymore.

"Make sure I don't turn. Don't let me end up as one of Moon's experiments…"

James racked a bullet into the rifle's chamber, "Of course…" James said.

Elliott Harding's consciousness began to fade. He fought to stay awake for as long as he could. In his last moments of consciousness, he watched as Agent Hanged Man jumped in to save him. He watched Agent hanged Man get bitten and clawed by a monster. He watched Agent Hanged Man fight back the monster as James rushed in after, gun in hand.

As the tranquilizers coursed through Elliott's veins and sapped the last bit of strength he had, Elliott couldn't help but think back to Capstone Creek. He remembered how he jumped in to save Adam, how he got attacked by the Doppelganger, how James came in to save them both. He thought back to the moment of his death.

As the last moment of Elliott's consciousness faded, he heard a gunshot ring out from Royce's room.

Chapter 10:
The Twists of Fate

01:

When Elliott regained consciousness, a bright, sterile light burned his retinas. He groaned and shielded his eyes from the light. Slowly, his vision focused on his surroundings. Elliott found himself on a large mahogany desk that sat in the intersection of four directions. Each direction led to rows and rows of bookshelves that stretched on until they faded into the distance. It was like he was in the center of a library or an evidence room, but impossibly large.

Elliott shivered and fought through his grogginess to sit up. Across from him, James Graves sat, eyes fixated intensely on Elliott.

"It really is you," James said with a shaky voice. For a man who was used to seeing ghosts, ghouls, and werewolves, James was stunned by the face in front of him.

"James..." Elliott groaned, head still spinning and disoriented, "Where am I?

"The Bureau Arcana archives," James said, "I had to make sure you were okay."

Elliott sat there for a moment as he processed James's words. He couldn't help but chuckle.

"The Bureau Arcana," Elliott repeated. "I've learned a lot about you in the past month."

James tried to hide it, but one of his eyebrows twitched upwards. "Oh?"

Elliott's lips twitched into a smirk for but a moment. "Oh yeah. You do a lot of good work, saved a lot of people..."

No one but Elliott could have seen it, but James relaxed. It made Elliott smile, and that made his next words cut all the deeper.

"So why?" Elliott asked, "Why didn't you save me?"

James went still, but Elliott heard his heart race. James kept his eyes locked on Elliott's and said, "I saved you this time."

"As I remember it, someone else saved me," Elliott

retorted, staring back at James. "What happened to him, anyway? Did you save him too?"

"There was no saving him," James intonede, closing his eyes. The Hanged Man's face flashed in his memory. He wanted to mourn but now was not the time.

"Is that what you said about me?" Elliott asked.

James opened his eyes, hiding his shock, "You can't save everyone, Elliott," he said, looking away. His guilt ate away at him… but Elliott was back, so perhaps he could atone for his sins.

"I just rolled the wrong dice, eh?" Elliott asked.

"What were you doing down there? How did you get there?" James demanded.

"What a wonderful question! What were *you* doing there?" Elliott asked, voice raising ever so slightly.

"Saving you," James repeated.

Elliott stood and gestured accusingly at James. "Is that why two suits were using Killian to push someone into Royce's room? Is that why you saved the other students at the academy? Saved Killian to do the Bureau's dirty work! You saved Royce to trick him into researching Project Moonlight! Saved Miles to bankroll it. What did you save me for? How are you going to use me?"

Elliott's words stung. James was being accused of everything he fought to prevent… He decided to play into Elliott's suspicions, at least for now.

"How do you know about Project Moonlight?" James said.

"Death hasn't made me any less of a detective," Elliott said, eyes smoldering with resentment.

James smiled, hands open with his palms up, "And what are you going to do about it?"

Elliott's eyes widened, stunned by James's apparent brazen evil, "I… I will stop you."

"Look around. You're in the belly of the beast. How do you plan to accomplish that?" James asked, gesturing towards the endless aisles.

"I guess I will have to slay it from the inside," Elliott declared with cold determination.

James stood, smile widening. He towered over Elliott before reaching out a hand. James's whole demeanor changed, he went from standing as an apparent adversary, to holding his hand out as an ally. An immense weight of apprehension lifted from Elliott's shoulders. He saw in James's eyes that he too was fighting the beast from inside. Elliott reached up and took James's hand.

"Good. Seems like we're on the same page," James said.

02:

In the basement floor of the academy dorms, Director Arthur Gecko, Agent Moon, and Agent Tower stood over the shredded corpse of Agent Hanged Man. His corpse was torn to shreds, copious amounts of blood soaking the carpet. There was a bullet hole in the dead center of his forehead, blood and brains painting the wall behind him. Despite such a violent end, Agent Hanged man's corpse had a peaceful smile across his face.

Royce, in his human form, was chained to his bed, shaking, eyes wide with shock. His voice had given out from his screaming. His nightmares had come true.

Between Gecko's fingers hung a smoldering cigarette that had burnt down to the nub without having moved once since lit. A cylinder of ash hung from the filter, ready to fall from even the slightest movement, yet the director remained motionless. Through the haze of smoke surrounding his head, his round glasses shone with the reflection of the carnage before him.

"Sir..." Agent Moon began. Director Gecko remained silent.

Agent Moon spoke again, "We can continue our work on Project Moonlight. We can take Royce to The Bureau and-"

"We are out of time," Gecko said, voice smoldering with cold, calculating fury, "Use Project Moonlight. Find the interloper. Find Killian. Find James and anyone who's working with him. Eliminate them."

"What about him?" Agent Moon said, nodding his head towards Royce.

"Take him to The Bureau. He can be patient zero for Project Moonlight," Director Gecko said. He flicked the ash of his cigarette onto Agent Hanged Man's corpse and disappeared in a cloud of smoke.

03:

When Killian regained consciousness, a bright, sterile light burned his retinas. He swore under his breath and rolled over to avoid looking into the light. He blinked his eyes into focus to see a stark white mask staring at him.

"Ack! What the hell?" Killian shouted, shooting up as a cold sweat ran down his back. Killian recognized his surroundings as the Academy Arcana labs. Maxwell stood in front of him and gave Killian a friendly wave.

"Oh yippee! Mr. Killian is finally awake!" Misha said, quietly clapping with excitement.

Killian turned around and saw Misha, Miles and the Cade twins. All of them watched Killian curiously, all of them had a hint of admiration on their face that made Killian existentially uncomfortable.

"What the hell am I doing here? Why are you all looking at me like that?" Killian asked, trying to scowl at his fellow classmates.

Quinton spoke up first, "Maxwell saw what happened last night. Apparently you saved Elliott's life. The Feds took him away so Maxwell saved you before they could take you too."

Killian turned to Maxwell with an almost offended look. Maxwell responded by giving Killian a head pat. Killian growled.

Andrew spoke next, "They just took Royce away. They were looking for you, too, but we hid you in here."

"Why the hell did you do that?" Killian said, voice starting to quiver. Did they know what he had done?

"Well, you saved Elliott's life. Apparently under that tough guy persona, you're quite a sweetheart," Miles said.

Killian winced. "No, I'm not. I tried to get him killed. I released a werewolf to maul his ass."

Andrew spoke up next. He turned to Miles. "Can't your elder god co-pilot read minds?"

Miles nodded. "Yes. Killian is lying. He saved Elliott."

"Wha? Why are you doing this!?" Killian screamed, voice cracking as tears filled his eyes. All the emotion he had been holding in since he became entangled with the Bureau finally exploded out of him. Killian just couldn't take it anymore. He craved consequences for what he The Bureau did, even if he was the one to suffer them.

"I'm a god damned killer!" Killian cried, "Do you know how many people I've made Royce infect? He experimented on people *I made him* infect! Did the masked freak tell you that I was gonna do it again! Read my mind, rich boy! You *know* I was!"

Miles fidgeted anxiously. Thanks to Zak, he had a direct line to the maelstrom of emotional turmoil swirling inside Killian's head. He clenched his fists and snapped.

"Oh, shut up," Miles said sharply, "I can hear your self-pity and it's nauseating."

Killian gasped, his eyes wide with shock. Everyone else stared at Miles.

"I beg your god damned pardon?!" Killian said, incredulous.

"Royce infected those people, not you," Miles said, almost dismissively.

Killian narrowed his eyes. "How dare you. How dare you blame him. He may have technically done the deed, but *I am the one who held his leash!* If it weren't for me, Royce wouldn't have done anything."

Miles's dismissive look quickly dropped like it was nothing but a mask. He locked eyes with Killian, "And who held your leash?" he asked.

Killian stared back, speechless as the rage he felt towards himself started to shift.

"Goddamn Bureau..." Killian and Miles said in unison.

"S-speaking of... Wh-what are they gonna do with Royce and Elliott?" Misha asked.

"What do you think?" Quinton replied. Everyone went silent as their imaginations answered.

"And you're just gonna let that happen, eh?" Miles asked Killian.

Killian stared at Miles before letting out a tired chuckle. He shook his head and asked, "What the hell can I do alone?"

Maxwell slapped Killian upside the head.

"Ow! What the hell!" Killian screamed.

Maxwell gestured to Misha, Miles, Andrew, and Quinton. Killian matched gazes with each of them. His face was twisted with confusion which slowly relaxed into a blush. Despite his best efforts, he wasn't alone after all.

"Seems like we're all on the same page," Miles said.

"So… What now?" Andrew asked.

Killian looked up with blazing determination in his eyes. "We're gonna burn The Bureau Arcana to the ground."

04:

The sound of approaching footsteps echoed down the aisles of The Bureau Arcana Archives. James instinctively moved in front of Elliott to shield them. Elliott tisked.

"Making up for lost time?" Elliott teased.

James flashed a stern look at Elliott before his gaze softened. He turned back down the aisle as three Bureau agents strode into view: Adam, Agent Wheel Of Fortune, and Agent Hierophant.

"Adam!?" Elliott cried, pushing past James to rush towards his best friend.

"E-Elliott?" Adam said, frozen in place. His eyes were wide with disbelief as Elliott's arms wrapped around him. "Is it really you?"

"Last time I checked," Elliott said with a playful snicker. Adam clutched Elliott tight and simply couldn't hold back his tears.

"And so, our twists of fate are again entwined," Agent Wheel said, taking a step forward. James teleported between Agent Wheel and the reunited friends. His hand was placed firmly on Agent Wheel's chest, halting their advance.

"Woah, woah! We come bearing gifts! Of a sort. Information!" Agent Wheel said, arms casually raised as if showing there was nothing up his sleeves.

"You sure have stirred up hell," Agent Hierophant said, hands held formally behind his back, "The Executive Director is looking for you three."

"Why?" James asked, voice stern and eyes focused.

Agent Hierophant didn't answer. He glanced towards Agent Wheel. Agent Wheel whistled to himself before noticing Agent Hierophant's gaze. His whistling stopped.

"Well!" Agent Wheel began, "You know Agent Hanged Man? Turns out that shadowy little scamp is great at gathering intel even when he's dead. His radio was turned on, and I heard Emperor and Moon scheming. Lucky, right?"

"Get to the point, please," Agent Hierophant prodded.

"Yeah yeah. So! Director Emperor wants to use something called Project Moonlight to uhm... Cull the Bureau. You and anyone helping you, gone," Agent Wheel punctuated his sentence with a zipping sound as he swiftly ran his thumb across his neck.

James looked between the two agents suspiciously. "Why are you telling me this? That would put you in Director Emperor's sights."

Agent Wheel chuckled, "I like betting against the odds."

"Inspiring," Agent Hierophant said dryly.

"And you, Hierophant?" James probed.

"Some of us still believe in doing what's right, my boy," Agent Hierophant replied.

"Agent Strength and Devil are on their way to help stack the deck a bit in our favor," Agent Wheel added.

Elliott chuckled and shook his head, finally releasing from his embrace with Adam, "All of this, just to balance the scales of fate."

The sound of those words made James's blood run cold.

05:

The Bureau Arcana headquarters was situated deep in the Redwood Forests. The dense forestry acted as a natural defense, but it also made it easy to get close without being detected. The building itself was a brutalist series of rectangular prisms where each floor was set back from the floor below to give the impression of a giant concrete staircase.

The entrance to the Bureau was guarded by two men in black suits and sunglasses, each with a patch on their lapel that depicted a Sword and a roman numeral that seemed to denote rank.

Miles Prince walked up to the two guards with an unshakable confidence.

"Halt," one guard ordered.

"Identify yourself," demanded the other.

Miles let out a theatrically offended gasp and said, "What? Did your boss not tell you? I'm Miles Prince with Prince Pharmaceuticals. I am supposed to meet with the Director of Research."

The guards looked at Miles with a cautious glance. Zak read their thoughts and relayed it to Miles.

What is a private sector company doing with The Bureau? one guard thought.

Pharmaceuticals and the arcane? Sounds like the setup to a horror movie. Are we doing something shady? the other guard thought.

That was his opening, put pressure on that insecurity to get past the guards. Miles put on a warm smile and let out a chuckle, "Although perhaps he didn't inform you. We are keeping this project classified after all."

The guards perked up, Miles looked around to see if anyone else was around before leaning in, gesturing for the guards to do the same. Like putty in his hand, the guards followed along.

"You two seem trustworthy, though," Miles said in a hushed voice. Zak could sense the anticipation and excitement in the guards. They both felt like they were being let into a secret inner circle. As Miles spoke, Zak sneaked a tentacle along one of the guards' belts, searching for a key card.

"It's called Project Moonlight," Miles explained, "We are helping The Bureau develop medication to treat lycanthropy. I'm sure Agent Moon would appreciate keeping the paper trail here at a minimum, so how about you just point me in the direction of the lab."

According to Zak, that statement satisfied one of the guards, but the other was confused why such a beneficial project needed such secrecy.

"I'll call Agent Moon and have him escort you to the lab," one guard said.

"Of course!" Miles said agreeably. He turned around so his

back was to the guards and sighed. Zak wiggled a tentacle for Miles to see that he successfully acquired a key card.

Miles subtly held a hand to his ear, as if brushing his hair back. "Alright. You're up," he said quietly into his earpiece.

"Finally," Killian said through the miniature radio, courtesy of the Cades, inserted into his ear. Moments later, the guards put their fingers to their ears.

"Fire at the northern perimeter?! How? Fine, we're on our way!" one guard said.

"Stay put, Mr. Prince!" ordered the other as both guards rushed off.

Once the guards were out of sight, Miles did not stay put. He used the key card on the door. There was a beep, a light turned green, then Miles opened the door and stepped inside.

The lobby of the Bureau Arcana was a three-story atrium. The floor was cold, polished concrete with a steel centerpiece embedded into it showcasing the Bureau Arcana's Raven and Eye emblem. At the far end of the lobby was a wall of massive, vertical flat screens. Each one cycled through a collection of promotional videos showcasing the Bureau Arcana. The wall of screens was flanked on each side by columns that connected to the balconies above, the balconies seeming to be a threshold between wings. Agents traversed the balconies, too busy on their own duties to notice Miles simply walk in. On the ground floor, the columns had doors that presumably led deeper into the facility. Just in front of the giant screens was a reception desk with no one sitting behind it. On it sat a computer and a pigeon.

Miles stared at the pigeon with a strong sense of apprehension before slowly approaching. The pigeon was perched on a bell. The bell was atop a note that read, "Ring for Communications."

Miles's radio crackled to life as Quinton's voice came through, "What's taking you? Find a computer and plug Andrew's flash drive in!"

"Sorry. There's a creepy bird here that's just… staring at me," Miles said.

"Oooo, real damn spooky," Killian teased. The sound of raging fire and shouting guards came through from his line.

Miles tisked over the radio and reached into his pocket to pull out a flash drive. He plugged it into the reception desk's computer, and the log in screen flickered before going black. The monitor flicked back on to show a BIOS or some technical submenu of the computer that Miles didn't understand.

Miles tapped anxiously on the desk. "What's taking you?" Miles teased over his radio.

Andrew spoke, "I'm sorry. The program takes time to execute!"

"Well, it better hurry!" Killian said, "They're gonna find me if I have to keep this up any further!"

"Just a little longer!" Andrew begged.

"Uhg!" Killian groaned.

Someone's coming, Zak said, sensing someone's approaching thoughts.

Miles moved to the front of the desk and acted like someone waiting for reception.

One of the column doors swung open and Agent Moon stepped into the atrium. He raised an eyebrow at Miles, who, with only a brief flash of panic, put on a salesman's smile and went to shake Agent Moon's hand.

Before Agent Moon could ask any questions, Miles took charge of the conversation. Thanks to Zak, he knew everything they were going to ask before they asked it. "Miles Prince. My father sent me to check on Project Moonlight's progress."

"Is that so?" Agent Moon said as he stared at Miles with a cold, sterile gaze, as if examining him under a microscope. He kept a firm grip on Miles's hand, asserting dominance.

Zak, what's he thinking? Help me out here. Miles thought.

He doesn't believe you... Zak replied.

Well damn...

"Well then by all means! Come, come!" Agent Moon said, pulling Miles close and wrapping an arm uncomfortably tight around his shoulders. He led Miles deeper into the Bureau, the door locking behind him. "You came at the perfect time..."

Oh god... Zak thought as Agent Moon's sadistic malice flooded his thoughts. He tried to communicate it to Miles, warn him what Agent Moon was planning, but he was simply too shaken. Miles hoped that the rest of the team could do their part.

06:

Outside The Bureau Arcana, Quinton anxiously drummed his fingers on a tree as Andrew hunched over his laptop. Maxwell lurked in the shadows as Misha sat meditating. Misha opened his eyes, "I can't sense Miles anymore…"

Quinton's drumming became quicker, more anxious. He moved to hover over his brother. "Andy…"

Andrew leaned in as if willing his program to work faster. Eventually, he yelped with excitement.

"I've always wanted to say this," Andrew said before lowering his voice, "I'm in."

"That's great, but now what?" Quinton asked.

"I'm searching for schematics to find a back door, vent or something for a more covert entrance." Andrew said, his fingers typing away hastily.

"About damn time!" Killian barked through the radio, "They spotted me, so I'm comin' in hot!"

"Wait, where?" Quinton asked frantically.

"Where do you think?! To you! Unless you get outta there!" Killian screamed.

"Any luck, Andy?" Quinton asked. Despite his anxiety, the adrenaline rush made him smile.

"West perimeter! There's a service door, but I need to disarm the security or else we'll be swarmed the moment we get in!" Andrew replied. The sound of commotion grew closer as Killian led a squad of guards their way.

Maxwell picked Andrew up by the back of his collar and started carrying them towards the bureau. Andrew yelped but kept hold of his laptop as he was carried. Misha and Quinton rushed ahead to cut a hole in the chain link fence surrounding the perimeter of The Bureau so Maxwell and Andrew could dash in without stopping. They saw the service entrance and sprinted in its direction. Andrew frantically typed in his laptop while in Maxwell's arms, trying to create any efficiency in his code he could to hasten his hacking.

At the last moment, Andrew let out a scream of victory. A red LED on the door flicked green right as Quinton slammed into the door. It flung open and the four fell inside.

Maxwell, Misha, and Quinton fell onto their backs, panting heavily, and Andrew fell onto Maxwell, unwinded.

"Phew! That was close!" Andrew exclaimed.

Quinton let out a satisfied, victorious laugh between deep breaths. He held his hand to his ear and spoke.

"Kia. Back door in the west. Shake the guards and get your ass in here," Quinton ordered.

"OH, JUST SHAKE OFF THE GUARDS!? THAT'S IT? I'LL GET RIGHT ON IT, BOSS!" Killian screamed, his voice just barely audible over the sound of chaos from his end.

"You got this, champ!" Quinton said.

Killian growled over the radio before it went silent.

The four students looked around to get a bearing on their surroundings. It appeared to be a storage room. There were crates packed in well-organized stacks, yellow paint along the concrete floor to indicate a mandatory clear zone, and logistics equipment parked around.

"Do you think Kia will make it?" Andrew asked.

"I do. He's too spiteful to let himself get caught," Quinton answered.

"S-so what do we do now?" Misha asked.

Maxwell gestured frantically to get everyone's attention. Once everyone looked at him, he brought a finger to the front of his mask in a "shhh" gesture. Everyone went quiet. The only sound in the room was the faint buzz of the lights hanging high above them. Maxwell held his ear to the back door. There was silence.

More silence.

Deafening silence.

Then Maxwell hopped up and out of the way moments before the back door swung open. Killian saw the four others and glared at them. He stepped inside as the door closed behind him. Andrew typed on his laptop and the door locked behind him.

Killian exhaled steam from his nostrils and said, "Next time, one of you is gonna be the distraction."

07:

Quinton, Killian, Maxwell, and Misha sat around Andrew's laptop as he showed off the Bureau Arcana's schematics.

"I saw Miles on the cameras being taken to the security wing. My guess is Royce and Elliott will be there too. We're going to have to sneak through some offices, but Killian's fire has bought us some time."

"It won't take them long to realize we are here, even if we aren't caught," Killian said, "So we will have to balance stealth with haste."

"Not to mention, we have to save our friends." Quinton said, staring sharply at Killian.

Killian rolled his eyes, "Yeah. I thought that part was self-evident."

Quinton chuckled, "Naw, I think you just wanna act like you still don't care about them."

"Huh? Hold on. Something's coming in over my radio." Killian said, holding his middle finger to his ear, and turning his head so Quinton could clearly see.

"This banter doesn't seem that stealthy or that hasty…" Misha said shyly.

"Anyway!" Andrew said, bringing everyone's attention back to the laptop, "So, we have a route through the offices and maintenance halls. Everyone ready?"

Everyone said "aye" in unison. Everyone except for Maxwell, who gave a theatrically formal military salute.

"Let's get going then," Quinton said.

Maxwell took the lead. He scooped Misha up to cling to their back. The two acted as a scout with Maxwell silently sprinting ahead to let Misha use his aura reading to sense for anyone around. Killian and the Cade twins followed, each of them imbuing their dominant hand with their brand of magic just in case things got dicey.

The halls of the Bureau were eerily quiet as they crept along. Killian kept hypervigilant and focused. As they breached further and further into the heart of the Bureau, Killian got very familiar with the different ways each Cade twin walked. Quinton stepped confidently, with a steady, almost mechanical rhythm, while Andrew's steps were more timid and uneven. Killian tried to get a read on Maxwell, but no matter how hard he tried, he simply couldn't hear his footsteps.

He was so intensely fixated on trying to discern Maxwell's footsteps that he missed it when everyone else dipped into a supply closet.

"Killian, where are you going?!" Quinton barked over the radio.

"What? I'm following you!" Killian whispered back over the radio. He turned a corner and ran square into a young man wearing office clothes that reminded him of his old job. He wore an ID badge that depicted a Pentacle and the roman numeral for 2. Killian only caught a glimpse of it before it was drenched in coffee. Killian heard the sound of a facepalm over the radio.

"Ack! Wh-wha?" the young man spluttered, looking at Killian's punk outfit with absolute bafflement, "W-who are...?"

"If I say I'm the janitor, will you pretend I'm not here?" Killian asked, a poor attempt at a friendly smile on his face.

"U-uhm... Y-yeah! Sure! Of course!" the man stammered, eyes flicking from side to side. It was obvious he would call for backup the moment Killian was out of sight.

Killian sighed and lit his hands aflame. The young man's eyes went wide as he opened his mouth to scream. Before any sound could come out, however, the young man's body tensed up and convulsed violently. The young man fell unconscious to reveal Quinton, fingers raised as electricity pulsed along them like the prongs of a taser. He gave Killian a smug look.

"I could have handled it," Killian pouted, picking up the young man's unconscious body.

"And risk setting the fire alarms off like you do at the academy? Not a chance." Quinton said, helping Killian carry the body to the supply closet where the others hid.

Quinton opened the supply closet to reveal the others packed in like sardines. Maxwell, taking up the most space, gave Quinton, Killian, and their unconscious guest a friendly wave.

"More are coming," Misha whispered.

"I am *not* cramming my ass in there with you lot," Killian

fumed.

"Too bad." Quinton said. He shoved the unconscious young man inside, then grabbed Killian. He slammed them both in and squeezed Killian between him and Andrew. The supply closet just barely had room to close.

In the hall directly outside the supply closet, a group of three office workers decided that was the perfect location for a conversation. One of them leaned against the supply closet door.

"Did you see that memo?" one of them asked.

"Yeah. What do you think Agent Magician did to piss off Director Emperor?" said another.

"Whatever he did, I'm sure Emperor has it comin."

"Shh! Don't say that out loud! There could be ears anywhere!"

"What? Like in the supply closet?"

Two of the agents laughed. The students started sweating.

"I'm serious! Why do you think the Major Arcana agents have been dropping like flies recently!"

There was a beat of silence.

"Well… If I were to choose sides, I'm siding with Agent Magician."

"That cold hearted bastard?"

"Hey, at least he's up front with it."

"I guess. But in case anyone's listening, I'm siding with our glorious Emperor."

The three agents laughed and finally walked off. Once Misha confirmed that they were gone, the closet swung open and the students poured out.

"Bleh!" Killian snarked, "I don't want to be that intimate with any of you ever again!"

"Oh, shut it." Quinton said, "We're almost there."

Killian sighed and gestured for Maxwell to retake the lead.

08:

Royce found himself in a holding cell surrounded by concrete walls with nothing to furnish it but an iron slab with a thin padding as a bed and a stainless steel toilet and sink. The front of the cell was made of glass that faced an octagonal room, each wall being 4 cells wide and 4 cells tall, with a series of catwalks and stairs connecting them to the ground floor. Royce had little choice but to gaze into the other cells. Each cell housed a humanoid creature that was somewhere on the spectrum of human and wolf man. Some looked mostly human but with muscles bulging and contorting their bones to fit the posture of a wolf. Others looked like a chimeric mix of wolf and man, with only one half of their face covered in thick fur and one hand a monstrous claw, while the other half remained human. As the cells moved from left to right, the creatures got closer and closer to what Royce recognized as the wolves he encountered in Westridge, though not one of them was quite right.

In the center was a collection of desks that normally served as a place for Minor Arcana Agents Swords to sit, but right now, all the desks had research equipment on them, or were being used as makeshift medical beds. Royce recognized the equipment as the same he used at the academy for his research.

Royce had time to contemplate what all of this meant. Despite how hard he tried, he couldn't escape the crushing fact that *his* research caused all of this. He should have known. He should have known how Doctor Moon was getting so many strange samples for him to work with… but he was blinded by his own obsession… Royce didn't care how he got the samples, just that he had samples to work with. He wanted to turn away, but almost as a form of penance, he forced himself to stare at these abominations.

A large, secure door opened, and Agent Moon strode in with Miles Prince under his wing. Miles looked around at the abominations and reflexively smiled. It was the same smile he so often used when entertaining the grossly out of touch socialites of the upper class. Poor Z'ak'Aroth was immediately bombarded with a cacophony of half-feral rage and confused agony coming from the Project Moonlight test subjects. The creatures were just human enough for Zak to receive their mental signals, but they were hardly sapient any longer. More disgusting than any of that though, was the sense of pride coming from Agent Moon.

"So, this is what my family is financing, eh? A bunch of

failures?" Miles said.

Agent Moon, without a second's hesitation, slapped Miles across the face with the back of his hand. Miles clenched his teeth, but his smile didn't waver. Zak no longer cared about anything else but ripping Agent Moon apart.

"A silver tongue to match your silver spoon. I suppose I should have expected nothing less from the Prince heir," Agent Moon spat.

Miles wiped the drop of blood from the corner of his mouth. "Given my father invested in this, I expected... more," he said, eyes locked on Agent Moon, twitching with hatred.

Agent Moon chuckled and walked over to one of his desks. He opened a drawer and pulled out a syringe. "Talk all you want. Your quick words are useless here."

Miles backed away, closer to Royce's cell. His face gave away nothing, but he was terrified. He felt as helpless as he did back when the Cult had him. "What exactly is your plan anyway?"

Agent Moon's glasses shined with excitement as his wide, sadistic smile gleamed in the harsh medical light. "I honestly didn't have one, but how could I turn away the opportunity to test on eldritch blood?"

Stay away from our blood. Zak thought, a pair of tentacles slithering around Miles protectively.

Miles pressed his back to the glass of Royce's cell. "Ah yes, I can see the headlines now, 'Prince Family heir becomes mad science experiment.'"

"Fear not," Agent Moon hissed, the point of his syringe glistened, "No one will know, and... frankly, I don't think your father will even notice."

Miles's smirk faltered. He was deep in the heart of the Bureau. If all of this was going on, obviously, they could just cover up and write off whatever really happened to him, just like they did with Killian and Beaumont Heights. He turned to Royce, who seemed in catatonic despair. His eyes twitched to meet Miles's

"I'm sorry... This is all my fault." Royce said.

Miles turned and placed a hand against the glass. He said, "Hey man, I knew what you were working on, and I could have warned you. Hell, I even came here to save you. I believed in your vision. I still do... We just gotta get rid of this... malignant influence."

A hint of hope flashed in Royce's eyes. A weak smile cracked his face, and a dry chuckle escaped his lips. "How? Look at us... Look where we are."

"Let's find out together." Miles said before closing his eyes. He took a deep breath and his body stiffened. He twitched, muscles jerking around erratically. He opened his eyes to reveal two deep green irises surrounded by black. His dignified smile was replaced with a crooked one.

Agent Moon was only a foot from Zak/Miles before Zak's tentacles violently splayed out, knocking the syringe from Doctor Moon's hand and rapidly climbing up the wall, dragging their shared body along. Doctor Moon screamed out in terror and pulled out his tranq gun. Wildly, he started firing in Zak's direction. Zak's tentacles moved with an insect-like speed as they wrapped around the catwalk railings, using them to swing up to the next floors as he evaded Doctor Moon's wild shots.

Zak eventually settled himself in one of the corners of the roof, watching Doctor Moon closely. Doctor Moon stared back. Slowly, he aimed the dart gun at Zak and pulled the trigger. It clicked; empty. Zak Smirked.

Zak wrapped a tentacle around a light fixture, yanked it off the ceiling, and threw it towards Agent Moon. He dove behind one of the central desks as the light fixture came crashing down. He frantically felt around his lab coat before finding a spare magazine and reloading. He looked up to see, under the desk across from him, a white mask was staring back at him. Agent Moon blinked and realized the mask was connected to a body... a large body... that waved at him.

Agent Moon lifted his tranq gun with a shaky hand, trying to level his sights at the white mask. Just then, a combat boot came crashing down on Agent Moon's wrist. He gasped out, in too much shock to scream. His shock only intensified when the wearer of the combat boot, Killian Wilkes, poked his head under the desk.

"I've wanted to do that since the moment I met your creepy ass, *doctor*," Killian snarled. He grabbed Agent Moon and dragged them out from under the desk, his hands burning the lapel

The Twists of Fate

of the doctor's lab coat before slamming him down on the top of the desk.

Misha did his best to meditate, to keep his astral eye open for any auras of guards coming their way, but it was difficult to see through the storm of distorted auras coming off of the Project Moonlight Test Subjects. He groaned with frustration and looked at Andrew.

"A-any luck?" Misha asked.

"I can't unlock the cells! It's an air-gapped network," Andrew said as he typed away at his laptop.

"Oh good. Old fashioned localized electronic locks. I can crack it, but it'll take a while," Quinton said.

"Or. We can get the not-so-good doctor here to open it." Killian said, shaking with excitement.

Quinton raised an eyebrow and looked at Agent Moon. He cracked his fingers which made them spark with electricity. "You know how this goes, Doc: the easy way or the hard way. I'm sure Killian has his own experiments he'd love to run."

Agent Moon clutched his shattered wrist and did his best to stifle his groans of pain. He opened his mouth as if ready to object, argue, or monologue, but nothing but a pathetic whimper escaped, completely undercutting anything he would have said.

"Fine... You win..." he said. He raised his arms slowly, one hand up while the broken one hung limp. Slowly, carefully, he moved along the series of desks, locking eyes with each of the students. On one of the desks was a panel with a series of switches and red LED lights that looked to correspond with the number of cells, and a keypad used for unlocking the console. He reached for the consol. Maxwell grabbed his non-broken wrist to stop him.

"How about you just tell us the key code and what cell to unlock." Quinton said, moving to the consol.

Doctor Moon tisked and backed away. He moved away from the center of the students, positioning himself so he was no longer standing between them and Royce.

"One-two, one-six, one-nine-three-three," Doctor Moon said, defeated.

Quinton typed the code in. He gave Doctor Moon one last glare before turning to Royce. Royce watched in disbelief. All these people... They hardly knew him, but here they were... Royce couldn't help but shed a tear.

Quinton smiled at Royce and pressed enter. Each of the switches on the panel turned from red to yellow. Before Quinton could open any cells, each and every LED began to flash green. An alarm blared.

"Son of a bitch! It was a trap!" Killian screamed, rushing towards Doctor Moon. Doctor Moon was already scurrying away, far from the cell doors.

Maxwell grabbed Killian's arm. Killian glared at Maxwell which quickly turned to wide-eyed horror. Every single cell was opening. Every single ravenous, rabid monstrosity was loose.

"Oh hell..." Misha said.

09:

The failed test subjects of Project Moonlight shambled from their cells, drawn to the scent of the students of the Academy Arcana. The more deformed subjects moved slowly, as if struggling to properly use the malformed muscles forced upon them. The more developed subjects on the upper floors jumped from the catwalks to block the prison's exit. They growled and stalked along the threshold, waiting for the moment to strike.

"I knew we should have brought a gun," Killian said, filling his hands with fire.

"Unless it shoots silver bullets, It wouldn't have made a difference," Royce said, hesitantly taking a step from his cell.

"Oh great," both Cade twins said in unison. They both charged themselves with electricity that jumped between them like a pair of tesla coils.

In the corner of the ceiling, Zak poised himself, tentacles ready to pounce.

Maxwell stood up straight and tall, cracking his knuckles.

Misha took Royce's wrist and said, "C'mon. We have to go!"

Royce was reluctant. He opened his mouth to speak, but before he could, he was interrupted.

"I swear to Z'ak'Aroth," Quinton shouted, "If you say one

single syllable of self-pitying garbage, I'm gonna electrocute you unconscious and carry your ass out of here."

Royce's face twisted with surprise and he rushed from his cell. From the neighboring cell, one of the Project Moonlight test subjects lunged for Royce, its single clawed arm swiped for Royce's neck. Before it could get to Royce, however, Maxwell's gloved fist intercepted the creature's face. There was a muted thud, a wretched crack, and the creature dropped.

At the same time, the test subjects guarding the exit pounced. The Cade twins each flung out an arm with two fingers extended. A bolt of lightning screeched across the air and struck one of the subjects. The subject seized up and convulsed as the lightning chained to the next closest subject, where it too, was incapacitated. The electrocuted subjects let out a garbled howl that didn't sound entirely animal nor quite human.

Zak remained in a corner towards the ceiling, evading a handful of test subjects that tried to leap and swipe at them. Every time one got close, Zak whipped a tentacle out, wrapped it around a test subject's neck, and threw it aside.

As a pair of test subjects pounced for Killian, Killian dashed backwards and thrust both of his hands out. A blast of fire sprayed from his hands, both propelling his dash and igniting the subjects. Killian looked around to see the test subjects slowly surrounding his friends... Friends? Yeah, at least they were the closest things to friends Killian ever had... He grit his teeth and let out a furious growl.

Killian held both of his arms straight out and spun, saturating his surroundings with a vortex of flame. While it wasn't effective at incapacitating the test subjects, it did direct their focus towards Killian. A cacophony of half-feral screeches filled the air as the singed test subjects stumbled, turned to Killian, and rushed to surround him.

"Now's your chance, idiots!" Killian called from the center of the prison, slightly fortified by the security desks. He launched fireball after fireball at the increasingly aggressive test subjects, just barely keeping them at bay.

The Cade twins, Maxwell, Misha, and Royce sprinted towards the exit. The twins chained their lightning along a string of subjects to clear the path, and Maxwell moved with surprising speed to evade the slower subjects, decking the quicker ones with heavy jabs before they could get to him.

"Miles, Zak, Killian! Cmon!" Quinton screamed. With the increasing number of burning but undeterred half-wolf test subjects, more and more of the prison caught fire. Soon, it would be entirely engulfed in flames.

"Working on it!" Killian screamed back. He tried to break through the wall of swiping claws and gnashing teeth, but there was simply no room.

"Damn idiot!" Quinton said, reeling an arm back to charge up an electric blast. Before Quinton could send out his charge, the threshold between the prison and the rest of the security wing became engulfed in flames.

Quinton gasped, eyes wide in shock. He just about dove into the fire before his brother grabbed him.

Quinton clenched his fists before screaming into the fire, "YOU TWO BETTER GET OUT OF THERE OR I'M GONNA KICK YOUR ASSES IN THE AFTERLIFE!"

Back inside the prison, the sudden combustion caused the catwalks on the upper levels to collapse, giving Zak an opening to breathe. He scurried down to the center of the prison as fast as his tentacles could take him. He wrapped his tentacles around the blazing test subjects surrounding Killian and ripped them away, flinging them across the prison with eldritch strength. The fire burned his tentacles, but it created an opening. Killian locked eyes with Zak and went wide-eyed.

Zak flung himself through the gap between test subjects and wrapped his tentacles protectively around Killian. Right before a hoard of the test subjects pounced, Zak flung a tentacle to an air vent, grabbed on, and pulled them both to safety.

Back outside the prison, Misha opened his eyes and let out a relieved sigh. Everyone else turned towards Misha.

Misha smiled warmly and said, "They made it."

10:

Almost on instinct, Zak's tentacles carried him and Killian through the vents until they reached a large open HVAC hub. The hub was roughly the size of an office, with a series of smaller vents running through it. The hub was fed air by a massive slow spinning fan blocked off by a safety grate.

Killian struggled in Zak's grasp before finally being let go. Once he was released, he fell to the aluminum floor with an echoing clang.

"Bleh! Slimy!" Killian said, wiping himself off.

"S-sorry," Zak said, gently holding one of his tentacles to examine how bad the burns were. He poked his wound and winced.

Killian glanced over and sighed. He moved over to Zak and took the burnt tentacle. He reached in his pocket and pulled out a burn cream. "Here. I used to burn myself all the time. I got in the habit of carrying a tube of this with me."

Killian rubbed the ointment on Zak's burn and Zak let out a sigh of relief.

"Thanks..." Zak said.

"Least I could do. You only got burnt saving my dumb ass..." Killian said, "Why the hell did you do that anyway?"

"It was Miles's idea. I'll have him answer," Zak said before closing his eyes. His body shivered and his tentacles slowly retracted. When he opened his now green and blue eyes, Miles sat, staring at Killian with a devilish smirk.

Killian's eyebrows twisted in a mix of confusion and concern. "Okay why did you of all people save me? And why do you look so pleased about it? I thought we hated each other."

"Well... You saved my ass; it felt only right that I returned the favor." Miles said.

Killian let out a dismissive tisk, "When the hell did I save your ass?"

Miles reached into his pocket and locked eyes with Killian. Slowly, he pulled out a playing card. It was a Jack of Spades with a burnt corner that had been drawn to look like Killian. The same card Killian gave The Jack Of Diamonds.

Killian's eyes went wide with realization, and his jaw went agape. He was overwhelmed with shock, horror, and disbelief...

"No..." Killian said.

"Oh yes," Miles said with a snicker, "I believe the words you used when you gave this to me were, and I quote, 'you're a goddamn hero-'"

Killian's face went bright red, "Shut! Shut up!" he shouted, tackling Miles to try and get the card back. Miles laughed and held the card just out of reach. The two rolled around in a scuffle before Quinton's voice came in over the radio.

"Hey lovebirds! We can hear you," Quinton said.

Killian groaned and stopped struggling, laying limp with defeat on Miles's chest.

"Copy," Miles said, all business. "Are you guys all safe?"

"Yeah. We're recovering in the maintenance halls. There's a vent nearby that you should be able to reach. Meet us there when you two are done fooling around," Quinton said.

"Copy. See you guys in a bit," Miles said over the radio.

Killian groaned in embarrassment and just closed his eyes. Being surrounded by killer monstrosities was less terrifying than this.

"Comfy?" Miles asked Killian who was still emotionally incapacitated on Miles's chest.

"No. I don't think I have ever in my life been less comfy," Killian bemoaned.

And yet, neither of them moved.

11:

Inside the Bureau Arcana Archives, James and his allies prepared for Director Gecko's next move. Elliott and Adam were by themselves sitting at agent Hierophant's desk, in between the 4-way intersection of the aisles, taking the brief respite to catch up. Adam told Elliott about becoming an agent, and Elliott told Adam about death and the academy. It all sounded so impossible, but here they were, living it.

James, Agent Strength, Agent Hierophant, Agent Devil,

The Twists of Fate

and Agent Wheel Of Fortune stood in one of the aisles of files, discussing their very limited options.

"So…" Jaq began, "Do you have a plan, James?"

"Perhaps it is not too late for Director Emperor to listen to reason," Agent Hierophant said, hands behind his back almost standing at attention.

"I tried," Agent Devil said, arms crossed as he anxiously gripped his coat sleeves, "No matter what I said, he remained convinced that you three are harbingers of some impending doom."

Agent Wheel laughed, "That is a bit dramatic, isn't it? What did he really say?"

Agent Devil sighed, "His exact words were, 'Graves and his interlopers will burn the Bureau to the ground.'"

"His interlopers?" Jaq asked, placing a hand on her cocked hip.

"I presume he means Elliott and Agent Fool," Agent Devil clarified, his glance shifting over to the two young men.

"Wait. I get Elliott being called an 'interloper,' but Adam?" Jaq asked.

Agent Devil's gaze met with James's, "Should I tell them, or will you?"

James returned Agent Devil's gaze. There was silence as the two simply stared at each other. James couldn't help but stare beyond Agent Devil to the ever-stretching aisle of the archives until they faded into darkness. Reflexively, his eyes twitched and focused on a point in the far off dark. He narrowed his eyes, and they began to glow. Then he saw it, the shimmer of light off the glass of a sniper scope.

James swept Agent Devil's legs, sending them to the floor.

"Mr. Graves! What has gotten into y-" Agent Hierophant screamed before James swiftly tackled him and Agent Strength into the archive aisle.

Just then, a bullet whizzed by, quickly followed by the thunderous sound of the bang that had propelled it. The bullet just barely nicked Agent Wheel's coat. Agent Wheel glanced at the damage to his coat and tisked, more annoyed than concerned.

Adam and Elliott dove behind the central desks as cover.

"What the hell was that?" Adam screamed.

"It was only a matter of time before they checked here," James said, eyes blazing white. He shrugged off his blazer and positioned himself in the way of the others, in the dead center of the aisle. He cracked his neck and waited, like a duel at high noon.

Another shot rushed through the air. James vanished in a flash of bright light, and Agent Wheel drew his platinum revolver. He pointed it towards the shooter and fired wildly until his cylinder ran dry. The click of the hammer repeatedly striking a spent shell filled the silence.

James blinked back into the aisle. He was panting but trying to hide it. He stared out into the darkness once more. The shimmer of the sniper scope was gone.

"Did I get 'em?" Agent Wheel asked.

The agents' radios crackled to life as Agent Tower's gruff voice broke in, "Well played. You shot out my scope. I was hoping to get more up close and personal anyway."

From down the aisle came a hiss, then from the darkness crept an opaque gray smoke. Agent Hierophant helped Agent Devil to his feet as James drew his sidearm. Agent Wheel pressed his back to James and reloaded. Jaq kept low and made her way to the central desk where Adam and Elliott hid.

James and the others slowly crept towards the central desk, eyes and ears vigilant for the approaching Agent Tower. One by one, the other aisles echoed with the sounds of metal bouncing off concrete followed by the bang and hiss of a smoke grenade going off. Every surrounding aisle filled with smoke until the only unobscured area was a 10-foot radius around the Hierophant's desk. James and the others formed a circle around the desk to look out in all directions.

James grit his teeth. Even he couldn't see through the smoke. He closed his eyes and focused on what he could hear… An alarm started blaring, reverberating off the endless aisles.

"Oh, for Christ's sake, what now?" Agent Devil groaned.

Agent Tower's laugh crackled in from their radios, "The wolf boy's academy friends seem to be tearing things up in the security wing. Don't worry. I'll clean them up once I'm done with you."

Agent Wheel tisked and pointed his freshly reloaded revolver out towards the smoke, "Oh yeah, what a skilled agent, taking out some academy students. Jeez, what a badass."

Agent Tower chuckled through the radio, "Sometimes you need to call an exterminator to deal with even the smallest of pests."

As soon as Agent Tower finished speaking, a knife flew from the smoke, straight towards agent Wheel. The blade stopped an inch from Wheel's forehead, James's hand on the knife's grip. In one fluid motion, James twirled the knife to face away from Agent Wheel, then threw it back into the smoke. He tried to hear the sound of impalement over the blaring alarms, but all he heard was a chuckle.

"You're outnumbered, Tower," Agent Hierophant said, "You can't take us all on."

"Heh. You're right. Let's even the playing field, shall we?" Agent Tower said. As he spoke, Agent Star emerged from the smoke. Her movement was poised and deliberate, like a black widow approaching its ensnared prey. She held a silenced pistol in her hand, the barrel of which was leaning against her shoulder. Her free hand was adorned with long, sharp nails that glowed with an astral energy.

Agent Wheel didn't wait for things to escalate and immediately fired upon Agent Star. Agent Star remained unphased. She only tisked and shook her head as another Agent Star emerged from the smoke, also shaking her head. Then another. And another… And another until there was one Agent Star for each of the defenders. They all pointed their guns towards James and his allies.

"Cheater!" Agent Wheel screamed, hastily trying to reload yet again.

"They are illusions. Only one of them is a real threat," Agent hierophant said.

"Yeah but which one?" Agent Devil asked.

"Aye, there's the rub," Agent Hierophant replied.

"You're fast, James, I'll give you that, but you can't protect everyone," Agent Tower said.

James immediately grabbed Adam and Elliott and dove to

protect them. At the same time, Agent Star opened fire. Although every gun appeared to fire, only one bullet existed, and it struck Agent Wheel square in the chest.

Agent Wheel cried out, clutched his chest, and fell to the floor with a heavy thud. Jacqueline dove on top of Agent Wheel, placing her hand on the bullet wound to compress it and stop the blood flow. Agent Devil and Agent Hierophant immediately repositioned themselves to rush the apparently real Agent Star.

Agent Star dropped her pistol and raised her arms as if in surrender, but once Agent Devil and Hierophant grabbed hold of her, she flared out her elbows, striking the two agents. With this opening, Agent Star turned and grabbed them both by the back of the neck. Once she had a solid grip on them, her and the two agents shimmered with an astral glow. The three sank into the floor until they were gone.

As they sank from one realm, they rose into another. It was laid out the same as the archives, with endless rows of aisles, but instead of fading into darkness, the endless expanse faded into a bright light that stung the eyes. The blare of the alarm was silenced, and the air was empty of smoke.

Agent Devil and Agent Hierophant broke free from Agent Star's grip and made distance between them.

"Where the hell are we now?" Agent Devil said.

"The astral plane. My archive is built on a ley line between realms," Agent Hierophant replied.

"It's lovely, isn't it?" Agent Star said, visibly brimming with astral energy. "It will make disposing of your corpses all the easier."

Agent hierophant tisked. He walked over to one of the archive shelves. "It is indeed a great place to hide things. I myself use the astral realm to store certain… artifacts."

As he spoke, he pushed some files to the side and reached into the back of the shelf. Slowly, he drew a flaming sword from the shelf. Once he fully withdrew the sword, six angelic wings burst from Agent Hierophant's back. He stood beside Agent Devil, sword raised towards Agent Star.

Agent Devil snickered and cracked his neck, "This is the perfect place to finally cut loose. I'm tired of being shackled to my desk."

The Twists of Fate

He turned to Agent Star. With one blink, his irises turned red surrounded by black, with vertical pupils like that of a snake. Two small red horns poked through his slicked black hair. He smirked, flashing a set of razor sharp teeth.

Agent Hierophant and Agent Devil, Nathaniel Cross and Damien Cross, the Seraphim and the Demon of the Bureau Arcana stood side by side.

Agent Star cracked a smile. "Oh good. I was worried I was facing two washed up old men."

12:

In the mundane plane of the archives, Agent Wheel let out a laugh as his bloodied hands clutched his bullet wound. Jaq pressed one hand against Agent Wheel's to help keep pressure on the wound while the other reached into her medical satchel. She pulled out a syringe, gauze, and medical tape. She began to work on patching Agent Wheel up, completely unfazed by the commotion around her.

Adam pushed James off and rushed to protect Jaq. James blinked himself and Elliott right beside Adam.

"Heh," James said, "You and I... Defending Jaq while she patches someone up. This feels familiar, doesn't it?"

"At least this isn't in a damn forest this time." Adam said. His eyes lit up with a bright white like James's, one hand crackling with electricity while the other blazed with fire. "Plus, I've learned a lot since Westridge. Watch this, Elliott! I dreamt I'd be able to show you this one day."

"Leave a piece for me," Elliott said, getting in a fighting stance, "I want revenge on this maniac for shooting me."

Agent Tower let out a loud, bellowing laugh that echoed from all directions. When he spoke, his voice came in over the radio. "Oh, this is rich. You thought I killed you?"

"Don't play dumb. You recognized me when we met at the academy last night. Remember? When you tried to feed me to Royce?"

Agent Tower's laugh only got louder, "Oh I didn't pull the trigger. I was there though if you wanna know who really did it."

"Oh? Enlighten me," Elliott demanded. He stared into the smoke, waiting for the faintest hint of Agent Tower to reveal himself. A slight disturbance in the smoke, a quick shadow, was all it would take...

"We are in the archives, you know. We could just pull out the file and read all its juicy secrets," Agent Tower taunted.

"Shut up!" Adam screamed, "There is no report. I checked. He's just trying to sike us out."

"Oh, am I? Why don't you ask your dear close buddy Agent Magician? He was there, after all," Agent Tower boomed.

Elliott's face twitched with uncertainty, and he turned to James. "Y-you were. What exactly did happen that day?"

"Shh," James said, "We have more pressing matters."

Agent Tower's boisterous laugh filled the archives. "Tisk. I'm disappointed in your cowardice, Magician."

Suddenly, there was an agitation in the smoke, it was subtle, but Elliott noticed it right away.

"There!" Elliott screamed, pointing in the direction of the disturbance. James and Adam whipped around to where Elliott pointed just as Agent Tower rushed from the smoke, combat knife in hand.

Together, James and Adam raised their hands. A loud, bright explosion filled the archives. When the flash faded, James and Adam were behind Agent Tower. Tower immediately swung his knife behind himself but, with an electrified grip, Adam grabbed Tower's forearm. This stunned Tower for only a moment before his free arm delivered an elbow towards Adam's throat. James threw his own elbow in to block the attack then followed up by extending his arm and driving his forearm into Tower's neck. Adam took the opening to deliver a lighting-imbued roundhouse kick to Tower's back.

Agent Tower swiped his arm down to try and grab James, but in a flash, James and Adam switched places. Tower instead grabbed onto Adam's arm which was now engulfed in flames. Agent Tower let out a surprised gasp and released Adam. Tower turned to face James who began delivering a series of quick strikes. Tower's arms moved to block each jab, but then Adam joined in, matching James's rhythm with a mix of electric and blazing punches. The electric attacks stunned Tower, and the blazing ones singed him, even when blocked.

Agent Tower rolled backwards to escape and in one quick motion, drew three knives and threw them. The knives flew straight towards Jaq. Adam blinked himself in the path of the knives, held his hands up and caught them midair with telekinesis. Adam flung his hands out and sent the knives straight back towards Agent Tower. Tower dodge rolled out of the way then took a knee. He couldn't help but smirk at the two agents as he panted heavily.

"Not bad," he said before tossing out a flash bang. It was for only a brief moment that the blinding light filled the archives, but when the flash was gone, so was Agent Tower

"Oh? Are you giving up?" Adam said with a proud laugh.

"Oh no no no," Agent Tower said over the radio, "I just wanted a taste of how you two fought together. The Ace and his Fool… it was a hard opportunity to ignore."

"That damn code name," Adam hissed before calling back into the smoke, "Yeah, well get used to it, cuz I'm not leaving his side."

"Heh. We'll see about that," Tower chuckled, "Elliott Harding, was it? Are you ready to learn the truth about your death?"

Elliott couldn't bring himself to vocalize an answer, but he couldn't fight his burning curiosity.

"Listen closely…" Agent Tower said, voice a low, gravely whisper that came in clear over the radio, "The person who ended your life… Was James Graves."

13:

In the astral plane of the archives, Agent Star stood with one arm crossed, her other arm propped up straight. On her raised hand, the tips of her fingers swirled with pale blue astral magic that made her nails shimmer like something between the spark of electricity and the crackle of fire. Damien, Agent Devil, and Nathaniel, Agent Hierophant, stood poised, preparing for battle.

Damien was the first to move, dashing towards Agent Star,

ready to slash her with his demonic claws. Agent Star grabbed Damien's swiping wrist, digging her astrally imbued nails in and twisted, causing Damien to let out a pained growl. In response, Damien gripped the arm that gripped his own and used his strength to throw Agent Star towards Nathaniel. Agent Star flew through the air, quickly reorienting herself to deliver a midair kick to Nathaniel. Nathaniel used the flaming sword to deflect the kick. The impact of Agent Star's kick pushed Nathaniel back several feet, whereupon he extended the sword to the side to steady himself.

Agent Star was now flanked by the two Cross brothers. She flipped her hair from her face and smirked, reinforcing her composure.

"Are you so sure James Graves is where you want to place your faith, Hierophant?" Agent Star asked.

"I am certain," Nathaniel said as a holy light surrounded him. He rushed for Agent Star, sword outstretched. Agent Star dipped backwards, performing a sort of limbo under Nathania's sword.

Agent Star returned upright and cracked her neck. She said, "Too slow, old man. My turn." Then she cracked her knuckles, creating four copies of herself that each rushed towards the brothers.

Nathaniel slashed his sword through the air, sending out a holy flame that cut through the copies, leaving only the real Agent Star staggering. He then stepped aside to let Damien lunge for her.

Like a knife fight, the two slashed at each other, Damien with his demonic claws, and Agent Star with her astral nails. The two seemed to dance with incredible speed, striking, dodging, blocking, all in quick succession. Damien's attacks were more aggressive and animalistic while Agent Star's movements were more fluid and elegant, but each were quick and powerful. Agent Star's rhythm was in perfect sync with Damien's moves, neither were able to gain any ground. It wasn't until Nathanial approached that Agent Star lost rhythm. Damian swiped and Agent star blocked with her forearm, leaving a bloody gash in her skin.

She created a copy of herself to give herself a moment to dodge backwards before being surrounded yet again. Damien swiped through the copy, the lack of any physical impact causing him to stumble and pant out of breath.

"And you, demon? Why do you side with James?" Agent Star said, gripping her bleeding forearm.

"Do I really need a reason to side with what's right?" Damian said, growling.

"Hah!" Agent Star said, slowly and carefully strafing to keep both brothers in her sights, "The Devil schooling me on what's right? How funny."

"What about you?" Nathaniel asked, approaching Agent Star, "Why stay loyal to Emperor Gecko?"

Agent Star shook her head, "Morality is of no concern to the cold, uncaring maw of the cosmos. When it comes to swallow us, we must be willing to do anything to protect our reality."

Nathaniel raised an eyebrow. He was now close enough to hold his sword up to Agent Star's chest. "If we must sacrifice our humanity to protect humanity, what are we really fighting for?" He asked.

"Thankfully, you won't have to worry about answering that," Agent Star said.

Nathaniel narrowed his eyes as Agent Star smirked. Suddenly, Damien screamed. The copy of Agent Star that stood before Nathanial laughed as it evaporated into astral mist. Nathaniel turned towards his brother. Agent Star wrapped one arm around Damien's neck then stabbed her nails into Damien's spine. A swirl of cosmic energy flowed around her before being channeled to her fingertips. She sent a powerful beam of blue light through Damien and towards Nathaniel. Blood shot from Damien's mouth as Nathaniel deflected the beam with his sword.

Nathaniel rushed for Agent Star, whom, still holding onto Damien, held her fingers to Damien's temple like a pistol. Cosmic energy swirled around Agent Star once more, charging up for another blast. Damian's lower half was limp while his top half clung to Agent Star, digging his claws into her arm to try and break free.

Nathaniel slowed, but continued his approach, staring into Agent Star with steely eyed fury. Agent Star kept hold of Damien, keeping his body like a shield between her and Nathaniel. Agent

Star focused her cosmic energy again into the tips of her fingers. Damien closed his eyes.

Suddenly... Nathaniel plunged the flaming sword through Damien and right into Agent Star's heart. She let out one quick gasp... then there was silence. The cosmic energy faded from her being. She went pale... limp... lifeless.

Nathaniel unsheathed the sword from its fleshy scabbard. Agent Star and Damien collapsed to the floor. Nathaniel fell to his knees beside Damien and pressed his hand against his brother's wound.

Damien let out a weak yelp, "Argh! Your damned holy touch burns..." he said.

"Deal with it. It's better than bleeding out," Nathaniel retorted.

14:

In the Mundane plane of the Archives, Agent Tower's words hung in the air.

"'The person who ended your life... Was James Graves...'" Elliott repeated. The air left his lungs in disbelief. He turned to James who had his back to him.

"James?" Adam asked, taking a step away.

"Tell me he's lying!" Elliott demanded, screaming. After all he went though, he was desperate not to believe it... that one of his closest friends had ended his life... It had to be a lie... It had to...

James's face hung low, somber... Guilty.

"Say something!" Elliott screamed.

"You were infected," James said coldly.

Elliott gasped in disbelief, shaking with anger. "So is Royce! Why did he get to live?"

"Werewolves are still human for 28 days a month. Once you turned, you were never going to be human again." James said flatly. His eyes never turned to meet Elliott.

"Oh, is that all?" Agent Tower taunted, "Why did you bring a civilian along on such a dangerous mission anyway?"

Elliott stared at James expectantly, waiting for an answer.

James didn't move an inch. Silent.

Eventually, James parted his lips. "Adam was going to die," he said.

"What?!" Adam yelped, "H-how could you possibly know that?"

James closed his eyes and said, "Fate."

"What the hell do you mean 'Fate?'" Elliott said sharply.

"Oh, ho ho!" Agent Wheel laughed before coughing up blood "I'm not the only one who made a bet with our resident Grim Reaper, eh?"

Adam gasped and rushed over to Agent Wheel, whose chest was wrapped up in gauze. There was a dark red stain seeping through his bandages, but it was surprisingly minimal. "You're alive!"

"The bullet completely missed Agent Wheel's arteries, heart, and lungs. If we get out of this, he'll make a full recovery." Jaq said, keeping two fingers on Wheel's neck to maintain a read on his pulse.

"Lucky, right?" Agent Wheel said, giving Adam a wink. Adam cracked a smile; it was a brief moment of levity brightening the dread around him.

"Deal with the Grim Reaper, eh?" Elliott prodded.

"Not quite," James said. His voice was somber, regretful, almost weak, "It's… complicated…"

As James tried to parse his thoughts, the air grew still. The perpetual swirl of the smoke froze. The temperature plummeted, but no one could shiver. Elliott looked around and noticed that Jaq and Agent Wheel seemed suspended in time while he, James, and Adam were free to move about. The twists of fate, alone in a fragment in time…

A soft, ethereal voice broke through the perfect silence. "Perhaps I can illuminate things for you," said the voice. Despite the wide-open space, the voice had no echo. A spotlight with no discernible origin came on and burned a hole in the smoke. As the smoke wafted away, it revealed a hotel door surrounded by art deco styled wallpaper. The door swung open to reveal a white void, and the silhouette of a sharp dressed man in a long-brimmed hat stood in the doorway.

"Agent Death..." James said, sounding almost breathless.

The Man In Black stepped from the hotel door whereupon the spotlight turned off and the smoke returned, engulfing the door. The Man In Black extended his arms and performed a deep bow, "Thank you for the introduction, but despite your honorific, I am not bound by your Bureau's... structure."

"Are you the Grim Reaper that Agent Wheel talked about?" Adam asked.

"Some call me that, yes," The Man In Black said, adjusting his bone-gray tie.

"Why are you here?" Elliott said, wary of whoever or whatever this entity was.

"To provide a service," The Man in Black said, "You see, I provide the Bureau Arcana with data: Possibilities, outcomes, causes and effects... Threads of fate for The Bureau to tug upon and change a course of events." As The Man In Black spoke, he held out his hands, fingers extended. He twitched and moved his gloved fingers as if pulling the strings of a marionette.

"In the case of you three..." The Man In Black continued, "Adam was destined to die. No matter what thread was pulled. Some threads led to Elliott becoming James's protégé, others with James dying alongside Adam. The thread The Bureau chose to pull would see Adam infected, and under the care of Bureau Arcana researchers. But at the end of the day, there simply was no thread where Adam made it out alive."

Adam felt his chest, as if feeling for a heartbeat, confirming that he was indeed still there. "Th-then why am I here?"

The Man In Black turned to James, "Somehow, James created his own thread. He brought Elliott along, tugging the thread so he would intervene. He would be infected; James would have to put him down. All so Adam could live."

Elliott glared at James before turning away. To know you were nothing more than a sacrifice for someone else was a profound hurt that Elliott simply couldn't process. He fell to his knees in despair.

"Then... why am I still here?" Elliott asked.

"Your thread is a knot that binds many together," The Man In Black said, "Of course, to restring your thread, I will have to take some from elsewhere." As he spoke, his head slowly turned to Adam. Adam was speechless. He almost seemed to accept his apparent fate. He stood there, waiting for this deathly being to sever his thread of fate.

"Wait," James said, a flash of panic in his eyes.

"I swear... You better not kill me again..." Elliott seethed.

The Man In Black chuckled, "That would be... unacceptable..."

James approached The Man In Black and leaned in close until his face, too, was obscured by the shadows of The Man In Black's hat. The Man In Black leaned in, listening to a whisper. After a long pause, The Man In Black spoke.

"That is... Acceptable," The Man In Black said. James returned beside Adam, face a ghostly pale.

"What have you done, James?" Adam said, voice grave.

"Shh," The Man In Black said, "Saying it aloud could affect the outcome, and we don't want to make any more of a mess of this than it already is," he said as he pulled out a reception bell. He pressed the tip of the bell which caused a loud ding to ring throughout the time-suspended archives. The bell's ding seamlessly morphed into the ring of an elevator that has reached its floor. A section of the smoke parted like an elevator door opening, then, with a final tip of his hat, The Man In Black stepped through, the doors closing behind him.

15:

Time returned to its natural pace. For James, it felt suddenly unrelenting. He stared into the smoke, his eyes absent of their arcane white glow. He faced the smoke with a grave steadiness. He took a step towards the smoke.

Adam gripped James's wrist, unsure of what to say, but certain he didn't want James to leave.

Elliott stared daggers at James, shaking with confused fury. Yes, James was the direct cause of his death, but... if he were in the same place... would he have done the same to save Adam? He honestly couldn't say...

James shook Adam's grip off and stepped towards the

smoke. He raised his arms out to each side, as if inviting Tower to strike. The messianic imagery infuriated Elliott.

"Heh," Agent Tower chuckled drily, "What's your game, Magician?"

"I surrender. You win," James said, affect flat, even more cold and emotionless than usual.

"Well…" Agent Tower said, emerging from the smoke, pistol in hand, "The guilt has finally caught up with you, eh?"

Jaq gasped. "James! What the hell are you doing?! Adam what the hell is he doing?" she screamed.

Adam looked away. All this chaos… to save him? He couldn't help but feel guilty, like this was all his fault. Adam couldn't understand why… He didn't think he was special… He didn't think he was talented… Not compared to everyone else around him. All he did right was being friends with the right people. Adam closed his eyes, unable to watch what was about to come.

Agent Tower turned James around and kicked the back of his legs, forcing him to his knees. Agent Tower made James hold his hands behind his head, as if awaiting execution. In this position, James locked eyes with Elliott.

"Take care of Adam for me," James said.

Something snapped in Elliott. He was tired of being a pawn of Fate. With a cold fury, Elliott turned to where Agent Star had spirited the Cross brothers away. He crept carefully over to Agent Star's dropped pistol. He heard Agent Tower cock his pistol, and in that moment, he raised the gun.

"Fuck your Fate," Elliott said, pulling the trigger. The first bullet struck James in the shoulder, the same shoulder James shot Elliott in back in Capstone Creek. James stared in disbelief, unable to even flinch from the pain as Elliott fired a barrage of bullets towards James and Agent Tower, indiscriminately riddling James's arm and Tower's legs.

Agent Tower's legs collapsed, leaving his head level with Elliott's aim. That's when Elliott's pistol ran dry. Without missing a beat, Elliott dropped the pistol and rushed to Agent Wheel. He took Agent Wheel's revolver and approached Agent Tower. Agent Tower raised his own pistol, but Elliott fired, striking Agent Tower in the hand.

    Elliott tried to steady his aim as much as his shaking hands would allow, firing one shot at a time until he closed the gap between himself and Agent Tower. Each bullet struck Tower square in the chest, the impact dulled by his Kevlar vest. Elliott pulled the trigger one more time, only for the gun to click.

    Agent Tower reached for his pistol with his shattered hand, but Elliott stepped on their wrist, causing Agent Tower to grunt in pain. Elliott tossed Agent Wheel's revolver aside and picked up Agent Tower's gun. Elliott aimed the pistol at its previous owner, Agent Tower's forehead. Agent Tower stared Elliott down and smirked. "Are you a killer, kid?" he said, blood dripping from his mouth.

    Elliott hesitated. Was he a killer? His aim wavered, and his gaze shifted. That's when he saw what was in Agent Tower's other hand. Agent Tower held a hand grenade, pin pulled so the only thing holding down the safety lever was Agent Tower's grip. If Elliott pulled the trigger, Agent Tower would release the grenade.

    Before Elliott could really react, James stomped onto Agent Tower's other wrist, causing him to release the hand grenade. Its safety lever sprang away, igniting the primer inside. Elliott gasped in shock before being pushed away by James. Elliott stumbled back, falling into Adam. He stared into James's eyes… Elliott's keen gaze noticed that James's eyes, ever brilliant and brimming with at least a tinge of arcane power, were a dull, dark gray. Purely and utterly mundane…

    Elliott hoped he was missing something, hoped that James would blink away at the last moment… But when the grenade went off, James and Agent tower both were engulfed in flames.

16:

    The smoke in the archives finally cleared. There was nothing left of James or Agent Tower but a smoldering splatter of blood and viscera. Elliott had seen his fair share of graphic crime scenes in his day, but even he couldn't stomach the sight of this. He turned to Adam who cried out in despair. Elliott approached and placed a hand upon Adam's shoulder.

"I... I'm sorry," Elliott said, voice cracking.

Adam gripped onto Elliott's coat with one hand while his other hand balled into a fist to pound Elliott's chest. Elliott grit his teeth and bared it until Adam tired himself out. Exhausted, Adam pressed his face into Elliott's chest and began soaking it in tears. Elliott wrapped his arms around Adam securely and protectively. He had just been reunited with James, and just like that, he lost him again.

Agent Wheel felt the urge to chuckle, even though he found none of this funny. He bit his tongue and forced himself to sit up. He groaned in pain, clutching the bullet wound in his chest. He looked at Jaq with an apprehensive expression.

"So uhm..." Agent Wheel began, "What about Hiero and Devil?"

Just then, Agent Hierophant rose up through the floor, clutching a hissing Agent Devil's wounds.

"Well!" Agent Wheel exclaimed, "Speak of The Devil, and he shall appear!"

Nathaniel Cross gave Agent Wheel a severe look before turning to Jacqueline. Jaq rushed to Nathanial's side and took over caring for Damien's wounds.

"Oh, thank god, hands that don't burn," Damien said, shaking from the blood loss.

"Thank god, you say?" Agent Wheel said with a snicker, which was quickly stifled by the pain in his chest.

Jaq groaned and got to work patching Damien up. "Is Agent Star..."

"Dead," Nathaniel said coldly. He looked around the archives, gulping when he did a head count. "Agent Tower and Magician?"

Jaq closed her eyes and frowned, "Dead."

Nathaniel's eyes widened in surprise, "Both of them? I... never expected him to go out to someone like Tower."

"I doubt it was just Tower," Elliott said, voice flat, as if still processing all that had happened, "Your so-called 'Agent Death' played a role."

Damien pounded his fist into the floor, causing blood to spurt from his wound, "Damn it, James! I told him not to make any more deals with him!"

"To be fair," Jaq said, hurriedly trying to clean up Damien's blood to make wrapping the wound in gauze easier. "You were a bit busy. Now stay still. Hierophant, can you keep Wheel from picking at his wound?"

Damien groaned in pain but forced himself to stay still while Jaq tended to his wounds. Nathaniel sat himself by Agent Wheel and grabbed their wrists to keep Wheel from fussing with his own gauze.

As things eventually settled down, so too did Adam. He let go of Elliott and reached into his pocket.

"You okay?" Elliott asked.

Adam pulled out a rifle shell casing and stared at it longingly. It was the same shell he caught from James's rifle back in Westridge, the same lucky shell casing he always had in his pocket... Eventually, he tapped the hollow end and filled it with light. He placed the casing down with the light emanating from the tip like a mourning candle. Elliott stared at the luminous shell casing, allowing a tear to fall from his eye. Elliott had mourned losing James once before... It didn't make the second time any easier.

Adam turned to Elliott and said, "I'm sorry."

"Why the hell are *you* sorry?" Elliott snapped.

"All of this destruction... For me... I don't understand it," Adam said.

Elliott pointed at the shell casing, "Look how effortlessly you did that, how effortlessly you fought alongside James. He must have seen the potential in you."

Adam let out a shaky chuckle as he wiped the tears from his face, "W-was it really worth all of this?"

"Well," Elliott said, "This place needed a bit of a purging- ACK! My classmates!"

"Wh-wha?"

"Remember what Tower said? 'The wolf boy's academy friends seem to be tearing things up in the security wing.' We have to make sure they're okay!"

Adam gasped, "Hell! You're right! Argh! I just want this to be over... I want to be able to mourn in peace."

Elliott let out an empathetic sigh, "Me too." Then he turned to the other Bureau Agents who were occupied with recovering from the previous battles. He turned back to Adam.

"I think it will be just us from here on out," Elliott said, holding a hand out for Adam.

Adam gently smiled and took Elliott's hand. "Let's go, then."

17:

Back in the maintenance halls of the Bureau Arcana, the motley crew of students rested near an air duct, awaiting Miles/Zak and Killian reconvening with them. Misha Woods stared anxiously through the concrete ceiling, waiting to see any hint of their friends' aura. Royce Grayson stared at the floor, fists clenched tight, shaking with rage, rage for both Agent Moon for using him, and himself for being foolish enough to be used. Quinton Cade tried to calm Royce down by patting their back... it did very little to help. Andrew Cade was staring at his laptop, looking through The Bureau's security cameras. Maxwell was nearby, but nowhere to be seen. He'd had enough of being observed.

Royce raised his fist, eyes hidden behind the glare of his glasses. Before anyone could stop him, he thrust his fist into the hard concrete wall with all his strength. To Royce's surprise, his fist cratered the wall.

Misha yelped out and clutched his chest due to the loud noise caused by the impact between Royce's fist and concrete.

"God damn... nerd rage much?" Quinton said, eyes wide.

"I mean..." Andrew said, "Can you blame him?"

Quinton shrugged and gave Royce another back pat, but with a hint of trepidation. "H-how's your hand?"

Royce carefully pulled his hand from the cratered wall and examined it with the analytical reflex learned from his intense research. "P-perhaps... Even when human... I have some latent lycanthropic... uh... strength?" he said, the spark of academic obsession soothing his rage. Despite Agent Moon's deception, Royce still had plenty to learn, to research... He would undo what Moon had done, he *would* find a cure for werewolfism.

Quinton clasped his hands excitedly on Royce's back and said, "You better use that latent strength to punch that screwed up doctor in his screwed up face."

Royce cracked a smile and let himself chuckle. Just then, the grate of the air vent was kicked out, Killian's combat boot thrusting from the newly created opening. Again, Misha yelped and clutched his chest. Killian slid out and hit the ground with a thud, covered in dust from the air ducts. Soon after, Miles/Zak followed, falling right onto Killian. Killian tried to scowl, but his face was stuck in a dumbfounded, embarrassed smirk. Quinton snickered, and Killian immediately shoved Miles/Zak off of him.

"What took you two so long?" Quinton said with a wide smirk.

"Bitch ass rich boy is bad with direction. *Sor-ry!*" Killian said, finally regaining his scowl.

Miles/Zak sighed and brushed the dust from his blazer with a measured and dignified steadiness. "Uh huh, sure," Miles/Zak said. He stood up and held out a hand for Killian. Killian narrowed his eyes and stood up on his own.

"I'm just glad you two didn't kill each other!" Misha said, hugging both Miles/Zak and Killian. Miles/Zak hugged back. Killian sighed and did the same.

"So, we got wolf boy, what's the plan now? Find the pipsqueak busybody?" Killian said, not sustaining the hug any more than he felt he needed to.

"Yeup," Andrew said, typing away on his laptop to cycle through security camera feeds. Each camera showed a similar sight: Minor Arcana agents fighting off Agent Moon's abominations which have now ventured from the security wing to wreak havoc throughout the whole of the Bureau Arcana.

Andrew flipped through the camera feeds until, finally, he found Elliott. "Security cams show him in the Admin wing with… Oh hey it's Adam! We like Adam, right?"

Andrew looked around to see everyone nodding, apart from Maxwell who stuck his arm out from behind a series of stacked boxes, giving a thumbs up.

Andrew flipped the screen around to show Elliott and Adam fighting Agent Moon's failed experiments. As Adam used all the magic in his arsenal, fire, darkness, lightning, even astral magic, each of the students smiled with a sense of pride, like somehow, through their individual experiences with Adam, they were partly helping protect Elliott.

"Oh god..." Miles said, "We just fought ourselves away from those monsters. Must we thrust ourselves back into the fray?"

"I might be able to provide you with some... assistance," came an ethereal voice that echoed through the halls. The students turned towards the source of the voice. Osric Ashford stood, leaning on his cane as his ghastly eyes met with each of the students.

The students, still wary of The Bureau, tensed up and looked ready to fight. Maxwell emerged from his hiding place and tried to grab Osric, but Maxwell's hand passed right through him. Osric turned towards Maxwell, an annoyed expression on his face as if a fly just landed on him. Maxwell blinked in surprise and slowly retreated back to the shadows. Osric's tired gaze slowly moved back to the other students.

Royce's eyes lit up like a nature documentarian catching a glimpse of a rare species of animal. "A spectral being! We read about these in 'Intro to Metahuman Biology!'"

"A g-g-ghost?" Misha said, hiding behind Killian.

"A ghost!" The Cade twins said in unison, rushing towards the ghost. They both poked into Osric's intangible form, shivering from the intense cold within.

"Guys...' Miles said, "Perhaps we shouldn't irritate someone who just offered us assistance."

"Verily..." Osric said. He stepped forward, walking right through the Cade twins. Both twins froze and shivered hard, like ice had gripped their very hearts.

"How do we know we can trust you?" Killian said, reflexively baring his teeth at the spectral Bureau agent.

"I suppose you can't. I can simply offer my intentions," Osric replied, gesturing with an antiquated formality, "It is my duty to ensure the sustained operations of the Bureau Arcana. Current management has... Well, you have seen. It behooves me and The Bureau to ensure you succeed in your goal. It is my hope that your younger generation can perhaps root out the systemic rot I have seen fester in the old bones of this facility."

Killian's tone immediately changed, and he let out a laugh. "Oh, I like the cut of this man's jib!"

Osric stared at Killian with confusion, "I beg your pardon?"

"Pfff. It's slang, old man," Killian said.

"Ah... I see," Osric said. If a ghost could blush, Osric would.

"So, what exactly are you offering us?" Miles said, speaking with the transactional charisma of someone used to witnessing backroom deals.

"Information. You see, these walls have ears..." Osric said, gesturing to himself, "...and I am always listening. Your friends are heading to the science and medical wing. Agent Moon is there waiting to ensnare them.

"And?" Quinton asked.

"Yeah, we're on the opposite side of the facility from the science and medical wing!" Andrew said.

Osric sighed and shook his head. "I know this building better than anyone on or outside this Earth. Shortcuts and secrets abound." He placed a hand on one of the many pipes running along the concrete walls. He turned to Quinton and gestured for them to approach.

Quinton ran up and placed his hand where Osric's was. He gripped onto the pipe. There was a click, then the sound of grinding stone as a part of the wall receded, revealing a dark, narrow path.

"This corridor should bring you straight to where you need to be. I wish I could provide more... hands on assistance, but alas..." Osric's voice trailed off, and his hand phased through the wall.

"Thank ya, ghost ex machina!" Quinton said, walking through Osric with one more intense shiver.

"My pleasure. Please. Take care of this place," Osric said before bowing, floating up through the ceiling.

Royce cracked his neck as he was the first one to enter the tunnel, "This all feels... very final. Are you all ready?"

"Certainly," Miles said before twitching, letting Zak take

over.

"Absoluuutly!" Zak said.

"As ready as I'll ever be," Killian said, arms crossed.

Maxwell emerged from the shadows and stood up straight and tall, giving an exaggerated and theatrical salute.

"Y-yeah!" Misha said, fist pumping with an excited but nervous determination.

"Hell yeah!" Quinton said,

"Let's go!" Andrew said.

Then, together, the rogue students of the Academy Arcana entered the tunnel.

18:

Agent Moon rushed through the sterile halls of the Science and Medical wing. He was gritting his teeth and clutching his shattered wrist as he ran as fast as he could, praying his abominations wouldn't catch up to him after they tore through the students. He ran until he made it to the observation theater's holding cell where he closed the door and collapsed onto the gurney to let himself catch his breath.

He turned his head to shield his eyes from the blinding, almost theatrical lights that shone into the observation cell, and his eyes fell upon the pair of manacles that originally bound Royce Grayson to this very bed. He narrowed his eyes, almost in mourning. All the time and effort he put into Project Moonlight, and it was all becoming undone.

There was a flash of movement in the corner of his eye, and he turned to look through the glass walls. Director Gecko burst into the theater's audience, a trail of smoke in his wake. He faced the open door, his favorite brand of cigarette casually hanging from his fingers in one hand, and his pure silver knife held firmly in the other.

Through the smoke obscuring the doorway leapt two of Moon's monstrosities. Gecko turned to the side as both creatures leapt past. At the same time, Gecko swung the knife upward, impaling the first creature under the chin. The creature went limp, held up by Gecko's strength.

The second creature pounced on Gecko from behind. In response, he grabbed the creature as he ducked, using its momentum to fling it across the audience and into the observation cell's glass. Before the second creature could reorient itself, Gecko unsheathed his knife from the first monster and threw it towards the second. With a wet, almost hollow thud, the knife buried itself in the second creature's forehead.

Agent Moon watched as the second dead creature slid down the glass, revealing Gecko, who took a drag of his cigarette. The reflection of his glasses through the smoke were fixed on Agent Moon.

Director Gecko spoke, an agitated edge to his voice. "Quite the mess you've made, doctor."

"Blame those brat students that Magician recruited. This all would have been much smoother without them interfering," Agent Moon argued.

"You got outwitted by a bunch of Academy students?" Director Gecko asked, stepping towards the railing at the edge of the observation gallery.

Agent Moon's face burned with humiliation, "How was I supposed to expect a bunch of students to break into our damn headquarters? Isn't this your show to run?"

Director Gecko aggressively cracked his neck and slowly transformed into a wisp of smoke. The smoke wafted through the ventilation holes of the observation cell, then Gecko morphed back into his human form, head still a swirl of smoke. He leaned over Agent Moon in a dominating pose.

"My 'show' is in the midst of a civil war, and thanks to you, not only are we dealing with Graves and his sympathizers, now we are dealing with a hoard of uncontrollable beasts," Director Gecko intoned, flicking his cigarette stub onto Agent Moon.

Agent Moon clenched his fists, including his shattered hand, and winced, "What would you have me do?"

Director Gecko reached into his vest pocket and pulled out his carton of cigs and a match. With the dexterity of someone who has done it thousands of times, Gecko ignited the match and lit his cigarette in one swift motion. He brought the cigarette to the horizon of smoke surrounding his head and inhaled. The smoke swirled from the filter of the cigarette and combined with the rest of the smoke around Gecko as he thought.

"The werewolf boy. Did you give him a dose of Project Moonlight?" Gecko asked.

"No," Agent Moon said, "I had it in a syringe and ready to go but..."

"Do you still have the syringe?" Gecko asked icily, cutting off Agent Moon.

"Yes, but without a subject... it's useless."

"Good thing we have a prime candidate right here," Agent Gecko said, the glare of his glasses shining intensely even through his smoke. They were aimed directly at Agent Moon.

Agent Moon's eyes flashed with realization. He opened his mouth to argue, but before any words could come out, a door in the observation gallery burst open. Killian and Royce led the charge with Miles/Zak and the Cade twins following close behind. Misha decided he worked better as support and stayed in the back. Maxwell refused to go through the most visible door and was somewhere in the shadows... Watching. Waiting.

Director Gecko's smoky head slowly turned towards the students. He let out a dark chuckle and glanced back at Agent Moon, "Another failure to add to your belt, Doctor."

Agent Moon's eyes drifted from Gecko to the students. His lips twitched into a crazed smile and started laughing. He was so close to something great, so close to completing his research... only to trip at the finish line. Well... Perhaps not quite. This last sample... Agent Moon pulled it from his lab coat with a shaky hand. If this worked... perhaps his legacy would be secured. If he did nothing, he was surely a dead man... but if Project Moonlight worked... He would be immortal, even if as a beast.

As Agent Moon eyed his life's work distilled, contemplating perhaps his final sapient choice in this life, Director Gecko hummed casually and turned to search the cupboards and cabinets housed in the observation cell.

"You still keep one of those lycanthropic repellent devices here, yes? Ah, perfect." Director Gecko said, pulling out the megaphone-like device that Killian recognized being used on Royce. Director Gecko held the device against his cocked hip, watching Agent Moon with a hint of amusement.

Agent Moon stabbed the syringe into his own chest.

In the halls of the Science and Medical wing, Elliott and Adam stood, doubled over and breathing heavily.

Elliott looked up at Adam and spoke between winded panting, "Looks like you learned more than any university could teach ya while I was gone, eh?"

Adam was panting less heavily and let out a sheepish chuckle. "James was a good mentor but... I only trained this hard in the hopes that I would somehow find you again."

Elliott shook his head, cheeks dusted with a light blush. "Well, it looks like it paid off."

As they spoke, a broken gargle of a howl echoed down the hall. A disheveled, skinny abomination turned the corner. Its fur was burnt, and its body riddled with bullet holes. Despite the damage, it relentlessly stumbled towards Adam and Elliott. The abomination's knee snapped from fatigue and caused it to crumple to the ground, but it continued... crawling, growling with a feral fury.

Elliott let out an anxious, annoyed whimper and raised his pistol. He pulled the trigger only for the hammer to click. "God dammnnn it! Of all the magic you've learned, you couldn't learn to conjure up silver bullets or something?"

"Sor-ry!" Adam groaned, "Looks like we gotta run some more. I'm pretty sure the observation theater has some silver bullets." Then he broke off in a run down the halls of the Science and Medical wing.

"Listen, I've been dead for a few years! I wasn't exactly keeping up with my cardio!" Elliott said, chasing after Adam.

Adam led the way to the observation cell and opened the door for Elliott to rush in. Adam followed and closed the door behind him, knocking a cabinet down to block the door...

...Then they turned around. Director Gecko chuckled, "Well, hello there, interlopers. You always seem to appear when you are least wanted."

Elliott's eyes widened. He reflexively raised the pistol.

Director Gecko whooshed through the air like a wraith of smoke and grabbed the barrel of Elliott's pistol. He twisted it out of Elliott's grip and disassembled the entire gun, throwing the parts casually onto the floor. Gecko then grabbed Elliott's wrist and twisted it too, bringing Elliott to the floor.

The motley crew of students in the observation gallery gasped and cried out Elliott's name. They rushed to the edge of the safety glass separating them.

Adam was stunned by fear for just a moment. Here he was, a mere rookie standing before the executive director of the whole of the Bureau Arcana. He fought through his nerves and engulfed his hands in flames. Adam wound up to throw a punch, but Gecko turned, and grabbed Adam's fist, snuffing out their flame with thick, smothering smoke. Just like Elliott, Gecko twisted Adam's wrist to incapacitate and bring him to his knees. Gecko made them both face Agent Moon.

All of Agent Moon's muscles tensed up, forcing him to curl into a ball. He writhed, and his muscles bulged. Fur slowly covered his entire form. Agent Moon's groans of agony slowly morphed into growls of hunger. His face contorted and morphed into a monstrous maw.

Elliott struggled fruitlessly in Director Gecko's grip and watched in horror as Agent Moon transformed. His eyes flicked around anxiously and landed on Adam who stared back at Elliott. Adam's eyes seemed to say, "I'm sorry." Did Elliott come back from hell just to die again here?

Elliott's eyes flicked to the students, his friends, who were all pounding desperately against the safety glass... All except Maxwell. Maxwell was invisible to everyone else, but Elliott saw him clearly, shrouded in shadow. Maxwell was still. His hand was pressed against the glass. Elliott's eyes locked onto Maxwell's bright blue eyes... Maxwell nodded, as if he knew it was certain Elliott would make it out, then he disappeared into the darkness.

By the time Maxwell was out of sight, Agent Moon stood eight feet tall, muscles bulging so large that they ripped through the skinny doctor's clothes. His claws were razor sharp and glistened under the medical lights of the observation cell. The culmination of all of Project Moonlight's data led to this... perfect specimen. At least that's what Agent Moon thought... or would have thought, had he any humanity left.

The Monstrous Moon took a step forward, and Director Gecko immediately let go of Elliott and activated his anti-lycanthropic device. A high-pitched whine filled the air and Elliott fell onto his hands and knees right in front of The Monstrous Moon, who growled and tensed up, seemingly frozen in place.

"Well, well, well," Director Gecko said, "Perhaps your replacement could make use of your research yet."

Adam watched as Moon was paralyzed. This was an extra moment to think... Don't waste it. He looked at the students pounding at the glass. Each and every one of them were here, involved with the Bureau, because of him... He couldn't just sit here and do nothing. After everything he's learned from them, there must be something he could do. He looked to Elliott. Elliott stared back with a determined gaze. The two old friends said nothing, but they nodded to each other.

Adam closed his eyes and took a deep breath. He focused as hard as he could. When he opened his eyes, a bolt of lightning shot from his free hand, but instead of being aimed at Director Gecko, or Moon, the lightning struck the anti-lycanthropic device.

The high-pitched whine of the device ceased, and in a brief flash of panic, Gecko let go of Adam. Adam took this opportunity and dove onto Elliott. Adam clutched Elliott tight, trying to wrap his arms as securely around them as he could.

The Monstrous Moon howled, free from the paralyzing eminence of the anti-lycanthropic device. Its feral eyes locked on Elliott and Adam, and it pounced.

Elliott was fully expecting the sharp sensation of his own impalement, but instead, he felt a cold rush. He looked around to find himself outside the observation cell and instead in the back of the gallery overlooking it. Adam let go of Elliott, and together, they looked into the observation cell.

Director Gecko was staring at them with stunned intensity. He simply didn't have time to react when Moon plunged his claw straight through his chest from behind. Gecko hung motionless from Moon's blood and viscera-covered claw. A long strand of ash fell from Gecko's smoldering cigarette. Director Gecko dropped the cigarette, and slowly... his body smoldered away into drifting smoke...

All of the students except Royce rushed to Elliott and Adam's side. Maxwell scooped Elliott up and squeezed them tight. "Aaaack!" Elliott wheezed. The breath was squeezed out of him as he hugged Maxwell back.

"Careful, you might break the poor pipsqueak," Killian said before yelping out in pain, "Ow!"

Miles/Zak slapped Killian upside the back of the head. Killian growled and narrowed his eyes at Miles/Zak. He reflexively wanted to curse out the privileged rich kid, but when he glared into Miles's eyes, he couldn't help but see the master thief he so deeply admired. An ever so slight blush dusted his cheeks. The twins noticed the blush and snickered to each other. This only worsened Killian's blush.

Misha gave Killian a pat on the back, and while it was meant with the best of intentions, Killian felt it as patronizing, so he grit his teeth.

Adam stood up and brushed himself off. "Glad to see you're all getting along!" he said, smiling at the motley crew of Academy Arcana students. He smiled with a bit of nostalgia for his days at the academy before his gaze drifted to Royce.

Royce was inches from the protective glass of the observation cell, a look of existential disgust on his face as he stared into the blood-crazed eyes of the transformed Agent Moon. Moon stared back.

The former Agent Moon slammed its fist into the safety glass, and while it was designed to withstand the impact of werewolves, or other potentially hazardous entities The Bureau may encounter, Agent Moon's Project Moonlight-enhanced fist cracked the glass. Royce, instead of flinching, bared his teeth and flashed large, sharp canines. Royce's classmates rushed to Royce's side as Moon smashed its fist against the glass once more, further cracking it.

Royce let out an almost feral sounding growl. He held out his arms, "One scratch and you will be just like me. Let me handle him."

"There should be some silver bullets in one of the cabinets in there," Adam said as he led the students away from the splintering glass.

"Anyone have a gun?" Elliott asked, looking around, "No? Well then we also gotta reassemble the one in there."

Moon pounded the glass again. Its fist broke through, leaving a jagged hole in the glass.

"Sounds like we have a plan then," Adam said with a nervous gulp.

"We'll help ya from the back, Royce!" Quinton said, giving a thumbs up.

Royce nodded and stared down Moon with a vicious intensity. Moon brought his fist back, and with one final punch, the glass wall shattered completely. Unrestricted by the safety barrier, Moon effortlessly climbed up onto the observation gallery, letting out a low, feral growl as he approached Royce.

Royce screamed as he threw a wild haymaker that made impact with Moon's monstrous jaw. Moon stumbled, swiping its massive claws wildly as it howled in pain. Royce dodged back, but he was a nerd, not a gymnast. He fell on his ass right as Moon's claw swung over him.

A deep growl escaped Moon's throat as it refocused on Royce. It arched its back, ready to pounce...

Suddenly, a bright flash filled the gallery. A gout of flame blasted into Moon, staggering it back. Two spears of lightning struck the monstrous wolf, causing the creature's muscles to convulse. Finally, a blast of blue astral energy drilled into the abominable doctor.

Royce turned to see Killian, the Cade twins, and Misha; all with their arms outstretched as they focused all their willpower into attacking Moon.

Moon's growl only got louder, morphing into a furious howl. Moon's fur smoldered but refused to ignite. Its muscles convulsed but continued to move. The monster was slowed, but it wasn't stopped. Even with their powers combined, it only hurt Moon, made it angrier...

Through the bombardment of magic, Moon slowly staggered towards the four attacking students. Royce growled and forced himself up, delivering a powerful uppercut to Moon's chin, redirecting attention back to himself. Moon thrust its claw towards Royce, but thanks to his classmates, he was able to dodge and respond with a counter jab. Each hit only angered Moon more and more, the magic barreling into him having less and less of an effect as the students energy waned and faded. It wouldn't be long before Moon would win this game of attrition.

While the two wolfen scientists brawled, Maxwell and Elliott dove into the now unshielded observation cell. Maxwell moved with almost blinding swiftness as he searched the cabinets, desks, and drawers for silver bullets. Elliott moved with sharp, precise dexterity as he gathered and reassembled each piece of the disassembled pistol.

Once the gun was reassembled, Maxwell tossed a box of silver bullets to Elliott. Elliott loaded the gun as fast as he could and took aim. Through the blur of fire and lightning and magic, he couldn't get a clear shot.

"Here!" Adam shouted. Elliott turned to see Adam, gesturing for the gun from the gallery. Without a moment's hesitation, Elliott tossed the gun to Adam. Adam caught the pistol full of silver bullets, then readied himself.

The next moment, Adam blinked. He warped himself between Royce and Moon, and he unleashed a tremendous arcane blast. The blast was a powerful cocktail of everything he learned working for the Bureau… And it was just enough to stagger Moon.

The observation theater went silent, nothing but the sound of ringing filled everyone's ears. The students recoiled and covered their eyes from the intense light. Adam lifted the gun… and his body failed him. With the last of his strength, he turned to Royce and thought back to the first time he saw Royce in the Westridge forest. He remembered how James had done this to save him. Adam supposed it was his turn. He collapsed, and the gun spilled from his hand.

Despite being closest to the blast, Royce was the first to recover. He saw Adam in front of him, unconscious, and the gun, feet away from him. Further ahead, he saw Moon already returning to its feet.

Royce, ever the obsessive thinker, the analyzer, the

scientist, didn't have time to think. He had to move on instinct. Royce dove for the gun right as Moon lunged. Had there been even the slightest hesitation, even a moment of contemplation, Moon's claw would have gone through Royce like it went through Gecko. But Royce stood firm and fired. Each pure silver bullet hit its mark.

The ringing in the air slowly faded… Agent Moon stood… but its eyes were dull… Eventually, the hulking mass of feral flesh fell back… and crashed into the observation cell. Dead.

19:

Royce stood, arm locked out straight, gun in hand. Smoke drifted from the pistol's barrel. Slowly, he took a step and looked over the edge into the observation cell. He stared down at Moon. Its chest wasn't moving.

After staring silently at the dead Moon for some time, finally satisfied with their demise, Royce dropped the gun. Killian was quick to scoop up the gun, reload it with more silver bullets, and emptied the magazine into the monster's corpse. He didn't stop until there were no more silver bullets to fire.

Miles/Zak watched the two and saw their pent-up pain finally have some release. Zak felt that catharsis along with Royce and Killian. Miles still had worry in his heart… His family was directly responsible for funding this after all. Miles shook his head and turned to the unmoving body of Adam Nolan.

Elliott rushed to Adam's limp body and gave him a gentle slap. "Okay. C'mon buddy," Elliott said, trying to wake Adam. The longer Adam didn't respond, the more panicked Elliott's voice became. Elliott's shakily hands pressed two fingers against Adam's carotid artery. He felt no pulse.

Elliott's face went white. He slapped Adam harder. "C'MON BUDDY!" He screamed, desperation in his voice. "Not now! Not after all this!" If this was in Fate's plan, Elliott was gonna strangle that bastard. In a panic, Elliott started performing chest compressions in a desperate attempt to revive his old friend.

Quinton rushed to Adam's side and coldly said, "Clear."
Elliott didn't even hear him.

"I said 'clear!'" Quinton repeated, more firm. Still, Elliott was unmoving. It wasn't until Maxwell pulled Elliott away that he grasped what Quinton was trying.

Quinton ripped Adam's bureau shirt open to expose the unconscious agent's chest. Quinton then rubbed his hands together, charging them up with a steady, even glow of electricity. Finally, he placed his hands on Adam's chest, one above their heart, and one below. Like a defibrillator, Quinton sent the electricity into Adam's body, which arched up from the jolt, before collapsing again. Andrew rushed to his brother's side and joined him.

"Clear," they said in unison before both sent a jolt into Adam.

Adam's body jolted up as he took in a violent gasp. The electricity coursing through his body made his muscles twitchy. His eyes were wide, pupils dilated, as if he had just been spiked with adrenaline. His shaky hands gripped onto the Cade Twins' sleeves, and he looked around, reorienting himself.

Misha gasped, "A-Adam! Y-your aura! I-I can see it!"

The words slowly penetrated Adam's newly conscious brain, and he started laughing. He clutched his chest and turned to Elliott.

"Do you think Fate is satisfied?" Adam asked.

20:

Back in the archives, Nathaniel Cross paced his aisles of files. Damien Cross and Agent Wheel were lying on the ground by Nathanial's desk, with Jacqueline Wells tending to their wounds.

"How are they?" Nathaniel asked, subtly but anxiously tapping his fingers along the spine of the file marked Adam Nolan.

"We're fiiiine!" Agent Wheel said, calling out to Nathanial. His voice had a self-assuredness in it that made Damien groan.

Damien rubbed his temples as he glanced down at the thick wrap of gauss around his chest. "As fine as I can be given the situation."

Jaq leaned against the side of Nathaniel's desk, "Yeah. I am certain they will make a full recovery," she said, feeling herself relax.

Nathaniel relaxed as well. He pulled Adam's file from the shelf and flipped through to the end. His eyes widened as he read through a summary of what had just occurred in the observation theater.

"Well, well, well," Nathaniel said.

"Eh?" Agent Wheel asked, tilting his head. In response, Nathaniel tossed the file over to Damien.

"Flip to the last page," Nathaniel said, "How do you think that would affect Magician's deal?'"

"Eh? Let me see!" Agent Wheel begged. Damien responded by flipping through to the last page of Adam's file. His eyes, too, widened.

"Well," Damien said with a pleased smirk, "Whatever deal made for Adam's life would be null and void." Then, finally, he handed the file to Agent Wheel.

Agent Wheel swiped the file and read it. He started chuckling uncontrollably. He handed the file to Jaq, who waved it off. She was tired of trying to understand the machinations of Fate.

Once Agent Wheel's chucking ceased, he put the file down and sighed, "That twist of fate surely is quite the wild card."

21:

The Executive Director's office was empty and silent… cold… The chaos flooding the rest of The Bureau seemed to be completely sealed off from this sanctum.

The silence was broken by a soft hiss as a faint wisp of smoke floated through the air. Slowly, a thick, faintly red cloud grew. From the cloud of smoke, the bloodied hand of Emperor Gecko emerged and slapped onto the top of his desk. The smoke around Gecko dissipated and he fell to his knees, his free hand clutching the gaping wound in his chest. The smoke that so often covered his face was faded and now only covered a third of his aged yet powerful features. Even losing blood, his brow was determined and dedicated.

Emperor Gecko slowly brought himself back to his feet when a gunshot rang out. A bullet struck the desk inches from

Gecko's hand. Gecko turned towards where the shot came from to see James Graves slumped against the wall, leaning against a streak of his own blood.

A gun hung from James's non-dominant hand, the slide locked back after firing the last round it had. James's right arm had been obliterated by Agent Tower's explosives. Along with his right arm, his right leg was a mangled mess of ripped flesh and shattered bone. James's clothes were half burnt and torn away, and half of his face was masked in his own dried blood.

Gecko sneered at James, his voice weak. "You... Ruined... Everything... Damn you..." The hatred he felt for James seemed to invigorate Gecko, and he began a slow, deliberate trudge towards James. "We are... doomed"

James lifted the spent gun in a daze and tried to pull the trigger to no effect. He dropped the gun and forced himself to move from the wall. James carefully limped towards Gecko, being sure to put as little pressure on his ruined leg as he could.

"Doomed?" James boomed with a steady, strong voice, refusing to let his voice be as weak as his body. "The Bureau, under your watch, with all its might and resources... couldn't even quell a handful of insubordinate agents. Whatever threat you fear... If you were in charge, we would already be doomed."

By the time James finished speaking, Gecko was only a foot away. Gecko's one unobscured and bloodshot eye stared into James with a deep resentment. Everything Gecko fought for... It couldn't be for nothing... He refused. He could still come out of this.

Gecko lunged at James and wrapped his hands around his neck. The sudden pressure on James's stance caused his damaged leg to give out. As the two men fell to the floor, James swung his undamaged fist into Gecko's face, shattering his glasses. Gecko seethed through the pain and only tightened his hands around James's neck.

James gripped Gecko's hands with both his good and shredded hand. He screamed through the pain as he forced his ruined hand to pry Gecko's from his throat. Gecko tried to keep his grip, but James's struggle made Gecko's hands slip on blood and release him. James tried to reposition himself on top of Gecko, but Gecko rolled away, leaving a trail of blood in his wake.

Gecko forced himself to his feet with great effort, clutching his wound as he stared at James. He just… had to outlast him… But James, too, forced himself to his feet. James stepped towards Gecko, arms raised in a fighter's stance. Gecko grit his teeth and did the same.

Both men shook as their bodies went into shock from blood loss. Still, they squared up with each other. Gecko threw the first punch. It hit James square in the bloodied side of his face. The impact staggered James, but he retaliated with a quick jab with his good hand. Gecko easily blocked it.

James could barely see Gecko's wicked smirk through the smoke. James's eyes focused and found an opening. He used all his willpower to force his ruined right hand into a fist and swung to deliver a devastating haymaker to Gecko's skull. The impact was so powerful that the whiplash of Gecko's head left a smear of smoke through the air.

Gecko stumbled to the side and fell to his knees. Gecko waited until James was close enough and pulled out his knife, swiftly swiping for James. James grabbed the blade with his ruined hand while his undamaged arm drove into Gecko's wound. He grabbed hold of the first thing inside Gecko he could and pulled. With a grotesque snap, James pulled a rib from Gecko's chest. Gecko screamed out in agony and released the knife.

James forced his wrecked hand to wrap around the handle of the knife and drove it into Gecko's neck.

Gecko staggered back and clutched his profusely bleeding neck, eyes locked on James's. Gecko fell to his knees. As the blood poured from his neck, the smoke around Gecko's face slowly dissipated. The last of the smoke cleared and fully revealed Gecko's dark gray eyes, ever locked to James's until… finally… the life drained from him and he collapsed.

James made as sure as he could that Gecko was well and truly dead, and only when there was no doubt left in his mind, he let himself collapse. His body fell right over the Bureau Arcana emblem embedded in the floor. Slowly, the raven and eye of the emblem were obscured by James's blood.

The rest was in Fate's hands now.

Chapter 11:
The Aftermath

01:

[[Director Of Archival, Agent Hierophant's report: Project Moonlight outbreak]]
Aftermath:
This section of the report is an attempt to pick up the pieces after the surviving agents of the Bureau Arcana contained and neutralized the entities related to the project identified only as "Moonlight."
I have cross referenced all notes, files, and reports related to Project Moonlight, and connected every distinct subject to a semi-lycanthropic corpse to ensure that each and every possibility for further outbreak was accounted for. Each subject was neutralized with a silver bullet to the head.
The Project Moonlight outbreak was devastating to the Bureau Arcana. A significant number of The Bureau's Major Arcana ranked Directors have died during the outbreak, or as a direct or indirect result of its development.

Fool (Rookies): Only one agent currently has the rank of Fool: Adam Nolan. Alive. Recovering from minor injuries. No injuries due to lycanthropy contact.
Magician (Director of Special Ops): While no body was found, Agent Magician is presumed dead. Presumed cause of death:

immolation due to Agent Tower's hand grenade in the Bureau's archives.

High Priestess (Director of Academia): Alive. Agent High Priestess was stationed at the Academy Arcana during the outbreak. Connection to Project Moonlight: None.

Empress (Director of Communications): Alive. Agent Empress was on the roof, caring for her birds during the outbreak. Since she is a frail old lady with little combat capabilities, she barricaded herself on the roof until the coast was clear. Connection to Project Moonlight: None.

Emperor (Executive Director): Dead. Cause of death: Throat slit in Executive office during the outbreak. Perpetrator, unknown.

Hierophant (Director of Archival): Alive. Primarily in the archives during the outbreak. Lead agent in charge of investigating the aftermath. Connection to Project Moonlight: Aware but opposed to its development.

Lovers (Director of Sociology): Dead. Cause of death: Lacerations caused by Project Moonlight subjects during outbreak while defending Minor Arcanas.

Chariot (Director of Engineering): Dead. Cause of death: Bitten by Project Moonlight subjects while supplying agents with arms and ammunition.

Strength (Director of Medicine): Alive. In the archives during the outbreak. Tended to the wounded before the science and medical wing was fully cleared.

Hermit (Director of Stealth): Dead. Cause of Death: Fell into the abyss during the Sharp Manor incident.

The Aftermath

Wheel Of Fortune (Director of Statistics): Alive. Recovering from minor injuries. No injuries due to lycanthropic contact.

Justice (Director of Ethics): Fired just before Project Moonlight began development.

Hanged Man (Director of Intelligence): Dead. Cause of Death: Severe blood loss due to lacerations received during lycanthropic encounter. Silver bullet gunshot sustained postmortem.

Death (Director of ▮▮▮▮▮▮▮▮): ▮▮▮▮▮▮▮▮▮▮▮▮

Temperance (Director of Arcane ops): Alive. Agent Temperance was overseas on an unrelated mission. Connection to Project Moonlight: None.

Devil (Director of Legal): Alive. Sustained significant injuries during the outbreak. Recovering. No injuries due to lycanthropic contact.

Tower (Director of Munitions): Dead. Cause of Death: Self-immolation by hand grenade in the archives during the outbreak.

Star (Director Of Astronomy): Dead. Cause of Death, blood loss due to altercation with Devil and Hierophant in the Archives Astral Plane.

Moon (Director of Research): Dead. Cause of Death, Multiple silver bullet wounds after subjecting self to Project Moonlight in the observation theater.

Sun (Director of Technology): Dead. Cause of Death: Executed by Director Emperor. Disposed of in the astral forest before the outbreak. Body has been recovered and will be given a proper ceremony.

Judgement (Director of Security): Alive. Lead the charge fighting of the subjects of Project Moonlight along with several Minor Arcanas. No injuries sustained. Connection to Project Moonlight: "vehemently opposed to its development."

World (Director of Facilities): For the sake of this report, Agent World is, for all intents and purposes, alive. Assisted with evacuation during the outbreak. No injuries sustained. Connection to Project Moonlight: opposed to its development.

During the outbreak, several Minor Arcana and Academy Arcana students were present at the Bureau Arcana Headquarters. I will go into more detail in a future report.

02:

It was the night after the outbreak of Project Moonlight. Miles Prince stood on the roof of the Academy Arcana's library. In one hand was a half-eaten hamburger that Z'ak'Aroth had been in the middle of enjoying. In the other hand was a cellphone whose ringing had interrupted Zak and his burger. Miles held the phone half a foot away from his head as his father screamed through its speakers. Mr. Prince was furious about the failed investment of Project Moonlight, and although he had no idea Miles was involved with its failure, the Prince heir was always the lightning rod for frustrations regarding any of his family's failures.

Miles stared at the moon, not listening to a single word his father said. He looked at the burger in his left hand and sighed. The sigh made Mr. Prince quiet on the other end of the phone.

"What was that?" Mr. Prince demanded, voice stern and furious, entitled to an apology.

Miles simply laughed. This only further irritated the man

on the other end of the phone. Miles only laughed louder.

"Miles Prince. What has gotten into you!?" came the voice from the other end of the phone.

"Oh. I just realized... I don't care," Miles said before hanging up on his father. Immediately, the phone rang again. Miles let it. Instead, he took a bite of his burger. Internally, Zak mewled with delight.

Behind him, Killian Wilkes stood, leaning against the wall with one foot pressed into it. He couldn't help but snicker. Miles/Zak turned to the source of the sound.

"Well damn," Killian said, "I didn't think you had it in you. I think your Jack of Diamonds persona is starting to leak into your Heir To The Throne persona."

Miles sighed and crossed his arms defensively. "What do you want, Killian?"

"Just to talk," Killian said, kicking off the wall and walking over to Miles. He placed his arms on the railing overlooking The Academy.

"*Just* to talk?" Miles asked.

"I dunno," Killian said. He stared up at the moon, an ever so slight blush dusting his cheeks.

"What do you mean you don't know?" Miles asked, narrowing his eyes at Killian.

"Well, I don't really need to say anything, do I?" Killian said, eyes flicking over to Miles's deep green eye with a knowing smirk.

Miles sighed and tilted his head. *What's he thinking?* Miles thought.

I... I think it would be rude to tell you. Zak thought back, seeming flustered.

Miles sighed and turned back to Killian. "He isn't telling me."

"Well tough. Cuz I ain't sayin'," Killian replied. His blush deepened.

The two stayed silent for a long time, simply staring at the moon together. After a while, Miles noticed just how close Killian was. The look of disgust Killian usually had around Miles was gone. Instead, he looked... comfortable.

Eventually, Miles broke the silence. "How are you holding up? Will you tell me that, at least?" he said, a genuine hint of concern in his voice.

"I'm fine. I'm used to violence," Killian said with a sigh. He was fine, and the fact he was fine was the most upsetting thing about all that's happened. Still, it wasn't something he felt was worth commenting on. "What about you?"

"I'm fine. I'm used to peril," Miles replied, "You wouldn't believe the sick things I've seen as the Jack of Diamonds."

Killian chuckled and shook his head, "Yeah, I bet those rich pricks would be into some crazy shit."

"Heh. Is that why you're here? To hang out with your 'hero?'" Miles teased, leaning closer to Killian.

"Shut it before I throw you off this roof." Killian growled. Miles snickered.

Miles's body suddenly twitched. He hunched over with crooked posture and looked at Killian with two deep green eyes.

"Just ask him already!" Zak pleaded before twitching again. Miles's body stood up straight as Miles was given back control.

"Ask me what?" Miles asked, head tilted as he stared at Killian.

Killian sighed before letting out an exasperated groan. "Misha invited me to go camping in the campus outskirts. I… wantedtoinvitemmphhmmmm…." He said, before his voice trailed off. Miles stared at Killian with a baffled look.

Killian took a deep breath and tried again. "You're joining us," he said, "I wanna see how a privileged prick like you fares in the woods."

Miles couldn't help but smile. "Oh? Fine, if I must."

"Good. Now come on. Misha is waiting," Killian said, stepping away towards the roof exit. Miles followed when Zak gently broke into his thoughts.

Hold his hand, Zak thought.

"What?!" Miles said aloud.

Killian froze and turned to Miles. "What? Pussing out- h-huh? What are you…?"

Miles huffed and took Killian's hand but refused to look at Killian. Killian's heart pounded hard. His blush burned his cheeks,

The Aftermath

almost bright enough to illuminate the dark library roof. Killian tightened his grip around Miles's hand.

Suddenly, Miles yelped and yanked his hand away. Killian's hand was smoldering.

"Ow! You almost burned me!" Miles shouted.

"Well, *sor-ry!*" Killian screamed back sarcastically.

He really is sorry; he's just pretending to be sarcastic. Zak thought to Miles.

"Oh what*ever!*" Miles groaned.

The two bickered with each other all the way to the academy's outskirts. In the shadows of the academy plaza, Elliott Harding and Maxwell Sharp sat under a tree as they watched the punk and the prep.

Elliott chuckled. "I never would have expected them to be a couple."

Maxwell used sign language to respond, *"Opposites attract, you know."*

"Heh. Maybe that's why we get along so well." Elliott replied. Maxwell tilted his head, confused. His innocent blue eyes shone bright behind his white mask. Elliott opened his mouth to elaborate but closed it again. He didn't want to vocally bring attention to his height, or lack thereof.

Elliott cleared his throat, "C'mon. Let's check on Royce. First one seen by anyone else buys lunch tomorrow."

Maxwell stood up excitedly and cracked his knuckles before signing, *"game on."*

Elliott and Maxwell snuck through campus and into the academy labs. There, Royce Grayson and the Cade twins sat on lab stools, each with a controller in hand as they played a retro game together. Around them, a concerning number of empty energy drink cans were strewn about the lab.

The round came to an end, and Andrew Cade shot up excitedly.

"Yes! Wooop!" he said, celebrating his victory with a level of energy that seemed impossible given how late it was.

Royce growled with frustration and Quinton snickered and pat Royce on the back.

"Oh? Is that a bit of wolf I hear?" Quinton teased.

Royce bit his lip to stifle his growling and moved over to his workstation.

"Sadly," Royce said, voice low, but excited, "I think there will always be a bit of werewolf there. But! Now that my research is free of... malignant influence... I think a cure, or at least a treatment is possible."

The Cade Twins moved behind Royce and watched over his shoulder as he worked.

"Hell yeah!" Quinton said.

"I believe in you!" Andrew cheered.

03:

A month after the outbreak inside the Bureau Arcana, the day after a full moon, the surviving agents held a funeral for those who had fallen. It was a bright, sunny day. The sky was clear, and the air was crisp. Birds were chirping, and the flowers were in full bloom.

Adam found it all so mocking, the earth was simply indifferent to the heartbreak within him. If nothing else, it made the all-black mourning suit even more uncomfortably warm.

He stood over the tombstone for the person he only knew as Agent Hanged Man. The dirt below his feet was freshly packed six feet deep, somewhere underneath was the body of a man he had never even seen. Nevertheless, Adam mourned him, missed him. He was always a comforting voice, a reassuring presence. And now he's gone. Death and undeath were things The Bureau Arcana dealt with, but sometimes, death can't be undone.

Adam read the name engraved on the tombstone. "Spencer Carter, huh? Pleasure to finally meet you," he said. He couldn't help but chuckle.

Behind him came another chuckle. Agent Wheel Of Fortune stood, hands stuffed unceremoniously in his coat. Adam thought he looked strange wearing a traditional necktie and full blazer instead of a bow tie and vest. It looked serious, too serious for someone like Agent Wheel.

The Aftermath

"How ya feelin', Rookie?" Agent Wheel asked, his voice tinted with a hint of mourning.

"Confused," Adam replied, "Someone I thought was dead is actually alive, someone I never met in person is dead, and no one knows or will tell me if James is alive or dead."

Agent Wheel chuckled louder, "Welcome to the Bureau Arcana."

Adam sighed, "How do you deal with it?"

Agent Wheel tilted his head. "Huh? Oh uhm…" he said, scratching the back of his head, "I never really thought about it. After a while here, the absurd just becomes another part of the mundane."

Adam stared at Agent Wheel with a tired look. He turned to see the fresh resting places of the others who died since he joined The Bureau.

"What comes next? For The Bureau, I mean," Adam asked.

"Oh jeez. All business, just like James, eh?" Agent Wheel said with a playful smile. When he saw that Adam didn't return the expression, his own smile faded.

"Well," Agent Wheel said, "Step one would be to fill the newly opened positions. Hiero and Devil are leading that effort. I'm supposed to be there, too, but… I'm not one for making decisions. I just play the cards I'm dealt."

"I see," Adam said. He felt compelled to nod, but his heart just wasn't in it.

"What about you? What are your plans while we figure out where to assign ya?" Wheel asked.

"I'm going back to my hometown to catch up with Elliott. In fact, I should really get going," Adam said, cracking a small smile. Agent Wheel nodded as Adam started to walk off.

"Oh!" Agent Wheel shouted suddenly.

"Ack! Wha?" Adam squealed.

"Wesley Colt," Agent Wheel said.

"What?"

"My name is Wesley Colt," Agent Wheel repeated with a bright, optimistic smile, "I didn't want you to wait until it was carved into my tombstone."

04:

Damien Cross sat at the end of a long table in the Bureau Arcana Board room. Beside him, Nathaniel Cross sat, taking detailed, studious notes. Around the table, the remaining directors of the Bureau Arcana, minus Agent Wheel, sat.

"The motion on the table," Damien Cross said, "Is to confirm the slate chosen to take on the roles of our open director positions. Agent Hierophant, would you mind reading the open positions and candidates for us?"

Nathaniel Cross cleared his throat, "Ahem. Of course.

"It is this board's recommendation that the following positions be filled by the following persons/entities.

"The Magician: Adam Nolan.

"The Lovers: Miles Prince and Z'ak'Aroth.

"The Chariot: Quinton Cade.

"The Hermit: Maxwell Sharp.

"The Hanged Man: Elliott Harding.

"The Tower: Killian Wilkes.

"The Star: Misha Woods.

"The Moon: Royce Grayson.

"The Sun: Andrew Cade.

"We also recommend we reinstate the role of the Director of Ethics and designate it once more as Agent Justice.

"Any questions or objections?" Nathaniel Cross asked.

Agent High Priestess raised her hand, "Yes. Besides Adam, aren't these candidates still students at the Academy Arcana? Is it not a bit premature to assign them to the roles of directors?"

Agent World, Osric Ashford raised his ghostly hand to answer, "Yes. Although they are still students, analysis of their actions while inside the Bureau Arcana during the outbreak shows that each and every one of them have excellent proficiency in the skills related to their considered role. They will of course still finish training and work as rookies before officially being designated as directors, but I find it difficult to see anyone else in these positions."

"Thank you, Agent World," Damien said, "Anyone else?"

The Aftermath

Jacqueline Wells raised her hand, "Forgive me, but... I can't help but notice that the role of The Emperor was not listed. Has that not been assigned?"

Damien sighed, "We have a candidate in mind, but Agent Death and I are... in disagreement about said candidate's validity... But rest assured, I will make sure the role of Emperor is filled."

05:

The streets of Capstone Creek had hardly changed in the 4 years since Elliott last stepped foot there. The smell wafting from his favorite coffee shop was exactly the same rich warmth that he remembered. The taste of the coffee was as bold and invigorating as he missed. Across from him, Adam Nolan sat. His face was the same bright and excited boy he grew up with, but "boy" hardly felt accurate anymore.

The two sat for hours. At first, the two had little to say, simply enjoying being reunited, enjoying the coffee they hadn't had in years, enjoying the peace. Once they did start talking, they talked until the sun went down and the moon rose. 4 years was a lot to catch up on.

"So," Elliott said, "You're the new Magician, eh? That was James's role, wasn't it?"

"Yeah," Adam said, looking up at the moon, "I hope I make him proud."

"Oh, I am certain," Elliott said, giving Adam a bright smile.

Adam couldn't help but chuckle, "How could you possibly know that?"

Elliott snickered and leaned back, hands behind his head. "Because I'm the future director of intel, apparently. It's my job to know things, even if- no- *especially* if it's impossible for mere mortals to know."

"Pfff. I don't think that's how it works, Elliott," Adam teased.

"Oh? How would you know? What intel do you have?" Elliott teased back.

The two laughed together. It was a cathartic laugh, a laugh

that eased the pain and heartbreak burdening their souls. It was the laugh of two severed strands of fate who finally came together once more.

    Across the street, shrouded by shadows, James Graves stood. He used his crippled arm to hold onto a cane that he used to keep weight off of his cripped leg. Slowly, he reached up and placed his good hand over his chest. He felt his heart beat. He was alive. Fate had decided it wasn't his time.

    Slowly, carefully, James Graves stepped from the shadows. Even with the aid of his cane, he limped across the street with great effort. Eventually, he stepped up to the occupied coffee table.

    "Do my eyes deceive me?" James asked with a deep, relieved smile across his face.

    Fate simply couldn't keep the three apart.

[[End Report]]

The Aftermath

Afterword

Thank you for reading! If you made it this far, I must ask a favor of you, dear reader. If you enjoyed this book, please leave a review on whichever platform is appropriate. Since this is my debut novel, it helps more than you could know. I am especially curious to know what your favorite characters were, it helps me know who and what to explore in future novels.

Special thanks to George Johnsen, Misha Petrov, Zachary Liebreich-Johnsen, Kasper Behrens, and Joyce M. Barros Matheu.

BureauArcana.com

```
                                        002 001 006
            024 005 011
                040 005 009


    052 009 001




                        114 036 009




                                181 010 002








184 024 002
```

About The Author:

R.G. Grayson currently lives in ██████████████. He writes fiction and is not well suited to biographies, especially autobiographies. I can promise you everything else in this book is more interesting than anything I could put here.

:)

www.ingramcontent.com/pod-product-compliance
Lightning Source LLC
LaVergne TN
LVHW010155070526
838199LV00062B/4377